"You are warmer?"

White Hawk's voice had a rough catch in it when he asked the question.

"Much warmer." Cloud Dancer turned to look up into his face. "Do you wish to set me from you?"

White Hawk could not understand what he was doing. He stilled his hand on her arm and shook his head. "No. I wish to have you close to me." He knew he wanted much more than to have her near.

"As I want you close to me," Cloud Dancer responded, feeling the warmth of his skin against her.

"You are not my wife. It is not the way of the Apache, but I want you, Cloud Dancer, as I have wanted no other woman. Among my people I would bring you disgrace and shame." He looked away as if he could not meet her gaze.

"But we are not among your people. Among my people it is not wrong. There is no shame in wanting me or in my wanting you."

His eyes again met hers, and Cloud Dancer saw them burning with desire, glowing with an inner light.

Dear Reader,

Harlequin Historicals has the pleasure this month of bringing you a new historical romance from Lynda Trent, *The Black Hawk*. Forced by circumstances into marrying an enigmatic sea captain, Lady Bianca Stanford has no inkling of the intrigue that will soon threaten her life and the lives of those around her.

Patricia Potter fans will be delighted by *The Abduction,* a tale of double kidnapping that pits an English nobleman and a Scottish woman, who is the leader of her clan, against their collective enemies.

In *The Loving Swords,* by Marjorie Burrows, Clemma Wells finds inner strength and love in the untamed territories of the American northwest. And Peggy Bechko's *Cloud Dancer* captures the tenderness and power of the love between a young Pueblo maiden and a seasoned Apache warrior.

Once again, join us for four historical romances from the line that always brings you your favorite authors: Harlequin Historicals.

Yours,

Tracy Farrell
Senior Editor

Cloud Dancer

Peggy Bechko

Harlequin Books

TORONTO • NEW YORK • LONDON
AMSTERDAM • PARIS • SYDNEY • HAMBURG
STOCKHOLM • ATHENS • TOKYO • MILAN

Harlequin Historicals first edition May 1991

ISBN 0-373-28676-7

CLOUD DANCER

Printed in the U.S.A.

PEGGY BECHKO,

a writer since the age of twelve, has loved the American West since childhood. After moving from Florida to Santa Fe, New Mexico, the author began seriously delving into the local history of the land and the different peoples that shaped the region's past and present; her stories reflect her success in capturing the heart of those cultures. Between working at her job in a college bookstore and writing, Peggy designs clothes, does sculpture, hikes, and goes country dancing "at every opportunity."

Prologue

November 30, 1598

Beneath the vast expanse of the shimmering blue sky, Juan de Zalvidar and his thirty soldiers rode hunched against the biting cold of the New Mexican winter. The wind, relentless, blew out of the east. The rhythmic scrape and thud of the horses' hooves was a familiar sound of comfort to the men as were the soft jingling of bridles and the clank of armor. There were no clouds this day, but already in days past the men had seen white patches along the river, and the smell of snow was upon the air.

As he rode at the head of the column, Juan de Zalvidar's stature and carriage easily marked him as the leader. At twenty-eight, his air of authority floated about him like a cloak; there would be none who would dispute it. He and his brother, Vicente, had already done much to explore and begin to tame this wild land. They were backed by the power of their uncle, Governor Oñate.

Juan's thoughts strayed as he rode. His tanned face creased in a smile as he remembered the tales his younger brother, Vicente, had told of his own attempts to capture the buffalo herds in cottonwood corrals built near a river. Vicente had returned after fifty-four days of travel to and from the buffalo plains with none of the beasts. When Juan had

taken his leave of his brother, setting out with his thirty soldiers to reinforce their uncle in the west, Vicente had still
been good-naturedly swearing that he would not give up so
easily; he would try again to capture the buffalo.

Putting aside the thoughts of his brother, Juan turned to
the young soldier at his side. "We will reach the pueblo of
Acoma soon. There we will get corn for our horses and meat
for us. The people of these pueblos raise turkeys in great
numbers. We may even have a feast!"

His companion chuckled against the chattering of his
teeth. "I relish food in my belly," he admitted, "but I relish even more the thought of being warm once again! I will
barter for blankets and firewood as well! There is so damned
little of it in this godforsaken country. I want a large, roaring fire. How these people can manage with such tiny fires
to warm their homes I don't know!"

"They are used to this miserable cold," Juan de Zalvidar
pointed out, bowing his head against the chilly breeze that
had suddenly sprung up out of the north at cross-purposes
with the wind from the east. "They were born here. They
were not softened and spoiled by the gentler climes to the
south," he said with wry amusement at his own discomfort
as well as that of his men.

He could afford to laugh, for soon they would know full
bellies and warmth again. The Pueblo peoples were tame
Indians, who would provide all that was needed. The king
of Spain had ordered his armies not to steal from the simple natives, but to trade instead, so Zalvidar's party had
brought along plenty of items, hatchets being of particular
appeal, to negotiate with the Indians.

But the Pueblos had recently begun to balk at trade. At
first they had been open and friendly with the Spanish, but
now they seemed reluctant to give up their corn, deerskins
or blankets. Still, Juan was not worried. Should it become
necessary he had a great enough force with him to take what
was needed from the Indians. After all, the king of Spain

was not riding at the head of a column of cold, hungry soldiers.

These Pueblo Indians were easy to manipulate or coerce. Oñate's colony had arrived too late in the year to build or plant in preparation for winter, so the colonists had traded for and taken what they needed from the Indians. Already they had dispossessed almost the whole pueblo of San Juan to obtain shelter from the bitter cold of the New Mexican winter. A few of the Indians of San Juan had stayed, making themselves useful in carrying wood and water for the colonists in exchange for being allowed to remain in their homes.

Juan knew that his uncle had stopped at Acoma on a past exploratory trip; the Kere of Acoma had been no more difficult than the other Pueblo Indians. And while Juan had no intention of bullying the natives unnecessarily, he and his men would have what they required to continue their trip to meet Governor Oñate at Zuñi.

"There!" The soldier beside Juan jabbed his finger in the direction of a great rock in the distance, thrusting into the sky. "There is Acoma! Soon we will be there."

Juan laughed. "Distances are deceiving here, my friend. We will camp tonight at the foot of Acoma. Tomorrow we will climb to the heights and obtain our supplies."

A wave of curiosity, excitement and apprehension swept through the Pueblo of Acoma when the report came that Spanish soldiers could be seen at the foot of the mesa. For months they had talked, planning what they would do if the Spanish arrived again demanding the food and blankets that the people of Acoma could ill spare with the long winter still ahead.

Standing with many of the Kere, Cloud Dancer peered down from the heights at the strangers. "They have come again," she said to her sister, Woman of the West Wind, who stood by her side. "I had hoped they would not."

Her sister nodded slowly in agreement. "I think we all hoped they would not come again." She touched Cloud Dancer on the arm. "Come, we must move away from here. Chief Zutucapan and the men will handle the Spanish, and they have said we should not stay outside."

Cloud Dancer nodded her agreement, but found she felt more than a little reluctance to be tucked away in a kiva or hidden inside one of the mud houses. Why must they always do what the men decided? She sighed and quashed the rebellious thought, returning with her sister to their home.

Both daughters approached their mother in respectful silence as they entered, for she was working the clay. Woman of the Willows smiled her greeting, her hands moving swiftly, dexterously about their chore, smoothing and shaping the clay into a vessel of great fineness and beauty. It was the Kere custom to work the clay in silence with respect for the spirit that it contained.

When Woman of the Willows finished, setting the pot aside to dry, Cloud Dancer informed her quickly, "The Spanish have returned."

Woman of the Willows's eyes darkened and her mouth set in a tight, grim line. Her eyes went to the small doorway open to the outside, searching. "Your father will be with the others. We must remain here."

"But what are they going to do?" Cloud Dancer demanded, forgetting her woman's place in her agitation.

Woman of the Willows smiled indulgently at her younger daughter. Cloud Dancer always had been the impatient one, always questioning, never satisfied with the way things were. "Your father has said it was decided we would give no more supplies to the Spanish. We will trade with a few old blankets and skins if they so desire, but they will have no cornmeal, pumpkin, pine nuts or other important stores. If we trade those, our people will go hungry when the deep snow comes. If the Spanish demand what we cannot willingly give, our men will attack."

Cloud Dancer's face glowed. Her older sister's paled.

"Good!" Cloud Dancer exclaimed. "The Spanish must be taught they cannot take whatever they wish from us."

"It is very dangerous," Woman of the West Wind murmured.

"It *is* very dangerous," her mother agreed.

They sat huddled close to the tiny fire on the hearth, for it was cold. Cloud Dancer nodded her agreement with the inescapable fact. "It is dangerous, but I do not think the Spanish are complete fools. If our men stand up to them, they will realize they cannot just take whatever they want. If our people do not stop it now it will only get worse. They would take the food out of our very mouths."

Cloud Dancer drew her heavy robe of fine down turkey feathers closer around herself and moved to the small window to look out toward the mesa's edge. Zutucapan and a handful of Acoma's men clambered over and disappeared from view.

"They go to meet the Spanish," Cloud Dancer observed.

"With the coming of a new day the Spanish will climb to the mesa top to trade." Woman of the Willows drew her bowl of ground cornmeal to her and began to fashion flat corn cakes to accompany the evening meal.

Woman of the West Wind immediately reached to help her mother with the preparation of the food, while Cloud Dancer lingered a bit longer by the window, gazing out.

"I am worried, Mother," said Woman of the West Wind. "What will happen if our men fight? Will the Spanish leave us in peace after that?"

"Only the gods know what will happen when the Spanish come." She sighed the patient sigh Cloud Dancer remembered so well from her youth. "There is nothing for us to do but wait."

Through the long, restless night, Woman of the Willows's words rang in Cloud Dancer's ears. Wait. All they could do was wait. She was restless. *She* could not just wait. She would not wait.

Before dawn Cloud Dancer had hidden herself where she would be able to hear and see clearly. Acoma was large with many houses and concealed passageways. The day was cold and overcast; a chilled wind wailed out of the north, promising snow. The first sound to reach Cloud Dancer's ears was the clanging and banging of the strange clothing called armor that the Spanish wore. Soon she could hear their voices, laughing and wheezing at the exertion of the climb of hundreds of feet in their cumbersome and awkward armor. Cloud Dancer was amazed they made it at all. After they labored up the great mountain of sand, they had to use the small handholds and footholds in the rock face of the mesa to reach the top.

Zutucapan, who had returned ahead of them, met them and welcomed them to Acoma with all courtesy, his low, guttural voice a contrast to the boisterous good humor of the arriving Spanish.

"It is no wonder that your people are warm in the winter and need only small fires," Juan de Zalvidar jested, speaking awkwardly in the language of the Kere, his face beet-red and his body sweating from the climb. "It is the mesa that keeps you warm. She is a stern mistress indeed!"

Zutucapan did not see the humor in Zalvidar's remark. Cloud Dancer could almost feel the chief's anger from her place of concealment. "The fires are small because there is little to burn," he said stiffly. "Our people endure the winter."

The men accompanying the Spaniard laughed when the words were translated. "No matter." Zalvidar dismissed the topic with a broad sweep of his hand, and continued in the language of the Kere. "We have come to trade. There are a few things we will need to continue our travels to meet Governor Oñate. We will not force your people to trade, but you must know that our need is great."

"Liar!" Cloud Dancer whispered the accusation with a fierceness that surprised even herself, the sound of her single word muffled and unheard beyond the mud walls that enclosed her.

"Come," Zutucapan said graciously, "I will show your men where to go to trade. All you need will be provided."

Cloud Dancer nearly choked. Zutucapan, too, was lying! She was surprised at the duplicity of their chief. Zutucapan was instructing Juan de Zalvidar to direct the troops who had accompanied him to various parts of Acoma, to different houses to trade for their needs.

"The men play a game with each other!" Cloud Dancer spoke to herself. "Many lives hang between them and they play a game of power!" How easily she could see what each was doing. The Spaniard, Juan de Zalvidar, swaggered, proclaiming with his lack of precaution how invincible he believed himself and his men to be, while Zutucapan was luring the Spanish deep into Acoma, dispersing them, making them vulnerable.

Zalvidar cooperated completely with the Acoma chief, sending his soldiers separately to the different places Zutucapan had indicated.

Cloud Dancer held her breath, waiting. Despite the cold there was sweat appearing across the smooth expanse of her forehead and above her upper lip. As the men moved away, she could hear only snatches of conversation.

"...must have cornmeal for our men and horses..."

"...will trade blankets for the hatchets you bring, but my people have little cornmeal to spare. The winter stretches long before us."

Cloud Dancer knew it was not her place to follow, but she had heard enough to awaken her curiosity and was desperate to know more. She was small, quick and silent. It was easy for her to slip after the men, finding places of concealment along the way, hearing only a few words now as they walked before her—and much Spanish laughter.

Laughter, until the indignant shriek of a woman split the crackling cold air. Cloud Dancer looked in the direction of the shout in time to see a young Spanish soldier brandishing a flapping, squawking turkey aloft out of the reach of the furious woman. She grabbed for the turkey and he brushed her aside much as he would have an irritating gnat. The woman hit the ground hard. After that there was no way to tell the exact sequence of events.

A terrible cry for battle issued from Zutucapan's throat, and wide-eyed, Cloud Dancer watched as the bloody war erupted around her.

"Treachery!" Juan de Zalvidar bellowed. "Draw your weapons!"

Every Spaniard within earshot immediately reached for his sword. Those near Zalvidar formed a tight knot, swords brandished before them in defense and warning.

"Do we retreat to the plain below and return to punish them later?" Zalvidar called out to his men.

"No!" one strong voice answered. "I will fight these Indians alone and dispose of them!" The heavy voice jeered, "We must teach them now! They cannot be treated as children! Their actions cannot be excused!"

Cloud Dancer shuddered. She understood none of what the Spanish soldier had bellowed, but could not mistake the vile, arrogant threat in his tone.

For a suspended moment of time the Kere hesitated. No one moved, nothing stirred.

"Take aim, but hold fire!" Zalvidar waved his sword above his head in a last effort to keep the peace. Pistols suddenly filled the free hands of many of his men.

Then the moment was gone. Cloud Dancer saw the men of her people pouring out of housetops into the streets. They sent arrows, lances, even their clubs against Zalvidar and his small band.

Juan de Zalvidar hesitated no longer. "Fire!" he called out to his men.

In another moment the battle was joined. More than one thousand Indians broke upon Zalvidar and his soldiers in wild combat, closing in and cutting off escape. They came from every direction, bellowing their hatred and anger, fighting against the superior weapons of the Spanish.

Blood flowed. Men died. Cloud Dancer cringed in her place of concealment, crouched low against the wall of a clay house, the sounds of battle assailing her ears. It went on and on. The thirty Spanish soldiers should not have been able to resist for so long the fierce onslaught of the many warriors of Acoma, but their superior weapons helped them. Still, all around Zalvidar his men fell wounded and dead. The Spanish worked their way back toward the cliff they had ascended to Acoma, leaving their fallen behind. Some soldiers climbed over the edge of the treacherous mesa face. Cloud Dancer saw several jump from the heights into space.

Zalvidar's courage was prodigious. Three times Cloud Dancer saw him fall only to rise and fight again. When he fell the last time, the men of the Kere, their blood boiling, stormed upon him, destroying him completely in an obscene mutilation.

Only five soldiers were left atop the mesa. It was difficult for Cloud Dancer to see much beyond the wall of dark, sweating bodies surrounding the Spanish defenders, but she was aware of them battling their way to the edge of the island of rock upon which Acoma perched. Then the five found an opening, turning from the battle to jump from the cliff to life or death as the fates might decree.

The great cries of battle started to die. Cloud Dancer stood, still hidden, shuddering in anguish at the sights she had seen. At last she rushed to the edge of the mesa to peer down at the long sand drifts against the base of the rocky cliff.

"What did I say when I told my mother we should fight?" she cried. The pain, the blood, the death. Many of the men of Acoma lay sprawled in hideous death among the bodies of the fallen Spanish.

Never had she dreamed of such horror as this. Yet, what other choice had the Kere had? To starve at the whim and greed of the Spanish? Cloud Dancer's stomach lurched in anticipation of the future, for she knew, as surely Zutucapan must have known also, that the Spanish would return to Acoma.

Chapter One

Excitement filled the camp of the Jicarilla Apache. Runners had arrived from the sky city of Acoma, sent by Zutucapan of the Kere. The Acoma tribe, fearing a second attack by the Spanish, who were invading the land, sought the advice of their warlike allies on how to defend themselves against this terrible threat. Bempol, respected war chief of the Apache, had called a council. Many warriors of the Apache camp, some standing, some sitting, were gathered to talk of Acoma's request for aid. Voices rose and fell around the circle as the gathering grew. The warriors looked to the war chief to open the council.

Bempol raised a hand for silence. Not a tall man, but with an imposing presence and a dark, shadowed look on his stern face, Bempol lowered his hands as quiet descended.

"The people of Acoma have turned to us for help," he began solemnly. "They are little experienced in the ways of war, though they have already fought bravely against the Spanish. They have traded fairly with us in the past and have shared their harvest when there has been little for us to eat. We count them our friends. They would stand beside us in war if asked."

There were some grunts of agreement from the gathering, and a few snorts of impatience; while the majority of the Jicarilla Apache considered themselves allies of the Kere, a segment of their tribe viewed the peaceful Pueblo people more as prey than friends. Other tribes of Apache raided the more accessible pueblos regularly for food and sometimes for women captives. Raiding was part of the Apache way of life—the way they provided for their families. They took pride in a productive raid with no bloodshed.

Bempol continued. "They have sent runners to our camp. They ask us to send some of our most experienced warriors to their sky city to teach their men more of the ways of war—of attack as well as defense—so that they may be ready when the Spanish come again. What say you to this request?"

White Hawk rose from where he had been sitting cross-legged upon the ground, uncoiling his tall, lithe frame in a smooth, fluid movement. "We have called the people of Acoma friends." White Hawk spoke with a rich, deep timbre that carried the weight of his respected position in the tribe, a position earned by his unquestioned prowess and bravery as a warrior. "I would not turn my back on those I name as friends. I will number myself among those who will journey to the sky city to teach the people of Acoma to better fight the Spanish."

With a snort, Standing Buffalo, White Hawk's older brother, leapt abruptly to his feet. "The people of Acoma are weak. We have traded with them and they have given us food, but they fear our strength. That is why they have helped us when the lean times were upon us—not because they thought us friends! We owe them nothing! They are lucky we have not raided their city as so many of our Apache brothers have raided other pueblos. That is enough. We do not need to go fight their war for them."

"They do not ask us to fight for them," White Hawk reminded his brother. "They ask our advice. I will go."

Standing Buffalo gave his brother a look somewhere between disbelief and pity, then shrugged. "Do as you will. I will do nothing to try to stop you from seeking your death.

They are weak, and we have seen the Spanish are a deadly enemy. If the Spanish attack while our warriors are among the Kere, then you and they will die, for the Kere will not stand beside you.''

"You do not change my mind." White Hawk's voice rolled like distant thunder through the council. "I will go."

"As will I.'' Another warrior spoke up, remembering how food from the Acoma tribe had saved his infant daughter from starving.

"And I.'' Another voice joined the chorus.

"And I.'' Yet another.

"As will I.'' Bempol added his powerful voice with solemn dignity. "Ready yourselves," he said to the warriors who had stood and stepped forward. "We will leave with the rising of the sun."

On the sidelines a young, unseasoned warrior watched the exchange with interest. Prairie Wolf would have gone with the group of older warriors in an instant, but he knew well he would not be asked to accompany them. He did not have the experience the leader of Acoma had requested of the warriors who would go there. They were to advise and teach, not fight. Prairie Wolf had not even counted his first coup. He remained rigidly unmoving, watching. How he would thirst for tales of battle when the warriors returned home.

In the wake of the battle, Acoma prepared for retribution from the Spanish. The runners to the allies of the Kere, the fierce Apache, had returned to Acoma with Bempol and his five warriors.

Cloud Dancer and her mother, Woman of the Willows, had just returned from a long trek, gathering wild onions far from the base of the great mesa for the long winter ahead, when they saw the Apaches. A deer had been taken in the hunt and laid out on fur rugs, covered with blankets and hung with precious ornaments of turquoise and shell to honor its gift to the people who would eat it.

Beyond the deer, one man stood out from the rest. Taller than his companions, he stood very straight with shoulders squared above a broad, deep chest. Cloud Dancer saw the hard angles and sharp planes of his face, and thought that it would have seemed carved out of stone if not for the gentling lines around his eyes and mouth, which spoke of much laughter. Now, though, his face was dark with thought and concern. He, like the other Apaches, had come with Bempol to advise the gentle Pueblo people in the ways of war—ways they had practiced little in the past. White Hawk, Cloud Dancer heard him called. A strong name. A proud name. One, she decided, that fit him well.

"Hurry, Daughter," Woman of the Willows called over her shoulder, a ghost of a smile playing about her lips as she saw where her daughter's eyes rested. "We must put these out to dry, then roast the pine nuts."

Cloud Dancer tore her curious gaze from the two Apaches deep in conversation with Zutucapan, and followed her mother inside their house.

"I have forgotten my digging tools!" Woman of the Willows exclaimed in dismay.

"I know where you left them, Mother," Cloud Dancer said, smiling. "I will get them."

When Cloud Dancer left the clay house, her gaze immediately returned to the spot where the men had been talking, but they were gone. With a little sigh, she retraced mother's steps to retrieve the tools. Bending, she gathered the tools and rose—running squarely into the tall Apache.

White Hawk's hands shot out to steady her on her feet. Despite the layers of clothing separating his hands from her arms, his touch was warm, his grip firm but not hurtful. His dark eyes were gentle, yet filled with strength, like those of a stag protecting his doe.

"You are not hurt?" he asked. White Hawk had reached out automatically to steady the girl when she had collided with him. Now, sensing her legs were firm beneath her, he released her and stepped back. Among the Apache a man did not touch a woman who was not his mate except out of necessity.

The Kere had no such restraints. Cloud Dancer frowned at his sudden withdrawal. His touch had been brief, but startlingly pleasant. "You did not hurt me," she said, stiffening her backbone to combat the inclination she felt to lean toward him. "I did not see or hear you." She boldly raised her eyes to meet his, liking what she saw, warming to him, yet at the same time disconcerted by his somber expression.

White Hawk was startled. An Apache maiden would have dipped her head and looked shyly away, hardly daring to exchange a word with him. But he did not want to move away or even break the contact of their gazes. He stared down into the tawny gold-green of her eyes. Cougar eyes, he thought. Memories of the visions he had had when he underwent the manhood rites and became a spirit warrior came back to him. He had seen a woman with these eyes in his visions. A beautiful woman warrior who fought at his side. But this was a child-woman. So small. No warrior. She lacked the fire he had seen burning in the woman of his visions. And yet he found himself staring into her face: the soft, full lips above a small chin, the elegant cheekbones and smooth, unblemished skin.

His thoughts whirled as if he were in battle. He did not doubt he gazed down upon her with an idiotic expression upon his face.

Then he collected himself, recovering from his shock. A faint smile touched his lips. Pride lit his eyes. "It has been said I move as a cloud moves over the land," he said, ignoring the long moments of silence that had stretched between them.

Cloud Dancer smiled in return, sensing the uneasiness in this Apache warrior. The Apache had been allies of her people for a long time. Her eyes brightened, gold glittering over brown. Meeting his gaze, she could not resist teasing him a bit. "More like smoke, for a cloud casts a shadow before it. I would have noticed the shadow."

Not accustomed to such teasing and banter, White Hawk frowned for a moment before he realized her words were full of gentle laughter. This woman of the Kere was not like those of his own people, and the difference did not lie merely in different backgrounds and beliefs. He sensed a depth in her that was lacking in the others.

"You have come with Bempol to help my people ready themselves for the return of the Spanish," Cloud Dancer said directly, her eyes fixed on him as if reading his face.

"Yes." For a moment White Hawk dragged his eyes from hers, a little unsettled by the boldness of her regard.

He looked around at the streets and houses of Acoma. The flash of his obsidian eyes gave it all away, there was compassion in those eyes—and a fear for her people that Cloud Dancer did not care to contemplate.

"You do not think the men of Acoma will fight well if they must face the Spanish?"

The question took White Hawk by surprise, as did their entire exchange. And the beauty of this small woman, her slim, womanly shape not concealed even by the heavy furs she wore against the cold, nearly took his senses from him.

He shook his head. The single white medicine feather he wore in his headband fluttered as a biting wind rose to rake across the mesa. "Your men are not as experienced as the Apache in war, but your warriors have great courage. They will fight and gain experience as any warrior does—in battle. It is you I was thinking about."

Cloud Dancer blushed. Did he share the strange and unexpected attraction she felt to him?

"I saw you and your companion come back up the trail from the valley below. It is no longer safe for the women to go below. We do not know when the Spanish might return. It would not be wise to go again."

"Are we to sit upon this rock and starve then?" Cloud Dancer snapped in return, the heat of embarrassment and anger staining her cheeks. She did not understand this man, she decided. This man or any man. Things must always be done in the manner they decreed, even if it meant hunger and suffering for others.

"It will be a hard winter," was White Hawk's simple reply.

"A hard winter!" Cloud Dancer spit out the words as if they tasted bad. "It will be a disaster if we do not add to our stores. The Spanish have already taken much of our corn. If they come again they will cut short our gathering season. No, I will go below again, as we have the opportunity, and my mother will, also. We will not cower before the Spanish even come!"

White Hawk gave an impatient sigh and stood aside to allow her to pass. "We were asked to Acoma to give advice. I have given that advice. You may follow it or not as is your will." His dark eyes were fierce, the line of his mouth thin and stiff. The Apache did not argue with women.

"I understood Bempol and his warriors came here to advise our warriors in the ways of war—not our women in the ways of food gathering." Raising her chin proudly, Cloud Dancer held herself at her full height. Despite that, she felt like little more than a child's doll beside him. Turning abruptly, she walked away from the angry Apache.

It was all right that he was angry, Cloud Dancer thought; she was angry, too! It was not his home and family that were being threatened by the demands of the Spanish. If the only advice he could give was for the women to remain on the mesa top, then the people of Acoma would have to take care of themselves!

With great dignity, her mother's tools clutched in her hands, Cloud Dancer walked back to her home.

Chapter Two

When each day dawned anew with no sight of the Spaniards' return to the mesa, the Kere of Acoma gave thanks and went about their daily chores. But apprehension grew daily that the next dawn would see an attack.

Cloud Dancer made many more trips to the valley below, bringing back much-needed roots, nuts and herbs to dry and store for the winter ahead, in addition to the corn, beans, pumpkins and gourds cultivated there all through the summer and already harvested. Cotton, too, was grown during the summer and harvested late in the year, the soft, puffy balls spun into long strands from which blankets and clothing could be woven through the long winter months. There would be a good supply this year to occupy the men—the weavers among the Pueblo Indians—all winter. That was, if the men did not perish when the Spanish returned.

Bempol and his warriors stayed on at Acoma through the slowly passing days, taking groups of warriors below to sharpen their skills and give tactical advice should the battle come to them. The Kere had never carried war to others, though in the past they had fought many defensive battles to protect their families and the fruits of their industry. But never had they faced an enemy like the Spanish.

Frequently, Cloud Dancer saw White Hawk walking through the dusty streets, or talking with some of the men.

Always, when he felt her gaze upon him, he would look in her direction. When their eyes would meet and lock, neither looking away, something in each reached out to the other.

Cloud Dancer had seen the good the Apache warriors had done in Acoma—the difference they had generated in the men—and her anger at White Hawk had long since evaporated. It puzzled her, really, that she now found herself looking for him much of the time while she did her outside chores on clear, sunny days.

Cloud Dancer's mother had more than once taken on the chore of cooking for one or two members of the Apache delegation, while others were cooking and providing for the remaining warriors. Since the Apaches had come to Acoma as allies, and without their women, the women of Acoma were expected to provide for them, take them into their homes. Cloud Dancer and Woman of the West Wind had helped their mother as was the custom among the Kere, though Woman of the West Wind was frequently absent, spending much time now with the man she would marry, Shadow Catcher. Cloud Dancer sighed and smiled, thinking of the many times she had seen her sister and Shadow Catcher huddled close together beneath a blanket, talking quietly together in her parents' home. The wedding would take place very soon.

"Your pot is truly a work of art," Woman of the Willows complimented her daughter as Cloud Dancer put aside the small eating bowl she had been carefully decorating with symbols calling for blessings from the gods. "You please the spirits. The bowl will live a good life."

Cloud Dancer dipped her head in deference to her mother. As was the custom, the young maiden never made a bowl or a pot with anything less than her utmost skill. Life existed in everything. The pot had life just as did all creatures, places and things. Its form must be directed with the greatest skill of its creator.

Woman of the Willows sat down beside her daughter, taking up the cylindrical bar of stone she used to grind the corn. She began her work in the sunshine, placing the corn to be ground upon a large flat stone, now hollowed out like a dish by time and long grinding.

In companionable silence mother and daughter sat before their dwelling, Woman of the Willows grinding corn and Cloud Dancer, forgetting herself, staring off in White Hawk's direction. It almost frightened her the way he captured her attention so totally whenever he was near. She was fascinated by nearly everything about him: his high brow and aggressive chin, his nose, straight above the firm line of his mouth, his obsidian eyes, so quick and bright, always moving except when they fastened upon her and she blushed from the intensity of his heated gaze. His slashing brows were the same gleaming blue-black as his long, braided hair, which shone in the bright sunlight with the brightness of a raven's wing. His body was strong and graceful, his neck corded, his shoulders wrapped in the soft curves and hills of well-developed muscles. She even admired the long, graceful shape of his legs and the subtle play of muscles beneath the bronze skin as he moved.

After a few moments Woman of the Willows laughed softly, the simple gaiety of the sound drawing Cloud Dancer's attention from White Hawk. "Daughter," she admonished her gently, "if you do not speak to him—spend time with him—you will never know where your heart will lead."

"I do not understand him, Mother," Cloud Dancer blurted, her surprise at her mother's words loosening her tongue. "His ways are not our ways."

"That is true," Woman of the Willows admitted, the heavy strands of necklaces fashioned from turquoise, bone and bright-colored stones rattling gently against her matronly bosom as she used the stone bar to grind the corn. "But it does not stop you from looking at him. Your eyes see little else."

"He is a good man," Cloud Dancer returned simply. "Bempol and the Apaches with him, including White Hawk, have been kind and helpful to our people. But they fear for us. I have seen it in White Hawk's eyes."

Woman of the Willows looked upon her daughter with kind brown eyes. "That is a reason not to seek him out? Your sister, Woman of the West Wind, spends more time with Shadow Catcher since we have all begun to fear. Perhaps if White Hawk's ways are so different, you could show him more of the ways of our people. He could tell you about the ways of his. Then you would come to know each other and your ways would not seem so different."

"But I could never go from here, abandon the home that you would pass to me, to follow him to his people and live upon the plains, always wandering, following the buffalo."

"You worry too far ahead," Woman of the Willows enjoined her daughter with a heavy sigh. "None has said he would seek you for a wife or you him for a husband. But if it would be so, perhaps he would come to live here in Acoma with us. He seems content here." She sat back on her heels and rested for a moment, smiling affectionately at her young daughter. "The ways of our people are simple. If you do not seek him out, you will not know."

"An Apache maid would not seek him out!"

"You are not an Apache maid. You have just told me that. You speak both ways at the same time. You must settle the matter in your mind to quiet your heart." She shrugged and climbed to her feet. "Perhaps it would be the first way you could demonstrate some of our customs to him. You must decide, Daughter," she murmured softly and went back inside their home.

For a few more minutes Cloud Dancer sat in the brilliant sunshine beneath the canopy of the dazzling, cloudless blue sky, pondering her mother's words. Then she climbed to her feet and started off in White Hawk's direction.

White Hawk saw her, but he expected her to walk past with a polite nod as she had so many times. Frequently, during the past few days, he had cast covert glances in her direction, watched her going about her duties, working near her home, or descending to the valley with a small party to collect more of autumn's bounty for the winter stores. He did not think her a fool for disobeying the advice he had given when they first met; she had great courage—stubborn courage to go below and gather food so her people would not go hungry if the Spanish imposed a siege against the red mesa.

White Hawk climbed to his feet, for it was becoming evident that it was he she was approaching. He did not intend to sit at her feet, since he was somehow certain she would be reluctant to sit beside him.

Cloud Dancer, her heart fluttering within her breast, raised her head a little to gaze past White Hawk's broad chest and firm jaw into his dark eyes. She faced him squarely, boldly meeting his black eyes, which were regarding her from his expressionless face. "The Spanish have not come, and I and others have made frequent trips to the valley below. We are still safe from harm." Cloud Dancer immediately regretted her choice of words. They sounded like an accusation! Whenever she was close to him her thoughts became muddled and she suddenly stumbled over her words.

"I'm sorry," she blurted, trying to recant her words. "I did not mean it the way it sounded. I simply meant we are fortunate that you were not correct in your assessment...." Cloud Dancer stopped, blushing again. Nothing she said now seemed to come out right. "I mean..."

White Hawk raised his hand in a restraining gesture. "It's all right. I know what you mean, Little One." The endearment slipped out before he realized what he had said, and when his words rang in his ears he hoped she had been too flustered to take notice of them. "It is good that the Spanish have not yet come. I am glad you have been able to collect the nuts and healing herbs you will need for the long winter." He smiled at her, and Cloud Dancer gazed at him in wonder at how it softened his strong, stern face, framing it in light. She expelled a heavy sigh of relief and returned his smile a bit hesitantly. She had known he would have a beautiful smile. It showed in all the lines of his face.

"You have come to me for more advice?" White Hawk's smile broadened, and the last signs of strain slipped away from his expression as he proved himself capable of laughing at himself—a facet of the stern Apache that Cloud Dancer had not expected.

He was not used to the direct exchange between men and women that was customary among the Kere, but he was quickly growing to like it. His black eyes glittered with amusement at the discomfited young woman before him. Still, she had come to him and he did not know how to deal with her. He was a respected warrior and hunter, a spirit warrior, yet this was beyond the realm of his experience.

"No," Cloud Dancer replied softly, realizing in a flash that he was gently teasing her. "I wanted to tell you that it was not that we believed your advice to be bad. It was simply that we must choose the lesser of the evils, and going below is that. You and the others who came with Bempol have done much good in Acoma." She bestowed upon him a radiant smile of her own, relaxing as they spoke. "You must find us strange, living high upon this rock, when your people roam the great plains. It is a pleasant life here, one that is safe and protected, but we do not travel far enough to see very much." She glanced away timidly.

"Your ways are different, that is all." White Hawk glanced around at the other people in the vicinity, sure they must all be staring at them, as would have been the case in the camp of his own people. But it was not so. It seemed he had to forever remind himself that this was Acoma—not the camp of his people, the Jicarilla Apache.

"Will you leave soon?" Cloud Dancer sobered at the thought even as she spoke.

White Hawk laughed softly at her directness. "Would you have me leave soon?"

Acutely embarrassed once again by the way her words had come out, Cloud Dancer crimsoned before his steady gaze, but did not lower her eyes. "No, I would not have you leave soon," she said in her soft, low-pitched voice.

"We will stay until Bempol says we will go." It was an answer, but it told Cloud Dancer nothing. White Hawk smiled again and relented. "It will not be soon."

White Hawk was surprised at how much he did not in fact want to leave Acoma now. The nearness of this small woman twisted his heart and played havoc with his reason. It was a sensation he had not felt before, save after a long fast and cleansing sweat when he had had visions in the past.

What was it about this child-woman that stirred him so? Perhaps it was that she was so different from the Apache maids. She did not dip her head and slip quickly out of his path when he walked through the camp; she did not cast him shy, speculative glances. She faced him directly and spoke without the blushing coyness of a young Apache girl surprised by a man's presence.

This openness puzzled him. Questions arose, but he did not find the answers. And it pained him to think of the future of Acoma. If the Spanish came in great numbers many would die. Perhaps Cloud Dancer would die. White Hawk pushed the unbidden thought from him.

"You and those with you will remain until the Spanish have returned here?" Cloud Dancer asked.

With a shrug, White Hawk answered, "It has not been decided."

"Perhaps the Spanish will not come again," she suggested.

White Hawk gave Cloud Dancer a pained smile and resisted mightily the urge within him to lay his hands upon her in a strengthening and comforting gesture. Eyes could be focused upon them from any direction.

"They will come. They have come to take over this land. In time we will all have to fight to drive them from our lands."

White Hawk's prophetic words stilled Cloud Dancer's heart. She had seen the battle that day. There had been deceit on both sides after the Spanish made their expected impossible demands. Worse, she had seen the Spanish fight, had heard their thunder weapons. Even with the double advantage of surprise and greater numbers, it had taken far too long for her people to win the battle.

"Zutucapan asked for your help and advice, but this is not your fight," Cloud Dancer said soberly. "Would you stay then to fight at the side of warriors so weak at the kind of fighting your men try to teach?"

"I am a warrior," was White Hawk's only gentle reply.

Cloud Dancer burned with fear for her people and fear for the handsome warrior who stood before her. The future was coming—rushing upon them—borne upon the wind, and Cloud Dancer felt the chill of its threat. Her glance moved from White Hawk long enough to catch sight of Woman of the West Wind and Shadow Catcher walking across the plaza together, and her eyes misted over.

"Many will die," she murmured softly to herself, her words not loud enough to reach White Hawk's ears. Then she lifted her tawny cougar eyes to his once again and offered him a pale ghost of a smile. "I'm sorry. I must get back and help my mother prepare our meal." With those words, Cloud Dancer turned and walked quickly back to her home.

White Hawk watched her go. He was relieved that she had gone—but even so, he felt an odd loss, an emptiness at her departure. He was entranced by her gentle ways, which were but a cloak around the inner strength of her courage. He had begun to note her departures from and anticipated her returns to the safety of the mesa. He felt a special warming of his body and tightening of his loins when she was near. He desired her. He knew, too, that among the Pueblo people, sleeping with Cloud Dancer—if she agreed—would be no disgrace. Even should she have a child from that union after he was gone, it would be no disgrace to her. She would be treated much as a widow with a child, and life would go on.

For White Hawk it was different. He could read the desire in her soft eyes as he knew it burned within his own. If he reached out to her, encouraged her, he would have her. But his life was very different. Among the Apache, chastity before marriage was prized above all else. A maiden who was not chaste and was discovered could expect a public whipping with a rope or a stick, administered by her father, and great disgrace could be brought down upon the family.

Among his own people he was allowed to slake his desires with a young widow when there was celebration and dancing after a raid or hunt. At those times such a woman was allowed to slip away with a warrior, to obtain a share of the plunder of his raid or bounty of his hunt while relieving the pressure of long abstinence, both her own and that of the warrior she chose. It was a much different life from that of the Pueblo peoples.

White Hawk shook his head, wondering at the direction of his thoughts. He had not expected to find a woman of Cloud Dancer's quiet strength and independence when he came to Acoma. She was an exception even to her own people. If he joined with her he did not know if he would be able to leave her.

Their lives were as far apart as the moon that shone in the night sky was from the ground they walked upon.

Chapter Three

Even though it was late in the year, the *koshare*—the clowns of the Pueblo people—had called a rabbit hunt in which the girls were permitted to participate. Cloud Dancer, laughing, ran to follow her sister and friends down the steep path from the mesa top. There were many rabbit hunts during the year when the men hunted alone, in honor of the chiefs or to feed the treasures of the kivas, structures built for ceremonies that housed kachina masks and sacred fetishes made by the medicine priests. All the people were in high spirits, for each day that passed without the return of the Spanish made life at Acoma seem normal again. Still, dread and apprehension remained. The people had to have meat for the winter stores, and many guards were posted to keep watch during the hunt.

"I am coming!" Cloud Dancer called to her sister, who was hurrying ahead to catch a glimpse of Shadow Catcher.

"Hurry!" came Woman of the West Wind's response from below. "We cannot be late!"

Cloud Dancer hurried her steps. She was sure White Hawk would be joining the hunt this day, and there were many customs he would not understand. She could not risk being late for the gathering and thus a victim of the *koshare*'s clowning antics. Because of her growing feelings toward White Hawk, Cloud Dancer did not want to chance the expression that might appear on his face if she became part of the entertainment.

Woman of the West Wind, her feet sinking into the loose sand where she stood, was waiting for her sister at the deep sandy base of the mesa. "Hurry!" she called again, and then turned to run to the appointed place as Cloud Dancer released her handholds and footholds in the red, rock wall of the mesa, and dropped the last couple of feet.

Though Cloud Dancer had gotten a later start than her sister, she was fleeter afoot and swiftly closed the distance between them, her shimmering black hair blowing free in the wind created by her passage. The air was crisp and cold; the sun was stunning in a sky the color of rich turquoise, cloudless and shimmering overhead.

"See," Cloud Dancer called out to her sister as they ran together toward the meeting place, "the *koshare* are already gathering, but we will be on time."

The *koshare* played about the edges of the gathering people, keeping an eye out for those who would come late. Painted white, with here and there a black stripe, they were naked, and used their nakedness in comic outrage. They leaped and ran, hazing the people sometimes to laughter, sometimes to shame in the spirit of irony and perversity. For this hunt the *koshare* were in charge, and the power of the *koshare* was absolute when they took charge.

All around them the men of the town were armed with throwing sticks for killing the rabbits. Farther out guards were posted to watch and warn if danger threatened. Though they were allowed to participate in this hunt, the girls did not kill. Both Cloud Dancer and her sister clutched the bundles of food they had brought along for lunch, and each searched for the man whose rabbits she would try to grab, for that was the man she would feed with the lunch she had brought.

"Have you seen Shadow Catcher?" Cloud Dancer asked her sister breathlessly.

A shake of the head was her answer.

"I have seen White Hawk!" Excitement raised the pitch of Cloud Dancer's normally mellow voice.

"Get closer to him," Woman of the West Wind urged, caught up in the growing excitement of the hunt, "so you can better see the rabbit he kills and go after it!"

Cloud Dancer hesitated.

"There! There is Shadow Catcher!" her sister exclaimed and, following her own advice, started edging off in his direction.

Cloud Dancer moved to position herself with the girls closer to the place where White Hawk and her father stood quietly speaking together.

White Hawk was aware of the press of young men around him and the laughter of the young women ready to take part in the hunt. It seemed strange to him that they could all be in such high spirits with the threat of the Spanish hovering near, yet he understood the need for food through the long winter. And he understood the reasoning of those who had decided on the hunt. It would raise the spirits of the people, make them feel less like prisoners atop their mesa, despite the danger. He would miss the hunt and Cloud Dancer's warm presence, but he would scout the surrounding country as he had for many days past and guard their safety.

His eyes met Cloud Dancer's, and he regretted again that he would not be taking part in the hunt. The softness of her eyes, the directness of her gaze told him she would run for his rabbits. And if she did, she would be sure to achieve her goal, he thought, for White Hawk had seen her run, and none among the women was her equal.

"It will be a good hunt," Soaring Eagle said to White Hawk. "I am sorry you will not take part. You and the other warriors who came with Bempol have taught us much. We would like the chance to teach you. There are many of our customs I would like to show you."

"It is my wish to learn," White Hawk said regretfully, his eyes wandering again to Cloud Dancer. "But, for now, I know it would be best if I scouted the dry riverbeds and low hills for some sign of the Spanish. If the Spanish are near, I will be able to bring word well in advance of their arrival."

Soaring Eagle sighed in resignation, but grinned when he saw the direction of White Hawk's gaze, and the look his daughter, Cloud Dancer, bestowed upon the Apache spirit warrior in return. "I can see neither of my daughters expects to go for my rabbits this day!" He inclined his head in the direction first of Cloud Dancer where she hovered near, then of Woman of the West Wind still edging her way closer to Shadow Catcher.

For a moment White Hawk's sober mood darkened further. "I am sorry, Soaring Eagle, that I will not be here to see Cloud Dancer run for my rabbits."

Soaring Eagle nodded. "The way she looks at you, there is no doubt it is your rabbits she expects to go after. She will be disappointed. Nonetheless, this is a time of celebration and joy. We have had a good harvest and it has been stored for winter. Cloud Dancer will chase my rabbits after all, or she will choose another." Knowing the growing attraction between this brave warrior of the Apache and his younger daughter, Soaring Eagle could not resist prodding the serious Apache a bit with the possibility that in his absence Cloud Dancer would seek another.

"Today is a day for a man like me to see his daughters growing to maturity. I would not deny them what I and their mother have had. They will marry and have families. Is it not the same among the Apache?"

"That much is the same," White Hawk agreed with a halfhearted grin. Then he sighed and hefted his lance. "I will go now so that Cloud Dancer will have time to choose another."

Ripples of excitement and soft laughter ran through the clutch of girls waiting for the hunt to begin, as the *koshare* capered around the edges of the crowd, now intercepting the latecomers for punishment.

For an instant, Cloud Dancer met White Hawk's searching gaze.

She felt a pleasant, warm rush when his eyes rested upon her, and a sinking feeling in her stomach. With the rising of each new sun her eyes hungered more to see him again, to be at his side. How these strange new feelings had arisen, Cloud Dancer did not know, but they became more deeply rooted with each passing day. She felt as though she were the earth, nurturing those tender roots as they spread throughout her heart.

But she had heard much of what had passed between White Hawk and her father. Disappointment was like a heavy stone upon her chest. White Hawk would not be here for the hunt after all. He would be far from her, searching for some signs of the Spanish. She clutched more tightly the bundle of food she had brought for them to share. When she had heard of the hunt she had planned it so well. She could not choose another! She wanted only to spend time with White Hawk!

He smiled a sad, apologetic smile, then turned and jogged away from the group.

Cloud Dancer's heart began to pound. She had to do something. She could not stand calmly here and join in the high spirits, when White Hawk would risk his life for their people! She shifted on her feet and bit her lip, undecided, her knuckles white from strain of clutching the food bundle.

"Whose rabbit will you seek to touch that you may take it home?" The bright, inquiring voice of Running Fawn disrupted Cloud Dancer's thoughts, drawing her attention for a few moments from White Hawk.

"I will gather the rabbits of the Apache warrior White Hawk." Cloud Dancer spoke softly to the excited girl, knowing White Hawk would be long gone when the hunt began.

Not yet truly a woman, Running Fawn giggled. "He is very handsome, but he is Apache. Soon he will be gone." She looked at Cloud Dancer with curiosity. "You would not go to live among the Apache, would you? Look over there. Little Fox and Morning Star are courting. I may run for his rabbits to tease her," she chattered while other young women gathered close around them, anxiously peering into the crowd of hunters to find their favorites. "There is still time. You can choose a hunter from Acoma and retrieve his rabbits. Truly you would not leave Acoma for the Apache?" the excited young girl babbled again.

Cloud Dancer looked at the girl thoughtfully, the repeated question battering her. White Hawk was moving farther away. "He has not asked me," she mused. But she was beginning to wonder—would she go with White Hawk if he asked? Could she leave behind all that she knew for a life so different from the one in Acoma? She wanted to follow him now, to be with him to share his dangers and his joys. What of later? Could she follow him from Acoma?

"Look!" the girl squeaked, her young voice again jostling Cloud Dancer's thoughts. "The hunt is about to begin!"

The *koshare* began the hunt. The party spread out and drove the rabbits within a loose circle, gradually closing it, driving the rabbits toward the center.

"I must get closer to Little Fox!" The young maiden laughed and ran off to accomplish her goal.

Her own decision made, Cloud Dancer turned from the hunt and began to run. Her feet carried her swiftly over the earth in White Hawk's wake. It was not her place to follow him, but she did not care. She would not slow him down, and she could share this time with him when they had so little to share. The threat of the Spanish was to all of them.

She could help him. Others, intent upon the festivities, did
not notice her slip away.

Soon the sights and sounds of the hunt were far behind
her and she had lost sight of White Hawk ahead. Her heart
did a little flip, but she continued on, slowing her pace
enough to catch sight of some signs of his passing.

She was congratulating herself on her heretofore undis-
covered talent for tracking when she rounded a bend in the
dry riverbed and almost ran fullforce into White Hawk.

Cloud Dancer gasped and almost tripped in her speedy
stop, but she recovered herself quickly and looked him dead
in the eye, when he asked, ''Why have you followed me?''

''I heard you speaking with my father. I know you intend to scout for some sign of the Spanish. I want to help.''

White Hawk eyed her with a niggling pride and growing
desire, as he remembered Cloud Dancer's graceful running
stride when she was coming down the dry wash behind him.

Bemused, he did not know what to do about the situation. He did not want to send Cloud Dancer back alone;
neither could he take her back. If the Spanish did appear,
she would be safer with him than caught in the open.

''You are a very swift runner,'' White Hawk complimented her, as always feeling a bit uncomfortable at the
close proximity of this young Kere maiden he desired so
deeply—uncomfortable with his own feelings, that was, not
with Cloud Dancer. She was stealing her way into his heart,
and he was coming to dread the day he would leave Acoma
with Bempol and the other warriors. ''Can you maintain the
pace throughout the day?'' Without waiting for an answer,
White Hawk turned and began walking swiftly through the
soft sand of the wash.

Cloud Dancer smiled faintly at White Hawk's obvious
discomfort—and equally obvious attraction to her.

''You do not have the skills of a warrior—stealth and
tracking—and you are not trained in the use of weapons,''
White Hawk said gruffly as they walked swiftly side by side.

"I will have to protect you this day." The weight of his words made it sound as if she were a heavy burden indeed.

Pricked, Cloud Dancer looked at him, finding his obsidian eyes already fixed upon her. "Then you must teach me," she said simply, and as the words left her mouth, she knew that that was really why she had come after him. That was what she wanted. She did not want to sit idly by or huddle in a kiva as others had done that day the Spanish had fought at Acoma. She wanted to learn; she *needed* to learn everything White Hawk could teach her.

White Hawk looked at Cloud Dancer with such an expression of surprise on his face that she could barely keep from laughing.

"Is it so much to ask?" Cloud Dancer asked clearly, facing him as he stopped and looked down at her. "I am strong, clear-eyed, and you yourself said I am a swift runner. I can learn as easily as any young boy. And—" she gave him a smile that reached clear to his heart "—I have brought food for us to eat."

"It is not much to ask," White Hawk said gently, stopping to rest the butt of his spear upon the ground. "There are some warrior women among the Apache."

This new fact astounded Cloud Dancer.

"Truly?" she asked, staring at him in a searching way, fearing he was but playing with her.

White Hawk laughed softly at the astonished look upon her face. Warmed by Cloud Dancer's scrutiny, he longed to take her in his arms and hold her close. It was a feeling he had never experienced, this strange tingling warmth that possessed him whenever she was near. He had slaked his man's desires on the bodies of other women, but never had he felt such sweet desire—made all the sweeter by his own self-denial.

White Hawk nodded in answer to her question. "They are accepted though they are rare, and some are highly respected."

"You *will* teach me?" Cloud Dancer asked cautiously.

"Yes, Little One," White Hawk said with quiet laughter. "I will teach you when I can—if you will feed me!"

Together they moved forward at a swift pace, running, then walking, then running again. Often they were able to run side by side; other times they went single file. Always White Hawk kept an eye on Cloud Dancer, but the burden did not seem nearly so heavy as he had first anticipated.

Cloud Dancer listened and watched intently as he pointed out things a warrior should know: how to read signs upon the earth, how to recognize what the small animals and birds might reveal about the nearness of an enemy, how to cover one's own tracks, how to watch the distance for movement such as dust stirred up by the passage of many men, or by the great animals the Spanish rode upon. He even gave her the spear to carry for a time, so she could become accustomed to the weight of it in her hand. It was his command that stopped them for food.

"We shouldn't stay here very long," Cloud Dancer said quickly, echoing White Hawk's own thoughts, as they found a narrow rock ledge protruding from a bluff and sat upon it to share the lunch she had brought. "There is so much I must learn."

"And not enough time to teach it all in one day," White Hawk observed, feeling more at ease now that they were some distance from the Acoma and the hunt. He eyed her speculatively and remarked, "I am beginning to enjoy your customs."

"There are many you would like," Cloud Dancer informed him confidently. "And there are many of yours I wish to learn. Have you no customs such as the rabbit hunt, where young men and women may get together?"

White Hawk shook his head. "We have dances where young men and women have a chance to spend time together, and sometimes, if the girls are not too bashful, they might invite some young men to accompany them when they hunt for wild plants to add to our food.''

''Tell me more about how it is between your young men and women.''

With a smile, White Hawk accepted the corn cakes Cloud Dancer handed him. ''Between young men and women there are many more restrictions than among your people. Even at the dances the girls are watched carefully by their mothers. The young people are forbidden to leave the dance place, and there are always chaperons policing the outskirts of the grounds to stop any from breaking the rules.''

''We would not be permitted to sit here together as we are now?''

''No.''

''But, despite everything, some Apache girls must find ways to be alone with the men they love?''

''Not very often. Girls are trained from birth to be reserved and bashful, and boys are taught from birth that it is unmanly to pay too much attention to women.''

As she passed him a handful of pine nuts and some deer meat, she felt herself opening to the tingle and rush of warmth where his hand had touched hers, as a flower opens to the radiance of the sun. The sensation made her giddy. She blushed and looked away; his closeness affected her so.

White Hawk impulsively reached out to touch her face, lifting her chin so that he might look into her eyes. Just touching her sent ripples of shock through his body and a warmth flooding his loins. He gritted his teeth, full-blown desire doing battle with the strict customs of his people. He hesitated, fingers barely trembling, then withdrew his hand.

Stunned by the brief contact, Cloud Dancer met his eyes and almost choked on the berry and nut mixture in her mouth. She drew a deep, steadying breath and tried to quell her embarrassment. She could see the desire burning in the depths of his eyes, and felt the answering rush of her own heated blood in her veins.

Despite himself, White Hawk found Cloud Dancer's demure embarrassment exciting. He hoped he would not embarrass himself now before Cloud Dancer, with evidence of his own desire. He ate the food she had given him, cutting off conversation. Cloud Dancer ate hers, flushed and confused by the sudden surge of feeling between them. In taut silence they finished the food, and when their meal was completed, White Hawk stood.

"We will come to know each other well, Cloud Dancer," White Hawk said firmly, and the words spoken had the ring of promise about them.

As the afternoon wore on, they began to circle back toward Acoma. Both were foot weary, and they had seen nothing of the Spanish. Cloud Dancer absorbed everything White Hawk taught her and thirsted for more. And when he tried to trip her up, to get her to do the wrong thing, she could not be fooled. He was proud of her accomplishments in so short a time, and surprised at her endurance and determination to continue. This goal of hers was not a young girl's whim.

White Hawk was carrying several rabbits he had managed to kill for the evening cooking pot, intending them as a gift to Cloud Dancer's parents. "Perhaps these rabbits will help make up for our desertion of the hunt," he said, humor glinting behind his eyes. White Hawk had been concerned that Soaring Eagle would be worried about Cloud Dancer, but now had a feeling he'd known exactly where his daughter was.

The gray sky began to darken to the northwest, as black heavy clouds drifted and built on the horizon. There was still a long distance to cover before they reached the mesa, and White Hawk saw Cloud Dancer glance frequently in the direction of the darkening sky. It did not seem like much at first—some distant clouds and the gray of a day approaching winter—but then the change came quickly.

The chilled wind burst upon them from out of the northwest in brittle warning. It stung their faces and tore at their clothes with its force, the sun swiftly disappearing behind the descending dark wall of clouds. The temperature plummeted, making even the warm clothes they had worn for a cool autumn day inadequate.

They were running easily, their faces to the wind, dust swirling around them when White Hawk stopped. The white medicine feather he wore turned down over his ear jerked and twisted in the heavy wind.

"We cannot make it back. The storm will catch us long before we reach the mesa!"

Cloud Dancer thought of the shelter the snug mud houses would offer against the coming storm and nodded dismally in agreement. "We must hurry and find shelter!" she called above the wind that snatched her words away as she spoke them.

"I know a place," White Hawk shouted back, gesturing in a direction that angled away from the trail to the red mesa. "It will give us shelter against the storm. I saw it when I came here with Bempol."

He cupped his hand beneath her elbow and began to hurry in the direction he had indicated, giving Cloud Dancer no chance to protest.

Within seconds the wind had gone wild, clawing its way through the valley, howling against the rock walls of the surrounding mesas and rattling through the winter-bared brush. The cold sliced through their clothes and flesh right to the bone as the first hailstones fell, causing dust to rise all around them. Seconds later the rich smell of moist earth began to fill the air.

The hail stung where it struck Cloud Dancer's exposed flesh or head. She could barely see a few feet in front of her to gauge direction, but White Hawk hurried them forward. Wrapping his arm around her, he used his body to shelter hers from the punishing hail.

There was no letup in the wind. The hailstones grew larger in size, with heavy drops of rain mixed in, falling at a steep slant nearly parallel to the ground. The hail pounded the ground without mercy, frozen bits of soft ice bouncing at their feet as they ran.

The distance seemed interminable and Cloud Dancer wondered what it would have been like had they attempted to climb the face of the red mesa. Finally she found herself being gently shoved by White Hawk into the dim interior of a sheltering cave.

Wet and chilled through, she huddled against the rear of the cave, arms wrapped around herself, clutching her bodily warmth to her as White Hawk disappeared again into the terrible storm, leaving her momentarily alone. The storms that came with the changing of the seasons were particularly violent and unpredictable, and Cloud Dancer was worried until White Hawk ducked back through the shelter's opening bearing a heavy burden of wood. She was amazed at how quickly he had collected it.

"The storm will rage for a while," White Hawk observed, arranging the surprisingly dry wood before him, then drawing a flint from the pouch he wore around his neck. "We will have a fire soon and it will warm you."

Cloud Dancer returned White Hawk's warm smile, then managed to still her shivering enough to look around the inside of the cave. "It is large!" she exclaimed, surprised at the size of the cave in contrast to its small opening to the outside.

The forces of nature had carved out of the foot of a rock mesa a cave that was larger than Cloud Dancer's small, mud home. The floor was covered with rounded stones of all sizes, and the roof sloped steeply toward the floor from its center toward the back, much like the stitched end of a pouch.

"There are some large boulders at the back of the cave and more near the front. They will help to hold the warmth when I have a fire burning.'' White Hawk blew tenderly upon the soft kindling where he had struck the spark from his flint, coaxing the tiny curl of white smoke to a small flame between his sheltering hands. "It looks as if some animals have been here before us. A fire will keep them from joining us now," he said wryly.

The struggling flame grew, and White Hawk carefully added larger and larger bits of wood until he could safely add bigger branches and urge the fire to respectable size.

Outside the wind shrieked and howled. Occasional puffs of air found their way through the heavy brush growing at the mouth of the cave, sending flickering shadows against the earthen walls and nearly smothering the fire. Hail and rain mixed, separated, then mixed again. Finally they combined for the last time to form a coarse, heavy snow that quickly blanketed the reddish-brown earth outside and clung to skeletal branches in glittering crystals.

"We must protect the flame or your work will have been for nothing.'' Cloud Dancer collected small rocks scattered about the cave floor and brought them to stack across the back of the exposed flame, protecting it from the wind.

"The kill must not be wasted.'' White Hawk pulled a large knife from the sheath at his waist and picked up the rabbits he had brought down.

Cloud Dancer removed her own smaller knife from her belt, and together they made short work of the chore of cleaning the rabbits. One was spitted and placed over the fire to cook as the storm showed no signs of relenting. The others they skinned and prepared to dry the meat. Their work complete, they cleaned their hands in the falling snow, then huddled close to the fire together to wait out the storm and watch their dinner cook over the flickering tongue of fire.

"Do you think the storm will last long?'' Cloud Dancer asked.

"It could go on for hours. Does that concern you?''

Cloud Dancer smiled at the tone of his voice and the question unasked in his words. "No. I am content. I just do not want my parents to worry when everyone returns to Acoma from the hunt but I am not among them."

"Your father knows you are with me, I think."

"M-My fa-ther?" Cloud Dancer managed between teeth clenched against further chattering as a new and sudden chill swept her.

"We spoke before the hunt began this morning. Your father is a wise man, and I think he is a man who knows his daughter." He frowned slightly at Cloud Dancer's huddled, shivering state. Strict upbringing warred with practicality, and he wondered what would happen when he actually took this woman in his arms. "Come," he offered, "let me warm you."

He held out his arm to her and Cloud Dancer sighed with relief, slipping into its curve naturally. She felt White Hawk twitch at their first contact, then fold his arm more closely about her. He pressed her side to his as his left hand stroked her with rough concern, urging the blood to flow faster and warm her small frame, while his right hand fed more wood into the fire.

She snuggled closer as the warmth they shared penetrated her damp clothing to warm her body. It was as if she had always known this strong, kind man of the Apache. She was content.

A familiar heat kindled in White Hawk from Cloud Dancer's body pressed so trustingly and intimately to his own. The soft curve of her breast pressed against his chest, the curve of her hip fit perfectly with him, and her hair, silken and drying quickly before the fire, smelled of the freshness of the storm without. He knew her not well and yet he felt that he had known her always. What would a life be like with Cloud Dancer, he wondered. Which life would they choose? Could he remain among the Kere and be content? Could she share his life among the Apache? It seemed so right, having her pressed closely against him. He shook his head to clear it of such thoughts and stared into the brightly burning flames, willing himself to hold at bay the emotions that threatened him.

The heavy snowfall continued, the wind at the cave's mouth whipping the sheltering brush to and fro. The dark sky was getting even darker as the sun dipped low in the west. The smoke from the fire rose to the top of the cave and found its way out through the opening in a slender wisp.

Cloud Dancer was no longer trembling from the cold, but White Hawk's stroking hand was doing wildly wonderful things to the beat of her heart. It brought a racing to her blood and a languorous heaviness to the lower part of her body. She breathed deeply of the masculine scent of leather and wood that clung to him and enjoyed the tingling heat that crept up her body.

"You are warmer?" White Hawk's voice had a rough catch in it.

Cloud Dancer nodded, the small movement against him a temptation he could hardly bear. "Much warmer." She turned to look up into his face. "Do you wish to set me from you?"

White Hawk could not understand what he was doing, but he knew as clearly as he could see himself in a still lake that he wanted this woman—wanted her more than anything he had ever wanted in his life. He stilled his hand on her arm, and shook his head in a firm negative. "No. I wish to have you close to me." He spoke the words clearly and knew he wanted much more than to have her near.

Cloud Dancer's wits spun in a whirlwind as strong as that thrown up by the storm outside the cave. Her stomach somersaulted. A tendril of cold air slipped past the fire, past White Hawk's sheltering embrace to send goose bumps racing along her neck and down her spine. Was it truly the cold that caused the sudden tingling rush of raised flesh? Or was it instead the subtle way White Hawk's rough, warming strokes had turned to a gentle caress?

"As I want you close to me," Cloud Dancer responded, looping her arm about his neck, feeling against her hand the incredible smoothness of his black braid, and the warmth of his skin.

"You are not my wife. It is not the way of my people, but I want you, Cloud Dancer, as I have wanted no other woman. It is wrong, but still I want you. Among my people I would bring you disgrace and shame." He looked away as if he could not meet her gaze.

"But we are not among your people. Among my people it is not wrong. There is no shame in wanting me or in my wanting you."

"You tempt me, woman, beyond endurance."

His eyes again met hers and Cloud Dancer saw them burning with desire, glowing with an inner light. She laughed softly. "I have seen no evidence of that yet."

"I would not hurt you, Cloud Dancer. I would not force you. I will only take what you can give." He stared into her small oval face, desiring to see into her heart.

"I do not understand this thing between us," Cloud Dancer admitted, "but there is no denying it exists. My mother says there is no way to tell what the future will bring. She has known from the beginning there was a feeling between us, even before I did. I would deny you nothing, White Hawk." Her words soft and breathless, Cloud Dancer turned fully into his arms, pressing their warmth between them, turning her face into his neck.

White Hawk gave an answering, shuddering sigh and gathered her closer to him, pulling her tightly against the broad expanse of his chest, pressing his cheek against the top of her sleek head. He did not know what to do with her. He loved her. That truth was becoming painfully apparent. He wanted her. But among his people this would not be right. Again and again he forced that thought upon himself, though it did nothing to slow the beat of his heart or cool the heat in his loins.

"Would you look upon me as something less if I gave myself to you now?"

"You are a maiden. You do not know...." He hesitated. "I would think of you always as a brave, kind, strong, beautiful woman. You could be nothing less."

"Then I know all I need to. You have touched something deep inside me. I watch for you each day when I walk from one place to another. My mind is filled with thoughts of you. We have walked separate paths until you came here, and now they merge together. For however long—whatever happens in the future—I wish to be with you now."

White Hawk caressed her cheek and pressed feather-light lips to her forehead. His hand nearly trembled with the passion and need that he had kept bottled so tightly within him. He feared for the future of Acoma and this beautiful woman in his arms. He had heard tales of the retribution of the Spanish. And he remembered the visions of his youth, when he had become a man. He knew somehow that those visions were for now. But that confused him even more than the unexpected feelings this young Kere maiden enlivened within him.

"I will not be a burden. I will not make your life less than what it is now. If you choose to return to your people with Bempol and leave me behind, then it shall be so. I want only what you can give while you are here with me."

White Hawk groaned in response and pressed a kiss to her neck, inhaling the heady fragrance of her rain-rinsed hair. The fire crackled its warmth close by them, and Cloud Dancer no longer trembled with cold. His hands held her with a fierce possessiveness, pressing her tightly against him as his lips explored the smooth column of her throat and made their way with soft, nibbling bites to her ear. His hand caressed a hip, then stroked her back, feeling the warmth of her flesh through the cloth of her mantle.

They delighted in slow, exploratory kisses, each stroking and touching the other, White Hawk leading, Cloud Dancer following. She was unsure of herself, for though it was the custom of her people to be uncensuring of such things, it did not allow for a woman to flit from one man to another. Cloud Dancer had been told much by her mother, and in the environment of the pueblo, where there was almost no privacy, she had seen much, but she had never lain with a man and had no experience now to guide her.

White Hawk pressed her down to the warm, sandy floor of the cave and smiled into her face. "You honor me, Little One." He knew her innocence despite the boldness of her words.

He caressed her once more, seeing surprise and anticipation leap into the depth of her tawny cougar eyes before he withdrew to shed his doeskin shirt. He drew her up gently to untie the knot that secured her long, decorated belt. It was wound several times around her waist, and he unwrapped it as if he were performing a ritual. He admired the beautifully intricate weaving in soft colors of the earth and laid the belt aside. Her mantle, wrapped under the left arm and over the right shoulder loosened immediately, draping into cascading folds around her slim body, teasing him with hints of the treasures that lay beneath.

Cloud Dancer went still; she barely breathed. Her flesh tingled and grew warm as White Hawk reached out to brush the cloth from her shoulder. She gasped, feeling the yearning within her growing, knowing what was to come, though she had never experienced it. The flame he kindled in her belly grew, and she ached to have him in her arms again, to feel him within her and know what it was to be a part of him.

White Hawk laughed softly at the expectant look upon her young, innocent face. He brushed the restraining strip of cloth from her shoulder, allowing her mantle to fall in a heap about her slender hips, baring her small, firm breasts to his gaze and touch.

She sat a little timidly upon her heels as the storm raged outside. White Hawk did not allow her more than a moment's uncertainty with him. His arms captured her in a gentle embrace, pulling her to him again, pressing the softness of her bared breasts against the smooth, broad expanse of his hard chest.

White Hawk felt her breasts against him, as her hands encircled his back, sliding over the roped muscles until they rested, gently curved, over his shoulders.

Her heart thundered its erratic beat. She closed her eyes, reveling in the feel of this man.

Gently, slowly, he nuzzled her neck, his fingers sliding into her hair to stroke the length of it. Then he pressed her back gently into the support of his arm, which was curled around her bare shoulders. Still on their knees, Cloud Dancer's mantle heaped in modest seduction about her hips, White Hawk cupped her breast in his hand, his thumb brushing gently across the budded nipple. He dipped his head, taking the bud between his lips in rough teasing that made Cloud Dancer gasp and cry out in surprise. Her hands moved from his shoulders to stroke downward, fingertips skating over the sheen of sweat that now coated White Hawk's body.

Her bones seemed to melt within her, and her mind lost its focus. She would have collapsed to the sandy cave floor if not for his support. Still her hands explored, stroking him in gentle, circular motions, seeking and beseeching. Filled with excitement and wonder, Cloud Dancer moved her hands to White Hawk's thick braids, freeing first one, then the other, so that his hair hung in a shining black curtain over his shoulders. His skin was smooth over firm muscles. She had never thought a man beautiful before this day, but White Hawk's body, hard and angled before the firelight, could be described no other way.

White Hawk's hands moved from her breasts to stroke up each side of her ribs, then down to where the heavy cotton of her mantle concealed her lower body from his eyes. Hands gentle and coaxing, one sliding up the curve of her back, the other clenched in the folds of the fabric, White Hawk drew the mantle from her and laid it with his shirt upon the sand, leaving her totally naked to his gaze. Quickly he divested himself of breechclout and leggings, adding them to the soft heap of their other clothes, which formed their bed upon the soft sand.

Gently pushing her back upon the clothes, White Hawk had to fight the gut-twisting need to take. She was untried; as delicate as any spring flower, and he had vowed not to hurt her. Sweat flowed freely from his body as he pressed it against hers, trapping the evidence of his arousal between them; his hand drifted lower to prepare her for him.

The roaring in Cloud Dancer's ears dulled the sharp crackling of the fire and deafened her to the sharp wind outside their warm, safe haven. Her world had contracted to this place and this moment. She shuddered against him, straining her smaller body against the length of his larger, more imposing one, and sought the culmination of her desires.

"White Hawk. White Hawk..." His name flowed as easily from her tongue as the spring rains flowed from the mountains. And it tasted as sweet.

She felt him touching her in her soft woman's place, drawing her strength and will from her body, leaving her hot and quivering in his grasp. He nuzzled her breast, sending thin tendrils of warmth streaking down the length of her body to join with the fire already kindled in her belly. Cloud Dancer stared up into his obsidian eyes as he continued his caresses, lighting fires to burn not just in her body, but in her heart and soul.

She clutched at White Hawk as he shifted his weight and nudged her thighs apart to settle between them. Sensations so sweet and strange bombarded her as she twisted and trembled beneath his heated kisses. But the true fire burned in his fingertips. First gentle and persuasive, then bold and demanding, his fingers, long and slender, touched and caressed, teased and tormented.

White Hawk ignited the dormant passions within her and delighted to her reactions. Firmly he held his own need in abeyance, demanding of himself that he wait, go slow and draw her with him to the clouds for which she was named. Each time he drew a breath it was filled with the scent of her. Each time he touched her he was filled with the heat of her desire soaring to match his own. Each time he looked into her eyes his already racing heart skipped a beat that she should offer herself so openly to him. Did she know how she stole his strength away?

Cloud Dancer gazed trustingly up into White Hawk's eyes as his manhood gently found the nest it sought and began to ease inside her. She tensed, and for an instant resisted, then he slid within her.

The sudden sensation of fullness took her breath away. There was pain, but only for an instant, and then it seared its way to a pleasure so intense that she cried out against his throat, arching against him to draw him nearer.

White Hawk hesitated, sweat beading across his upper lip and forehead as he forced himself to wait for her to adjust to him. He fought with all his strength to refrain from plunging on to his own satisfaction. The pulse within her throbbed around him, and only his determination to be gentle kept his wits from spinning off into the void of love's passion. The muscles in his arms quivered as he braced himself above her and looked down into her small oval face, alight with the desires burning within—desires he had kindled and would satisfy.

Then he began to move, slowly at first, urging her with the movements of his body to join him; Cloud Dancer took up the rhythm easily. It was a relief from the squirming, reaching for the unknown that had preceded it, and Cloud Dancer's eyes widened as White Hawk's tempo increased.

"Meet me," he whispered, "lift yourself to me. Let me be a part of you. Hold me and we will soar together."

White Hawk's voice roughened and deepened, and Cloud Dancer gave herself over to the sensations running riot within her body, building and racing through her. Her breath felt locked in her throat. She wanted to cry, but more, she wanted to laugh. It was like sunshine breaking through the clouds after the rain. It was like light filling all the lost, dark corners of the heart. Her head arched back, her blood sizzled in her veins. White Hawk's movements quickened, his thrusts deepened and he touched that place deep within her that burst the sun in shimmering shards across her brain.

They lay quietly in each other's arms a long time after, each listening to the quieting of the other's heart. The snowfall was tapering off outside the cave and the slate gray of the sky was lightening. Soon they would return to Acoma.

White Hawk squeezed her gently, one hand sliding the length of her body while the other fed more fuel into their fire. He cradled her in his arms so that she was nearer the fire, and brushed the soft, tangled mass of her hair from her face.

Cloud Dancer looked up into his face and saw again the warm, gentle strength in his eyes. "It is much more than it appears," Cloud Dancer whispered with laughter in her voice.

"And you are even more beautiful that your laughter carried us to the clouds."

Cloud Dancer sobered, peeping at White Hawk through lowered lashes. She had not realized she had actually laughed! "I'm sorry. I did not mean to laugh."

With a chuckle that warmed her heart, White Hawk playfully nipped her bare shoulder. "It pleases me, Little One, that you would find joy so great in my arms that it brought laughter to your lips. There is nothing for you to be sorry for." He hugged her close and buried his face in her hair, drinking in the sweetness of her.

"We'll have to return soon," Cloud Dancer said with a sigh. Return to Acoma meant the return of apprehension, of standing guard, of waiting for the Spanish.

"Yes."

Sensitive to her meaning, knowing she was thinking of the Spanish, White Hawk could find no other words to say. The future would come whether they welcomed it or not.

Cloud Dancer shivered, not eager to think about the future when the present was so beautifully fragile and slipping so quickly out of her grasp. But she had reaffirmed her decision, lying here in White Hawk's arms. She had tasted of life most fully, and she was prepared to fight for it.

"Come," White Hawk said as the snow outside dwindled nearly to nothing, "we must dress and eat, then we must return to Acoma. It will be dark soon."

Within half an hour they were dressed and had collected the remaining rabbit meat for the trek back. They emerged to a fantasy land of shimmering white blanketing the earth. The fading rays of the sun sneaked between the parting clouds and gleamed and winked off the surface of the snow.

Rested and refreshed after their stop in the cave and the meal of fresh rabbit, White Hawk and Cloud Dancer set out at a swift jog, the ground falling easily away beneath their feet. Everything was draped in the pristine white of the snow; scrubby trees had taken on the look of veiled goddesses, rocks the look of huddled, stooped, old men. The cold was so intense it snatched the breath away and stung color high into their cheeks, but they were not far from Acoma, and would come soon to the warm mud houses.

They rounded a bend in the wash where they had been running and took the easy ascent up a low hill, then another, until they reached a knoll giving a view of the countryside for miles around.

Abruptly White Hawk stopped, waiting, listening, eyes sweeping the distance. Instinctively, Cloud Dancer remained silent, her eyes, too, raking the distant expanse of the gleaming white countryside. Sound carried far on the cold stillness, and there drifted to her ears an odd, rhythmic clanking. It was not a sound she could place.

"There." White Hawk spoke in a soft, unedged voice, muffling the sound behind one hand while he pointed into the distance with the other. "They are coming as your people feared."

Cloud Dancer squinted against the fading light and its glare upon the snow. Far in the distance, little more than oversize specks, she could see the movement of something against the snow. A few more seconds and she could make out shapes of men on horseback.

"What is that sound?" Cloud Dancer asked, knowing it was what had first alerted White Hawk to the approach.

"Their weapons make that noise as they ride," White Hawk responded grimly.

"They will be here soon. And when they arrive we will fight."

White Hawk nodded. "We must hurry. The snow will slow them some, but you are right, they will be here soon. We must warn your people."

Together they turned toward Acoma, their long strides filled with new purpose.

Chapter Four

"No!" Cloud Dancer's shriek was cut short by the report of a Spanish musket as the young warrior who guarded her and the other women and children in the underground kiva toppled from his perch near the top of the ladder with a gurgling cry.

Dark, bearded visages clogged the kiva's small opening, blocking out the gray sky. The Spanish began to fire indiscriminately. Mothers threw their bodies over their children in a vain attempt to protect them. Dust and gunpowder sent up a choking cloud that drew streams of tears from tortured eyes, but failed to hide anyone inside the kiva from the withering blanket of death cast by the Spanish soldiers.

The dying were all around. Cloud Dancer held her mother flat against the earthen floor and whispered urgently to her, "Do not stir! Perhaps they will think us already dead!"

Cloud Dancer's singular hope was dashed as the faint light from above was completely blotted out by the bulk of descending soldiers. Survivors screamed and whimpered when the soldiers kicked them to see who lived, then with savage laughter hauled those few out of the kiva's depths.

With clenched teeth Cloud Dancer managed to keep her silence as rough hands dragged her upward, forcing her up the ladder. Behind her she heard her mother's wail as she scrambled after her. Others were left to die in the next barrage or to try to clamber up the ladder in the face of the Spanish weapons.

Outside the stifling kiva, death screams and blood-curdling war cries filled the air around Cloud Dancer, punctuated by the explosive thunder of the Spaniards; weapons and the deafening clash of arms. Already crimson splashes of blood were everywhere, the sweet, gagging, coppery smell of it heavy upon the frigid air.

The Spanish soldier who held her threw Cloud Dancer to the frozen earth and fell upon her, but she had rolled clear even before Woman of the Willows screamed and flung herself at the soldier's back in a mother's frantic attempt to protect her child. The soldier tried to shake the slight woman from him and gain his feet, but Cloud Dancer reacted swiftly, knocking him off balance so that he fell heavily in his armor.

"Come, Mother." Cloud Dancer grabbed frenziedly for Woman of the Willows, pulling her to her feet. "We must run! We must find safety!" She steadied her mother, until she found her feet.

Frantically, she looked all around her for some sort of weapon. Everywhere, her people were dying; children screamed and fires erupted from houses where the Spanish threw burning torches.

Cloud Dancer stared past her mother, back toward the kiva from which they had emerged. She saw Spanish soldiers wreaking their punishment upon the helpless, watched in horror as they fired their thunder weapons again into the kiva. She imagined she could hear the pitiful cries from that kiva more clearly than any around her. Spinning, Cloud Dancer lunged forward, drawing her mother with her.

Woman of the Willows's legs were pumping now, her round face contorted in anguish. She caught sight of her daughter's expression, and looked back over her shoulder in shared horror.

The Spanish reloaded and fired yet again. As a few survivors tried to clamber out of the kiva, they were cut down by the terrible spiked weapons of the Spanish, which had the head of a hatchet facing one way, a blade curved like an eagle's beak facing the other and the point of a spear at the top. The women they did not kill instantly they threw to the frozen earth and raped before ending their lives.

Cloud Dancer shuddered. She and her mother had been spared, but for how long? Again she sought a weapon, racing ahead of Woman of the Willows. She had to find a place of safety for her mother; after that she would take her place to fight at the side of the warriors. Wheeling, Cloud Dancer started to urge her mother to greater speed, but already it was too late.

Woman of the Willows was crumpling to the snow-covered earth, blood erupting from her chest, a look of stunned surprise upon her gentle face.

"Mother!" Cloud Dancer shrieked and tried to race back across the slippery, blood-splattered snow to the mortally wounded woman's side. Without warning her feet went out from under her on the ice, throwing her to the earth—and below the path of a buzzing miniball spit from a Spaniard's gun.

She got to her knees and began to crawl, flailing her way forward. Her hand came into sudden contact with the lance of a fallen warrior: the weapon she had sought. Instinctively her fingers curled around it.

"Mother!" she screamed again, her voice barely audible in the cacophony of battle.

Somehow, through the chaos and carnage, Cloud Dancer reached her mother's side. Woman of the Willows's mantle was soaked in her blood. Tears welled in Cloud Dancer's eyes, but she did not shed them. They had escaped the kiva. Fate had saved them both for a few moments. Now her mother, sweet, gentle Woman of the Willows, who'd never raised a hand in anger to anyone, was lying in the snow dying. Grief clawed at Cloud Dancer's heart.

She pressed her hand against the terrible wound in her mother's chest, trying to stem the flow of blood, trying to make a difference in what was going to happen—knowing she could not hold back death.

"Mother?" she whispered.

Unbelievably her mother's eyes flickered open. "You were right, daughter." Woman of the Willow's whisper was painracked, scarcely able to be heard above the battle sounds around them. "They are dead, all dead...."

"Shh, Mother," Cloud Dancer whimpered.

"No," Woman of the Willows responded. "The others are gone." Her hand fluttered feebly. "I wish I could stay with you, my daughter...."

Cloud Dancer huddled over her mother, trying to shield her body from sight and harm, and they went unnoticed as the battle surged in bloody carnage on all sides of them. A cold rage so deep it caused her to tremble held Cloud Dancer in its grip, and she longed to throw herself into the heat of battle, to destroy as her mother had been destroyed; yet she could not leave her mother while she still lived. She had to move her! She had to hide her somewhere, to protect her from the Spanish! If she could hide her, protect her, she would heal. She would yet live.

As those thoughts were forming in Cloud Dancer's mind, her mother sighed deeply and slipped away in death. Cloud Dancer's throat went dry and she choked on a sob, easing her mother's still body to the earth. She didn't want to leave her here!

Cloud Dancer rose, intending to drag her mother's body clear of the main surge of fighting, when something ripped her arm. She could feel the white-hot sear of her torn flesh, and she rolled away as a Spanish hatchet whistled above her head. Her hand clenched tightly around the shaft of the spear she had picked up and taken with her. She rolled to one knee to face the danger confronting her and saw the leering, eager face of a Spanish soldier, who towered above her. Her stomach turned as she stood to meet him and she knew the icy chill of imminent death.

Before Cloud Dancer could raise her spear in defense, another pair of combatants careened into the Spaniard, sending him reeling.

Crouching, Cloud Dancer ducked and slipped around the corner of the building, leaving them behind. Blood from the ugly gash in her arm ran down its length, dripping from her hand and fingers. She stopped only long enough to fashion a makeshift bandage, then was moving again, heart pounding, mouth dry.

Spear clasped tightly in her hand, Cloud Dancer dashed around one of the mud buildings close to the moving battle. Quickly, she guided some terrified children away from the heart of the fighting. Then with a savage yell she ran straight for the fray, spear held aloft, small, moccasin-clad feet pattering over the snow in a bare whisper of sound.

The Spaniard she charged, a big, square man, his bearded face twisted into a battle snarl, half turned at her charge. Cloud Dancer's spear went beneath his arm and banged against his heavy armor, inflicting no more than a prick to the flesh beneath, where the slender spear point slipped beyond the protective mail.

The impact jarred her arm and Cloud Dancer fell back in openmouthed horror. Was there no way to kill these butchers?

The Spaniard turned on her with a leer. His frame dwarfed her own and he came after her. Nimble-footed, Cloud Dancer dodged. The Spaniard fell to the ground at her feet, and in numbed surprise Cloud Dancer tore her eyes from him.

"He is not dead," White Hawk said hoarsely, "but we will be if we remain." He dropped the heavy club he had used to fell the Spaniard and pushed her in the direction of some untouched houses. "Conceal yourself. Night is coming. The Spanish are withdrawing. You can do nothing more now but save yourself!"

Cloud Dancer raised her eyes to White Hawk. "This time I will not hide and watch. I will fight them."

White Hawk blanched. "You have not had enough time to learn the skills of a warrior. If you take up weapons against the Spanish, they will kill you."

"If I don't, do you think they will not?"

"I do not know," White Hawk said with a deep sigh. He knew, looking at her, that he could not turn her from her course. "You must decide when the time comes. But know this, Little One, my heart will be with you wherever you are, whatever you choose to do."

Cloud Dancer nodded, the ghost of a smile touching her trembling lips. "I will do what I must, but my heart will be with you also."

He touched her, his hand caressing her cheek with infinite tenderness. He wished to say more, to hold her longer, but the fighting surged around them and there was no time. "Be safe, Cloud Dancer." He uttered the words as a blessing, pressing her toward the safety of the nearby mud houses, then turned and ran to rejoin the fighting.

When White Hawk raced off again, Cloud Dancer moved quickly toward where the slaughter continued beneath the orange-streaked sky of sunset.

Splashes of blood stained the pristine surface of the snow, appearing as dark shadowy pools in the night's darkness. The silence of death hung heavy upon the frigid air. Many had died; many more shivered in the snow and prepared to meet the battle again with the coming of the new day. Some still huddled in the kivas, sunk deep into Earth Mother. There they found warmth and the comfort provided by their nearness to one another. Dawn would bring with it more death.

Stony faced and exhausted, Cloud Dancer stood on the fringes of the huddle of warriors, listening as they spoke in council. She should not be here. It was not her place. Women of the Kere did not attend warriors' council. Neither did women of the Kere kīll in battle. She clutched the spear a little more tightly in her small fist, butt braced against the earth, sharp tip pointed toward the heavens. She no longer cared what her place was or what she *should* do. She had seen death—enough of it to last several lifetimes of memories.

She would never go back to what she had seen. She would not cower or hide, nor was she prepared to give up her life easily or to kill herself as so many already had done. She would not trust her life or death to another; she would fight as the warriors fought. The gods and her own hand would decide her fate.

Only the pale shadow of a fire flickered at the center of the circle of warriors, its yellow light illuminating the features of the men nearest it in sharp crags and dark hollows. The rest fell away in deep shadow. The night wind rose off the mesa and all drew tighter the furs they wrapped around themselves against the terrible cold.

Shivering, Cloud Dancer pulled her own thick fur more closely about her. She had tried to kill this day and on the morrow would kill a Spaniard without hesitation.

"When the sun rises they will come again. You, Chief Zutucapan, and your people must decide. Surrender to their demands, or stand against them. But know this," declared Bempol, respected war chief of the Kere's Apache allies, "if you stand against them it will be at a terrible cost." The proud Apache war chief spoke now not in defeat, but in truth; he knew what must be faced.

"You have seen their weapons—the great stick that throws death with the sound of thunder, the smaller ones they carry in their hands. They wear shirts of metal that turn your knives and spears from their bodies. I joined with you in battle as did the men from my camp. I did not see one of the Spanish fall not to rise again. Did any man here see such a thing?''

The deep, resonant voice of Walks Tall spoke up from the shadows. ''They have offered us terms of surrender. They will accept tribute, our submission—and the deliverance of those who led our people in the destruction of the Spanish party.''

All eyes shifted toward Zutucapan, who had led the Kere in the massacre of Juan de Zalvidar and his men that day in December, not two months earlier.

''They take vengeance for the death we visited upon their number when the snow first fell.'' Walks Tall's tone was accusing.

Zutucapan nodded. Even in the dim light of the small fire, Cloud Dancer could see—and feel—Zutucapan's full attention turn in dark temper toward Walks Tall. ''And what of us? Are we to allow what they have done to our people without taking vengeance for our own? Are we to allow them to abuse our women, to steal from us, even to kill us?''

Another spoke up from the gathering, voice steady, but underlined with apprehension. ''What are we to do? They will slaughter us all if we fight, but our families will starve if we give them what they demand.''

''What has happened in the past is no longer important here,'' Bempol said, his words raw as an open wound. ''You have a decision to make. Will you accept their terms for surrender, or will you continue to fight?''

''It is all lies and treachery!'' Cloud Dancer blurted from the wellspring of misery that had become her soul. She was hardly aware of all eyes turning in her direction.

''It does not matter if we give them tribute. We could give them every pot, blanket and kernel of corn in our stores, but it would not be enough! They wish only to kill us and that is what they will do!'' Cloud Dancer thumped the butt end of her spear against the frozen ground for emphasis. "There is no point to surrendering or giving them tribute. They will but take it and many more will die. If we are to die, I say we die in defiance!"

Walks Tall found her with his censuring gaze. "You are but a woman, Cloud Dancer. You should be in a kiva with the other women and children," he said sharply. "You do not fight as a warrior."

"I have fought this day! If I had not been dragged from the kiva I would be dead with all the rest who took refuge there," Cloud Dancer retorted violently, "But I was dragged forth! I have faced death. I have fought as you fought. And *my* blood, too, colors the snow, mingling with the blood of those who have died!" she snapped. Defiantly, unable to believe they would discount her words at a time such as this, Cloud Dancer jerked her arm from beneath the warming furs to expose the bloodied bandage covering most of her arm.

A quiet moment of wonder passed over the gathered warriors. Women did not speak at the council fires—and *never* did they speak like this. Never before had a woman of Acoma taken up arms and fought as the warriors fought; none knew how to react.

White Hawk, Apache spirit warrior, stood beside Bempol and regarded Cloud Dancer intently, her small figure wrapped in furs save the arm she had freed to display her wound. This night, in this light, she seemed hardly more than a child. And it was her youth that hit his senses the hardest. So young, but so much a woman. White Hawk's heart swelled with pride in Cloud Dancer. Many had died, but she still lived, thank the gods. He bridled silently at the Keres' dismissal of Cloud Dancer's courage.

"Cloud Dancer—" the name was musical to White Hawk's ears as he spoke "—is probably right. There is no guarantee, if you offer them the tribute they demand, that the killing will stop. Or do you have reason to trust the Spanish?"

"Cloud Dancer is a woman, but her words are true," Chief Zutucapan said in agreement with White Hawk of the Apache. "The Spanish have deceived us in the past."

Walks Tall stood, towering over others of the Kere, fur wraps falling away. "The woman should be sent from this council. Whether what she speaks is true or not has no bearing on the decision we must make. I say we should meet the terms the Spanish have offered us. We must try to end the killing."

Murmurs of agreement rippled through the gathering.

Zutucapan stood and raised his hands for silence. When it had descended he paused, looking from Bempol to White Hawk, then back to his people gathered before him. "We shall accept the offer of the Spanish," he said quietly. "Let those in the kivas know that with the rising of the sun we must gather together blankets, pots and clothing. We will take these things to their camp. I will offer myself, for it is I who led our people against the soldiers of Juan de Zalvidar."

There were many uncomfortable murmurs and more shifting of positions, but none protested Zutucapan's declaration that he would turn himself over to the Spanish to meet their demands.

"Then it shall be so," the Kere leader intoned with dignity. "With the rising of the sun the fighting will be at an end."

Cloud Dancer gave a derisive snort. "You will give them tribute and they will kill you. They do not want tribute—they want death. They do not fight only the warriors of our people. They kill women and children who are helpless to fight back. Tomorrow you think to end the dying, but it has just begun. Our people will crawl to them and they will destroy us utterly, because there will be no plan, no defense."

She looked suddenly directly into White Hawk's eyes. "And what of the Apache? What will they do?"

It was plain the question was directed at White Hawk, but Bempol gave Cloud Dancer the dignity of a reply. "We came to aid our brothers and allies in whatever way possible. This day we have fought at the side of the Kere warriors. With the coming of the rising sun we will do what must be done."

Cloud Dancer's eyes glittered. So, the Apache would be prepared to fight. They would respect the decision of the Kere council to offer tribute, but they would nonetheless stand ready to fight if the need again arose. Plainly they did not believe as Walks Tall and the council did, that the killing was ended. She looked again at White Hawk. The hard set of his face echoed Bempol's words. But there was something more in the lines of his face. What he felt for her was mirrored there. The memory of their time together was as strong in his mind and heart as it was in hers.

White Hawk did not take his eyes from Cloud Dancer as those gathered at the council fire disbanded, leaving them alone, standing a few feet apart, staring at each other. Much had happened this day; he had not known if Cloud Dancer lived or died after he left her in battle.

In silence, he regarded her a bit longer. He took a couple of steps toward her and was rewarded by Cloud Dancer's following his example. He could see the bright color of her eyes, tawny brown and aglow with the light of the mountain lion's soul. The cast of her features was grim now, from the experience of bloody death and fear that had swept through Acoma that day. He remembered her face filled with laughter: lips, soft and full, turned up at the corners; eyes twinkling with mischief. He looked at her with a mixture of joy and pain, dreading what might come again with the dawn.

Already many in Acoma who were not warriors—women and children—had perished. It grieved him to think of

Cloud Dancer, too, dying atop this stone fortress at the hands of the Spanish.

"You fought like a warrior today." White Hawk acknowledged her. "Has someone cleaned the wound?"

Cloud Dancer shook her head. "I have done what I can. It can wait."

"And you face tomorrow," he said softly. "You have seen the war of the Spanish. You are not afraid?"

Cloud Dancer shrugged and the heavy fur she clasped around her slipped a little lower on her shoulder. "Yes, I am afraid. Are you telling me that you are not? Should I be more afraid to fight as a warrior and perhaps live then to fling myself off the cliff and go certainly to my death?"

White Hawk moved closer and stared down into her upturned face, marveling at the depths of her golden-brown eyes. "You were right when you spoke at council. Few will survive this." His words crackled with emotion. He could feel her spirit reaching out to his. The warmth they had shared was so near, yet there atop that cold rock, it seemed so far from their grasp.

She smiled wanly. "Perhaps I will be one who survives." She frowned and winced as she drew her injured arm back into the warmth of her furs. "And you? You will fight as well?"

He smiled in return. "I have no choice. I am a warrior."

"And I am not, yet you do not tell me to go hide in the kivas with the other women and children."

"Would you go if I told you to?"

"No. If I am to die I wish to die beneath the clear sky, breathing free air." She looked at him boldly and felt a stab of fear within her breast. It was not fear for herself; she had learned quickly to live with that and keep going. This was a fear for White Hawk. The thought of him among the dead tore open the ugly wound of her mother's recent death and squeezed her heart until the pain threatened to choke her.

"You are Apache, not Kere," Cloud Dancer murmured, trying to control her sudden shakiness. "It is not your fight."

"The Spanish do not care. To leave this place we will fight as the Kere must. Or the judgment of Zutucapan and your warriors will prove true, and the fighting will stop with the payment of tribute and the surrender of Zutucapan. Perhaps the taking of his life will at last satisfy their need for vengeance."

Her mouth dry, Cloud Dancer looked away, then back, ensnared by the black-eyed gaze of White Hawk. "I fear Zutucapan is a fool. He will die for nothing."

White Hawk did not want to leave her. This child-woman-warrior of the Kere was entrenched in his heart. Even the bulky furs she clutched around her for warmth could not hide the slim womanly shape he had come to know so well. There was fire in her eyes and in her soul. He no longer doubted; this was the woman of his visions when he had gone through the manhood rites and become a spirit warrior—a medicine man and a warrior. He had also seen much death and destruction, and he had seen the fire woman fall in battle. Had he come so far then just to have it come to nothing? Could such a thing be so? He laid his hand upon her shoulder and drew her close to him; he needed to feel her in his arms again.

"Our people have different customs, Cloud Dancer. Among the Kere a woman is permitted to talk as you do now to me—and to look at me as you do. Among the Apache this would not happen, and I would not speak so boldly," White Hawk said passionately.

Cloud Dancer blushed furiously at this sudden change in his manner. "If you speak what is in your heart, there is no harm."

"I will not tell you not to fight if it begins again, for I do not think you are wrong. But I will fear for you, Cloud Dancer, and if I fall, my last thought will be of you."

Gently, his hand touched her cheek. "If we live," White Hawk said softly, "there will be much to talk about between us."

Cloud Dancer's heart swelled, and without thought she turned her cheek into the warmth of his broad palm. Hope struggled and strained against the threads of the cocoon she had wrapped it in, surging forth in a rebirth within her. Her mother was dead. Of her father and her sister, she knew nothing. But White Hawk, spirit warrior of the Apache, was here before her and with his love he sought to give her a reason to live.

White Hawk took his hand away and stepped back from her, though it was not easy to do. He wanted to take her into his arms and love her once more before the rising of the sun. But there was no time; soon he would be called to join the other warriors.

"We will live," Cloud Dancer said with sudden conviction, her voice stronger now that a small distance separated them and she could gather her wits.

Older, and much more experienced in war than Cloud Dancer, White Hawk could not capture her idealistic optimism, but he had a will of steel and he would not be easily defeated. "Do not go close to the camp near the head of the trail," White Hawk advised her. "If the tribute is not accepted, that is where the fighting will begin. If it starts do not run to it. Let the fighting come to you. Do not let your emotions rule your head. Many will die, but you cannot stop that. Do not let the cries of the wounded and dying cause your death. You can save yourself, perhaps. You can help some others, but you cannot save them all. If you are dead, you can do nothing."

Cloud Dancer nodded solemnly as Bempol called for White Hawk to join him. Tears prickled behind her eyelids and she blinked rapidly to keep them from spilling over. She did not know if she would ever see him again.

Giving her one last, lingering, caressing look, White Hawk laid his hand briefly against her cheek and then was gone.

The warm impression of his hand, the feeling of where his fingers had touched her flesh, remained. Cloud Dancer stared after him as he, Bempol and Zutucapan moved in the direction of the cliff camp of the Spanish.

In the east the sky was beginning to grow pink with the promise of a new day. Already the hopeful Kere women, with their children, were emerging from kivas to return to their homes and their stores to collect the tribute, believing it would buy peace. Some were forming a column heading for the place where the Spanish waited.

There had been no sleep for Cloud Dancer. She stood now quietly, her spear clenched tightly in her hand, her injured arm aching. She watched her people moving in obedience to the Spanish command. Her heart ached at the destruction all around her. It contracted with the wrenching pain of loss and emptiness.

She watched her people herded together like animals to do the bidding of the Spanish, the bile rising in her throat as the hairs prickled along the back of her neck. Her throat clenched tight against an involuntary scream, and everything inside her body vibrated with what was to come.

Chapter Five

The first cry echoed eerily across the mesa. The terror of it brought the previous day's bloody horrors flooding back to Cloud Dancer in an overwhelming wave, and she would have vomited in the snow at her feet if there had been anything in her stomach to bring up. Instead, she froze for a moment, unmoving while White Hawk's words of advice passed again and again through her mind like rolling thunder.

Let the fighting come to you. If you are dead, you can do nothing. What White Hawk had spoken echoed through her. They were good words. They were sane words. But the powerful pull of that first awful cry of death reached into her soul and she felt herself being drawn to her people.

Another cry followed the first, then another. Confusion reigned. Cloud Dancer heard the sound of many people running. More shrieks followed and distinctly male bellows of pure fury thundered across the mesa, followed by the fearsome call to battle. Zutucapan then still lived; his battle cry was not to be mistaken.

A girl burst into Cloud Dancer's place of hiding as if materialized by the gods. "Run!" Running Fawn shrieked, her eyes so wild and strange in terror that at first Cloud Dancer did not recognize her friend who'd been so gleeful at the rabbit hunt. She ran on, strewing a swath of clothing, blankets and cornmeal. "Treachery!" Her hands, freed of their burdens, tore at her hair in a frenzy of grief at the horror she had witnessed. "They will kill us all! Run! Run!"

The echoes of White Hawk's words of warning were forgotten as Cloud Dancer started to run after the irrational girl. Her feet pounded against the hardness of the frozen ground. Somehow she had to bring reason back to the girl, direct her path, or she would be lost.

"No!" Cloud Dancer cried. "Not that way!" But her voice was lost in the tumult of screams and yells and the roar of Spanish weaponry. Her spear hefted and clenched tightly in her hand, she ran toward the chaos.

Cloud Dancer did not hear the single shot that took young Running Fawn, but she saw the back of her dress suddenly splash with glistening crimson. The soft, creamy buckskin soaked red in an instant. Two more steps and her thin legs became suddenly useless, folding beneath her, plunging her headlong into the snow, her spine severed by the Spanish ball.

The battle cries of Acoma's men racing to engage the enemy rose in volume, joined by the hoarse bellows of the advancing Spanish. Slowing her steps, Cloud Dancer reached the frail maid she had sought to help and dropped to her knees on the ground beside her. Gently, her own heart beating a frenzied tattoo, she turned the body, oblivious of the continuing battle around her. Unblinking in death, sightless, staring eyes looked up at her. Rigid, her jaw clenched against a scream, Cloud Dancer eased Running Fawn's limp body down to the ground.

A terrible, aching void was all Cloud Dancer had left inside. A violent, boiling hatred together with an almost sweet longing for retribution grew in her heart.

A thunderous explosion buffeted her eardrums. The force of it ripped the very earth and threw its remnants into the air.

All around, people ran in every direction. The Spanish thunder weapon spoke again and again. Smoke drifted upon the air, sometimes choking in its density, and the fires the Spanish set spread throughout Acoma. There was no order, no hope. It was not a battle, it was a slaughter.

Some of Cloud Dancer's people ran toward the fighting, men picking up anything that could be used as a weapon. Some were armed only with sharp sticks and large stones. Some women ran to protect their children, dragging them away from the terrible battle and screams of pain and death. Others ran toward the fighting to share the fate of their husbands.

Throwing her head back, Cloud Dancer gave an almost inhuman cry of rage and pain as she stood and turned with determination toward the battle, the fur that had warmed her through the night of horror falling away. She would join White Hawk if she could. If there was to be nothing left to her, she would fight and at least know he was near—if he had not fallen already.

"White Hawk has not fallen." Cloud Dancer spoke the words over and over again, like a litany against the din of death and horror that surrounded her. "I will not fall until I have taken a Spaniard with me," she vowed, nursing the bitterness and hatred seeded within her, taking no notice of the tears trickling in quiet warmth down her cheeks.

Her feet pounded the frozen ground. Children screamed pitifully, carried off as prisoners of the dark-faced Spaniards. One boy threw his small body into a fire set by the Spaniards rather than be taken by them. Others, older, calmly walked into flaming houses to die.

The mingled smells of burning flesh, blood and gore hung moist and warm upon the dry, freezing air. Cloud Dancer gagged again, but ran on, legs pumping mechanically without conscious direction.

Smoke from the spreading fires continued to billow and curl like a clinging fog almost everywhere. She ducked in and out of its screen, using it to pass undetected toward where the worst of the fighting raged. Gunshots cracked across the frigid air. All around her, men fell not to rise again as the metal balls of the Spanish found their targets. At the edge of the cliff, Spanish soldiers were hacking her people down, throwing their lifeless bodies from Acoma's heights. Children, quick and agile, avoided the hands of the Spanish to throw themselves over the cliff in the wake of their dead parents.

A cry, thin and reedy, filled with the despair of a dying animal, diverted Cloud Dancer's attention and changed her direction. The cry had been familiar; she raced toward it. A small figure struggled on the ground beneath a heavy, squat, black-bearded Spaniard. The face of his pinioned victim jerked toward Cloud Dancer as the Spaniard prepared to use her body, knife in one hand poised for the kill.

"Cloud Dancer!" Woman of the West Wind cried in recognition of her sister. "Run!"

The soldier, distracted from his first intent, glanced sideways to where Cloud Dancer sprinted toward them before he plunged the knife into Woman of the West Wind's chest.

Woman of the West Wind screamed only once, then lay still, saved at least from one last humiliation. Cloud Dancer did not run as her sister had bidden. For her sister she would sip the sweet nectar of revenge that she had sought while traversing this hellish horror. Her foot lashed out with all her strength. The soldier's nose pulped in a bloody spray, and he yowled in pain, dark eyes fastened on Cloud Dancer in a killing fury. He rose from her sister's still body, knife in hand, and lunged for Cloud Dancer. She hit him again, this time with the butt end of her spear, feeling a savage satisfaction, a singing of the heated blood in her veins, as his ear was nearly torn from his head and a new flow of blood joined with the first.

"Beast! Pile of dung! You have destroyed my sister!" Cloud Dancer shrieked at him, enjoying his pain while her

sister's body lay at his feet. She knew he did not understand a word she hurled at him, but did not care. The rage
tearing at her insides had to have release. "Murderer of
women and children! Spanish dog! I will have your life for
hers!" She wanted to kill him by inches, but there was not
the time.

Cloud Dancer flipped the spear so its point was forward
as the cruel-faced Spanish soldier came at her, brandishing
the knife that still dripped her sister's blood. She did not
know if his fury blinded him so that he did not see or if he
was so stupid that he believed she would turn and run before his obvious black rage.

Her courage did not fail her. She held her ground and let
him charge. She had seen in the past how the metal shirts the
Spanish wore deflected the points of the Kere spears and
arrows. Cloud Dancer was determined to have her revenge.
Beneath the shirts they were just men like the warriors of
Acoma.

Until the last instant Cloud Dancer stood firm and
waited, feet braced in the snow. Her warming fur long lost,
she found the cold not debilitating but bracing, clearing her
head for what she would do. Her injured arm ached and
pinched, but it was not useless.

The Spanish soldier came on. Lithe as a cat, Cloud
Dancer dropped in front of the charging, bloodied Spaniard half rolled and brought the spear tip up from below. He
all but fell upon it, the sharp point finding soft flesh below
the mail. He groaned and shrieked, limbs flailing uselessly,
the knife flung from his hand as he grabbed the shaft of the
spear close to where the mortal wound gouted blood from
his belly.

For an instant they were suspended that way, the bulky
soldier impaled upon the spear above, Cloud Dancer braced
against the ground, holding the spear firm, twisting against
the earth to roll clear of his inevitable fall. In death, his
squat body relaxed and the spear pierced him through, its

exit blocked by the shirt of metal in back. "Ahh!" Cloud Dancer screamed in horror as the body on the spear above her descended upon her. She rolled free, but lost her spear.

Coming to her knees, she searched for the knife the soldier had dropped, her eyes rising to a heated battle beyond. Bempol and the Apaches fought the Spanish with savage determination, leading a small band of Kere warriors who still stood and fought. There, among them, White Hawk battled, feet braced in the blood-spattered snow. As if he felt her eyes upon him, White Hawk's gaze flashed in Cloud Dancer's direction, a look of pain flitting across his angular features.

Then the Spaniard clubbed him. His head snapped back with the impact before he fell, half-dazed. In casual contempt, the Spanish soldier with whom he had fought pointed the thunderstick carelessly at White Hawk. The sharp crack of its explosion followed.

True to his word, White Hawk's last thought was for Cloud Dancer as darkness, complete, fell heavily about him.

Cloud Dancer staggered to her feet. "No!" The shriek of her denial pierced the din of battle, drawing attention to her even as the fights around her continued.

Another of Bempol's warriors discovered the secret of the shirts of metal as Cloud Dancer snatched up the falling soldier's knife. Reeling toward them, the Apache warrior sank his knife into a soldier's belly beneath the mail, disemboweling him with a ripping stroke side to side. The soldier was dying on his feet, but he lunged forward, clasped the body of the Apache to him and slashed the warrior's belly wide. Blood flowed and the two men fell, entrails grotesquely entwining against the glistening white snow.

It was too much. Cloud Dancer no longer saw the horror, the blood, the death around her. She saw only White Hawk's fallen body, knew only her desire to reach his side. There was nothing left for her. Her family was destroyed. Acoma was burning. Her people were lost. White Hawk, he who had given her something to live for, had fallen. She would die at his side.

Cloud Dancer never saw the Spanish miniball that knocked her legs out from under her, cutting short her desperate attempt to reach the fallen Apache warrior. It brought with it a white-hot pain that seared through to her soul. She saw only for the briefest instant the young Spanish soldier racing toward her, his club upraised to deliver the killing blow. She saw his face, contorted in an expression that twisted together fear, pain, horror and anger; he was young—so very young—his swarthy face barely fringed by the distinctive black beard of the Spanish conquerors.

She tried to rise. Youth did not matter! The Spanish had no mercy, she would have none. She would kill this one if she could! Or he would kill her.

Pain shot through Cloud Dancer anew with the sudden movement, and weakness washed over her like a spring flood as warm wetness spread rapidly from her new wound. She saw the club falling, rolled to avoid it and barely felt the pain that brought with it darkness and an end to struggle.

Chapter Six

The killing, the mutilation, the blood, all swam before the darkness of Perez de Ortega's tightly closed eyes. He had come to realize the enormous wrong they had committed at Acoma, and he himself had not been without guilt. His head drooped and he cried.

Fear, pain and loneliness penetrated every corner of Perez de Ortega's heart. "What will I do if you should die?" Perez opened his eyes and spoke to Cloud Dancer, who rested a little more quietly now upon the bed he had prepared for her. "I can never go back to my own people. They will not see the value of what I did. They will see it only as desertion. They will think me a coward. And if they finally believed the reason I fled with you was not one of fear, if they knew why I truly ran from Acoma, it would be worse. Many helped when I ran, laughing and making vile jokes about where I was taking you. They will be very angry when they realize I never returned to battle." He buried his face in his hands and again wept.

It was three days since he had taken her and fled from that damnable rock upon which Acoma stood, leaving behind the blood and the killing frenzy—three long days since he had taken Cloud Dancer from the carnage as the single act of reparation he could find to carry out amid that hell. He had not known if she would live or die. He had looked upon the face of this beautiful Pueblo woman and remembered the savagery with which she had fought. He had cleaned her wounds and wrapped her in furs, keeping a fire burning close by to allow her to rest after he had found a safe place to camp.

He knew little about healing save what his mother had taught him about herbs, and of those whose properties he did remember, he had only the ground alum root he carried in a pouch to treat minor wounds. He did not carry a large quantity of it, and certainly had not expected to be treating wounds as extensive and bloody as those dealt the young Indian maiden, but he had applied the little he had and the bleeding had stopped almost instantly. That had given him some small hope.

Kneeling now beside Cloud Dancer, Perez soaked a cloth in cool water and mopped her face. She had a fever. He prayed it would not get worse. "Are you coming back to me?" Perez spoke to her softly in Spanish, though he knew she wouldn't understand even if she could hear him. He knew only a little Pueblo language.

Cloud Dancer tossed and turned on the edge of consciousness, murmuring time and again about death and the end of all she knew.

"You are not dead." Perez spoke with some difficulty in her language, hoping the familiar words would draw her forward into the waking world of a cold, gray winter day. "You are not dead, and you are safe. The fighting is over. We are far from Acoma."

He was not sure his last words had been wise—if she could understand him. Being far from Acoma might frighten her, just as, if the truth were known, he was afraid being so far from those who had been his friends and comrades and the city of San Juan on the Rio Grande. The shock of what he had done had yet to fully engulf him. He had thrown away all he had been taught to believe in for the Indian maiden stirring restlessly beside him. Perez sighed deeply and ran the cooling cloth once again over her delicate face with its small chin, straight nose and uptilted cat's eyes.

In all of his eighteen years he had never done anything that so mystified him. Why *had* he done it? The horror of his memories of Acoma caused his stomach to roll and his throat to go dry.

At first he had believed the retaliatory raid against Acoma, as punishment for what had been done to Juan de Zalvidar and his men, was justified. There had seemed nobility in their aim: punishment and a returning of the peace through war; peace—according to the friars—was the principal object of war. And as the object of war was to establish peace, then it was justifiable to exterminate and destroy those who stood in the way of that peace. The war had to be waged with good faith and without covetousness, malice, hate or ambition for power, but during the execution of that war, the wrongdoers and their possessions would be at the mercy of their conquerors.

Such had been the declaration of the friars when the governor had asked what conditions were necessary to wage a just war. Such had been the words spoken to the men as they had armed themselves with broadswords, halberds, muskets and brass artillery, preparing for the march to Acoma. Everything had been polished and oiled and inspected repeatedly. Every man's knapsack had been filled with his issue of emergency rations, gunpowder and bullets. They had worked day by day after Christmas and into the New Year, and they had come to love their weapons and equipment, as absorbed as children in a new game; awaiting danger, anticipating the fight, they were happy.

By the order of the governor all men in the party went to confession and communion before leaving with the army, for was this not a war blessed by the friars? Then, on the morning of January 12 in the year 1599, the army against Acoma left San Juan. It had taken them nine days to reach

Acoma; at first good humor passed through the men in rippling waves, but soon they felt the tension growing.

And then it had started. Vicente de Zalvidar, Juan's brother, was under orders to call upon Acoma for peace, and submission. This he did, but he did more. He demanded that those who led the insurrection against his brother be turned over to him for punishment. He demanded that tribute be paid as recompense for those who had fallen, for were not the possessions of these murdering rebels at Vicente's mercy as the friars had said?

The terms had hardly been expressed before the killing started. Perez squeezed his eyes tightly shut, sitting close beside Cloud Dancer, and tried to force the memories of the slaughter, rape and destruction from his mind. Bodies had been hurled from the cliffs above even as the last of the soldiers ascended the heights of Acoma using the steep and treacherous pathways of the Indians. Perez had not been able to block from his heart the humanity of all those who died at Acoma that day. He buried his face in his hands again.

Cloud Dancer's mind was reeling. Was there truly pain after death? she thought, swimming in her sea of darkness, resisting the exhausting return to consciousness.

And the bluster of the cold wind. Did she feel its bite because there had been no one to see properly to her burial? Yet there was warmth, too. She felt wrapped securely in a cocoon, unable to move; it was muffling and constricting. Uncomfortable, she began to squirm.

"My people are all dead." Cloud Dancer's voice, soft and weak, could not have startled Perez as much if she had screamed at him.

When he looked down into her face he saw the anger sparkling in the depths of her tawny eyes, and he knew at that moment that if she were not so weak and at his mercy she would try to kill him. It was no more than he had expected. He smiled at her—a tentative gesture of kindness in the face of overwhelming hatred.

Cloud Dancer stared at him. She was not dead; she was alive and she was alone with this young Spaniard with the sparse fringe of beard and sad face. Her thoughts were confused, but she was sure he was the one she had seen coming at her with a club after she had fallen before the weapon of the Spanish. He had raised it above his head and then ... darkness. She was not dead; neither was she in the camp of the Spanish. Coming out of her fog, she had thought she heard this young one crying. Was she a prisoner? Were there others? What of Acoma?

She hurt everywhere. She was hot, but felt cold. Her head throbbed in an agonizing rhythm. Her arm pinched and prickled, filled with heat. Her leg knew a piercing pain that stabbed through it at uneven intervals; that was more reassuring than the fuzzy pain of her lacerated arm. She had not cleaned it properly. She had not expected to live to regret it. Poisons were gathering.

"My name is Perez de Ortega," the young Spaniard said very haltingly, in what sounded vaguely like her own language.

He turned toward the fire where he had kept a broth warm; he had brewed it from wild roots he had recognized as edible if not palatable, boiled with some of the dried meat from his emergency rations. "You need to get some strength back," he murmured as he filled a dented cup and turned toward her. Over the past days he had fed her drops of the broth when she was close to consciousness, and able to swallow. But now it would be different. What would he do if she would not eat?

Cloud Dancer stared at him a few long moments. Taking stock of the condition of her body, she became aware of a persistent gnawing feeling in her stomach when the smell of the broth reached her nose.

Perez could read in her face that she was searching for answers. "I will help you eat," he offered, picking up a spoon.

Cloud Dancer drew back. She wasn't sure she wanted to eat if it meant taking help from his hand.

He waited, wisely not pushing her, watching her eyes.

Returning his stare, Cloud Dancer looked up into his square swarthy face, his brown eyes filled with unfathomable emotions. She would not die now unless she, in essence, killed herself. There did not seem to be anything to live for, yet she could not be like so many others at Acoma. She could not give up her life easily. She had planned to die at Acoma with the others, but this young Spaniard had not allowed it. That he had saved her and not some other had to be the doing of the Great Spirit.

"It grows cold," he said patiently.

Her hunger was becoming worse with the titillation of the steaming broth so close at hand. But being fed by the hand of her enemy was intolerable—unless she could find a rationale she could live with.

He was giving back a tiny portion of what had been taken from her people. The thought was almost enough to allow her to accept the nourishment. Then she came up with another reason to eat at his hand. If she lived to kill one more Spaniard because of the help provided by this one, then it would be worth it. Cloud Dancer set her chin stubbornly. "I will sit up."

Ridden by the demons of his guilt, Perez would have refused her nothing. This was a small enough request. He set the cup on the ground, then wrapped a wiry arm around her to lever her up to where she could lean against a large rock, keeping the blankets tucked securely about her.

Cloud Dancer frowned at the sudden clamoring of her senses the movement set off. Her stomach rolled and her head spun. She felt as if she had run uphill for miles, and darkness threatened to close in on her once again. A wave of heat rolled upward from her feet to swamp her face in a flush that brought a sweat to her forehead.

"Are you all right?" Perez asked anxiously. "Would you like to lie down again?"

With a stubborn shake of her head that set bells ringing in her ears, Cloud Dancer said, "I am all right," but she was drained by her own weakness.

Perez picked up the cup from the ground, dipped the spoon into the broth and held it to her lips with an expectant air. Cloud Dancer sipped the liquid and felt its soothing effect all through her body. It had not much flavor, but it filled her stomach and warmed her limbs. She consumed most of what the cup contained that way, one small spoonful at a time while the silence stretched between them like a chasm.

When the first cupful was gone, Perez filled it again. Cloud Dancer hesitated at the sight of the refilled cup, and Perez smiled faintly and waited, spoon poised. He had to clamp down his force of will tightly to keep from laughing and shouting his joy at each small success. He must tread carefully. It was like nursing a small, frail bird. He did not want to rush or frighten her.

"What are you called?" Perez asked Cloud Dancer when she looked away from the proffered cup.

This skinny Spaniard with the furrowed brow and slight frame, not yet having reached his maturity, was reaching out to her. Cloud Dancer could feel it. Should she tell him her true name? Did it really matter? What did matter anymore? She was too weak, tired and confused to give it any deep thought.

"Cloud Dancer."

He nodded and held the spoon to her lips once again. "A name of great grace and beauty," he said with a solemn nod. "How old are you?"

She took more of the broth and said, "I have seen sixteen summers." She flicked her gaze at him. "How many summers have you seen?"

Perez grinned, heartened by her curiosity in response to his own. "I'm eighteen."

She sipped the broth and grunted.

"Tomorrow I'll catch us a rabbit," Perez promised, "but I think the broth will have to do for today. Since you haven't eaten in so long, too much too soon might make you sick. At least that is what *mi madre* told me after I had been very sick.

"I'm sorry about what happened to your home. I know that doesn't help, but I want you to know I'm sorry. I . . . I just couldn't think of anything else to do, but carry you away. I had to change something. I am only one man. There was nothing else I could do." He hesitated, realizing he had begun to babble in Spanish, as Cloud Dancer allowed another mouthful of broth to slide down her throat. "I understand how you feel. The loss, the loneliness. You are very young to be so alone," he said speaking still in her tongue.

Cloud Dancer was too weak to rail at him in her fury, her voice too stiff. What did he know? What could he know of her grief and loss? He was the enemy. His people had slaughtered hers. All she had ever known and loved was lost: her family, her home, her friends. Even the brief moment of closeness, of love, she had shared with White Hawk had been snuffed out. Perez had been there with the hated Spanish. He was one of them. What could he know of what she had suffered? She would never again feel her mother's arms around her or hear her sister's plans and laughter. She would never again work the clay in reverent silence with her sister, and she would never again participate in the joy and excitement of the harvest dance. Gone, it was all gone; swept from her life by the Spanish.

Then the sudden realization hit Cloud Dancer like a dash of cold water from a mountain stream: this Spaniard had left everything behind to take her from Acoma. He could never return to his people. He was an outcast—alone—just as she was alone, her people lost to her in death. Perhaps he did know something of the pain of loss. Her anger subsided. She could not see him as a friend, but she had to accept what he had done. He had sacrificed greatly.

Perez de Ortega's face mirrored his soul. Every emotion he felt was plainly imprinted there for the world to see. And pain was the predominant emotion expressed. Yet Cloud Dancer knew that to have survived what he had, to have brought her here, he could not be a weak man. He confused and disarmed her.

"Your people were wrong to demand so much of the Kere that they would starve if they agreed," Cloud Dancer said when at last she spoke again.

Perez did not argue the point. "Both our people were wrong. Zalvidar should not have demanded so much. Your people should not have killed him and his soldiers." He hesitated. "One must kill at times to survive, but that was not such a time."

Anger flared again in her eyes. "You were not there." The words were hurled at him like sharp pebbles. She had been there. She had seen and she remembered.

"I am a soldier," Perez returned. "Until I took you from the mesa top, I had no choice but to fight. But that was not fighting there, it was killing, just as it was no more than killing when your people attacked Juan de Zalvidar's men. Now there are many choices to be made. I will make them and you will make them. We are both without a home now. Neither of us can return to our people."

He put down the cup and spoon he had so patiently fed her with. "The first choice is rest. You must rest and get better so we can leave this place soon. I don't know how long it will be before they look for me, or even if they will, but we cannot remain here long, and it has already been three days."

Cloud Dancer wanted to protest in anger when he gently lowered her to the ground, but she did not have the strength, and sleep seemed such a wonderful thing that she could not fight against it.

Perez smiled down at her. "If you awake hungry, call me and I will give you some more broth."

When Cloud Dancer awakened the next morning, Perez de Ortega was not there. She felt an instant of panic. Where was he? She could not take care of herself. She was not strong enough. What would happen if he did not come back?

She moved within the constricting embrace of her sleeping furs. Most of the aches and pains of yesterday came back, though they seemed a bit muted. The ache in her head was nearly gone. The pain in her leg was sharp, but it was a healing pain. She turned, then allowed sudden fear to jerk her to full, clear consciousness. Her arm lay beside her like a dead log. It was terribly swollen, the skin stretched so tight it looked ready to burst. Save for a fuzzy, distant prickling, there was little feeling in it. The hand was almost totally without color or feeling.

Quickly she loosened the bandage with her good hand. The skin beneath was ugly and discolored. Red and black mottled the flesh, and the whole of the wound oozed a yellow liquid. The bandage was not her own. It had to have been Perez who had changed it, but the poisons were still gathering.

In a panic Cloud Dancer tried to sit up, but fell backward, the short fall jarring her and setting off new sensations of pain. Breathing heavily, she closed her eyes, squeezing back the fear. She had to think. She was sure Perez would return. But where had he gone and how long would he be gone? She had seen such festering wounds as hers a couple of times in the past. She knew well that hers must have herbs and roots to draw the poison, or if not that, heat. And the skin would have to be pierced where the poisons gathered, to allow them to exit along with the demons who would steal her arm, and probably her life.

She looked toward the place the campfire had been the night before. The fire was still burning. Perez could not have been gone long. Did that mean he would be gone a long time more, or that he would be back soon?

Gently, Cloud Dancer laid a hand upon her injured arm, feeling the heat emanating from it, touching it fearfully as though the slightest pressure would cause it to burst. Tears swam in her eyes and her throat closed upon a sob. It was not fair! To have survived so much, to have been brought here from Acoma against her will; she could not lose her arm!

Cloud Dancer knew she could not wait for Perez to return. She craned her neck until she saw much of the small, tidy camp. An animal skin was lying a little to one side of the fire, near a pack. That would do for something to hold the hot water against her arm. She could put it into steaming water and apply it as a poultice. Also near the fire were several small sticks Perez had brought for kindling, and there was a pot that still contained some of the broth he had fed her. Propped up among a few small rocks was a gourd of water. The effort cost her much, sapping her flagging strength, but Cloud Dancer dragged herself nearer the fire and the supplies. Sweating with weakness and exhaustion, she managed to cover those few feet.

Loath to waste the broth, Cloud Dancer nonetheless dumped the pot and refilled it with clear water. She picked up the skin while she waited for the water to heat. It was soft and would be absorbent. When the water began to steam she would soak the skin and apply it to the wound. She winced at the thought, but there was no other way.

She leaned back against her furs and nearly fainted, keeping her hold on consciousness only by sheer force of will. Sprawling half in and half out of the furs Perez had so carefully wrapped her in, feeling the chilled bite of the air, she shivered as its dryness swept the dew of her sweat from her skin.

Cold and confused, but determined, Cloud Dancer lay waiting for the water to heat when she heard the sound of a horse approaching. She blacked out a few times, but somewhere in the coming and going of the darkness, she realized it was Perez who suddenly appeared to hover over her.

"*¡Madre de Dios!*" Perez exclaimed, laying aside the rabbit he had trapped and dressed. "What are you trying to do?"

Then he saw her arm. Cloud Dancer smiled weakly as Perez's face showed a look of pure horror. He dropped to his knees beside her and gathered her up to wrap her in the warmth of the furs and his arms.

Cloud Dancer trembled in her weakness. "I must draw the poisons with heat. Then, when the poisons are near the surface you must open the wound and allow them to flow out until the blood runs red."

"I'm not sure. I haven't done anything like this before." His words were drawn out, nearly a moan.

"I am sure," Cloud Dancer whispered intensely. "We have come this far. There is no other way."

He gave a tight nod and glanced almost fearfully toward the pot where the water heated. In grim silence he berated himself for not taking better care of her, for not paying closer attention. And yet the wound had not seemed so bad just the day before, when he had changed the bandage as she lay unconscious.

"I do not want to hurt you," Perez protested when he saw the thick steam beginning to rise from the pot of water.

"Pain is not as permanent as death," Cloud Dancer pointed out softly, trying herself not to think of the moment when the hot cloth would touch the raw wound. "It is time. Take the skin, and when you have soaked it, use a stick to place it on the wound. You must hold it there."

With a less than steady hand, Perez did as Cloud Dancer bade, trying without success to divorce himself from responsibility for the act. This was her desire, her idea, not his. If he had not returned, she would have accomplished this herself. He knew something had to be done and he himself did not know what, so they had to rely upon her knowledge.

He dropped the soft chamois skin in the pot of boiling water, poked it with a stick and fished it out again, soaked and steaming. He brought the skin close to the wound on Cloud Dancer's arm and she flinched.

Immediately Perez drew back. How could he bring her pain when she had already suffered so much?

Cloud Dancer's eyes sprang open and their tawny depths sparked with anger at his reluctance. "Do it...now!" she snarled, arranging her face into an expression of rigid control.

Startled by her savage whisper, Perez did not think any longer, but laid the steaming, dripping skin across the ugly, festering wound. Cloud Dancer was too weak to do anything more than gasp and faint.

Perez de Ortega had never had to do such a thing in his life, and it tortured him that he had to do it to the beautiful, delicate woman who so gently touched him. She was stubborn, she was angry, and she brooked no overtures of friendship, yet she was stealing her way into his heart the way the dawn cast its light over the night.

Allowing the heat to penetrate a few minutes, he then dipped the chamois into the water and applied it a second time, grateful that Cloud Dancer still sought escape in unconsciousness.

After the third application the wound looked different. The ugly discoloration seemed to be centering, drawing in around the jagged red gash that was the original wound. Yellow fluid oozed in tight, infrequent drops from the wound. He applied the hot compress again. And again.

Most of the day passed that way, with Cloud Dancer in and out of consciousness, incoherent even when her eyes opened. Perez rearranged the furs so that they covered all but her pitiful arm, then built a windbreak to their north. After that he steeled himself and continued the treatment she had demanded. The wound changed tremendously, the yellow fluid collecting in a tight knot close to the surface of the skin. It gave him hope; it had to be an improvement. She had told him he would have to lance the wound when it reached this point. His stomach dipped, but he put his small dagger into the flame to clean it.

He had always hated waiting, and this was by far the worst. While he sat beside her, huddled against the cold, Perez gazed down into her small oval face. She was so beautiful. High cheekbones set off the uptilted cat's eyes. The chin was also small but squared with a stubborn set, and the soft, rosy tone of her tan skin almost seemed to make her glow. He sighed deeply. Cloud Dancer was so very young. Sixteen. Only a year older than his own sister.

He gave a twisted, pained smile at the irony. Cloud Dancer accused him of youth when she was younger than he; but perhaps what appeared to be so was not true. Even though they had shared the same experience at Acoma, she had experienced it from a different perspective. Perhaps she really was older. He gazed steadily down at her as the time slowly passed. She stirred within him feelings of protectiveness and emotions he could neither name nor understand.

Sweat broke out upon Perez de Ortega's upper lip as he lifted the dagger from the flame and allowed it to cool a few moments in the icy January air. The knife was razor sharp. It would not fail him. The blood pounded at his temples. He could only bear to look once at the yellow, swollen place where he would put his knife before he plunged it in, opening the wound anew from top to bottom.

Great clots of putrid-smelling yellow and green liquid spilled from the wound in the path of the knife. The smell of it was so overpowering it made Perez gag, but he did not relent. He put the knife aside and began applying gently increasing pressure from the bottom of the wound toward the opening.

More of the yellow liquid burst forth, both watery and in more solid clumps. That was followed by blood, nearly black in color. Cloud Dancer moaned softly, but did not awaken. Still Perez worked at the wound, kneading it and cleaning it, remembering Cloud Dancer's instructions. Until the blood ran red, she had told him. He had to continue until the blood ran red.

Sweating profusely now, though the air could not have been much above freezing, Perez peered intently at the wound. Blood, bright crimson, was beginning to ooze up through the wound. Doubling his efforts, Perez was rewarded by the clean, steady flow of red blood untinged by discoloring poisons.

With a joyful cry he sat back on his heels and allowed the wound to bleed a little bit longer, cleansing itself. Then he soaked the chamois once more in the hot water, this time allowing it to cool a bit before he used it to wash the wound. Satisfied at last that he could do no better, Perez applied the last of his mother's alum root to stem the bleeding and bandaged the wound before tucking Cloud Dancer's arm back beneath the furs.

She would be all right. He knew in his heart. There was nothing more he could do for her now. She needed rest. With a silly grin quirking his lips and lighting his face, Perez retrieved the rabbit he had cast aside when he saw Cloud Dancer's distress. In a very short time he had the rabbit roasting on the spit over the fire, a fresh broth begun and his horse watered and cared for.

Cloud Dancer was awake when Perez returned, and looked up at him with gratitude in her eyes. She realized she would not have had the strength to poultice, lance and cleanse her wound. She was having a hard time reconciling her anger at him for taking her from Acoma with her gratitude for all he had done.

The swelling in her arm was down dramatically and the arm ached with an unforgiving, but welcome pain. She found she was ravenous, as well, the smell of the rabbit cooking over the open fire causing her stomach to growl softly in anticipation.

Perez squatted beside her, his hand automatically going to her forehead to check for fever. She was warm, but not hot. "You're going to be all right." He had a shy smile. "What you told me you wanted me to do worked. All the poison is out. It will heal now."

"You are a good man, Perez de Ortega." It was the only thing Cloud Dancer could think to say that did not lay bare before him her gratitude.

Perez chuckled softly, the sound rich and soothing to Cloud Dancer's ears. He tore off a piece of the cooked rabbit and fed it to her. He looked at her again and shook his head.

"*¡Madre de Dios!*" he whispered to himself, realizing what had been happening to him as the days had passed. He had fallen in love with this small stubborn woman.

Chapter Seven

Whatever it was that woke Cloud Dancer, she was grateful for it. She had slept long enough over the past days. It was time for her to begin living again. Her wounds were healing. There was less pain with each sunrise. It was difficult for her to focus on exactly how many sunrises had come, melted into early day and dissolved into sunset followed by the icy grip of the night, since she and Perez had come to this place.

Perez de Ortega had hovered over her as if she were a helpless child. He had hunted for their food between cleansing and dressing her wounds, helping her to move around, feeding her and talking to her throughout her convalescence. He had eaten little and seemed to sleep even less, as he was instantly at her side each time she had awakened.

They never spoke of the nightmares they each suffered during sleep. They were still enemies, despite the easing of tensions between them over the days spent close together. They could not yet share their pain.

Perez de Ortega was standing on a slight rise of land a short distance from their camp, looking out across the rolling landscape, dotted with scrubby pine. The air was cold and fresh, bearing the scent of the pine on biting, though gentle breezes, and the sun was brilliant against a clear blue sky, bringing warmth to the winter land. It was good here, but they would have to move soon; already they had lingered too long in one place.

When Cloud Dancer stirred, Perez de Ortega was instantly aware of it. He hurried the few strides back to her. She was sitting up in front of the windbreak he had fashioned, warmed by the fire before her and the reflector he had built behind it.

"You must be careful," Perez said softly. "It would be a bad time to rupture one of your wounds."

Cloud Dancer frowned, ready to snap her reply, but marshaled her emotions and glanced up at him through lowered lashes. "You aren't going to tell me I can't get up? That I will injure myself if I dare to move?"

With a shrug and a smile, Perez shook his head and squatted beside her on the ground. How he wanted to hold her close, to be more to her than savior and protector. But as yet he saw no possibility of that reflected in her tawny eyes.

"If I did, would it stop you?" The words were an echo of White Hawk's on that fateful day at Acoma.

"No."

"Then that is even less reason to say it—but I would not have said it anyway. Soon we will have to leave here. The only way for you to regain your strength is to begin to walk, and as soon as you're ready, to do some light chores."

"You want me to work for you." Cloud Dancer frowned. She said the words not out of belief of their truth, but to prick the young Spaniard.

Perez's lips gave a wry twist. Always this young Pueblo maid could color his words to make him seem a monster. She clung to the enmity she believed should still exist between them. But, he thought with an inward smile, it was apparent that doing so was more and more difficult for her.

"No," Perez answered her patiently, "I want you to work for yourself. Now come, I will help you up. You can lean on me if you tire. We will go sée my horse." Cloud Dancer's language came a bit more easily to him now, with her help.

Instantly she brightened. In his ramblings to keep her distracted during the time it took her body to begin to heal, Perez had told her much about the big animal he rode, which carried him with ease. It did not matter that he was playing on her interest in and attraction to the horse. The Kere had no such thing as these god-dogs, which Perez referred to as horses. None had ever touched one of the great beasts and never had there been the opportunity to ride one. Her greatest desire was to spend time near the horse. She put out her hand to Perez and he took it in his own, warm and dry despite the coldness of the air.

Her breath left her in a small whoosh as Cloud Dancer gained her feet, and she swayed before Perez wrapped his arm around her waist to steady her.

"You're all right?" he asked, holding her up. At the same time he made sure that the thick fur was wrapped tightly around her, as they were about to leave the warmth of the fire.

"I am well," Cloud Dancer murmured, too stubborn to admit otherwise, though for a moment the land had tilted crazily away from her as though on a separate axis from the earth beneath her feet. She breathed deeply. She did not like the way Perez was holding her, but knew if he did not, she was likely to fall.

"You must try to walk a few steps as soon as your head stops spinning," Perez advised, remembering well his own long illness when he was small. He found it a little awkward to talk to Cloud Dancer when he held her like this, but at the same time, it seemed so natural. She fit the curve of his arm just so. And though her stubborn strength, emanating from some deep spring within her, stiffened her against him, Perez was aware of a warmth spreading throughout his body such as he had never known before.

Cloud Dancer fixed her gaze straight ahead, refraining from answering Perez with a nod. "I am ready," she announced firmly, then emphasized her statement with a step forward.

Perez moved as one with her, avoiding any jarring motions on his part. "We will go slowly at first," he said softly, hoping to reassure her and encourage her with the same breath.

Cloud Dancer's leg pinched, and was reluctant to take her full weight, so she limped. Her arm throbbed slightly, though Perez took care not to touch the injured limb, and her head felt as though its top were floating somewhere high above. She was aware of nothing around her—not the birds, or the cold, or the vaulted blue sky overhead—but knew only the effort it took to place one foot in front of the other and move forward in her dragging gait.

The horse nickered at their approach. Accustomed to a lot of attention, as she was in truth Perez's pet as much as his property, the mare was not used to spending long periods alone with no one to brush her or feed her, or just talk to her and scratch her ears. She tossed her head and nickered again in greeting, pressing forward as far as her generous picket line would allow.

Perez grinned when they got close enough to feel the mare's hot breath on their cheeks as she sought to nuzzle him.

Cloud Dancer felt she was in the way. "She is very strange!" she said breathlessly in an attempt to cover her apprehension at the mare's familiarity.

Aware of her straining back against his arm, Perez said teasingly, "Bonita has been lonely. She thinks I have been paying too much attention to you!"

Cloud Dancer could not suppress the wisp of a smile at his words, and her tension eased slightly when the mare did no more than nuzzle Perez and pluck at his clothes with her teeth in search of a treat. "What does Bonita mean?"

The shy, warm smile that weakened Cloud Dancer's reserve toward Perez tugged at the corners of his mouth. "It means something like 'pretty girl' in your language."

"You named her well," Cloud Dancer replied. This was about as close to a compliment as she had come with the young Spaniard, and he warmed to her praise.

"It's a pet name, really, and I'm afraid I've made a pet of her. Even so, she does do her job, and none can say she doesn't do it well."

The light-headedness had receded, giving Cloud Dancer a clearer view of the world. She removed one hand from the depths of the fur robe to hold it before the roan mare. Bonita responded by snuffling the proffered hand.

"She likes you to stroke her nose and pet her neck," Perez suggested. He felt Cloud Dancer straighten, and eased a bit of his support away from her.

Lifting her hand, Cloud Dancer placed it on the muzzle of the friendly mare. It felt like warm velvet! Bonita blew softly and gazed upon Cloud Dancer with fathomless brown eyes so warm and gentle they melted Cloud Dancer's heart.

"Feels nice, doesn't it?"

"Like the fur of a baby rabbit." Or a lover's touch. Her rebellious thoughts brought back memories of White Hawk's tender touch in their last moments together at Acoma.

Unaware he was competing with a ghost, Perez gently took Cloud Dancer's hand and placed it upon Bonita's neck. "There, and what does that feel like?"

They were like children sharing a game. Cloud Dancer's happy face was alight with excitement. Her cheeks were pink in the cool breeze, her eyes sparkling as Perez had never seen them. What a glory it would be to hear her laugh! he thought.

Cloud Dancer stroked gently, the mare's neck smooth beneath her touch. "It's like the finest cloth! So smooth! Or maybe like the softest leather, tanned until it is suitable for delicate tasks." Her small hand crept into the mane where it hung long along the arched neck, shining a rich reddish brown in the brilliant morning sunlight.

The mare, obviously reveling in the attention, stood very still, reaching her nose out to Perez to be stroked as the girl continued her gentle exploration.

"You can lean against her," Perez prompted. "She won't move."

"The hair here is coarse and strong," Cloud Dancer exclaimed, allowing the mare to support some of her weight instead of Perez. "It could be used for sewing, or braiding into rope!"

Perez laughed. "Horsehair has been used for that. Once I heard it was used to sew up the wounds its master had received in battle."

Bonita shook her head and switched her tail. Cloud Dancer jumped, and in her weakened state would have fallen had not Perez's steadying arm been there. The mare craned her neck, bringing her face close to Cloud Dancer's, a questioning look in the depths of her liquid brown eyes. She obviously was not used to dealing with humans so unsteady on their feet.

"Bonita, stand!" Perez's sharp command was a reaction to the need to protect Cloud Dancer, but it brought a wounded look to the mare's eyes.

"She is standing!" Cloud Dancer almost allowed a soft laugh to escape. "It's not her fault I cannot stand upon my own two feet! Oh, Perez, she is so very gentle."

He nodded in agreement, instantly contrite for the sharp tone he had used. He stroked the mare's neck gently in reassurance that he was not angry with her. "Bonita is very gentle, but you must always remember, Cloud Dancer, that it is not so with all horses. Some are full of energy and would prefer not to be ridden. Those who would be their masters must fight them every day they ride. Others have bad habits, like biting if they are annoyed, and some are like some people—they are simply mean. You must always be cautious until you know an animal well."

"You speak as if I will one day have an animal such as this for my own."

"Won't you, my little warrior? Horses are here now in this land, and they are multiplying. There are not many yet, but there will be. I don't think you will be content until one of them is yours."

Cloud Dancer hugged Bonita. "Not one—many!"

"So be it!" Perez laughed softly. "But it will have to be later. You should rest now. We will visit Bonita often, and maybe she will not be so jealous." He grinned and promised, "In a couple of days I will let you sit upon her back."

"Does it feel strange to sit upon her back when she is moving over the earth?" Cloud Dancer asked, not resisting his suggestion that she rest after her exertions.

"It did, a little, at first," Perez responded as they walked back together toward the campfire and its beckoning warmth, "but not any longer. Now when I am astride I feel almost like a part of her."

Bonita gave a plaintive nicker at their backs. Cloud Dancer was struck with awe and fascination, thinking of the many uses her people could have made of horses if they had had them. Horses could carry heavier burdens farther than her people could carry the same loads upon their backs. They could carry hunters farther, increasing their range in search of game to fill their pots. Perhaps they could even drag a pointed stick to till the soil when it was time for planting.

Perez walked beside Cloud Dancer back to the windbreak before the fire, his steadying arm hovering around her, but it seemed she gained strength with every step now. She leaned against him hardly at all. Nonetheless, she was breathing heavily and limping badly by the time he helped her ease back down on the ground amid her bedding near the fire.

"Are you hungry?" Solicitous as usual, Perez held the offering of warm rabbit stew in a small bowl in his hands before she had the chance to accept or refuse.

Cloud Dancer remained sitting up and accepted. She was ravenous most of the time, though Perez pushed food of one kind or another upon her constantly.

"I will take Bonita and go hunting, if you will be all right here alone while I am gone."

Cloud Dancer frowned. "Of course I will be all right. I am not a child. I am not afraid to be alone," she declared with that stubborn lift of her chin that Perez had come to know so well.

Perez paused, looking at her with tender regard, then turned to delve into the small pack of his possessions. He pulled out a single-shot cap and ball pistol and turned to Cloud Dancer.

"You are proud, Cloud Dancer, but you are not yet strong. If anyone or anything bothers you while I am gone, you can use this."

Cloud Dancer gasped. "The stick that thunders!"

"It's a pistol, and it doesn't take strength to protect yourself with this—unless you count how it can knock you over backward when you fire it."

He squatted beside her. "Here, you take it like this." He pressed it into her small hands and curved her finger around the trigger. "Point it at what you want to shoot, and pull this back." He gently tapped the trigger.

"You are not afraid to give this to me?"

"Are you going to shoot me?"

"No."

"Then why would I be afraid?"

"Sometimes I do not understand you!" Cloud Dancer exclaimed in frustration.

Perez's face softened. "It is not something I can explain. I have no people. You have no people. Until we can find a place to live where we will be happy, we must take care of each other. Later, when you are stronger, I will teach you to reload it. Now,'' he said softly, ''point the pistol and fire it for me once before I go.''

Cloud Dancer cringed. In her hands she held the terrible weapon that had destroyed her people. Now this man of those people who had brought the weapon to Acoma was asking her to use the thunder weapon herself. Her impulse was to drop it as though she held fire. But something stayed her hand. She looked at the pistol, grasped loosely between her hands, and was aware of the roiling storm of her own emotions.

For a moment Cloud Dancer was dizzy. Then she fixed Perez with large, round eyes and gathered her tattered strength to do as he bade. She would not point out to this young Spaniard that after this she probably would not have the strength to awaken if anyone threatened their camp while he was away. He was offering her the secrets of the Spanish and she would accept his gift. One day soon, she would be able to use that knowledge against the tyranny of the Spanish invaders.

Cloud Dancer raised the gun, pointed it in the general direction of a large scrub tree and pulled back the trigger, as Perez had instructed. The pistol roared. The sound at this close range was even more earth-shattering than Cloud Dancer remembered it from Acoma. Her arm spasmed, and pain raced along its length with the unexpected force of the pistol's explosion. She was knocked back against the wind-break, her heavy clothing and furs cushioning her against the force of the impact.

A large chunk of bark flew away from the tree. It was not exactly where Cloud Dancer had intended, but it awoke within her a swelling feeling of power. She pulled herself upright before Perez could extend his hand to help her.

He took the pistol from her, the acrid smell of gunpowder still heavy upon the air, and deftly began to reload. He poured the powder, added the shot and applied the packing. It seemed to Cloud Dancer only an eye blink until he handed the weapon back to her, still warm from its previous firing.

"If you were pointing the pistol at the tree, you did very well," Perez said after a long moment of silence between them. "If you were not pointing at the tree, make sure whatever it is that is attacking is very close before you pull the trigger."

He stood and collected the longer thunder stick from his belongings. "I'll be back soon. Maybe I'll be able to get us a deer."

"If you do, thank the spirit of the deer for its sacrifice that we may eat."

Perez nodded and strode purposefully away. Cloud Dancer placed the pistol close beside her and eased back upon her bed to rest.

There was a dusting of snow upon the ground, more granular than crystalline since the cold was so intense. Every breath Cloud Dancer and Perez expelled formed a vapor cloud upon the air. The dry cold crackled; the stirring of the gentle breezes rattled the bare branches of scrub brush together and even made strange clattering noises—like the rattling of bones—through the branches of the occasional cedar trees.

"Soon we will be leaving," Cloud Dancer spoke softly into Bonita's ear. The horse twitched the ear and nuzzled Cloud Dancer. The young woman from Acoma had made friends with the mare as Perez had said she would. She had spent time with her every day and ridden upon her back on numerous occasions, with Perez leading the smooth-gaited mare. "You are not to worry because you will be carrying two of us," Cloud Dancer continued. "We will let you rest often and be sure you are well fed. Perez is teaching me much about you. Our friendship will grow over this journey."

Perez, packing the last of their meager possessions into a tight bundle, glanced in Cloud Dancer's direction. He was proud and pleased with the way she looked. Her cheeks were highly colored by the cold, but beneath that was the glow of returning health. She stood straight, limped only a little and could now use her arm in performing easy tasks about the camp. He could see her strength returning with each day that passed.

It would have been beneficial to her health to spend a few more days here, beneath the brilliant blue skies and the warmth of the winter sun, but they would move very slowly at first, allowing Cloud Dancer to accustom herself to hard travel by degrees. Perez felt strongly that they must be moving. They had lingered here too long already. He was not too good at gauging danger, but the first law of escape was to keep moving.

It was a fact that each day was more dangerous than the last. Isolated as they were, they had no way of knowing where the Spanish were patrolling, or if they were searching for him—or even if they realized what he had done. For both their sakes they could not risk running across any of the Spanish army.

"Bring Bonita," Perez called to Cloud Dancer. "We will be leaving soon. We must get ready."

The sun was barely up, its rays not yet producing enough warmth to penetrate the night's lingering cold. Perez had planned the early start in consideration of Cloud Dancer's still weakened condition; he believed it would be best to travel as far as they could early in the day, before she tired. Then they could stop early to camp and he would be able to hunt for their dinner.

They had eaten well, camped here at the foot of this mesa. Perez de Ortega was a good hunter, and Cloud Dancer had provided plenty of knowledge about setting snares to catch small animals, as well as how to cure and tan the skins properly so they could be used. While Cloud Dancer was gaining strength, she had fashioned from these skins a pair of thick-soled, high-topped moccasins for Perez that he cherished. He wore them whenever he went hunting, because the moccasins allowed him to move over the ground much more quietly than in the heavy boots he had worn previously.

And, although Cloud Dancer was much more used to wearing clothes made from cloth—either of cotton or of yucca fibers—she and Perez constructed for her a pair of breeches and a loose-fitting shirt from the skin of the deer. The garments were soft, supple and warm. For further warmth there was a cloak made from the furs of small animals. Had she been back in Acoma she would have been wrapped in a cloak fashioned from turkey feathers, the soft down of the turkey's breast and body tied with yucca fibers.

Cloud Dancer led Bonita to Perez, talking to her gently as he himself would have done. He greeted the mare in Spanish—a few words of which Cloud Dancer was coming to understand. He stroked Bonita's neck and prepared to place the heavy Spanish saddle and accoutrements upon her back.

Cloud Dancer frowned. "Would she not be more comfortable carrying us both if we rode without that?"

"Maybe," Perez said, acknowledging the possibility, "but I need the saddle to ride well. And if I did not, I still would not leave the saddle behind because I could sell it in one of the settlements and use the money to buy supplies."

"She is not very large to carry such a load," Cloud Dancer offered tentatively.

"She is stronger than she looks," Perez reminded her, "and we will not travel hard at first." He smiled down at Cloud Dancer. "You have a gentle heart."

Cloud Dancer blinked, caught unprepared for the compliment. In Acoma she would have been honored; now it seemed almost an insult. He saw in her what she believed she no longer had. During the battle at Acoma she had striven to stamp out all traces of that gentle heart. She had told herself that as long as the Spanish were upon the land, there would be nothing gentle about life.

Now Perez de Ortega saw and acknowledged what she sought to conceal. Always she was so confused where this young Spaniard was concerned. There was a sisterly fondness growing within her heart that could not be denied, and yet beside it resided the black anger of her hurt and loss. He had saved her, but he was a Spaniard. Before he had saved her, he had killed. It was so, or he would not have been there to carry her away. He was one of them, but he was also a single man. A man who had seen a wrong and sought, in some small way, to create a right.

Perez handed Cloud Dancer the bundle of skins and furs they had not had time to make into something useful and finished saddling Bonita. Intrigued, as always, when he slipped the bit into the horse's mouth and put the bridle on, Cloud Dancer watched intently with puckered brow. Each time she felt there should be a a a better way.

Handing Cloud Dancer the reins, Perez scattered the last remnants of their fire and concealed, as best his meager experience in such things would allow, the traces of their camp. He even used pieces of scrub brush to wipe the dry earth beneath the fine dusting of snow clean of their footsteps.

"I don't know how good a job I've done," Perez said when he rejoined Cloud Dancer, "but I can't do any better. It's time to leave." He sighed, then climbed up on Bonita, turning to extend his hand to help Cloud Dancer mount behind him.

Cloud Dancer accepted his help, swinging up behind him with something less than grace in consideration of her healing leg. She was none too experienced in the ways of concealment—one of the specialties of the Apache, not her people of the mesa—but she felt compelled to express some encouragement of Perez's efforts. "You have done well," she said crisply. "The sun will melt the snow in only a few hours, and then there will be little to betray we were ever here."

Pleased at her words, Perez de Ortega smiled softly, enjoying the closeness of her behind him as she settled herself for the long ride ahead. He gathered the reins as Cloud Dancer's arms crept around his waist to keep her from falling off Bonita. After hesitating a moment to be sure Cloud Dancer was ready, Perez touched his heels to the restive mare, the animal even more eager for the trail than they were. They started off to the northeast.

Cloud Dancer, who had never been more than a few miles from her home at Acoma on the mesa top, was now severed from that world like a piece of driftwood upon the ocean. She was facing distances heretofore not even contemplated and a future unimaginable. She remembered the talk she had heard of a great river that lay to the east of Acoma and wondered about it.

"Will we see the Great River?" Cloud Dancer asked Perez with a twinge at the remembrance of White Hawk's words that he would one day show her the Great River.

Perez gave the mare her head and let her pick her own pace. The sturdy little mare took to the trail with long, confident strides. "Yes," he answered Cloud Dancer. "We will not get there for a while, but when we do, we will follow the river north. I don't know too much about the other Indian tribes, so we will have to be careful."

Cloud Dancer squeezed Perez in her excitement and laughed, the sound a new and unexpected delight to Perez's ear.

He laughed, too, and called over his shoulder. "Hang on, Bonita is well rested and eager for a run. I'm going to let her gallop."

Chapter Eight

The sun was coloring the western sky, painting the vaulted heavens a brilliant peach, turquoise, then purple beyond the western mountains when Perez and Cloud Dancer first came upon the Great River.

"Rio Grande is what my people call the river," Perez said softly, respectful of the awe Cloud Dancer appeared to feel.

Never in her life had Cloud Dancer seen so much water at one time. Acoma was an environment of dusty red stone perched four hundred feet above the somewhat greener valley below. The summer rains had come there in torrents that ran for a time then dissipated. And the time of rain had been a time when the Kere had worked hard to direct the flow of the precious liquid to the crops upon which their lives depended.

"It is so big. Does it never stop? Where does it come from? Where does it go?" Cloud Dancer's questions were breathless.

With a chuckle, Perez touched his heels to Bonita and guided the mare down the soft embankment. Tonight they would camp on the shores of the Rio Grande for the first time. The river that seemed so large to Cloud Dancer was, in fact, little more than a stream at this spot.

"It is not so large," Perez corrected her, hating to cause disappointment, but feeling responsible to impart such knowledge as he possessed. "It begins a long way to the north of here and runs until it reaches an ocean called the Gulf of Mexico. There, where the river meets the great waters of the gulf, you would be able to stand upon the shore and look out across an expanse of water that seems to go on forever, but even that is a small body of water compared to other great oceans."

Cloud Dancer stared at the meandering river, trying to envision what Perez told her. For a few moments she was silent. "If you do not think it is so large, why do your people call it the Rio Grande?"

"I did not name it," Perez said, drawing Bonita to a halt and dismounting. He turned to help Cloud Dancer to the ground. He knew she was stiff and sore at each day's end, but she never complained, never asked to stop sooner or rest more often. "But," he continued, leading the mare to the flowing water to drink, "I would guess it was named that by a man who saw the river at flood in the spring when the melting snows feed it." He stroked Bonita's neck thoughtfully. "Or maybe," he said with a sly grin, "it was named by a man who by the time he got here was desperate for water and any stream would have seemed a Great River!"

Cloud Dancer could not help smiling at that. It was true. Water was precious here. On either side of the river beyond the spreading limbs of the tall cottonwoods, bared by winter's cold, stretched vast expanses of dry land, almost desert.

"The river makes a beautiful music," Cloud Dancer observed, her ear tuned to the soft rippling and rushing of the water over stones and through the silt of the riverbed. She knelt and scooped some of the icy water into her mouth. "It is sweet and cold! I think it tastes of the mountains. Will we go into the high mountains on this journey as well?"

There was such a beauty in Cloud Dancer's innocent wonder at the world, such a contrast to the angry warrioress he had taken from the mesa, that it took Perez's breath away. He looked at her, and though he did not want to, he felt a man's desire tighten his loins. Now was not the time, he reminded himself. She was not yet healed of her wounds, and the long days of travel were exhausting. It would be different when they found a place to stay. Then, when the wounds of her flesh and the wounds of her soul were more fully healed, he would approach her as a man did the woman he loved and desired.

"The sun is setting quickly," Perez said, changing the subject and totally forgetting Cloud Dancer's last question. "We must make camp and start a fire."

"You are all right, Perez?" There was a queerness in the set of Perez's face that Cloud Dancer could not understand. During their days on the trail together she had come to like him, even to think of him as a friend, and she had believed she had become sensitive to his expressions and moods. But this one was a puzzle. It was a look that almost resembled pain, yet how could it be pain? He had not injured himself. And when he rode with her and the days passed, it was with laughter.

"Yes, I'm all right," he answered quickly, feeling his face flush red that she had seen the longing in his face. "It's going to be bitter cold once the sun is behind those mountains. We need to get the fire going fast. Gather some small branches and dry leaves. There should be plenty around here." He still spoke quickly. "I'll get some bigger logs to add after the fire is started. Then I'll leave you to take care of Bonita, and I'll see if I can get a rabbit or two."

A little startled at Perez's sudden recital of every task that was to be done, Cloud Dancer nonetheless moved to do as he asked. Already she could feel the cold penetrating her clothing. Without the brilliance of the January sun to warm them, they would be huddled and shivering in only a few minutes.

There was plenty with which to start a fire, and an abundance of forage nearby for Bonita. It was a good place to spend the night.

Perez swiftly got the fire started. Then, wearing the moccasins Cloud Dancer had fashioned, he disappeared into the encroaching night in search of their dinner.

Cloud Dancer did not like being relegated to the chore of camp tending while Perez did all the hunting. She was learning to hunt; Perez had taught her how to shoot and reload the small thunder stick. There were the snares she had learned to set, and the throwing sticks her own people had used to hunt with. But learning to hunt took time and practice, both of which were scarce at the end of a long day on the trail. She would learn, but for now she would be patient, feed the fire and wait for Perez to return.

The moon, full, cold and bright, was rising behind the jagged silhouette of some distant mountains when Perez returned with his catch. More rabbits.

"You are going to have to teach me about the plants that grow here—ones we can eat—or we will get very tired of eating rabbit," Perez said, busily finishing cleaning the rabbits and spitting them above the fire Cloud Dancer had nurtured.

"I will teach you," Cloud Dancer agreed, "but we will hunt together."

Perez eyed her speculatively. She was healing quickly, gaining strength with each day. And she wanted to learn to hunt, to be independent. He could not fault her for that. Even though he could not fault her for it, it was still so unusual in his experience that it was difficult for him to accept. Still, he recognized that in this changing land it would be the best gift he could give her: the ability to take care of herself if something happened to him.

"We will hunt together," Perez agreed, and wondered a moment if he should tell Cloud Dancer what he had found while he was out alone.

He turned the spit slowly, deep in contemplation. He had been raised to respect women, to protect them, even though there were many who would tell him that such teachings by his parents did not extend to the women of these primitive peoples. Some claimed the Indians were dirty, backward and slow. Perez did not see these people through those eyes. Cloud Dancer flew in the face of all the detractors' claims. She was bright and quick, strong and independent and industrious. She did not understand the ways of the Spanish, but she knew the ways of life. She deserved to know the truth, to know what dangers they faced.

"There were tracks near the river when I hunted," Perez said in a low voice.

"Tracks?" Cloud Dancer was puzzled for a moment and waited for him to continue. His tone and attitude telegraphed the fact that this was not good.

"Tracks made by horses other than Bonita. I couldn't tell how many there were, but it was plainly several. And where there are horses, I cannot help but believe my people are nearby."

Cloud Dancer shuddered. Much of the peace of the night left her in a rush. She drew the cold night air deeply into her lungs to steady herself and turned large, fear-rounded eyes upon Perez. "Do you think we will see the Spanish?" She referred to them as though Perez did not share their heritage. Over the time they had spent together she had come not to think of him as Spanish and she as Kere. They were just two people.

"I don't know," Perez replied. "It is a big country. Perhaps we will pass each other. But also because it is a large country, it is possible they will see us from a long way off. If we try to avoid them then, they may think it suspicious and follow us. I cannot tell what may happen. We will have to wait and see."

Cloud Dancer's answer was to shudder again and look away.

"We are far from Acoma," Perez offered. "If they do not know me they will not know we are from there. Not unless they are searching for me."

Wrestling with his guilt for both participating in the destruction of Cloud Dancer's people, and betraying his own, Perez was not sure how he felt about the possibility of meeting a group of his own people out here, so far in time and place from what had happened at Acoma.

Her gaze fixed on the distant stars lighting up the night sky, Cloud Dancer could not meet Perez's eyes as a sudden thought shook her to the core of her being. She asked the next question. "If they know you, what you did at Acoma, what will they do to you?"

Perez stopped turning the spit and took the crisp rabbit meat from the stick, handing a piece to Cloud Dancer when she at last turned her gaze upon him. His whole body tightened and then he drew a breath. "I'm not sure exactly how, but I think they would kill me. At least that is how the soldiers would handle it. The officers, the leaders, would call a trial—a council of the chiefs—and then they would order me shot."

He smiled wanly and took a bite of the juicy meat, savoring its rich flavor. "If we meet them we can only hope they will not know who I am and what I have done."

"You are a good man, Perez," Cloud Dancer said firmly. "It is not right that you should have to be ashamed of what you have done."

Perez felt the full weight of her words. His heart warmed as a wave of emotion swept over him and he smiled at her, a full, dazzling smile that conveyed much more than words could. "In my heart, Cloud Dancer, I will never be ashamed of what I did that day at Acoma. My shame lies in that I could not do more."

"You did what one man could. You did more than many men would. There is no shame that you should suffer."

"You are kind, Cloud Dancer, kinder, I think, than you want to be noticed. Your words are a balm to the wounds of my heart and soul, but I must live with that day for the rest of my life."

Never had Perez looked so young to Cloud Dancer as he did then, speaking earnestly to her. His square face, fringed in sparse black beard, seemed so old, yet so very young. Slender as a reed, he had proved himself time and again to be nonetheless as tough as rawhide, despite the softness of his coffee-brown eyes and the lines of bitter experience that surrounded them.

Cloud Dancer tamped down the wellspring of her own grief and met his eyes directly. She had hated Perez once, but she could hate him no longer.

"You will live with that day, Perez," Cloud Dancer assured him, "and when the years have passed and you have gained the wisdom of the elders, you will see the words I spoke to you now are true."

Perez sighed and swallowed a bite of the rabbit meat around the lump in his throat. "I hope that time will indeed prove you right," Perez murmured, not eager to upset Cloud Dancer further with denials, but knowing in his heart with a chill of premonition that he would die with that day of horror as vivid upon his conscience as it was now.

Chapter Nine

With the rising of the sun they were riding again, Cloud Dancer astride Bonita's back behind Perez. Perez guided Bonita up the slopes and across the ridges, sketching a trail parallel to the Great River, moving against its flow, yet keeping clear of the riverbanks. That was where the riders were most likely to be, he decided—hugging the banks of the sluggish river.

Cloud Dancer clung to Perez. Aware of the swifter pace he set today than in days past, she said nothing. She watched the winter-sparse, rolling hills, dotted with only an occasional twisted cedar tree, slip away on either side of them, and her eyes anxiously scanned the dense greenness that screened the river from their view for some sign of the dreaded Spanish.

Through the long hours of the sun's climbing high into the sky, they saw nothing. Then, with Bonita tossing her head, eager for water, they turned to the river intent on only a brief pause to slake the thirst of them all, and suddenly the Spanish were there, in front of them, as if they had materialized out of thin air.

Perez's instinct was to jerk Bonita up short, wheel her in her tracks and run, but he curbed that first impulse and allowed Bonita to continue moving forward at her brisk walk, making for the water as if there were nothing more on their minds than to quench their thirst with the river's sweet waters.

"Don't move and don't say anything." Perez forced the words between clenched teeth, words edged with desperation.

"Turn away!" Cloud Dancer pleaded, the bile of remembrance rising suddenly to clog her throat. She trembled and could not stop it; every moment of Acoma's horror replayed itself upon her consciousness. In the bearded countenances of the Spaniards on the bank of the river before them, she saw again the faces of the plundering soldiers. She felt again the bite of th it morning's piercing cold and heard the screams of her people.

"It's too late. It was too late the moment they saw us. There is a friar among them. The soldiers are probably escorting him somewhere. We'll be all right," he finished with a confidence he didn't feel.

Their reception by the Spanish was one both of puzzlement and of wariness. It was not common for a Spanish soldier to be traveling these distant wilds with only one of the natives for company. It was a dangerous land to travel alone.

The friar stepped boldly forward to greet Perez. He was a short, thimble-shaped man, appearing bowed beneath unutterable burdens, and yet there was a stiff regality about him, dressed in his simple brown robes. He projected a strong presence, born of devoted certainty—a presence belonging to a man who, in his own quiet way, was used to command.

Perez drew Bonita up a few feet from where the friar stood. The man regarded them for a moment before moving closer. "I am Fray Francisco de San Miguel," the friar announced, waving his escort back, brushing off their tendency to hover around him in a protective wall. "We are traveling to the pueblos, my friends and I. Please, won't you get down and join us for some food. We have plenty, and it is not usual for us to meet one of our countrymen out here alone. Perhaps we can talk and you can tell me where you are bound."

The hood of the friar's robe was pushed back to drape over his shoulders and hang down his back, revealing thick, sandy hair and a fringe of reddish beard accenting a hard, square jaw. His eyes were gentle, his manner patient.

Cloud Dancer stiffened at Perez's back. "I will not get off Bonita to stand among my enemies," she hissed.

With a nod, Perez swung his leg over Bonita's neck and slipped from the saddle. "I am Perez de Ortega," he said, deciding against lying about his name—surely they would not recognize it. He was not good at lying and did not wish to jeopardize himself and Cloud Dancer with small mistakes. "We have traveled a long way and have much farther to go, but we were going to stop for a meal and the fresh waters of the great river. I would be honored to share your meal, but the woman I am taking to Santa Fe—" he lied then for there was no way to explain Cloud Dancer "—is very shy. She will not get off the horse."

Fray Francisco nodded his head as if he understood, surprising Perez, who began to relax just a little. He did not have much respect for the men of God in general after what their pious decree had wrought in Acoma, but there had to be some good men who took up the holy life. Perhaps Fray Francisco was one of them.

"The native peoples of this land are uniformly quiet and shy," Fray Francisco observed. "I have seen none any other way. At least not those of the Pueblo peoples," he qualified. "Of the other tribes, well, it is a difficult and dangerous time to be traveling these lands alone." The question was spoken plainly in the friar's tone. He wanted to know what Perez was doing out there. "There has been trouble even at the pueblos." He sighed. "It is difficult sometimes to understand what is in the hearts and minds of people. I am bound for the north to teach the Pueblo people the ways of our gentle Lord, but I am afraid it will be a long time before we reach them in any great numbers and peace comes to this land.''

Perez felt the knot of his tension easing further. Here, before him, stood a reasonable and gentle man. ''You've been traveling long?'' Perez's statement was really a question.

''It seems like months!'' Fray Francisco said with a laugh. ''But in truth, it is only a string of days since I passed through San Juan. But, come, let us eat together and talk in comfort. You are sure the girl will not get down? I would not like to see her go hungry.''

Perez froze at the mention of San Juan. The friar had been there only a matter of days before. Yet he did not react to Perez's name. Could it be that there was no talk about him? That they were not searching for him as he had believed they would be? Perez's breath caught in his throat, and fear, like the quick, searing touch of the Devil, raced through him.

''She will not get off Bonita,'' Perez tightly reaffirmed Cloud Dancer's statement. She was a stubborn woman, and not even for appearances would she budge.

The friar's expression did not change. Perez could not read even a flicker of guile or deception in their black button depths. Perez's blood raced hot, then cold. He could feel a fine sheen of sweat forming across his forehead despite the chill of the February day. His emotions roiled and snapped like pennants driven before a fierce wind. How could he get back on Bonita and away from this place quickly if the friar was deceiving him?

But Fray Francisco was not deceiving him, Perez thought in an attempt to calm himself. The friar had not recognized his name. He knew nothing of what he had done. And the soldiers with him were not familiar to Perez. None of them was from the garrison at San Juan, for Perez would have recognized them if they had been. He began to relax again.

"Then we will have to bring her some food," Fray Francisco said with cheery good humor, his words seeping through the haze of Perez's scrambled thoughts and emotions.

Perez doubted Cloud Dancer would eat any food coming from the Spaniards' hands, but he did not voice his conviction. They went to the small campfire where the meal had already been prepared, and Fray Francisco placed a generous portion on a tin plate. The soldiers who were his escort, their plates filled, drifted off at the friar's wave of a hand, to eat at a distance.

The friar talked easily as they shared a companionable meal. He was a man of God and Perez believed he was honestly disturbed by the mistreatment of the Indians he had witnessed. Fray Francisco mentioned nothing of Acoma, but Perez knew the man could not be unaware of it if he was aware of the Indians' plight elsewhere.

Cloud Dancer remained astride Bonita, keeping her distance, her face a stone mask, revealing nothing. She waited with stoic patience as quizzical glances flicked frequently in her direction. She heard much of what was said, and even understood a little, for Perez had been teaching her some Spanish. She was worried for Perez, since she did not trust these men. But Perez, she saw, was weakening. These were his people, she forcefully reminded herself. He was reaching out for what she would never again possess: a sense of belonging.

"She seems very young to be so sad." Fray Francisco's voice was soft and fueled the deep-seated guilt Perez nursed, both at the destruction of Acoma and his own desertion of his companions that day on the mesa.

"She has seen more grief than anyone should see in a lifetime, yet she is little past sixteen."

Fray Francisco nodded sadly. "Yes, it is the way of this land. Indeed, it seems to be the way of life. If you would tell me, Perez, I would like to know the source of her grief. Perhaps I could be of some comfort.''

"She has suffered greatly at the hands of our people." Perez shifted uneasily, not sure how to address the friar's offer. His voice was tightly controlled. "She will not be easy to talk to."

"How did she come to harm?"

Perez took a deep breath. "She is from Acoma."

Instantly Fray Francisco's eyebrows knitted together in consternation. "Tell me her story." His voice was soft and reasonable, a strange weariness punctuating the few words he spoke. "And tell me yours."

Perez could have sworn only hours earlier that there was no one alive to whom he would tell his story, that it would live only in his heart and mind for the remainder of his days. Yet he had been raised to believe in God, to put his trust in those representatives of God's teachings on earth. He had come to doubt much, to trust little, and yet, when he was confronted with Fray Francisco, those old teachings surfaced with such strength that something broke loose inside Perez. As if hypnotized, he heard himself relating the tale that had brought him together with Cloud Dancer.

He did not spare the friar's sensitivities, but told Fray Francisco every grisly detail of the slaughter, the abuse and death that cold morning at Acoma. So caught up in his telling of the story and his reliving of that horror was Perez that he did not notice the tightening of the friar's lips, the deepening of his frown and the gathering of deep creases at the corners of his dark eyes.

Then Perez told Fray Francisco what he had done. And, when Perez stopped and his eyes met the friar's, his blood turned to ice in his veins.

Fray Francisco de San Miguel's face was not softened by pity or the understanding Perez had thought he read in the friar's demeanor when he had begun the tale. It was stiffened with anger. It was the face of an avenging angel, not of a man of God who would bestow forgiveness.

"You must see what a terrible thing you have done, my son." Fray Francisco's voice was like steel swaddled in silk. "Acoma did fall to Vicente de Zalvidar that day. His troops returned to San Juan with a glorious victory and more than five hundred prisoners to be sentenced for their part in the uprising."

"It was not an uprising," Perez protested. "They were defending themselves even as we would if we were attacked!"

"It was not the same at all." Fray Francisco adopted a patient voice, but one that was edged with the unbending certainty of a fanatic. "The people of Acoma were like children—children too long without direction. They had to be punished severely so such a thing would not happen again."

Perez was quickly regaining his equilibrium, emerging from the self-imposed haze of confession being good for the soul. His mouth went dry at Fray Francisco's last words. "What were the sentences Oñate imposed?"

"Males over twenty-five were sentenced to have one foot cut off and twenty years of servitude. Males between the ages of twelve and twenty-five and all women over twelve received sentences of twenty years of servitude. Girls under the age of twelve were turned over to Fray Alonso Martinzez to be distributed in this kingdom or elsewhere and the boys were given to Vicente de Zalvidar. It is hoped that the children will learn to be good subjects of the king and forget the past."

"My God." Perez whispered the words in a tattered voice reserved for dreaded things and glanced quickly in Cloud Dancer's direction. He knew now that he had made a terrible mistake in telling Fray Francisco all he had.

"There was a rumor in San Juan when I was there that one of Zalvidar's men had fled Acoma. This man did not return with the soldiers to San Juan and his body was not found, but no one really believed such a thing of one of our soldiers of the Lord. It was widely accepted that the missing man was dead. Now you say you are that man and what was rumored is true. You fled Acoma with this girl!'' Fray Francisco's voice grew louder, his words vigorous, rising in accusation. ''I cannot grant you the forgiveness I can see you seek. You must return to San Juan! You must beg God's forgiveness for your desertion and turning from your duty. And that one—'' he pointed his finger imperiously in Cloud Dancer's direction ''—must be given over for punishment fitting what she has done, just as the others of her people were punished.''

Perez almost cringed before the friar's stentorian declaration, his ears ringing before the onslaught, but his eyes flashed with sudden anger. Anger beyond reason. All his apprehension of being pursued and caught had been for nothing. They had not even sought him. But now he had betrayed himself; worse, he had betrayed Cloud Dancer.

''No! It is not I who needs forgiveness,'' Perez snarled, ''for I, in the end, saved a life. It is Vicente de Zalvidar who needs to be forgiven. He and all the soldiers with him who remained to kill and rape and destroy! It is Juan de Oñate who needs forgiveness, and those who condoned his actions. Men like you, Fray Francisco! Men of God who recommend extermination as a way to peace! No! I will not turn myself in and beg forgiveness from God and men such as those, and I will not allow Cloud Dancer to be treated as a criminal because she killed in defense of her own life and those she loved and survived the hell our soldiers created at Acoma!''

Perez was on his feet by the time he finished, his face suffused with crimson rage, lips twisted into a feral snarl, eyes filled with a hate so black he feared it would scar his soul.

Cloud Dancer sat still upon Bonita, who shifted nervously beneath her, agitated by the strident voices raised in anger. She knew they spoke of Acoma, and saw the robed man's hand pointed damningly in her direction. She raised her chin a little higher and did not allow her stone mask to slip.

"She raised her hand against the Spanish soldiers!" Outrage jerked Fray Francisco to his feet beside Perez, his face darkened by fury. "She, a woman! She killed a soldier of our king and our Lord? You have damned her by your own words! Such a thing cannot be forgiven! Her soul will burn in hell for eternity!" He spun around, robe flapping in his fury, and called to his soldiers. "Arrest them! Arrest them! They have committed crimes against our God and our king! We must return them to San Juan for judgment!"

Cloud Dancer saw it coming. She did not understand all the words, but she understood the gesticulations, the tirade unleashed in a storm of fury and the implacable expressions upon the faces of the men. Perez had made the mistake of reaching for too much of his lost life.

Without a moment's hesitation, Cloud Dancer pulled the smaller pistol Perez had been teaching her to use free of the sling hung on the side of the saddle and urged Bonita forward with her heels. The horse, trained in the ways of battle, did not hesitate. Together Cloud Dancer and Bonita surged forward as Perez was suddenly surrounded by the friar's military escort.

"No!" Perez shouted in the language of her people once he spotted Cloud Dancer and realized her intent. "Go back! Run!"

Cloud Dancer did not even consider running. She would not abandon one so brave and strong as Perez to the cruel judgment of the Spanish.

Bonita surged through the wall of human flesh surrounding Perez and struck out with her hooves to clear a path as Cloud Dancer swung her sideways into another soldier. "Quickly! Get on!" Cloud Dancer called, and raised her pistol to fire. She did not care where the ball struck just so long as it did not strike Perez.

Pistols filled the hands of the Spanish soldiers as they realized the fight was escalating beyond simple physical restraint. Perez had a second pistol in his belt and drew it.

"Surrender yourselves!" Fray Francisco bellowed above the shouts of his soldiers.

One of the soldiers had his hand on Perez's arm, grabbing for the gun to direct the ball heavenward. Cloud Dancer's foot shot out with stunning force, catching the soldier solidly in the chest, breaking his grip on Perez and sending him reeling backward. She leveled her pistol on a soldier grabbing for Bonita's bridle and pulled the trigger.

The explosion jolted her in the saddle and sent a ringing through her ears. The soldier tumbled backward as Perez wheeled, his back against Bonita. He aimed his own pistol in defense of Cloud Dancer. The pistol cracked. Another soldier fell. Other pistols exploded around Perez.

He felt the terrible roaring pain as one ball ripped into his chest and another into his abdomen. Blood gushed from the wounds in a warm flood, instantly soaking his clothes. He was dying on his feet and he knew it. Bonita's great body was all that was holding him up.

"Get on, Perez! Get on!" Desperation ripped through Cloud Dancer's words and she grabbed at him, wrapping her fingers in the cloth of his shirt in an attempt to drag him upward as Bonita danced sideways and hands grabbed at her from all directions. She saw the terrible spill of his lifeblood, but would not accept the inevitable. "They will kill us both! Get on!"

For an instant Cloud Dancer's words jerked Perez from the sliding glaze of impending death, and an icy spear of truth pierced his heart and mind. She was going to die, too. All he had worked to accomplish would be lost.

Perez turned to her, looking up into her beautiful face as blood rose in his throat to bubble upon his lips. "I am already dead," he whispered. "Save yourself."

Then with a surge of superhuman strength he shouted a command to Bonita and hurled himself at Fray Francisco—knowing full well the soldiers would turn to protect the friar—hoping desperately Cloud Dancer would be able to hang on.

Well trained, Bonita obeyed Perez's last forceful command. With a flailing of hooves and a piercing whinny she broke from the melee and ran. It was all Cloud Dancer could do to hang on to the powerful animal as she stretched out, hooves pounding the dry earth, at a dead run without direction.

Cloud Dancer tried to pull her up, to turn her back to go to Perez, but her slight experience at handling the horse made that impossible. She looked back over her shoulder, and she knew Perez de Ortega was dead.

Her heart pounding, her head matching the rhythm, Cloud Dancer gasped air into her lungs and felt her chest give a painful lurch. Perez de Ortega was dead. Now, for the first time, she knew what it meant to be truly alone.

Chapter Ten

Cloud Dancer stuck to Bonita's back like a burr, and together they put many miles between themselves and Fray Francisco and his soldiers. When she finally drew Bonita to a stop at the crest of a hill to let the horse catch her breath, Cloud Dancer saw they were no longer being followed by the Spanish soldiers, and she started to cry.

Tears flowed down her cheeks, cutting wide, hot trails down her dusty face, dripping unheeded onto her breast. She stared into the distance but saw nothing. The scalding tears continued and soft sobs forced their way past the lump in her throat.

When she regained consciousness far from Acoma and knew all those she loved to be dead, she had not cried; she had not really felt. She had been conscious only of cessation—an ending of all she had known—a hollow emptiness, a shell that had taken the place of her heart.

Now anguish overflowed, rushing into the empty corners of her heart, flooding it with an intense grief. No longer was there anyone for her to fight, or to vent her anger upon. There was no one to help her learn the things she had to know, to smile at her, to encourage her. She had lost her parents, her sister and her way of life. And now she had lost her friend, Perez.

She cried, too, for her lost love, White Hawk, who had been taken from her too soon.

Of all the deaths, White Hawk's seemed most unreal. She did not feel his death, deep within her, as she felt that of the others. She felt the pain of his loss, but somehow his death did not register as reality in that part of her that stored all the other pain. Somehow, he seemed not really dead, just lost to her. It confused her, sending her thoughts into turmoil as sobs continued to debilitate her and more tears spilled down her cheeks.

Once the tears had begun, Cloud Dancer believed they would never stop. Pain clawed at her heart until she threw her head back and screamed a guttural cry of anguish that ripped the fabric of the cloudless day and sent a hawk soaring from his perch, his own cry mimicking that of Cloud Dancer.

Bonita shifted beneath her, rising on her toes to dance lightly beneath the feather-light burden Cloud Dancer was. She loosened her grip on Bonita's reins, and the mare began to move of her own accord, walking briskly toward the north and east.

It was two more days before she reached the pueblo of Isleta, the destination she and Perez had chosen with hopes of finding sanctuary for both of them. When she arrived she was met with open arms. Her coming created quite a stir, especially since she was astride Bonita. All seemed to know of Acoma's fate and embraced her as one of their own. It felt so good to Cloud Dancer to be accepted that she did not notice the first of the niggling doubts that arose almost as soon as she entered the pueblo.

Here, the heartbeat of life was so like what she had known in Acoma. That was why she had gone there despite Perez's death. She understood when the people pressed forward, filled with questions about the beast she rode. The people of Acoma would have done the same. Many of the Kere were curious about the horses the Spanish rode, but few had ever been near them. Cloud Dancer enjoyed the warmth and welcome, and she enjoyed answering questions while she held Bonita still for the many who wanted to come and touch her.

It was easy for Cloud Dancer to fall back into the old ways she had known and accepted from childhood, working with clay, grinding corn, sewing clothes. The days passed quickly and easily. But the shadow of the Spanish lay across the land. On the surface things appeared to be the way they had always been, the rhythm of life pulsing as it had for hundreds of years, but underneath it all was a current of change. The people were cheerful, stretching what supplies they had, but it was plain they were not prepared to face what remained of a long, hard winter. Already they were hungry. The men hunted constantly to add meat to their pots, but game was scarce when the weather was extremely cold, making the pickings lean.

The rhythm of life in Isleta was a stabilizing comfort, but despite the generosity of the people and their consideration, Cloud Dancer discovered she needed more. The death of Acoma and the life she had led after its destruction had changed her. The old taboos and restrictions made her restless. She spent a lot of time with Bonita and even more time sneaking off—when she should have been gathering food—practicing with a bow, throwing her knife or the spear she had fashioned. It was difficult leading a double life now, and yet she found she could not completely go back to her old ways, the ways of a Kere maiden.

A voice cut into Cloud Dancer's mental wanderings. "The horse is very beautiful. I can see why you spend so much time with her."

Cloud Dancer looked up, only a little startled, for many of the people were so interested in Bonita they came by frequently to see her or to ask if they could stroke her. Since the horse was such an oddity, spending time with her was one of the few strange things Cloud Dancer could do in Isleta with impunity. There was no rule of behavior concerning men and women and the care of horses; who took care of the horse and who stood back and watched was not an issue, because Bonita was the only horse, and she belonged to Cloud Dancer.

"I like being alone with her," Cloud Dancer said simply. "We have an understanding."

The young man nodded. "Do you remember me?"

Cloud Dancer stared hard at him. There was something about him that was familiar; perhaps it was the bold, black eyes or the crooked nose. Then recognition hit her. Little Fox! "I'm sorry," she said sincerely. "So much has happened. I did not expect to see anyone from Acoma here."

"Nor did I," Little Fox confessed. "May I come in?" He hovered at the gate of the small enclosure that had been fashioned for Bonita.

Cloud Dancer smiled slightly, feeling a bit awkward with the young man from Acoma. She recoiled from any thought of her lost home, and yet she wanted to know all he could tell her; she craved to share what knowledge she had with him.

"Bonita likes company," Cloud Dancer said in what she hoped was an encouraging tone of voice. "She likes to have her nose stroked very gently, and her neck patted."

Eagerly, Little Fox joined Cloud Dancer inside the enclosure, moving confidently up to Bonita, stretching his hand out to her. "She is very strange and wonderful."

Cloud Dancer nodded. "She is more. She is my friend."

Little Fox looked puzzled at the statement, but did not question it. Instead he asked, "How did you come by her?"

"She is a Spanish horse," Cloud Dancer said grimly.

"They are all Spanish horses, with few exceptions—such as this one."

Softly Cloud Dancer laughed, setting aside her pain. "Yes, that's true. But the Spaniard who owned her was different. He befriended me. He took me from Acoma and saved my life.''

"That is how you survived the attack?''

"Yes.''

Little Fox continued to stroke Bonita's neck, pausing to gather his thoughts. ''I was knocked unconscious when one of the Spaniards' thunder weapons ripped the earth. When I awoke I was confined with many others who had survived. Some were badly injured, others were like me. They took all of us from Acoma to San Juan, where their leader decided what was to be done with us. I was to have one foot cut off and be made a slave.''

Cloud Dancer involuntarily glanced down at Little Fox's feet.

He smiled ruefully. ''I still have them both—and I escaped. Many others did the same. When someone found a small way out, that person would disappear like smoke upon the wind. Many have found new homes among other tribes, Pueblo and their allies. They are being sheltered and hidden.''

"You escaped alone and came here?''

Stepping back from Bonita, he patted her sleek neck, enjoying the unusual feel of the warm puffs of air from her sensitive nostrils as she turned to appraise him. ''Yes. Only one at a time were we able to slip away. If we had tried to go together or to fight again we would have been destroyed.''

"There are others, then, who escaped?''

"Yes, many others. There is talk here that some went to the camp of the Apache. Others went farther north to join the Utes or Comanches. I do not know what their reception would have been at any of those places.''

"Did any of our people escape with our brothers, the Apaches with Bempol?'' Cloud Dancer steeled herself for the answer. The Apache were much fiercer warriors than the men of the Kere. Could any of them have survived?

Little Fox frowned. "I do not know. Some have said Bempol himself and one or two of his warriors survived Acoma and escaped the Spanish. It is possible."

Hope flared within Cloud Dancer like a scalding flame. For a moment it burned white-hot, as everything within her, every fiber of her being, focused suddenly on White Hawk. If Bempol and one or two of his warriors escaped, could White Hawk be among them? Was it possible he was still alive?

"Did you hear who among Bempol's warriors survived?" Cloud Dancer's words were strained, her voice a whisper.

"No." Then, as if sensing her distress, he added, "I am sorry."

Cloud Dancer smiled weakly, the white-hot flame of hope subsiding to a tiny flickering spark, almost dying entirely. She had to accept White Hawk's death. She had seen him fall. She had seen the Spaniard point his thunder weapon at him and fire. He could not be alive.

"Perhaps if you told me the name of the one you ask after?"

"White Hawk." His name was like dust upon her tongue.

Little Fox frowned in concentration, then shook his head slowly. "I did not hear that name, among neither the living nor the dead. I do not know."

"I saw him fall," Cloud Dancer admitted.

"So many died," Little Fox agreed.

"But I did not, and you did not. There are those who would have seen us fall."

"That is true, but I hold out hope for no one. We cannot live in the past. We cannot return to Acoma. We must build new lives for ourselves."

Cloud Dancer sighed and let go of the beauty of her short-lived hope. Little Fox was right.

Cloud Dancer and Little Fox spent much time together in the days that followed. Quickly he became as a brother to

Cloud Dancer, a friend, one with whom she could share memories.

For a while life in Isleta was one of numb contentment. Cloud Dancer was only occasionally plagued by memories of White Hawk and by the unsettled feeling left behind at his loss. There was no ruler in Isleta, as there was no ruler among the people of any pueblo. As in Acoma, life in Isleta was organized, all the people giving continuity to ways inherited over centuries by common agreement. Everybody in the pueblo owned all the land together. Early in the spring, Cloud Dancer and Little Fox would be assigned the use of some land by the council of elders. Already, they had been given permanent possession of rooms in the pueblo. Those rooms would be theirs as long as they or their families existed. Now, the small space was enough, but they could build more space when needed, perhaps when one of them married and brought forth a family.

Cloud Dancer spent much time with Bonita. She had eliminated the heavy Spanish saddle, and rode the mare with only a folded blanket between herself and the horse's back. At first she had felt strange and unbalanced without the saddle, but little by little she had come to feel even more at home upon Bonita's back—almost as if she were a part of the mare.

Cloud Dancer loved to ride the mare in the hills not far from Isleta and along the riverbanks. When she did not have to work for the pueblo, she rode or groomed Bonita, or conversed quietly with Little Fox. Sometimes they rode together, Little Fox beaming at the deference she showed him in teaching him to ride the horse.

And, too, as the days quickly passed Cloud Dancer was drawn inexorably into the fabric of the pueblo's society. She made new friends and worked the clay in companionable silence with women of the pueblo. Except for the continuing interest in Bonita, her arrival in Isleta had not changed the day-to-day lives of the people there. They simply accepted her. Life continued in Isleta as it had for centuries.

The only flicker in the life at Isleta was the knowledge of what had befallen Acoma—combined with the continuing presence of the Spanish upon the land. Like a small flame shuddering before a draft, Isleta balanced before the dark cloud of the Spanish presence.

Chapter Eleven

The coming of the new day brought with it more than the simple herb- and food-gathering Cloud Dancer and Little Fox had planned on. It seemed the gods were smiling upon their endeavors, for they had quickly gathered wild onions near the riverbanks as well as some stray juniper berries and even some osha for the doctors' use in warding off visits from witches. And Little Fox had taken four rabbits.

They were returning to Isleta when Cloud Dancer drew Bonita to a stop at the crest of a small hill, gazing around her in all directions, looking for signs of movement as White Hawk had taught her. There had been so little time for him to teach her, yet what he had imparted, Cloud Dancer utilized and tried to improve upon.

She sat perfectly still, the sun brilliant upon the land, the north wind nipping at her ears, and listened. Bonita shifted nervously beneath her, her delicate ears twitching as she waited beneath Cloud Dancer's restraining hand.

"What is it?" Little Fox asked, sensing Cloud Dancer's unease.

Her eyes swept the distant hills again. "I am not certain." She had begun merely to practice, to look for the sake of looking, but there had been something....

Then she spotted the telltale cone of dust moving up from behind a hill, caught upon the blustery winter winds.

"There!" She pointed, drawing Little Fox's attention to what could barely be seen. "Horses are moving there." She pointed again toward the almost indiscernible speck moving forward above the base of a hill. Then she realized the direction they were taking and nearly groaned. "They are heading for Isleta."

"How can you be sure?" Little Fox peered in the direction Cloud Dancer pointed, at last spotting movement in a dark line. "Are they Spanish?"

Cloud Dancer's face darkened. "There, now that the wind is shifting our way, do you hear it?"

Straining his ears, Little Fox hesitated, then grimly nodded. It was the clank and rattle of the Spanish on the move.

"I hear. But perhaps they will bypass Isleta."

"Perhaps." The old anger and hatred seethed up within Cloud Dancer with the power of a summer storm. "We must hurry and return to Isleta. They must be warned the Spanish are coming this way. They may want to make preparations."

Little Fox laid his hand upon Cloud Dancer's shoulder. "Do not think they will fight—they will not."

"They will fight if the Spanish attack as they did at Acoma!"

"The Spanish will not attack. They will demand and threaten, and the people of Isleta will give them what they want."

Little Fox sighed beneath the burden of his knowledge, and went on. "You have been hardened, Cloud Dancer, by what you saw at Acoma. These people did not see what we did. They have only heard the horrible stories, and they are afraid. They are not cowards, but they fear the Spanish. They may resist, but in the end they will give the Spanish what they want."

The words of Little Fox stiffened Cloud Dancer's spine. "What you say may be true, but if the people of Isleta will not see the danger, if they will allow the Spanish to take their stores without resistance when already there are many starving, then I do not belong among them. If I do not belong among them, I will leave Isleta."

"There is nowhere else you would belong!" Little Fox returned in some alarm. "And where would you go?"

"That does not matter now," Cloud Dancer answered. "We must hurry. We must hide Bonita far from the town and tell no one where she is hidden lest their weakness betray us. I will die before I allow the Spanish to take Bonita." She spit the words as though she tasted something bitter.

The vehemence of Cloud Dancer's words worried Little Fox. Never had he seen a woman like her. They had become friends since her arrival in Isleta, but he had come no closer to understanding her than when she first arrived. He would not see her suffer and yet she was as aggressive as the Apache warriors he had known at Acoma. How was he to protect her?

Cloud Dancer turned Bonita and guided her toward Isleta, giving the fleet-footed mare her head. The rush of the winter wind through her hair and the warm kiss of the sun upon her face would have been sheer joy if not for the urgency of their mission.

They flew over the hills and rocks, dodging scrub brush and animal dens dug in the earth. Cloud Dancer, long accustomed now to riding with only a blanket upon Bonita's back, clung with her legs and wrapped her fingers in Bonita's flying mane. Little Fox was left to cling to the horse and the bounty of his hunt as best he could, slipping and sliding on Bonita's sleek back, but managing to remain astride.

They thundered into Isleta with the suddenness of a summer storm. Little Fox quickly slid from Bonita's back as many of the people gathered around them, surprised, curious and a little fearful of the manner in which they had arrived.

"We have seen the Spanish, and they are coming this way," Cloud Dancer called out. "You must hide what you value and be prepared to fight!"

One of the tribal elders stepped forward, gazing at Little Fox, all but ignoring Cloud Dancer. "Is this true?"

Little Fox nodded. "If they continue on as we saw them, they will arrive here soon."

"If we feed them, perhaps they will leave us in peace."

"If you feed them, more of you here will starve!" Cloud Dancer exploded.

The old man's face hardened. He plainly did not like looking up at Cloud Dancer where she sat astride Bonita. "If we resist, they will destroy us as they did Acoma." His words fell like rocks upon her heart.

He turned from her to the gathered people. "We must prepare. Hurry!"

For a few moments Cloud Dancer seethed. It was the same here as at Acoma. She was a woman. They did not wish to hear her speak at council. She was to have no say in the fate of the people, or if they had their way, in her own fate.

"I will go hide Bonita and come back." Cloud Dancer bit out the words to Little Fox.

Gently, Little Fox said, "Go, hide Bonita, but do not come back until the Spanish have left Isleta. Stay with Bonita."

"I cannot," was Cloud Dancer's answer, and she turned Bonita away from the town, leaving at a gallop.

Little Fox watched carefully the direction Cloud Dancer had taken, hoping she would return the same way so that he might intercept her.

The word of the coming Spanish spread through Isleta like wildfire. Swiftly the people disappeared from the streets between the adobe houses, taking refuge behind the thick mud walls.

When Little Fox saw Cloud Dancer returning, he saw she moved as a warrior, crouched and wary, a bow and arrows clutched in her hand. He had his own weapons close at hand, but he had not seen Cloud Dancer fight at Acoma; nor did he know of the training White Hawk had promised to undertake.

He blocked her path when he saw she intended to move nearer to the town's plaza. "Cloud Dancer, you must take shelter! It is too dangerous for you here!"

"It is not dangerous for you?"

"Yes, but it is what I must do."

"It is what I must do as well."

The argument went no further, for the head of the Spanish column entered Isleta and one of the elders stepped forward to meet them.

Quickly Little Fox drew Cloud Dancer into the shelter of a thick wall. "We must be careful. What if one of them recognizes us from Acoma?"

"Do not fear they will recognize us." She laughed softly, almost inaudibly, her words laced with sarcasm. "They cannot tell one of us from another." She hesitated and stared at the bearded leader of the troop of Spanish soldiers. "But what is really funny," she added bitterly, "is that I cannot blame them for that, because with the hair on their faces and the way they dress, I cannot tell them one from the other either."

Little Fox gaped at her. There was nothing he could find funny about this situation. He did not appreciate irony or twisted perversities of fate, though when he thought about it, Cloud Dancer's words had about them the ring of truth.

Little Fox had been growing into a steady man when Acoma was destroyed. He went at life straight on. He looked and he saw what was before him—and what was before him was a troop of Spanish soldiers, soldiers just like the ones who had raped, destroyed and murdered at Acoma.

Little Fox knew he would fight if necessary, but he did not disagree, as did Cloud Dancer, with the decision of the elders of Isleta to attempt to turn away the Spanish with offerings of food and necessities. It was true the people of Isleta were already hungry. But the men could hunt. The fate of starvation was not nearly so certain as what would happen if Isleta resisted the demands of the Spanish.

The leader had climbed off his horse and was speaking now to the representative of Isleta. Cloud Dancer could understand his use of the Indians' language, and found, to her surprise, she could understand a few of the Spanish words he called over his shoulder to the soldiers with him. Silently she thanked the spirit of Perez de Ortega for all that he had given her.

Then it began. It was not like Acoma. There was no killing. The people of Isleta brought forth some maize and humbly offered it. The Spanish took all they were offered and demanded more.

"We can spare no more. Already our people are starving," the chief protested in his humblest manner.

"You have plenty more in your stores. You and your people are now the servants of His Royal Majesty the king of Spain. What is yours belongs to him, and we are his servants in need. You will show us where you have stored the corn, and we will take what we need. We will leave enough to feed your people."

"No," the old chief answered firmly. "We have given you already what we can ill spare. You will take that and leave."

Another of Isleta's chiefs joined the first in a show of solidarity, but it did little to impress the Spanish, or to turn their attention from what they had come for.

Cloud Dancer's hand almost lovingly cradled the bow and arrows she had taken up. She could feel the heat rising to race through her blood. Her fingers itched to notch an arrow and send it flying into the broad chest of the Spanish leader. But like the soldiers at Acoma he wore heavy mail; she knew the arrow would not penetrate.

The leader of the Spanish barked an order over his shoulder, and a moment later the two chiefs were surrounded. Other soldiers were swaggering from one adobe house to another, searching until the hiding place of the town's maize supply was revealed.

Cloud Dancer watched in horror and once tried to raise her bow, but Little Fox restrained her. "They do what they believe is best for Isleta. They do not fight because they believe that is best."

"How can giving up everything, food, pride...everything, be best?" Cloud Dancer's breath came in short gasps. Acoma had been a horror, but this, this was almost worse; it was a destruction of the soul. These people were defeated and dying. It would just take longer than in the heat of battle.

"Come," Little Fox urged, "you must move away from here. We must conceal you where they will not find you."

"I will not hide. If they come for me I will fight. It is my choice."

"Do you not see?" Little Fox asked anxiously. "Yes, if they come for you, you will fight. If you fight, you will cause what the people of Isleta have sacrificed so much to avoid. The killing will begin here as it did in Acoma! You must conceal yourself and wait for it to be over. The people of Isleta have taken you in. Do not destroy them for it!"

Cloud Dancer tensed, but abruptly a rush of reason washed over her. She remembered White Hawk had once said that a great warrior must be a mighty warrior, able to defeat his enemies, but more important, he had to know when to fight as well as how. She bowed her head in defeat.

"You are right," Cloud Dancer admitted with great sadness. "These are good people and my heart weeps for them, but I will not fight in defense of those who will not fight themselves."

Her decision weighing heavily upon her, Cloud Dancer turned wearily from the sight at Isleta's plaza and allowed Little Fox to draw her into the shelter of a weaver's house and conceal her beneath the cloth being readied to fashion into garments.

Alone in the darkness, Cloud Dancer slipped into her greatest despair. She could not fight, but she could not stand to watch. And her spirit would not allow her to cower each time an enemy came near.

"Oh, White Hawk," she whispered into the darkness of her shelter, summoning her lost love. "What am I to do?"

When the Spanish were gone, Little Fox returned to the house where he had left Cloud Dancer and called out softly to her. "It is over. The Spanish have gone."

Cloud Dancer emerged from her place of concealment with stiff dignity. She gazed directly at Little Fox and did not see cowardice in his eyes. He, too, had wanted to resist, but his compassion for these people—their people—had overridden his desires. He had stayed his own hand even as he had stayed hers.

"I must leave Isleta," Cloud Dancer said clearly.

"Why? How? Where would you go?" Little Fox wrestled with his distress at her calm statement, managing to hide his greater agitation. "You cannot mean it. Think! This is your home now. These are your people."

"No." Cloud Dancer spoke plainly, slowly. "I have changed. I cannot live among these people any longer. I cannot stand by time and time again and watch what happened here today. I must go where I can be what I am and be accepted. I must be able to fight when I am faced with an enemy."

"That makes no sense, Cloud Dancer. You are a woman. You are not a warrior. You work the clay and grind the corn. It is not your place to fight beside the men."

"It is not a woman's place to die in battle, either, yet many died at Acoma."

"That was not battle, that was slaughter!"

Cloud Dancer shrugged. "It does not matter what you call it. Will it change now that the Spanish put their mark upon the land?"

"Our people have known battle before," Little Fox said sternly. "We have fought to protect our homes."

"I saw no man lift a weapon this day," Cloud Dancer returned.

"The memory of Acoma is still fresh."

"No." Cloud Dancer shook her head. "These people are dying. They are being ground beneath the heel of the Spanish. They will not fight."

"You think fighting and killing are good?" Little Fox tried another tack. "You think more killing will bring an end to killing?"

Again Cloud Dancer shook her head. "No," she said sorrowfully. "I do not want to have to kill. I do not want to fight. I was never so frightened as I was at Acoma. But I do not want to lie down at the feet of my enemy and die before the deathblow is struck.

"There is little left of the people here. Can you not feel their fear and desolation in the very air around us? Perhaps if I go north and find the Apache of Bempol, the people of White Hawk, I will be able to begin a new life. Perhaps the reach of the Spanish will not extend so far. But whatever happens, I know I must go."

Cloud Dancer turned to walk away.

"Wait!" Little Fox pleaded. "There must be something you will listen to, something that will change your mind. Think! The life of the Apache is nothing like that of the Pueblos."

Pausing, Cloud Dancer smiled wanly. "That is the reason I will find them and ask them to allow me to stay." She softened her voice and met his eyes. "Now I have to go back and take care of Bonita. It may be a long journey. I will leave with the rising of tomorrow's sun." She turned again and this time began moving away.

Little Fox was confused, his heart thudding within his breast. Cloud Dancer was the last link he had with Acoma; she had become like a sister to him. He did not want to see her go. All the same, her words were true. He had felt as she had this day. His gorge had risen and he had wanted to fight despite his meager experience as a warrior. He had stayed his own hand as surely as he had stayed hers.

He had not been content in Isleta, not really. He had made friends, and the customs were little different from those of Acoma, yet he had felt uneasy, unsettled. Acoma had changed them both. Blood and death had wrenched loose the moorings of the old life and set them adrift as bits of wood were swept along the Great River.

"Wait!" Little Fox repeated. When Cloud Dancer again turned, his bold black eyes told her even before he spoke the words. "You cannot go alone. I will go with you to the land of the Apache."

She stared at him a moment, still clutching her bow and arrows in her small hand, her eyes boring into his as though she could read there what was written on his soul. She gave him a quick denying glance, but did not speak, something within her making her hesitate.

Little Fox's face tightened at her hesitation. The lines deepened around his eyes. "Do not deny me this, Cloud Dancer," he whispered, his dignity preventing him from saying more.

"I could not deny you, for you are free to go where you will," Cloud Dancer said softly. "I will say only this. I would welcome you as friend and companion—not as protector," she warned him.

Little Fox accepted her terms. "We will leave with the rising of the sun."

Chapter Twelve

Six days from Isleta they were still working their way in a mostly northerly direction—grateful not to have seen another living soul—when Cloud Dancer directed Bonita to skirt the base of a hill then ascend to its crest to survey the sprawling land on all sides. Little Fox jogged at Bonita's side, his lance carried easily in his right hand.

When she rode, Cloud Dancer's bow was slung over one shoulder, her arrows tucked in a hide pouch nestled against her knee within easy reach. The small thunder stick Perez had taught her to use shared space in the bottom of the same pouch. Her spear she kept in her hand. Without the heavy Spanish saddle, it took very little to guide Bonita and telegraph her commands to the mare. The only disadvantage was the lack of places to hang things they needed to have with them, causing them to tie much of what they carried to their persons.

With a clear view in all directions, Cloud Dancer and Little Fox stopped at the top of the hill. After five days of brilliant sunshine, snow was threatening again. The sky was overcast, gray clouds hanging close to the ground, curling and snaking on the rising wind like wisps of smoke. The general grayness made it difficult to pick out details at a distance, but still Cloud Dancer and Little Fox rested and let their eyes roam the distance in search of movement.

"We will need to find shelter soon," Little Fox said as the freezing wind snatched at his clothes and slapped a high color into his cheeks.

Cloud Dancer nodded her agreement as the first fine flakes drifted down from the darkening sky. "It will give us more time to fashion arrows and use the skins we have to make warmer clothes." She spoke the words as though caught in a trance and hesitated a moment longer on the top of the hill.

"It is strange," she said to Little Fox at last, "but I feel something is very near...that I could see it if... There! Look!"

To the northeast, Cloud Dancer picked out the movement of a line of men appearing from a valley between two imposing mesas; they were on foot. No horses were visible. It could not be the hated Spanish, but there were others besides the Jicarilla Apache who struck down into this land to hunt or raid. There were the Comanche and the Ute and the many different Apache bands. Unless she and Little Fox got closer, they would not know who the men were.

An erratic pulse fluttered in Cloud Dancer's throat and her eyes burned with the effort to see more clearly. There were many who would be willing to try to steal Bonita from her, or even to kill to get the horse. Both she and Little Fox knew the risk well. He had been true to his word on other matters, not attempting to impose upon Cloud Dancer what he considered her woman's place, and they had spoken of this danger. They would do now what had to be done.

"Come, get on Bonita," she said. "We must hurry if we are to catch them before the storm breaks."

Little Fox hesitated, but only for a moment. "It would be better to find an encampment and approach it. It is not possible to tell if those before us are a hunting party or a raiding party."

He swung easily upon Bonita's back despite his encumbrances of a bundle of half-tanned furs and a sack of dried meat and cornmeal.

"That would be better," Cloud Dancer agreed, "but this is what we have." She touched her heels to Bonita and sent her down the slope of the hill to intercept the party emerging from the valley.

The sky was leaden with heavy clouds and white with lightly falling snow when Cloud Dancer and Little Fox caught up with what she counted now as six warriors. There were no women with them, and long before their arrival the group had turned to meet them, weapons at the ready. They had laid upon the ground a deer that had been slung between two of them, evidence that this was, after all, a hunting party. All were bundled in heavy clothes and cloaks against the rising wind and falling snow. Cloud Dancer had drawn her own cloak of pelts closely about her, up to her chin, and partially covering her head. She held Bonita to a walk once she realized they had been spotted, moving steadily toward the party until one signaled her with a raised hand to stop.

Cloud Dancer sat astride the mare, watching carefully while Little Fox slipped off to stand beside her. Something about the way the leader moved, the way he held himself, was compellingly familiar. The snow swirled about them in a gossamer curtain, blurring and distorting vision, but the familiarity remained.

Little Fox took the initiative instinctively, moving a step forward, planting the butt of his spear against the ground, point toward the heavens. "We seek the Apache band of Bempol. We would speak to the leader of his people."

"You have found us. Bempol is war chief to our people." The rich, deep timbre of the voice of the leader of the hunting party took Cloud Dancer's breath away.

She jerked the cloak away from where it protected her face against the wind and freezing snow, and slid from

Bonita's back, her heart beating wildly in her chest. This could not be! Yet it was. She had felt it to be true from the beginning!

"I seek the warrior, White Hawk!" Her voice came out strong and steady, and she stood proud before the warriors, her knees trembling and her belly feeling as if it had dropped to the snow at her feet. Her mouth went chalk dry after she got the words out, and she was sure she could not have spoken another word if her life had depended on it.

That voice again, this time with an odd, strained quality as its owner turned to fully face Cloud Dancer, jerking back his own cloak. "You have found him."

Cloud Dancer's breath left her in a rush and returned to her just as fast. Here, standing before her, was White Hawk. She did not understand. He could not be alive. She had seen the Spaniard point the thunder stick and fire. But it was true. He stood before her now.

Her head spun, and she rushed forward to throw herself into his arms. She shivered in the cold; her head pounded and her heart sang. She looked up at him, eyes shining, and smiled with pure joy.

"You are alive," she whispered, feeling reborn, as if her world, previously a dead, dark place, had suddenly been bathed in sunlight. "You are truly alive!"

Dizzily happy, oblivious to the other Apaches around them, she touched him, knew the warmth of his flesh against hers and verified it was truly White Hawk before her and not a ghost.

Slowly, Cloud Dancer realized White Hawk was not returning her embrace. He stood within her arms, a frozen statue, rigid and unyielding. She felt the tension within him even as she felt the warm throb of his heart against her.

Bit by bit she loosened her grip and stepped back beneath the hard-eyed appraisal of the other Apache warriors. She felt rejected and confused. How could it be like this? How could he be so cold when they had just discovered each other again? She loved him, but he turned from her in spirit as well as in flesh.

Cloud Dancer's heart was a wounded thing, rent through by the jagged blade of White Hawk's indifference. Her eyes began to water and she blinked furiously to vanquish the tears before they spilled. She swallowed repeatedly against the thick knot that had formed in her throat. She had believed he loved her. She had never stopped believing, even when he was lost to her. But time had passed, flowing like a river between them. Could it be that he no longer felt for her what she did for him? Had he found another woman, one of his own people, who better suited his needs? Apprehension and pain melded with her joy. She trembled and stared into his gentle black eyes, waiting—but the wait was too long and she looked away.

White Hawk softened, looking at Cloud Dancer as a man dying of thirst would look upon a pool of water, but Cloud Dancer had cast her eyes to the ground at his rejection of her and did not see. He had gone rigid at the first clear sight of her, cloaked in the swirling snow. Now his ears still rang with the clear bell-like tones of her voice. A great exultation filled his chest to bursting. His emotions set his senses reeling. She had been dead! He had seen her fall. And when the battle was over no sign of her could be found. Yet now she had clung to him like some wraith, only slowly relinquishing her hold.

The snow whipped wildly about them, fine grains of it catching and settling on the angles and plans of White Hawk's stern countenance as he stared, dumbstruck, down upon her.

"I thought you dead," he said quietly, his words as cool as the winter winds that enveloped them. "When it was over, we searched but could not find you. My heart wept for you. Yet you are here, now, alive. How can this be? Are you a ghost to stand before me now?" His words spoke of his concern, but his tone did not. He would not touch her, though his hands burned with the desire to do so. Cloud Dancer had forgotten herself when she had flung herself against him. He could not.

"I am not a ghost," Cloud Dancer responded in a tight voice. "I am as real as you. You felt my flesh beneath your hand. I, too, thought you dead, and wept for you. I was taken from Acoma, but that is a long story," she added, glancing over his shoulder toward his companions. "How did you live? How did you come here, when I saw you fall and the soldier fired his thunder weapon at you?"

White Hawk turned. "This woman and her companion are from Acoma," he said to the men of the hunting party who accompanied him. Then he looked down again at Cloud Dancer, his gaze steady, his eyes unfathomable. "I saw you near the head of the trail, and when I turned something struck me down. I knew nothing of the thunder weapon until I awoke among the dead. I don't know how much time passed while I lay there barely able to move. Bempol appeared beside me, urging me to rise, telling me we must make our way from Acoma before the Spanish found we were alive. Bempol, too, was injured and not strong, yet he got me to my feet.

"The dead were everywhere and I was confused. When my senses returned, I searched for you and urged Bempol to leave me, but he would not." White Hawk stiffened at the memory and Cloud Dancer thought he felt regret, but the granite set of his face betrayed no emotion. "We searched for you together among the dead and found no trace. When we had no more strength and sought shelter, concealing ourselves from the Spanish, I still searched the faces of the prisoners, but you were not among them."

"Yes, I was not among them." It tore her heart, but Cloud Dancer now adopted the same cool, formal tone that White Hawk employed. She sorely regretted her impulsive greeting. Confusion still threatened to scatter her thoughts like dead leaves before an autumn wind, yet she retained her

control. She would not expose her feelings so openly to him
again. She stiffened her spine and met his eyes directly,
brutally forcing the warmth from her gaze.

"I have come now with a friend to ask the Apache if we
might live among them. We can no longer live among our
own people." That much had not changed and would not
change, no matter what White Hawk's reception of her. She
lifted her chin stubbornly and stilled the quivering of her
lips. If they were accepted by the Apache, she and Little Fox
would make their new home with them. She stifled the aching pain in her heart and stood straight and proud before
these Apaches, waiting.

There was laughter in White Hawk's heart at the mere
sight of her, but his words were brittle and forced and he
knew he had hurt her. He did not wish to hurt her, but he
was an Apache warrior. She would understand, he told
himself. She would have to understand.

"You will be welcome," he said. He glanced at Little Fox,
who all the this time had stood like a part of the scenery,
then back to Cloud Dancer. "Hurry, the storm grows worse.
We must return to camp."

"Put the deer across Bonita's back," Cloud Dancer pro-
posed through stiff lips. "She can carry the weight, and we
will be able to return to your camp faster."

Once the deer carcass was hoisted across the mare's withers and Cloud Dancer swung up behind, White Hawk said,
"When we are inside a tepee with a fire to warm us all, I will
ask you how you came to possess a horse."

How he wanted to take her into his arms and crush her to
him! How he wanted to feel the beat of her heart so close to
his own and the touch of her hand gentle upon his body.
From the instant he had seen her, ghost or not, he had
wanted nothing else; yet he could do nothing. The strict
moral code of the Apache dictated his behavior, and though
he had seen the hurt in Cloud Dancer's eyes when he set her
from him, he could have done nothing else. She had come

to him. She was alive. He could do nothing to endanger her acceptance among his people. He could only try to explain away her unorthodox behavior as part of her past life in Acoma, and pray it did not blacken her in the eyes of the men accompanying him.

He looked up at her, his hand brushing her leg as he stood sheltered by the bulk of the mare's body, his action unnoticed by the others. Cloud Dancer stiffened, her eyes clashing with his, glittering like ice crystals that he should touch her so now, after he had put her from him. Her gaze was full of loathing and contempt, tawny cougar eyes flashing a furious warning; she was not to be played with. If he did not want her, if he could not take her to him before them all, then he would not steal touches when they were out of sight. She kneed Bonita away from him, putting cold distance between them. She could not let him see the pain he caused her, the way her blood still raced at his touch despite his cruel rejection of her.

White Hawk winced. Since that terrible day at Acoma when he had sought her, though grievously injured himself, and found nothing, he had tried to forget her. He had returned to his own people and had tried to resume his life, but always she had occupied a small corner of his mind and all of his heart. He had looked upon other women, but none had meant to him what Cloud Dancer had. He had come to believe he would marry one day, but it would be to have a home, a woman in his tepee and sons, not out of love.

In the blink of an eye, that had changed. She was here with him now. She would learn the Apache customs. She would come to understand. He could not lose her now to the differences in their cultures—not now that he had found her again. White Hawk turned from Cloud Dancer to lead the hunting party home, half-afraid that if he looked over his shoulder she would disappear like the hallucination suffered by a freezing man.

The Apache camp was not far and they traveled fast, but by the time they reached it the wind was howling like an enraged beast and the snow fell in blinding, writhing curtains.

The young brave, Prairie Wolf, took the deer from Bonita's back and disappeared into the falling snow. White Hawk urged both Cloud Dancer and Little Fox toward a tepee larger than the rest, but Cloud Dancer balked.

"I must take care of Bonita! We must find her shelter before I can enjoy the warmth of a fire!" she yelled above the shrieking winds of the growing storm. She held the mare's head low, sheltered by her own body, waiting for White Hawk's reply, uncertain how he would react, uncertain about everything since his strange reception of her in the valley.

"There!" White Hawk pointed into the storm, at what she could not guess, since she could see no more than a few feet in front of herself. He guided her through this storm as he had guided her before on that long-ago day at Acoma, but this time Little Fox followed. The horse's hooves thudded against unseen rocks and hard ground in quickened rhythm.

They threaded their way between several tepees aglow with fires inside against the rising cold, to where the camp apparently backed up against a natural rock outcrop thrust from the side of a hill. Combined with a thick copse of stunted juniper, it formed an enclosure with three walls, creating a natural windbreak for the few horses the camp already possessed. The force of the wind was much less here, though it could be heard howling on all sides.

"Stay here!" White Hawk yelled to be heard, then disappeared into the curtains of falling snow.

Cloud Dancer worked fast to withdraw Bonita's tether line from her possessions, looping it over the mare's neck to tie her, then freeing her of the Spanish bridle and reins. There was little grass here, and both she and Little Fox

quickly gathered more from the surrounding area, returning to wedge their offering between the low rocks so it would
not blow away.

They had barely gathered the grass when White Hawk
returned with several long poles and heavy skins. "Between
the rocks there, and the trees there—" he pointed at the
outcrop and then toward the stubby tops of the sturdy,
twisted junipers "—we can tie these hides and make a roof
for the horse."

Little Fox nodded enthusiastically. "I will help!" Using
fingers and toes, he scaled the rock face easily, clinging there
like a fly on the wall while White Hawk flung him the first
corner of a skin and the rope to tie it.

Together they worked swiftly until the small corner of
rock and brush almost resembled a flat-roofed house like
those constructed of earth at Acoma. Satisfied her friend
would be safe, Cloud Dancer went with White Hawk and
Little Fox to the beckoning warmth of the tepee.

The hunters returning with White Hawk had quickly
spread the word of the arrival of strangers in camp, and
many Apaches were congregating at the tepee of the chief to
see the newcomers. Places were made for Cloud Dancer and
Little Fox nearest the fire, Little Fox on one side seated with
the men, and Cloud Dancer on the other, seated with the
women. With nowhere to leave her few possessions, Cloud
Dancer laid her pouches and weapons before her on the
ground. White Hawk sat across the fire from her, to the
right of the chief. To his left, her eyes rested upon Bempol,
war chief of the Jicarilla Apache, he who had originally led
the small band of Apache warriors to Acoma. His gaze was
steady, his eyes lively and filled with interest. He spoke a few
low words to White Hawk, who nodded, and then the
Apache chief, Claws of the Bear, proclaimed that he would
hear the tale of Little Fox's and Cloud Dancer's escape from
the horrors of Acoma.

Little Fox spoke first as Claws of the Bear indicated, telling of his part in the battle, his capture and his eventual escape.

The warmth of the tepee, with so many bodies gathered close and the fire built high, wrapped itself around Cloud Dancer. Bit by bit she felt herself relaxing in the presence of these people so different from her own. She occasionally caught the great war chief's eyes upon her with interest, and once she boldly met his eyes. As she shed the stiffness of the cold that had permeated her bones, she was aware of the growling of her own belly. Food was passed to her by the chief's wife, and she accepted it gratefully.

She could feel White Hawk's gaze steady upon her and returned it with pain in her eyes. She was still stunned by the shock of his rejection, but she knew, if he no longer cared for her, she would live with this new, wrenching pain as she had learned to live with others. Time would dull the hurt.

There was another who regarded her intently as he sat beside the fire listening to Little Fox; Cloud Dancer could feel the hard stare of the one White Hawk had called Prairie Wolf. When she glanced his way, she met the bold appraisal of his dark eyes.

There was an air of disapproval about Prairie Wolf when his gaze raked her, and for the moment Cloud Dancer could but wonder at it. He was young and more than easy to look upon. His oval face was marked by strong features: an angular jaw, slightly crooked nose, lips compressed into a straight, disapproving line, and dark, fathomless eyes set beneath a slightly protruding brow. Others looked upon Cloud Dancer with curiosity that she could see in their faces, but it was obvious something more was bothering Prairie Wolf.

White Hawk's voice interrupted her contemplations. "Cloud Dancer, our chief has asked to hear your tale." He spoke kindly to her in her own Kere dialect, but his words reflected none of the special warmth that had touched her in Acoma. "Little Fox has already told us how bravely you fought and I have said how I had seen you fall and believed you dead."

Cloud Dancer nodded curtly and, tamping down her riotous emotions, began her tale. The Apache were great storytellers and listened in rapt attention to a well-spun story. Cloud Dancer was truthful, but she did not leave out anything. She did not skirt around details when she believed she had been lacking, or felt she had done the wrong thing in battle. She bared herself to these still-faced strangers who sat all around her, in hopes now of little more than acceptance.

Chapter Thirteen

Cloud Dancer was out of her sleeping robes before sunup. The old woman with whom she shared a tepee now was still asleep. She collected her weapons and the saddle pad she had fashioned for Bonita and slipped from the tepee, warm from its banked fire, into the freezing bite of the early-morning air.

She had seen little of White Hawk during the days since her arrival at the Apache camp, and she had resolved to harden her heart toward him. But in other things she was content. She was honing her hunting skills, gleaning acceptance and, in some cases, admiration from the men of the tribe. She had been taken in by the old woman, She Who Seeks Wisdom.

She Who Seeks Wisdom was the tribe's wisewoman: the keeper of the knowledge of the ancient ones, the conveyor of women's knowledge to the young ones and the midwife. She was venerated among these Apaches, and there was always a young hunter to bring meat for her pot. But since Cloud Dancer's arrival, there had been little need. Cloud Dancer took great pride in bringing the meat they would share in exchange for the lodging and kindness the old woman bestowed upon her.

"The warriors do not treat me as they do other women of the tribe," Cloud Dancer whispered to Bonita as she first rubbed the mare's nose, and then slung her saddle pad across the horses's back and tied it in position. She worked deftly in the darkness of the predawn. "It is partly because I have you." The horse had become her friend and confidante since Perez's death had left them together.

Bonita dipped her head and gently nudged Cloud Dancer, as she slung her quiver of arrows across the mare's withers. The maid jumped up from the side and pulled herself astride as Bonita stood patiently waiting.

"But, in truth, I know it is more than that," Cloud Dancer said softly, her hand stroking Bonita's mane before she guided her out of the enclosure where the few horses of the camp were kept. "The Apache have these few horses they have traded for or taken on a raid. No, you are not the only reason I am treated differently." She put the mare to a gentle canter, intending to get the game needed quickly and return to camp.

She knew her desire to become both warrior and hunter was accepted because of White Hawk's words, and for that she was grateful to him. When she had told her story that first night before the fire of the chief, White Hawk had added afterward how she had taken up the spear and knife and fought at Acoma. To Cloud Dancer's ears, his tale had made it sound much more than it had been. But the people had listened and they had accepted.

The people had accepted, but what of White Hawk? He had remained so formal, so aloof. Cloud Dancer had resolved repeatedly to harden her heart toward him, yet the pain of his abrupt rejection remained. What had happened in the time they had been apart to change his feelings toward her? The question nagged at Cloud Dancer, but her pride would not allow her to risk another rebuff at his hands. She had learned she must depend upon herself alone, and it was a lesson she would not forget.

Cloud Dancer urged Bonita up a steep incline and toward the tall trees on the slopes higher above. For now, the

Apaches with whom she lived were camped on the long slopes of the gracefully rolling hills, midway between the sluggishly flowing river and the much higher mountains to the east. Game was plentiful everywhere, but Cloud Dancer gravitated more toward the high mountains. The life was so very different from the one she had led at Acoma, yet she reveled in it. She heard the mountains whispering her name in the sighing of the wind through trees so tall they would have reached from the valley floor to the mesa top of Acoma. The old way of life at Acoma had slipped away from her as skin shed water. This was her life now. These were her people.

A brilliant golden light flared in the east as the sun rose swiftly above the mountain peaks, spreading a warming bath of sunlight before it. Cloud Dancer turned her face to enjoy the warmth and even the mare neighed her delight as the few wispy clouds streaked across the sky took on the iridescent orange-pink of morning.

Cloud Dancer rode a little farther, then, taking her weapons, slipped from Bonita's back and proceeded on foot. She had left her lance in camp, but she carried with her her bow and arrows as well as her knife, which was tucked inside the high-top deerskin boots She Who Seeks Wisdom had fashioned for her.

She skirted a clump of boulders, paused behind a thick tree trunk and worked her way forward, alert to any movement that would signal the presence of game either large or small.

Then, as she paused behind some brush, Cloud Dancer spotted a large buck grazing at the edge of a clearing. Quickly she raised her bow, arrow notched and ready, but she paused for a moment, thanking the spirit of the deer for its sacrifice, and praying to the Great Spirit to guide her arrow for a quick, clean kill.

She drew the bowstring a little more taut and let the arrow fly. The zip of the finely crafted arrow through the air brought the buck's head up an instant before it struck. The buck leaped into the air, then crashed to the earth and, in moments, lay still.

Cloud Dancer whispered her thanks for the true flight of her arrow and rushed out into the clearing to claim her kill. When she reached the motionless body of the deer, she stopped dead in her tracks, gaping at two arrows, not one, protruding from the carcass. Both were fatally placed. Another hunter had taken aim at this deer even as she had done!

Her heart leaped into her throat. There were many enemies and she was in the open! She spun away from the fallen deer, eyes probing the shadows among the trees, searching for the owner of the second arrow.

"Do not fear, Cloud Dancer." The voice was familiar, low and husky, its rich timbre going straight to Cloud Dancer's heart, despite her determination that she would be as aloof as he. The rich tones reached out to her upon the clear morning air. "Even without my tutelage you have learned much. The deer is yours."

Cloud Dancer shook her head firmly, allowing her breath to escape in a deep sigh of relief that no enemy stood before her. "No, White Hawk, both our arrows were true. We will share the meat." She held herself stiff and straight. They were as two strangers meeting for the first time in the clearing.

White Hawk moved toward her, a smile as brilliant as the early-morning sunlight upon his lips. "As you wish," he said softly.

She did not understand that warm, liquid smile after his coldness of the days past. Cloud Dancer returned White Hawk's smile with a placid expression of patience. All the uncertainties that had plagued her since their reunion, all the pain of his rejection, flooded her heart and she sought to strengthen the wall against those feelings. Raising her chin to its stubborn tilt, she allowed her lips to curve from her first hesitant smile to an ironic twist. They were alone. For the first time since she had found White Hawk again, they were truly alone. But now, it meant little to her. That was what she firmly told herself.

The sunlight caressed his ebony hair. He stopped a few feet from her. "We are alone, Little One. Here there are none to see or condemn." His words were gentle, beseeching. "Even now when I see you I cannot believe you are truly here before me."

White Hawk dropped his bow and arrows and opened his arms to her. His gesture was so unexpected by Cloud Dancer after his coolness toward her in camp that she stood stunned and unmoving, rigid and mute. Her traitorous heart cried out for her to throw herself into his open arms, but the pain of his past rebuff caused her to wait, feeling as though her feet had become rooted to the earth. Her eyes glittered with uncertainty and rising anger.

How could he do this? How could he act as if he cared nothing for her as the long days passed, yet now suddenly stand before her, arms open, and expect her to fall into them? Did he care only to use her? Was there only lust in his heart?

White Hawk frowned as the moments stretched long between them and Cloud Dancer did not come to him. Slowly he allowed his arms to fall to his sides, pain and sadness darkening his black eyes, sapping the light from them.

The confusion in his gaze was plain, but it served only to fan the flames of Cloud Dancer's anger. She stood rigid and unyielding before him, her bow clenched in her small white-knuckled fist. "We have taken the same deer, and I have said we will share the meat," she murmured through stiff lips. "What more do you want of me?"

The question took White Hawk aback, the bite of her words stinging like the lash of a whip. He drew himself to his full height, the angles of his cheeks hardening his handsome face to stone. "You have changed much since Acoma," he accused.

"No!" Cloud Dancer returned more sharply than she intended, for the wall she had so carefully built around her heart was quickly crumbling before the pain in his eyes. "It is you who have changed," she said, her tone softened.

"I do not understand. I have not changed."

"If you have not changed, why did you put me from you? Why do you avoid me in camp? Why have you not come to me before now?"

The hard angles of White Hawk's face softened slightly. "You are among the Apache now," he said simply. "Not the Kere."

"I do not understand!"

White Hawk sighed; of course she did not understand. He had expected too much. She had to learn the ways of the Apache, to know in her heart the Apache ways were far different from the customs of the Kere of Acoma. "I could not come to you openly. I would have destroyed your reputation as a maiden, caused you to appear an easy woman, which would make you unwelcome in the camp of the Apache. I could not risk that. And I could not embrace you before the warriors as you did me. It is not the way of the Apache warrior." He searched her eyes for understanding and continued.

"I have looked for you each day when you hunt!" The words came from White Hawk in a soft, quick whisper. "I followed your tracks, but each day you would take your game and return to camp before I could find you. If I had not found you this day I would have gone mad!"

Cloud Dancer still looked doubtful, the hurt in her heart a stubborn thing.

White Hawk grunted in frustration and quickly moved to embrace her; she stood rigid against him.

"I have missed you so much, White Hawk," she finally choked out. The admission was painful, but brought with it the surge of old feeling they had shared.

"I have wanted nothing more than to touch you and hold you close to me since I saw you in the snow. Your life at Acoma is no more. I would not have you bound to me if it is not your choice. Much has changed since we were together among your people."

"We have been separated by time and pain—nothing more. I had felt in my heart that you were not dead, yet I could not believe it."

"I, too, felt your heart calling to mine. You have walked with me in my dreams and I have seen you in my visions. If the Great Spirit had not brought you to me now, I would have begun searching for you. I could not have remained here."

She did not relax against him and he did not release her.

Cloud Dancer lifted her head to allow her eyes to gaze into the depths of his, seeing there her own reflection. She was beginning to understand some of White Hawk's behavior as an Apache, but the hurt of his denial of her was still like a raw wound within her.

She longed to snuggle close and enjoy his warmth, his strength and the fierce throbbing of his heart beneath the palm she had braced against his chest. She was weakening, but still she feared. At Acoma she had given herself willingly to him in the way of her people. But now, here among the Apache, the differences were becoming painfully clear. What if he wanted her only for what her body could give to his and not to share a life?

White Hawk drew her down upon a small hillock and leaned back in the crackling grasses, drawing Cloud Dancer into the bend of his arm. He stared up into the cloudless sky and stroked her gently. He desired her deeply, felt the rush of warmth to his loins—but now was not the time.

He breathed in the sweet essence of her and drew a deep, steadying breath. "To have you with me now, after I saw so many die, is more than I believed possible."

Cloud Dancer winced at the pain etched into the lines and planes of White Hawk's face. "I am sorry I was taken from you. But Perez did what he believed was right."

"Do not be sorry," White Hawk responded gently, his hand wrapped possessively about her waist, holding her close to him, despite the feeling of her resistance. "I have no love for the Spanish, but if it were not for the one you call Perez, I *would* have found you among the dead."

He paused, then went on. "Bempol and I stayed in the cave where you and I were sheltered against the storm the day of the rabbit hunt." He squeezed her gently, indicating the cave had been much more than shelter when they had occupied it. "Like animals we stayed there licking our wounds, until we were strong enough to return to our people."

Cloud Dancer raised her hand and pressed it to the buckskin shirt beneath which lay the healing flesh, scarred by the Spanish miniball. She gazed up into the handsome visage of her love. "The others with Bempol were all lost?"

White Hawk nodded.

"You must curse the day you and your people came to advise your Kere brothers in the ways of war."

He brushed the top of her head with his lips. "No, Little One, I do not curse that day. Those who died at Acoma died as warriors. It was their choice to go there. If I had not gone there I would not have found you. No, Cloud Dancer, it is you who should curse me, for I claim my love for you at the same time I endanger your remaining among my people— the people you have chosen after the loss of your own."

Cloud Dancer sat up abruptly and stared down at White Hawk, a horrified expression on her face. "You could not do that!"

"But I already have. If we were seen here...alone together, you might be forced to leave. That is the way of my people in these matters. You would be disgraced, and it would be at my hands. Even now, like this, we are at risk. There has been no one for me since our time in the cave at Acoma. There will be no one again until we are married."

"Married?" Cloud Dancer stiffened all over again. Did he mean it, or were these just words?

White Hawk nodded. "When we return I will court you the Apache way. You will see. Meanwhile you will stay with She Who Seeks Wisdom and learn the skills of a warrior as you wish."

"But how long will that take? Already we have been apart so long!" She took a deep breath and raised her eyes to his.

"I will welcome your courting." Her fingers trembled with the emotions she had suppressed as the wall about her heart crumbled away completely. Her fingers rose to touch his face, tracing his eyes and sliding over his lips.

White Hawk gasped, amazed at what the mere touch of her hand could bring forth within him, and caught her slender wrist in the firm grip of his hand. He gave her a slow, sensuous smile before playfully tumbling her backward into the dried grasses. "You tempt me almost beyond endurance, Little One," he chided her gently, "but you are among my people now and must learn their ways. Here we will spend our lives, and while what we do beyond the reach of prying eyes will be between us, we must take care not to break the taboos set forth by our elders."

Cloud Dancer frowned and reluctantly nodded her agreement. She truly realized, for the first time, how hard it had been for this Apache warrior when he had not found her at Acoma, and how hard his people could make it for their love to flourish. In that moment she gained a whole new respect for his love and his strength.

White Hawk laughed. "It will not be so bad," he teased her. "The courtship will be short—but long enough to have the anticipation make it all the sweeter."

Rolling to his feet, White Hawk put out his hand to her. "Come," he said softly, "we have stayed long enough. The kill must not be wasted."

Cloud Dancer gained her feet, and together they made short work of cleaning and dividing the deer carcass.

Chapter Fourteen

She Who Seeks Wisdom's lips were sucked into a rosette, her face folded into a complex set of wrinkles, while she intently watched Cloud Dancer's hands slide and skate over the surface of the clay, forming and smoothing. Falling Leaves, sister to Prairie Wolf, was sitting at Cloud Dancer's elbow. She, too, watched in rapt attention and respectful silence, as the clay bowl took on definite shape.

The Apache wove baskets and grass mats, but they did not work the clay, for the nomadic life they led made the proliferation of pots impractical. Yet they found it fascinating, this delicate forming of the clay into vessels of practical worth.

Both Falling Leaves and She Who Seeks Wisdom knew how to work the clay now, having learned from Cloud Dancer, but both remained in awe of the young woman's skill and the almost trancelike state she attained while working the soft, moist clay between her hands.

"You have magic in your hands," She Who Seeks Wisdom stated quietly when Cloud Dancer set the bowl aside to dry. The wisewoman's normally resonant voice was muted in awe of this wonderful gift the young Acoma maid possessed. "But that does not surprise me. You have success at all you put your hand to."

"Not all, Grandmother," Cloud Dancer said with a sad smile, "but of late, enough."

"You do not lie!" The older woman chuckled, then sobered. "I will miss you when you marry and erect your own tepee, even though it is such a one as White Hawk whom you marry." Her eyes twinkled at the reference to White Hawk's courting of Cloud Dancer. Then she laughed again. "But you may yet change your mind. Others bring meat to our pot and court my favor for your hand. Perhaps Prairie Wolf will yet sway you."

Cloud Dancer grimaced. "He does not even like me. At every turn he ridicules the skills I learn for hunting or fighting. He has even tried to take Bonita from me, arguing at council that a woman should not have that which the warriors so desperately need. I do not know why he tries to court me. I will not accept him."

"That is why he courts you!" She Who Seeks Wisdom exclaimed. "He is a man. If you accepted him he would control you. He would not feel shamed by your abilities being greater than his own, since he would not allow you to continue. You would no longer be the only unmarried war woman. And he would get Bonita."

"Then why does he think I would accept him?" Cloud Dancer railed in frustration.

She Who Seeks Wisdom shrugged. "He hopes you are a fool."

"Cloud Dancer is not a fool," Falling Leaves interjected seriously. "She will marry White Hawk. Prairie Wolf is my brother, but I fear *he* is the fool."

Bursting into laughter, her soft topaz-colored eyes twinkling in merriment, She Who Seeks Wisdom slapped her young friend on the back. "That is true, but let no one else hear you say it!"

She turned to Cloud Dancer. "Do not worry about Prairie Wolf. If he continues to bring meat for our pot as he does, you continue to hunt, and White Hawk does as well, we will have enough dried meat to feed the entire camp! None will go hungry for the rest of the winter!''

Cloud Dancer sighed. "I am sorry if I bring you trouble, She Who Seeks Wisdom. It was not my intention when I came to live with you.''

That statement evoked even heartier laughter from the old woman. "Trouble? This old woman has not had so much fun since her youth! They swarm to you as bees to honey. This old woman will never go hungry!''

"You need not worry about going hungry again, for that will never happen while I live. And you are not an old woman,'' Cloud Dancer chided gently, for she had seen the child looking out from behind She Who Seeks Wisdom's old eyes. "You will see many more summers.''

"Yes, I will, but then I will be a *very* old woman.'' She smiled and shifted her position near the fire, the sharp crack of her joints popping loud to their ears. "I have known you not long, Cloud Dancer, yet I know there is much more to you than first appears. You are strong—much stronger than Prairie Wolf could dream—and you are true. There is much I would teach you if you would learn. You would become a vessel, carrying the knowledge I impart for others and passing it on to your daughter one day, so that she will take her place as wisewoman when the time is right for her to carry on the tradition of our line.''

Falling Leaves smiled radiantly and rested her hand upon Cloud Dancer's arm. "It is a great honor she offers you,'' she put in.

Recognizing the seriousness of the older woman's tone, Cloud Dancer nodded. "I will listen, She Who Seeks Wisdom, but I am not of the Apache. Should you not choose one who is?'' She turned to Falling Leaves. "Perhaps Falling Leaves?''

"Falling Leaves is like another daughter to me, but there is none such as you for what I would teach.''

"And if I am killed in battle?''

"You will not be."

"And will the Apache accept what you will teach me?"

"Yes. They have already accepted you. You have come to us from Acoma, but you are Apache now. You live as we live. You learn our customs. If it were not so, there would be many against a joining between you and any man of the tribe. There is much pressure among the Jicarilla Apache to marry within the tribe."

"White Hawk has told me this."

"It is so!" Falling Leaves exclaimed. "Yet he courts you now."

"All will be as it should be," She Who Seeks Wisdom said softly, then awaited Cloud Dancer's answer.

Cloud Dancer fell silent for a few moments, deep in thought. "I will accept your teachings, She Who Seeks Wisdom, if in turn I may teach you and Falling Leaves the ways of my people as well so that their ways will not be lost."

"So be it," the wisewoman agreed.

"Ho, Old Woman!" White Hawk's voice rumbled from without, "I bring meat to honor you who shelters Cloud Dancer."

She Who Seeks Wisdom grinned across at Cloud Dancer. "Do you wish to walk with him?"

Cloud Dancer nodded eagerly.

"Then take your bow and arrows and go outside. White Hawk's aim is among the best of the warriors of the Jicarilla Apache. Perhaps you can improve your aim," she suggested, a slight squint of the eye all that gave away her pretext for allowing Cloud Dancer to spend time alone with White Hawk. "Just do not go beyond the sight of camp. All must see he is instructing you with the bow. We do not want tongues wagging."

"Yes, Grandmother," Cloud Dancer replied humbly, then, unable to suppress it, broke out laughing.

The soft, melodious sound preceded Cloud Dancer from the tepee, and she stopped short, almost colliding with the broad wall of White Hawk's buckskin-clad chest.

White Hawk's lips were already curving into a smile at the sound of Cloud Dancer's laughter, but when she stepped through the flap of She Who Seeks Wisdom's tepee she took his breath away. She was radiant in a new buckskin tunic over heavy leggings and thick, fur-lined moccasins. Over the tunic she wore a caped jacket, fashioned no doubt by She Who Seeks Wisdom from the woolly skin of the shaggy buffalo. In her hand she clenched her bow and quiver of arrows.

But it was the slender grace of her, the dancing lights in the depths of her gold-flecked brown eyes, the flush of her cheeks and the unmistakable joy she radiated when she saw him that pierced him through to the heart. He wanted to enfold her in his embrace, but held himself aloof, the proper Apache warrior courting the woman he would have as his mate. Only the gleam in the depths of his obsidian eyes spoke to Cloud Dancer of his desires—and his restraint.

She Who Seeks Wisdom poked her head outside long enough to accept the haunch of venison White Hawk brought, then disappeared within.

"I was going to practice with my bow," Cloud Dancer said softly, eyes meeting White Hawk's. "She Who Seeks Wisdom has said you are the most skilled among your people. Perhaps, if there is nothing you must attend to, you would demonstrate your skill."

White Hawk smiled at the old woman's strategy. Cloud Dancer had become an exception to many of the Apache customs with her acceptance into the tribe as an aspiring warrior and owner of one of the few horses within the tribe. When she was practicing or off alone hunting, she was not seen as a woman, but was respected as one of the providers of meat for the tribe—a proved hunter and declared warrior. It was only when she was in camp, performing a woman's duties, that she was expected to behave as a proper Apache maiden.

"Come," he said seriously. "Demonstrate for me your abilities, and I will help you to improve."

Together they strode to the edge of camp, and White Hawk set up a target. He quickly fired a couple of arrows, hitting his target nearly dead center, then turned to Cloud Dancer.

"I have yet to see you use the bow and arrows, Little One, though I have seen the result," he said softly, referring to the deer they had shared, his words beyond the hearing of anyone but Cloud Dancer.

She took up his playful challenge with a small, tight smile, notching an arrow and drawing the bow to full cock before letting the arrow fly. The arrow whispered through the air to the target, striking it to the left of White Hawk's, a little wide. A second arrow followed much the same path.

It did not take long for what had started out as an excuse for them to be together to turn into an earnest lesson with the bow. Time after time White Hawk let his arrow fly, then watched critically while Cloud Dancer did the same. He adjusted her grip on the bow and the way she drew the string, smoothing her movements. After a few more tries he adjusted her stance, steadying her foundation for shooting, thus shrinking the circle where her arrow would strike.

Cloud Dancer had been good with the bow before, but what She Who Seeks Wisdom had said was true: White Hawk was among the best she had seen. And he had the gift of imparting his knowledge and skill to others. He could see immediately the small adjustments that would begin to make her an excellent archer.

Her arm tiring from the repeated stress of pulling the bowstring taut, Cloud Dancer lowered her bow and walked to the target to retrieve their arrows once again, as she had so often during their session.

When she turned, Cloud Dancer saw Prairie Wolf standing beside White Hawk, gazing fixedly in her direction. His hawklike features were arresting, but a shadowy sneer hung about his heavy mouth, drawing those features into sharp crags and hollows.

"She shoots like a woman," were the jeering words Cloud Dancer discerned passing from Prairie Wolf's lips to White Hawk's ears.

"I *am* a woman." Cloud Dancer met his gaze directly, boldly refusing to drop her eyes, and handed White Hawk's arrows back to him. "Do you shoot like a young boy?"

White Hawk sent her a warning look, but his lips quirked with the effort to suppress a grin.

"A target does not move," Prairie Wolf snapped back. "And a target is not a man, little warrior. I would not want such as you at my back during battle."

"Then she can stand at my back," White Hawk said evenly, stepping between them.

"You are a fool. She has blinded you, bewitched you."

White Hawk's face darkened like a storm cloud. Such an accusation was tantamount to condemnation. "You have spoken strong words. Their claim cannot be left unanswered." White Hawk's tone was low and menacing, drawing the attention of a few onlookers who had paused to watch Cloud Dancer shoot the bow and arrow. "If you do not have proof of what you say—that Cloud Dancer is capable of witchcraft—then you will say so...now!" Fury held White Hawk in its grip.

"I have no proof," Prairie Wolf admitted, his face twisting in his anger, bold black eyes defiant. "But it is not right that you train her as you would a warrior."

"She is a warrior."

"She is a woman."

White Hawk frowned and stared directly into Prairie Wolf's angry young eyes. "We have warrior women. There have been others in the past."

"They are not like her! She is not married!" Prairie Wolf protested. "Wives who accompany their husbands on raids remain behind in the temporary camp to cook, clean and nurse the wounded. They go only if their husbands are warriors or to avenge the loss of one of their family. They are not without mates as she is, tempting and distracting the warriors. War women fight only in defense."

"So has Cloud Dancer fought in the past." White Hawk's gaze did not waver. "Perhaps it is that you fear your abilities are not as great as hers. Perhaps you would like to draw the bow against her and see who is the best."

Cloud Dancer blanched. Already she had enough trouble with Prairie Wolf's ridicule and ill will; she did not wish to look foolish. She did not wish to make him look foolish. And yet, if she pitted herself against him in a match, she would not be able to do any less than her best. For a moment anger at White Hawk flamed within her at the position he had placed her in. Then Prairie Wolf spoke.

"I do not fear her! I will put an arrow in your target, but it will prove nothing. You train her as a warrior. I would teach her it is not necessary for her to be a warrior. If she were my woman," he said directly to Cloud Dancer, "she would soon learn *I* provide enough meat for our pot and *I* protect our home. I would put a baby in her belly and she would not leave the child to fight like the men. There would be no need for her to join the war women."

A few other members of the tribe had gathered closer, aware of the disturbance, watching intently.

"Cloud Dancer is a woman, but she is also a warrior." White Hawk looked directly into her eyes. "I saw her in my visions before I saw her fight at Acoma. If she were my woman," he said softly, "I would have her never be helpless again. I would have her stand beside me always, and I would be proud to have her stand at my back in battle when there was need." His words were as close to a declaration of love as he could publicly come.

With those few words White Hawk lifted his bow and let the arrow fly, nearly hitting dead center of the distant target. "Whoever puts their arrow closer to mine wins."

White Hawk's declaration on her behalf nearly staggered Cloud Dancer; it was rare for a stoic Apache to say so much in defense of a woman. But, his speaking out was not so different from Prairie Wolf's diatribe, and she could hear the uncomfortable rumbling from those near them who had heard the exchange.

Prairie Wolf waited no longer and raised his bow, drew back the string and let his arrow fly. Out of the corner of her eye, Cloud Dancer saw Little Fox join the growing assembly, glancing first at her, then at White Hawk, his eyes finally following the path of Prairie Wolf's arrow to where it vibrated in the wood of the target only a couple of inches above White Hawk's. There was empathy in his gaze; he understood her uncertainty among these people the two Keres hardly understood.

Cloud Dancer looked at White Hawk, seeing the light of encouragement in his eyes despite the stony set of his face, then raised her own bow. The arrow flew true, burying its tip where it nearly touched White Hawk's arrow, quivering with the impact. Then all eyes turned toward Prairie Wolf.

Disbelief, frustration and rage seethed behind the cool mask of the young Apache's face. He stood stiff and straight, eyes moving over the gathered crowd, finding, to his embarrassment, his sister, and beyond her, Little Fox of Acoma.

Seeing Little Fox and Falling Leaves standing close together, knowing that already the entire camp spoke of Little Fox's courtship of Falling Leaves, was too much. Prairie Wolf's eyes met Cloud Dancer's in open warfare and malevolence. "See the great woman warrior!" Prairie Wolf proclaimed in a thundering bellow, waving his bow above his head with one hand, pointing toward Cloud Dancer with the other. "She comes from a people whose women learn to kill and whose men—'' he cast his sneering look in Little Fox's direction ''—know nothing but farming and weaving! Is it any wonder that such a people fell to the attack of the Spanish?''

Cloud Dancer watched the color drain from Little Fox's face. She felt his anger and his pain. No man could stand being made to play the fool before the woman he loved. Falling Leaves dropped her eyes for a moment. When she looked up, Little Fox took a step forward, fists clenched by his sides, eyes burning with fury. He was not the warrior Prairie Wolf was, but he would have challenged the jealous, hotheaded young Apache warrior if Falling Leaves had not spoken urgently. Her words were for Little Fox alone.

''Wait, please! She Who Seeks Wisdom says my brother is a fool,'' she said with a soft sigh, ''and I fear she is right. But worse, I think he envies Cloud Dancer. If you fight him it will change nothing!''

Little Fox was puzzled. ''Envies her? But she had lost everything before she came here.''

''And now she has everything Prairie Wolf had come to believe belonged to him!'' she whispered urgently. ''As White Hawk recovered from his wounds, it was my brother he spent much of his time with, showing him how to improve his aim and fashion better weapons. Now it is Cloud Dancer White Hawk teaches. It is Cloud Dancer the other men of the tribe watch with interest and praise, not Prairie Wolf. He cannot tolerate any of the young men to be better with a bow and arrow than he, and yet Cloud Dancer, a woman, has just bested him before the entire camp! My brother has much pride and it has been sorely wounded since Cloud Dancer arrived among us. Let it pass. Please...''

At her pleading, Little Fox's anger subsided, and he gritted his teeth against raising his hand to one Falling Leaves cared so much about. He loved Falling Leaves. Her words had tempered his anger. He would not raise his hand against her brother.

"Cloud Dancer's shot was clearly the better," White Hawk announced, having no patience with Prairie Wolf's petty jealousies. "You may shout to the heavens, but that you will not change." He paused, allowing silence to settle over the onlookers. "The people of Acoma fought and died bravely. Many died. Many who lived were scattered to the winds. I was at Acoma. I saw this, as did Bempol, our war chief. Prairie Wolf has seen none of this," he told those gathered. "Their lives were different from our own, but the Kere of Acoma were our brothers, our allies. They were destroyed by the Spanish, who are our enemies as well. Now Little Fox and Cloud Dancer have come among us, asking to remain and learn our ways. We have accepted them and they have proved their hearts are true. They learn our ways. For now, it is enough."

White Hawk's last words fell like rocks, their weight ending the discussion. They warned Prairie Wolf to hold his peace. White Hawk's stony gaze swept the younger, less proved warrior, who at last saw the wisdom of refraining from further outbursts, and fell into a sullen silence.

Standing Buffalo watched the exchange from a short distance, face set firmly in thought. Never had he seen his younger brother, White Hawk, so impassioned. Prairie Wolf was young and hotheaded, but Standing Buffalo wondered if there were not some truth in the words he spoke. The woman of the Kere had a strange hold upon his brother. It was a situation that would bear careful watching. She might have great power. If so, that was good. But if Prairie Wolf was correct in his impulsive accusations, if she truly was a sorceress, she would be capable of upsetting the balance of nature, of creating a situation where evil would befall the people. No matter how impassioned White Hawk's oratory, such a one could not be allowed to remain among the Jicarilla Apache.

White Hawk, Standing Buffalo knew, had great power. He had journeyed to the sacred mountains, had fasted for four days and four nights, and on the last day his power had been bestowed upon him. Many times White Hawk had been able to see the future. In addition, he was a great shaman with the power to heal wounds when others failed. He was respected and honored among their people. He would be a potent force to be reckoned with should Cloud Dancer prove to turn her own power to evil. But to fight her power, he would have to recognize it, and for the moment, if there was danger, White Hawk was blinded to it. Standing Buffalo decided he would watch and wait.

The stern, implacable look of the warrior upon her face, Cloud Dancer kept her voice low and breathed a sign of relief after Prairie Wolf stalked off and the curious onlookers dispersed. She and White Hawk were alone except for Little Fox and Falling Leaves.

"She Who Seeks Wisdom has told me if an Apache couple does not mind risking a scolding from their parents, they may arrange a rendezvous with another couple." She nodded in the direction of Little Fox and Falling Leaves. "Perhaps, if I asked, they would take such a risk. Would you?"

White Hawk chuckled. "Perhaps." He smiled down at her, a surprising softness coming over his face. "There will also be a dance three days from now. But go now, conspire with Falling Leaves. Set up your rendezvous, and I will be there with Little Fox."

Cloud Dancer dipped her head, hiding her spreading grin from White Hawk's view. Gripping her bow and quiver of arrows firmly in her hand, she strode toward Falling Leaves, her heart singing.

Falling Leaves giggled softly as she and Cloud Dancer hurried toward their rendezvous with Little Fox and White Hawk. The spot Falling Leaves had suggested for their meeting was some distance from camp, on the banks of a chuckling creek among the fragrant pines.

"Hurry!" Falling Leaves said in a giggled whisper. "We must not be late or they will think we are not coming."

"Perhaps it would be good if we were a little late," Cloud Dancer suggested. "Just enough to make them wonder if we are coming." Or, she thought to herself, late enough to give her longer to prepare, for the very thought of spending this time so near to White Hawk sent chills of yearning spiraling through her stomach.

Falling Leaves laughed softly, the sound blending with the musical tinkling of the stream, and slowed her pace just a little.

They continued on in silence, Cloud Dancer pondering the unfamiliar way of the Apache, so different from that of the Kere. It was difficult for young Apache men and women to meet out of the sight and reach of morally strict parents—thus their secret meeting. If caught, the young Apaches could be severely scolded before the entire camp. Cloud Dancer knew she ran little risk, since She Who Seeks Wisdom would merely laugh. Little Fox had no parents, and White Hawk would be little reprimanded. It was Falling Leaves who was taking the biggest risk in meeting with her love. If Prairie Wolf discovered it, her action would not be allowed to pass.

Yet is was not Falling Leaves who was likely to commit an impropriety, Cloud Dancer thought. She did not know how she and White Hawk could be so close and yet remain prudent after they had been apart so long. Just the thought of his nearness caused her to tremble with anticipation. She deepened her breath and calmed her body, reminding herself that soon they would be together always.

"There they are!" Falling Leaves pointed through the trees where White Hawk and Little Fox stood together on the stream bank. "They have arrived before us."

The two young women slowed to a sedate walk as they drew nearer, Cloud Dancer's heart quickening its cadence with each step forward.

White Hawk's dark eyes gleamed at the sight of Cloud Dancer, as desire, hot and searing, surged through him; Little Fox, beside him, appeared every inch the anxious suitor.

As if by mutual consent they all sat upon the earth a few feet apart. Cloud Dancer mused that young girls brought up to be terribly shy and reserved before men were expected, in this circumstance, to make all the advances.

Falling Leaves smiled demurely and picked up a small pebble, tossing it at Little Fox. Cloud Dancer followed her example, smiling brightly at White Hawk, who appeared to be enjoying the play, his head cocked as if questioning what was to come next. She watched him closely, the familiar tingle caused by his nearness rushing up her back and neck. They could be close as they were now and yet not touch more than a feather's breath. The enforced abstinence created a tension that sparked and crackled between Cloud Dancer and White Hawk.

In contrast, Little Fox, following newly learned Apache ways, tossed the pebbles back and Falling Leaves blushed and looked away, then shyly back at Little Fox.

They tossed the pebbles back and forth for a time, then slowly moved closer together. White Hawk felt the fine sheen of sweat when it broke out across his forehead. He could breathe the scent of his love, light upon the early-evening air, yet that was all.

Little Fox's heart was filled with love for Falling Leaves. He loved her shy modesty and her quick smile; he loved her enthusiasm and her loyalty. When he was near her everything seemed as if it would work out. Silently he thanked Cloud Dancer for bringing them all together.

"The winter has been long." Falling Leaves broke the silence with a barely heard murmur, speaking of commonplace things as was the Apache custom.

"Yes," Little Fox replied, "and it will be longer yet before we feel the warmth of spring."

"We must ask the Great Spirit to help us find game when the sky darkens and the snow flies again," White Hawk added, his hands clenched tightly against the urge to take Cloud Dancer into his arms.

They spoke of common things, yet all White Hawk could think of was the memory of Cloud Dancer pressed against him, her passions rising to match his own. He longed to have her in his arms and to hold her close to him. He, too, had to satisfy himself with the knowledge they would soon be together and away from prying eyes. He, too, drew a deep, steadying breath, yet found it did little to ease the fire in his veins.

"The hunting has been good," Falling Leaves said softly. "We have not gone hungry."

"And we will not," Cloud Dancer put in, speaking softly as they did, but her voice was tight with restrained desires. Oh, how she hated these strict Apache customs. By the Great Spirit how she wanted him! How she missed him! It had taken this simple meeting to make her realize just how much.

"I have returned with meat each time I have gone to hunt," she added in a lame attempt to keep their idle exchange moving.

"You are a fine hunter," White Hawk complimented her. "Others have not been so fortunate, though there has not been a great hunger in our camp."

White Hawk would have reached out to touch Cloud Dancer then, if he had not known that to do so would unleash the powerful desire he fought so hard to contain. He glanced at Little Fox, marveling at his innocent demeanor. If he was plagued by the same desires and emotions that unsettled White Hawk, he did not reveal the fact by look or gesture.

"If there were more horses in the camp we would be able to range even farther in search of game," Little Fox put in. He looked at Falling Leaves, his thoughts wandering to the gift he might offer when he asked for her in marriage. Horses, though few among the Apache, were already becoming a mark of wealth. White Hawk had acquired a horse on a recent raid and would stake it before Cloud Dancer's tepee. He himself would follow the old ways and offer many fine skins and other well crafted items for Falling Leaves's hand.

"We must find a way to get more horses," Cloud Dancer said in response to Little Fox's observation.

"It will be dangerous," White Hawk interjected, "but it is something that must be done." For a few moments he was distracted from Cloud Dancer's sensuous allure.

Falling Leaves frowned at the serious direction their conversation had taken. "There will be a dance very soon!" she chirped. "Then I will have the chance to dance with any unmarried man in camp," she teased Little Fox.

"I am not so fickle," Little Fox retorted in jest. "I will wait for you to ask me to join you."

Falling Leaves's face colored, and her eyes dropped to stare intently at her hands. She smiled shyly, replying in a whisper, "I will ask no other to dance."

"And you?" White Hawk asked Cloud Dancer, wondering how he would get through the night of the dance without crushing her to him. "Whom will you choose as your partner?"

"Prairie Wolf still seeks to court me," she mused, even as her heart beat faster at the heat in White Hawk's eyes when he let his gaze rest upon her. "So do others."

Falling Leaves snorted. "I love my brother—but you do not. You will dance with White Hawk."

It was Cloud Dancer's turn to blush and she did it with grace and true art, dipping her head and looking demurely away in the manner of an Apache maiden, using Falling Leaves as her example.

They lingered a while longer, speaking only of light-hearted matters until the shadows lengthened and the sun began its journey to the far western horizon.

"We must return to camp," Falling Leaves said gently. "We will be missed."

With a feather-light touch, Little Fox touched Falling Leaves's leg as she sat beside him, causing her to blush furiously again. She drew away from his touch out of propriety, but not so quickly as to make him think she truly wanted to move away.

White Hawk's eyes met Cloud Dancer's, and the familiar spark leaped up between them. To Cloud Dancer and White Hawk it seemed as if the very air thrummed with the power of their emotions. But for tonight, it was not to be. It was time to return to camp.

Together Cloud Dancer and Falling Leaves rose, leaving the bubbling stream and their loves behind them. Cloud Dancer's heart was light with the happiness of White Hawk's courtship. The Apache ways were so very different; not being able to touch, or wrap a blanket close about them both, creating their own small haven, was frustration itself—but he *did* love her!

"It was so short. And so stiff," Cloud Dancer said quietly as she and Falling Leaves walked back to camp.

"It is our way," Falling Leaves replied. "Girls are very shy, as they are taught to be, and young men do not display emotions openly. If a man shows affection for a woman in public, he will be laughed at. You will see after you learn more of our customs," she added seriously. Then her face lightened with a brilliant smile. "Though I would not mind learning some of the ways of the Kere, as well!"

The next few days passed quickly. Cloud Dancer, White Hawk, Falling Leaves and Little Fox gleaned no scolding from their meeting. Little Fox practiced with a bow and a lance frequently now, no doubt planning to prove Prairie

Wolf wrong about his fighting and hunting abilities. It was plain to see he was crazy in love with Falling Leaves, but there would be no more meetings among the four of them, for Prairie Wolf had begun to shadow his sister's footsteps as though he were her guard. Cloud Dancer sympathized, but perhaps that was good for Little Fox, who was having difficulty proceeding along the traditional Apache paths of courtship. He and Falling Leaves were trying to follow the Apache restrictions, but Falling Leaves was eager to learn the ways of the Kere, as well, and Little Fox was hard-pressed to resist her entreaties.

There was so much yet for Cloud Dancer to learn among the Apache, yet she felt she belonged here and her past life in Acoma was becoming only a shadow upon her memory.

Cloud Dancer ducked into the tepee where She Who Seeks Wisdom sat before the fire, tending a savory stew while her granddaughter patiently wove a small basket. The rabbit Cloud Dancer brought would make a welcome addition to the stew.

"Come, sit by me," She Who Seeks Wisdom said at the first sight of Cloud Dancer, patting the hides and fur robes covering the hard ground beside her. "You have risen with the dawn and return with meat for our pot. Rest and we will talk."

With a smile Cloud Dancer did as the old woman bade, handing over the rabbit to be quickly cut up and added to the stew. The flames of the fire did a graceful dance beneath the paunch in which the stew cooked, its soft light and gentle warmth caressing Cloud Dancer's face. She Who Seeks Wisdom's tepee was always filled with smells that spoke to Cloud Dancer of home: delicious food cooking over the fire, smoke, earth and well-tanned hides. It was particularly cold out this day and Cloud Dancer was glad of the opportunity to sit before the fire.

"Warm yourself," She Who Seeks Wisdom advised, pressing a cup of herbal brew into Cloud Dancer's hand.

She shifted her position, leaning closer to her young charge from Acoma. "Now, tell me what troubles you."

"You see through me easily, as you would through the flowing waters of the river to the bed below," Cloud Dancer said with amusement. She sipped the brew, savoring its rich taste and aroma. "Since I have come here I have learned many of your ways, but there is so much more I need to learn. There is much I do not understand. You heard what happened with Prairie Wolf the day you sent me with White Hawk to practice with the bow?"

She Who Seeks Wisdom nodded. "Falling Leaves spoke of it. I wondered how long it would take before you came to me," she added with a pleased quirk of her lips, her wise, deep-set jet-black eyes bright and bemused.

"I do not understand Prairie Wolf."

With a snort She Who Seeks Wisdom shook her head. "That is what troubles you? He is a fool. He is not worth thinking about. He has been a fool since he was a child. He will either find his way out of it one day, or he will remain a fool."

"He does not accept me," Cloud Dancer said simply.

"Did you believe that everyone would?" She Who Seeks Wisdom stared into the fire for a moment. "Acceptance takes time. You are not of our people—and yet you are. Most know you are trying to learn our ways, and that you are doing so quickly. They accept you for that reason alone. You are honored to be allowed to remain among the Apache; the Apache are honored by your true heart. All the same, some accept more quickly than others. They are not all fools like Prairie Wolf."

Cloud Dancer turned her head and met the older woman's steady gaze. "But you accepted me...."

"That is why they call me a wisewoman," the old woman said, chortling.

"I do not want to cause trouble among the Apache, splitting the people into those who believe the words of

Prairie Wolf and those who do not. I do not want to cause trouble for White Hawk."

"Then do not cause trouble for White Hawk or the people."

"I have not!"

"No, you have not." She Who Seeks Wisdom grinned. "The fool has."

"Yet it is because of me," Cloud Dancer protested.

She Who Seeks Wisdom shook her head. "It is because of Prairie Wolf."

"But there must be something I can do."

"Learn patience. Be as you are. Prairie Wolf is an impatient man. What he wants he seeks to grab. But most of all he wants control, power. One day he will find his own power inside, here—" she thumped her chest over her heart "—then he will be content."

Cloud Dancer paused, considering the words of She Who Seeks Wisdom. "Tell me about the Apache, the Indeh. I struggle to learn your customs and there are many to teach me, but I have learned little about the children, how they are taught, how they learn all I am learning, but with so much more time!"

"One day they will call you wisewoman, too!" She Who Seeks Wisdom slapped her knee with merriment. "You would see the roots to determine how the tree grows! Very well, I will tell you. Many of the skills our young girls learn you have already learned among your own people. Food gathering, building and taking care of the sick or wounded. But though the chores involved with the home and children are considered most important, girls, just like the boys, are taught to be strong, to rise early, run often and work hard.

"Look outside the tepee," She Who Seeks Wisdom directed as the high-pitched voices of children at play cut into their conversation. Several young boys and small, short-legged girls dashed from one end of camp to the other in a fiercely competitive footrace. "If there is an attack the children need to be able to reach safety quickly. Because of this, they are taught the same. While they are young, girls are encouraged to practice with bows and arrows and spears, as are the boys." The wisewoman's words fell like a gentle rain.

"I have seen the smaller boys and girls together," Cloud Dancer said.

"It is not until the boys and girls grow older that they are separated and girls gradually turn to home and family and boys to hunting and raiding. Indeh girls marry young. They marry young because they know it is forbidden for a man and a woman to lie together until they are married." She Who Seeks Wisdom quirked an eyebrow at Cloud Dancer. "In this you are different. You are older. Your life at Acoma was different. Your ways were not the same, so the people overlook what has gone before. But remember, what has gone before in your past life cannot happen here, among the Apache." Her last words were heavy with meaning.

Cloud Dancer ducked her head, concealing her tawny cougar eyes from She Who Seeks Wisdom's penetrating gaze. She knew! Somehow the old woman knew she had lain with White Hawk before she had come to the Apache. The past days and weeks had been difficult, but White Hawk had been right not to allow them to meet alone again. It could have meant disaster for them both.

"Falling Leaves, then, will marry soon."

"Yes."

"And I . . ."

She Who Seeks Wisdom squinted her eyes in amusement, deeper wrinkles gathering at the corners at odd angles with the deep furrows of her aged face. "You will marry White Hawk, and it will be soon or both of you will surely burst."

Cloud Dancer shared the older woman's laughter, and when it died down she smiled. "I do love White Hawk and hope to give him many children. You are right. When I carry his child I will not think of fighting and raiding, yet knowing I possess those very skills, that I may protect all that we love in his absence, is what will make me content."

She Who Seeks Wisdom grunted. "It is good. You will bring much, one to the other."

Cloud Dancer looked at She Who Seeks Wisdom. "White Hawk spoke of a dance. You must tell me what to do."

The old woman laughed. "I will show you the movements for the dance—the rest you will have to do for yourself!"

Chapter Fifteen

The fire leaped brightly at the center of the dancers, throwing warmth against the wintry night chill and light so that they might see to place their feet. The singing and chants had already begun, the heavy throb of the drums forming the background and pulsing through Cloud Dancer's veins, awakening memories of other dances in a past now lost.

"He looks for you." She Who Seeks Wisdom chortled in Cloud Dancer's ear, nodding in White Hawk's direction. "His eyes see no one else."

It was true. White Hawk's eyes had found Cloud Dancer when she first appeared at the fringes of the dance, and had not wavered since. Other maids glanced his way, but he did not meet their eyes, plainly oblivious of their attentions.

"It is no different with me," Cloud Dancer admitted to her friend and guardian.

"Then go to him. Choose him for the dance. It is what he waits for."

Cloud Dancer hesitated, her eyes moving around the circle until they lit on Falling Leaves. Eyes glittering in the firelight, the Apache maid glanced Cloud Dancer's way and smiled a slow, confident smile, one that was meant to encourage. Beneath the stern, condemning gaze of her brother, Prairie Wolf, Falling Leaves walked with graceful movements to where Little Fox sat. She lifted her chin slightly, her heart fluttering, then softly kicked the sole of Little Fox's moccasin, inviting him to join her in the dance.

Little Fox saw Prairie Wolf's scowl and admired his love's courage as he came to his feet to join her in the steps and movements of the dance.

Cloud Dancer left She Who Seeks Wisdom's side, walking boldly across the circle of dancers to where White Hawk sat, not quite successful in imitating the shy, humble pace Falling Leaves had demonstrated. She met his gaze steadily for a moment, before modestly dropping her eyes in respect of the Apache custom. Softly she kicked the sole of White Hawk's moccasin, following Falling Leaves's example to invite him to join her.

Graceful and powerful as the hawk for which he was named, White Hawk swiftly stood, a slight smile flickering across his face. His eyes, luminous in the pale orange light of the fire, caressed her and warmed her blood.

"She Who Seeks Wisdom has taught you well." White Hawk allowed his amusement to touch Cloud Dancer in the lightness of his words.

"Did you fear I would not know the proper Apache way and embarrass you?" Cloud Dancer whispered in mock indignation.

"No," White Hawk said softly in reply, the ache within him to reach out and touch her almost beyond his control, "I feared that with so many fine warriors and hunters to choose from, you would not choose me."

Cloud Dancer's soft, tinkling laugh, gentle as a spring breeze, was lost to all but White Hawk beneath the insistent throbbing of the drums. The magic of those drums filled the night, and Cloud Dancer slipped into the steps, matching the movements of her feet to the beat. White Hawk smoothly joined her in the dance, moving around the campfire with the other dancers.

The moon hung bright, full and heavy in the dark night sky, as together Cloud Dancer and White Hawk danced. Cloud Dancer's feet were light upon the earth; White Hawk's pounded with the heavy beat of the drums. The current that flowed between the two grew up out of the power of the drums and the chants sung by the old men. It wove a web between them, propelling them slowly, almost in a trance, around the circle.

"You are my heart," White Hawk whispered for her ears alone, as he, too, was swept up in the spell the drums cast. Sweat beaded his forehead as they continued to dance, and he held her close, if only within his fevered regard.

Cloud Dancer's spirit soared. "You are my life," she responded, looking full into his face and knowing the instant she said it that it was true. While she had believed White Hawk was dead, she had been only half-alive.

But here, now, with White Hawk, Cloud Dancer's blood sang in her veins, humming with the pulsations of life, and she swayed toward him, transported by the throbbing beat. All traces of past misunderstandings and hurt were banished. She felt her body transformed by the night. She was a boneless thing, a willow bent before the wind, a she-panther stalking. She was all of those things as her small, supple body lithely followed the movements of White Hawk, their feet beating a harmonious rhythm upon the ground.

They moved closer to the leaping flames of the crackling bonfire. White Hawk felt the heat of the flames against the flesh—or was it the warmth of Cloud Dancer's nearness? The hypnotic pulsings of the drums continued, the spirit filling White Hawk until he felt that his feet did not touch the ground, though his tread fell heavily with the beat.

The sparks passing between the dancing couple could not be ignored. Some onlookers smiled. She Who Seeks Wisdom chuckled and the parents of White Hawk nodded their approval, while others frowned in consternation, remembering Prairie Wolf's words.

Cloud Dancer was totally enveloped by her happy haze, until she chanced to meet Prairie Wolf's gaze. His eyes, flat and black, held hers in thrall, causing a shiver to run the length of her spine. His anger reached out and touched her from the distance as though it had a spirit of its own. He wanted her, yet she knew for a certainty that he hated her.

Drawing a deep breath, Cloud Dancer lifted her chin and put defiance in her eyes, meeting his glaring stare until she and White Hawk moved past where he stood, arms crossed, at the edge of the circle of dancers.

"Beautiful woman," White Hawk teased at her distraction, "who has caught your eye?" The sharp angles and flat planes of his face were softened by the firelight's glow.

Comforted by the love she felt emanating from White Hawk, Cloud Dancer swung her softened gaze back to him as they danced closer together toward the farthest edge of the circle of dancers. "My eyes see only you," she whispered.

Prairie Wolf nearly choked on the bile rising within him when his eyes rested upon Cloud Dancer. He did not want her, yet he was angered she had not turned her attentions his way when he made it known he could court her. How else was he to have some control over her? But she rejected him. He had had no impact upon her with his frequent offerings of meat for the old wisewoman's pot. He suspected She Who Seeks Wisdom herself was urging the young Kere woman toward White Hawk. Now his sister had befriended her, and worse, his sister was welcoming the courtship of Little Fox!

In the simmering heat of his anger, Prairie Wolf spotted White Hawk's brother, Standing Buffalo, nearby and moved to join him. He nodded in the direction of White Hawk and Cloud Dancer and kept his voice low. "She weaves her spell well," he said dryly.

Standing Buffalo gave Prairie Wolf a sharp glance, but uncertainty also appeared in his dark look. "My brother makes a fool of himself over this woman but that does not make her a witch."

"No?" Prairie Wolf asked slyly. "Did he not mourn her long after his return from Acoma, though he had known her only a short time? Did he not speak of her as though she were alive, and then she arrived among our people truly alive? Did he not journey again to the spirit mountain for guidance?"

"Yes." Standing Buffalo could not deny it. His brother had done all those things, and more that even Prairie Wolf did not know about. Did his brother love this woman, or was he bewitched by her as Prairie Wolf claimed?

"You are too impatient, Prairie Wolf," Standing Buffalo said calmly. "Time will reveal if she is indeed the sorceress you claim her to be. We will wait and watch."

Prairie Wolf stiffened at Standing Buffalo's quiet words, but he did not press the point. He had planted his seed; now he would see if it would grow to bear fruit.

The old men were resting from their playing of the drums, and drinking the juice of the mescal to revive their voices after long chanting when White Hawk and Cloud Dancer moved away from the others. White Hawk wanted her to himself, but was careful to stay near enough to the leaping fire that Cloud Dancer would not be disgraced in the eyes of the tribe.

He touched her hand and spoke. "Your spirit travels far from here, leaving only your beautiful form to stay with me." He hesitated even bringing up Acoma. "You were remembering your home." He knew this to be so as surely as if she had spoken the words to him. Her heart, in silence, had spoken to his.

"Yes."

"It will take a long time to put the past behind you."

"I will never forget."

"It would not be possible to forget what happened at Acoma. But you will put it behind you as time heals the hurt. We are your people now." He smiled tenderly and reached out to touch Cloud Dancer's hand, briefly enclosing it within the warmth of his own. "We have waited long enough. I would have you with me always."

White Hawk dropped his hand from hers before his small gesture of comfort could be considered an impropriety.

Cloud Dancer studied his face and saw the depths of his love reflected in his eyes. "You will find your horse left before my tepee would not go long without food or drink," she softly assured him, having learned about the custom of the Apache warriors who had a horse to leave it before the tepee of an intended bride. If she took care of the animal, his petition was accepted. If she did not, he was not acceptable as her husband.

An Apache maid would not have spoken as Cloud Dancer had to one who courted her. It was bold, not in keeping with their inherent shyness. Despite all her efforts at learning the customs of the Apache, her reaction was Kere. After she spoke, Cloud Dancer was overwhelmed by a wave of uncertainty and her eyes reflected her unsettled emotions.

"Beautiful woman," White Hawk said softly, his spirit soaring as he rushed to reassure her, "I could want nothing more than you. I will cherish you all the more for the ways that are different from our own and yet so much the same. You will know no hunger in my lodge and our children shall know the ways of both people. I have said it."

White Hawk smiled at her and longed to take her into his arms, but refrained. He knew the need of Cloud Dancer to learn the language and customs of the Apache, but he wished her to retain her own culture as well—which he had fallen in love with at Acoma.

An Apache maiden would have been confused by his declarations and his expressions of affection, but not Cloud Dancer, beautiful woman of another people. With another, a few stolen touches, a few sly exchanges of unimportant words spread over a long period of time, and it would have been decided the night he staked his horse before the maiden's tepee. The bride-price would have been set and the wedding arranged.

With Cloud Dancer he felt there would be the customs to steady their lives, but there would be something more. Much more. He would share everything with her. They were two halves of a whole. He felt bound to her. He knew now that he had been bound to her since their first meeting at Acoma.

"Look for my horse when next the moon rises full," White Hawk said firmly, speaking of the following night.

Cloud Dancer dropped her gaze, then returned it to White Hawk's strong face, meeting the soft regard of his black eyes. Her lips curled slightly at the corners and she could not resist teasing.

"Do you think I am so eager to marry that I will steal out of the warmth of She Who Seeks Wisdom's tepee in the middle of the night to feed and water your fine horse?"

White Hawk knew well that when a warrior staked a horse before his intended's tepee, a woman who went too hastily to take care of the horse was thought to have an unusual desire to get married; her too ready acceptance was severely criticized by the people. Clearly, Cloud Dancer knew this, too. In truth, he doubted she cared, yet she played the role of the affronted Apache maid well. White Hawk enjoyed this verbal play they shared. It was another joy she brought to his life.

He put on a face of mock severity. "He is a good horse, and there are few among our people. Fewer still would offer such. I would not place him before your tepee if I believed he would go long without food or drink."

She smiled up at him and cocked her head. "How long is too long?"

White Hawk frowned more deeply, then responded, "More than a day."

Cloud Dancer appeared doubtful. She had been well instructed by She Who Seeks Wisdom and was aware that she should not lead the horse to water before the second day, then secure it in front of her future husband's lodge.

"It is a matter for consideration," she murmured, her brow knit in thought. Then she brightened. "I do not yet understand this custom. What would happen if I were to feed and water the horse, but not tie him before your lodge?"

"That is not acceptable," White Hawk whispered, his head bent near hers. "If you feed and water him you must return him."

"Hmm. If I took him and placed him with Bonita to care for him?"

A shake of White Hawk's head was her answer.

She sighed and looked down at the ground at her feet as the drums began again, signaling the return to dancing. "Look for your horse a day after you have staked him before my tepee."

"You are the joy in my life, Little One," he said with simple honesty.

As they again joined the others moving in rhythm to the songs and drums, Cloud Dancer saw Falling Leaves and Little Fox again among the dancers. She smiled faintly, nodded her head to direct White Hawk's attention toward them, then grimaced at the sight of Prairie Wolf, whose glowering attention they had already drawn.

"Do not worry," White Hawk said quickly after his eyes had found the couple, dancing closely together, heads bowed. "Little Fox is stronger than Prairie Wolf believes. And it is not Prairie Wolf, but his parents, who will accept or reject Little Fox as a suitable husband for Falling Leaves."

"I know," Cloud Dancer murmured. "Little Fox is a good man. Falling Leaves could do no better."

As Cloud Dancer and White Hawk spoke in low voices, their words hidden by the powerful continuing beat of the drums, standing Buffalo watched from the sidelines. He had eyed the beautiful maiden from Acoma with interest at her arrival among the Apache. Now he watched the exchange between his younger brother and Cloud Dancer and frowned. She did not drop her gaze respectfully, but met White Hawk's eyes boldly; they spoke for long periods. He did not understand this way of the Kere and he did not understand White Hawk's tolerance, even embracing of, her custom. She was supposed to be learning the ways of the Apache, and yet White Hawk allowed this behavior. Perhaps, he thought, there was some truth in what young Prairie Wolf believed.

A soft voice spoke from outside She Who Seeks Wisdom's tepee, asking permission to enter.

She Who Seeks Wisdom granted it and Cloud Dancer was not surprised to see Falling Leaves duck into the tepee, a twisted smile of confusion and surprise leaping to her lips as her eyes met those of Cloud Dancer.

"I thought I would talk with you alone," Falling Leaves said softly to She Who Seeks Wisdom, dropping her soft fawn eyes away from Cloud Dancer.

"If that is what you wish," She Who Seeks Wisdom replied gently, as Cloud Dancer began to rise to leave the tepee. "But I think what you wish to speak to me about might be better put to the woman of the Kere, Cloud Dancer."

The old woman's words froze Cloud Dancer in place, standing face-to-face with Falling Leaves. She knew immediately that what Falling Leaves wanted to say had something to do with Little Fox and herself.

Already, Cloud Dancer had learned much from She Who Seeks Wisdom. Some were practical things, such as herbs to prevent a woman from conceiving a baby, to bind wounds, to ease a woman's moon flow if it was too heavy or to help in a hard childbirth. She knew how to summon the Earth Mother to their aid, and was learning about the power each Apache could possess or gain.

She had also learned much about people. She Who Seeks Wisdom had opened her eyes to the good and the bad, to the many odd twists of human nature. To live among people, the old woman had taught her, one must know them, understand them and, finally, despite differences, make peace with them. To that end, Cloud Dancer had put her efforts toward understanding Prairie Wolf, and though her anger with him did not disappear, she now understood many of the things that motivated him. In time, she was sure, they would make their peace.

"I will listen if you would have me hear," Cloud Dancer said gently. "If your words are for She Who Seeks Wisdom's ears alone, I will leave."

Her head bowed, Falling Leaves shifted on her feet, looking terribly young and plainly embarrassed. "I have come to speak of Little Fox." She and Cloud Dancer had grown close, but in this she felt awkward.

"Ha! What did I tell you!" She Who Seeks Wisdom was not at her most tactful, but Cloud Dancer could see through the old woman's ploy as easily as she could see the thin tendril of smoke that rose from the fire. The wisewoman was gently nudging Falling Leaves to confide in her.

Falling Leaves looked startled.

"He is a good man, but I have told you this before," Cloud Dancer said firmly. Then she added, "I saw you dance with him last night."

She Who Seeks Wisdom impatiently gestured toward the fire and the space around it for Falling Leaves and Cloud Dancer to be seated. "Sit," she commanded imperiously. "If you have come here for my advice, I do not intend to get a crick in my neck waiting to impart it."

Both Cloud Dancer and Falling Leaves obeyed the older woman's command, making themselves comfortable.

Falling Leaves was obviously very insecure and, in fact, a little in awe of Cloud Dancer. Very slender of build, she seemed to be tucked in everywhere, peering at the older girl anxiously.

Cloud Dancer finally managed to meet the girl's eyes directly, though Falling Leaves had tried repeatedly to elude her gaze.

"Little Fox is a friend. You came to speak of him," Cloud Dancer prodded, placing a gentle hand on Falling Leaves's leg in a reassuring gesture.

"He is of your people...."

"My people are the Jicarilla Apache. Little Fox strives to make them his people, as well. That makes him of your people, too, Falling Leaves. But what is this about? He courts you, not me."

"Some of his ways are strange," Falling Leaves blurted out a little breathlessly. "The way he talks to me..."

"Perhaps he forgets and treats you as he would have treated a woman he cared for at Acoma."

Her eyes widening, Falling Leaves gasped. "The day we went off together with you and White Hawk, I knew it was different." She threw a surreptitious glance toward She Who Seeks Wisdom, wondering if she was giving anything away in revealing their rendezvous several days previously. "Other Apache maidens have done it in the past. I have heard of it. But it did not seem so frightening that night. You and White Hawk and Little Fox seemed so happy and without care. Only I was frightened. Do the men of Acoma really treat their women so differently?"

"You did not seem frightened, and in truth there was nothing to fear," Cloud Dancer said gently. "And yes, there are great differences between the people of Acoma and the people of the Apache. White Hawk is patient with me, and he is kind. Already I know his horse will be tied before my tepee with the coming of this night's moonrise."

She Who Seeks Wisdom frowned slightly at this revelation, not so much because Cloud Dancer knew what White Hawk planned, but because she had revealed her knowledge to someone as innocent as Falling Leaves.

The young girl's eyes became rounder still. "Then there can be no doubt you will marry White Hawk—if you take his horse to food and water."

It was all Cloud Dancer could do to keep from laughing at the look of vast amazement that lit and colored Falling Leaves's delicate features. How could this shy, delicate creature be sister to a man like Prairie Wolf? It was easy to see why Falling Leaves held such a warm spot in She Who Seeks Wisdom's heart.

"Yes. There is no other. Is that so hard to understand? Would you want any other but Little Fox now that you have come to know him?"

Falling Leaves dipped her head, dropping her eyes to the fire at the center of the tepee. "No," she whispered so softly Cloud Dancer could barely hear the single muted word. Then Falling Leaves's voice grew stronger and her words came out in a rush. "But Prairie Wolf has said feelings are not so important, that I would come to feel about another as I feel about Little Fox and that there are other matters to consider when looking for a husband. It is more important to have a very good hunter and brave warrior for a husband than one such as Little Fox. He says the Spanish are coming and that Little Fox has already shown how little his worth is against them. But I love Little Fox, and as it is between you and White Hawk, so it is between us. Prairie Wolf does not want me to marry Little Fox, but I want no other!" Falling Leaves still looked unsure of herself, despite her impassioned words.

"Prairie Wolf was not at Acoma." Cloud Dancer's words fell brittle as ice tinkling about them.

"Prairie Wolf is a fool," She Who Seeks Wisdom interrupted, raising a hand to still any further words from Cloud

Dancer. She eyed Falling Leaves affectionately, raising one eyebrow questioningly. "Does Little Fox bring meat for the pot?"

"Yes," Falling Leaves managed though she was a bit upset at again hearing her fiery-tempered brother referred to as a fool.

"Then he is a suitable hunter."

"Yes."

"You have heard White Hawk speak of the bravery of the men of Acoma in the face of the Spanish attack and the thunder weapons they use to fling death?"

"Yes."

"Then there is no reason to believe Little Fox is not a brave warrior."

A gulp followed by another single-word reply. "No."

"Would you have us go to war before you accept him so that he might have the chance to prove himself a warrior?"

Falling Leaves looked down, her youth painfully apparent. "No." She hesitated as if fearing her words might be construed as an insult by She Who Seeks Wisdom. "But Prairie Wolf has said a warrior may prove himself by counting coup on a raid."

"So he may," She Who Seeks Wisdom mused, "and he no doubt will.'

"You are young," Cloud Dancer added gently, knowing that in years she herself was not much older; yet in comparison to Falling Leaves she felt ancient. "There is time and Little Fox will be patient. Perhaps Prairie Wolf will come to accept." Cloud Dancer surprised herself with her deep concern for Little Fox. In the short time she had known him well he had become as a brother to her, in some small way filling the gap created by the loss of her family. She looked at Falling Leaves as she would a prospective sister and found she liked the idea very much.

"Prairie Wolf will one day grow out of his foolishness," She Who Seeks Wisdom promised with a soft cackle. "Until then remember, you are wiser than he. Just don't let him know that you know it.''

Falling Leaves turned to Cloud Dancer. ''My brother is a fine hunter and warrior. He has said he wants you, that he would take care of you and that your tepee would never know hunger. He has said it would be a great thing if you would allow your husband to use your horse to hunt and raid and you of the great heart and spirit remained in camp to care for your sons and daughters. Is it that you do not want him because of this foolishness She Who Seeks Wisdom speaks of?''

''No,'' Cloud Dancer said with a shake of her head. ''It is because I want only White Hawk—and because Prairie Wolf does not really want me.''

''She would be a fine wife for Prairie Wolf, would she not?'' She Who Seeks Wisdom interjected. ''She has no family Prairie Wolf would be bound to care for. He need not leave this band to go live in another because she is not of this band. There are few horses among the Apache, but Cloud Dancer possesses one. And, if he chose, he could take another wife another time.''

Falling Leaves acknowledged the painful truth of She Who Seeks Wisdom's words. ''Yes,'' she murmured, ''Cloud Dancer would make a fine wife for Prairie Wolf if he had his way.'' She looked to Cloud Dancer, more sure of herself than when she had entered the tepee. ''But my brother will not have his way. You will marry White Hawk soon.''

Feeling enveloped by the warmth of this young girl, Cloud Dancer nodded her agreement. ''Very soon.''

White Hawk sat astride his horse, one of the few in the small remuda of the Jicarilla Apache, and stared off into the distance. He had set out before dawn, having had very little sleep after the words he and Cloud Dancer exchanged at the dance. The place he wanted to take Cloud Dancer for the seclusion of their first days together as husband and wife was not far from the camp of the Apache band. There was a valley, up higher in the mountains, among the tall pine and swiftly flowing creeks. It would be quiet now, cloaked in winter's white silence, the snow heavy upon the earth, the creeks frozen and still, but it would be no less beautiful for its winter sleep.

"Come, Dark Sky," he said to the sleek stallion, so black that he gleamed blue fire in the sunlight, "we must hurry if we are to do what we came for and get back in time for Cloud Dancer to feed you and return you to me."

He nudged the stallion with his moccasined heels and pressed on, reaching the clearing before the sun passed the tops of the tall pines at its zenith. It was indeed as beautiful as he had remembered it. A broad open expanse, which would be a rolling green meadow in the spring, sloped gently toward the north hills, fringed by towering pines. The air was redolent with the crisp bite of the pine scent, even more pronounced because of the cold. The snow had drifted deeply in several locations, and at others had barely dusted the earth. The tiny creeks that laced the valley were frozen on top, but water flowed swift and gurgling beneath that hard shell. It would not be difficult to break through to its cold sweetness.

White Hawk worked swiftly, unloading the sling that trailed behind Dark Sky on slender poles. He chose a sheltered spot where the snow had not accumulated in deep drifts and cleared away even that sparse snow in a wide circle. Then, with economy of movement, he erected the poles of the tepee, ending by attaching the hides that formed the walls. It did not take much longer to gather the stones needed to circle the fire and to carry inside all the other bundles he had brought along: furs for sleeping, tools, leather parfleches of dried meats, nuts and berries. Another couple of trips into the trees produced enough firewood to last many days. This he stacked near the entrance flap of the tepee, placing an additional large bundle of wood inside. Quickly he buried the parfleches to insure they would not be disturbed until he returned with his bride, then went outside to survey his handiwork.

White Hawk smiled and braced his legs, gazing up to the vaulted blue heavens and raising his arms to give his thanks to Ussen, the Life-Giver, for his good fortune and happiness.

Chapter Sixteen

"All is well, wife? You seem so far from me. Is there something you wish that I have not provided?" White Hawk continued working, furiously twirling the fire stick between his palms to start the fire in their secluded tepee. "I have looked forward to these days," he said with simple honesty, the directness of his words piercing Cloud Dancer's heart with their sweetness.

"I could ask for nothing more, my husband." She sent him a fiery, seductive smile that aroused White Hawk's senses.

She watched her husband almost in awe of the strength and grace of his movements. It was the little things, the small movements and gestures that brought thoughts of their time together at Acoma. Her heart began to pound strangely as the memories flooded back. She remembered the day in the cold cave with the snow falling outside, remembered the feel of his hands, gentle upon her body as they brought her to heady fulfillment, the rich male smell of him in her nostrils—the same rich scent that now reached between them, bridging the distance easily. It was good for them to be together—alone. It was good to be away from the camp of the Apache, from the prying eyes of those who stared at her and White Hawk with speculation, and from Prairie Wolf and his jealousies. The Apache were her people now and she would welcome the return to camp when the time was right, but for now, in the custom of White Hawk's people, they would spend these first days as husband and wife alone.

They were truly alone for the first time since she had come to live among the Apache, and there would be no need to fear what others would think of their behavior—more particularly, *her* behavior. A quiver of joy raced through her, pursued by the heat her husband raised in her blood with just a look. She and White Hawk were husband and wife, and for now, there would be none to see. Nights and days of love and sharing lay before them. And when they returned to the camp, they would be treated differently. She would still be strange, but she would be White Hawk's wife. His parents had approved of her; She Who Seeks Wisdom was delighted with White Hawk. Life would finally fall into a comfortable rhythm when they returned from their seclusion. Cloud Dancer drew a deep breath filled with the essence of her new life, filled with the essence of White Hawk.

White Hawk divided his attention between patiently spinning the fire stick, watching for the first faint signs of fire, and watching his wife. How she stirred him in all ways! Her gentle presence was both a balm and a torment to his soul. He could barely wait to take her in his arms again, yet he *would* wait until the fire was burning, warming their tepee.

Cloud Dancer was dressed truly as an Apache now, wearing creamy white deerskin leggings and a matching tunic that hung to her knees, the fringe dangling well below. Upon her tiny feet were hard-soled moccasins, draped around her shoulders delicately beaded and quilled, and for added warmth was a heavy buffalo robe. But it was her face that touched White Hawk most—the small, perfectly formed beauty of it, set off by a stubborn chin, elegant cheekbones and smooth, unblemished skin. There was a soft, rosy hue to the rich earth tone of her skin, almost a glow, and emotions expressed themselves in fleeting sketches against the gentle canvas of repose her face presented. He glimpsed sadness, contemplation, anger sometimes; but most of all he saw joy, and if his eyes did not deceive him now, desire.

White Hawk was content. He was whole again. He still did not understand how this woman of another people could be so much a part of him that he did not feel complete when they were apart. Only Ussen, the Life-Giver, knew the answer. Perhaps one day it would be revealed to him.

The small flame White Hawk had been coaxing erupted into life, sending a tiny curl of smoke spiraling around the stiff swiftly spinning stick. Its acrid smell tickled Cloud Dancer's nose and reassured her; it represented a bastion against winter's cold, a fire to warm them when passion's storm was spent.

"Quickly! Add kindling to the flame!" The excitement of success roughened White Hawk's voice as much as the desire he curbed to finish his work.

Cloud Dancer acted swiftly, dropping bits of dry grass and wood into the struggling flame, seeing it grow larger until it was possible to place sticks and finally small logs upon the popping, crackling flames. Their fingers touched as each reached for the same log, and a fire much hotter than the flames surged between them. Cloud Dancer gasped, but now there was no need to retreat. A soft, slow smile curved her full lips and a wicked, teasing gleam lit her eyes.

The fire burning brightly, White Hawk set aside the fire stick and sat back beside Cloud Dancer, drawing a second buffalo robe about himself. For a time each felt a sudden awkwardness in the moment. They had burned so long for each other that now they hesitated. Then White Hawk laughed softly, the roughened edge of the sound sending a shiver of anticipation through her body.

"Come, sit with me. We will share our warmth. The air still has the chill of winter." White Hawk lifted a buffalo-cloaked arm, beckoning Cloud Dancer nearer.

The huffing movement of the buffalo robes admitted a tendril of cold air that sent a swift chill through Cloud Dancer, causing her to press more tightly against White Hawk, inviting the soft stroking and questing of his gentle hand. She trembled against him, awed by the riotous feelings his touch always set off within her body. Would it always be the same when they were together? A sweet, tender voice within her heart answered it would be so.

Together, as if borne upon the softness of the first spring breeze, they tumbled in a glorious tangle of heavy buffalo robes and twisted clothing.

"I have missed you, Cloud Dancer. The wait has been long." The tickle of his warm breath sent riotous sensations cartwheeling through Cloud Dancer's body; White Hawk's hands were busy beneath the thick robes, stroking, pressing, molding her smaller body to fit perfectly to his own.

"Do you want me?" Cloud Dancer whispered, "the same way you wanted me when first we joined?" Her voice trailed off in a soft sigh, her senses throbbing with the strength, feel and scent of him.

White Hawk laughed softly, whispering Apache love words in her ear.

His obsidian eyes blazed with the answer. His fingers sent fire through every nerve in her body. She melted beneath him, hands clutching at the broad wall of his shoulders looming above her. There blossomed between them a renewed intense physical awareness of each other.

As White Hawk pressed his sinewy length against her, the heat of his body sent more fire tracing the path through which her blood coursed. He nuzzled her neck and smiled when she threw her head back to give him better access, a gentle moan of passion issuing from her lips. Her hands skimmed over the softness of his buckskin shirt, feeling beneath it the flex of heavily roped muscles and the rising heat of his body.

Cloud Dancer tingled with excitement as White Hawk moved gently against her, lowering by degrees his full weight upon her. He settled between her legs, pressing his belly to hers, separated only by their clothes as he rocked gently against her. Then he raised his head to gaze into the depths of her golden eyes. She felt the drumbeat of his heart so close to her own, and knew the heat of his rising desire. Cloud Dancer thought she would go mad with White Hawk's touch. Ragged whimpers of need passed in heated little breaths from her lips to his ears.

White Hawk continued to sweetly torture her with gentle touches and caresses, his lips tracing a soft, warm path down the side of her neck to where it met the gentle curve of her shoulder. He wanted to move slowly, to prolong their first joining after being apart so long, yet he wanted her with a fierceness he had never experienced before. He had been without a woman since their joining in the cave.

Eagerly, White Hawk rose to strip his buckskin shirt from his body, the heavy buffalo robe falling away. Then he pulled the cord to strip off his leggings, leaving only his breechclout as he turned and saw Cloud Dancer, slipping the creamy buckskin she had worn for their wedding ceremony from her slender body. Her eyes dipped shyly away from him, her body glowing warm and welcoming in the golden firelight. She opened her arms to him and lifted her eyes to meet his steady gaze.

He took her hands, drawing her to her feet and into his arms again. Cloud Dancer gasped, feeling the raw warmth of his skin beneath her fingertips, the moist heat of his lips upon the tender flesh of her neck below her ear, and the throbbing evidence of his arousal pressed tightly between them. Her hand drifted down the sweat-slicked length of his body, jerking the cord that held his breechclout, freeing that part of him that she longed to have inside her.

White Hawk groaned, his stomach twisting with the hard knot of need. "You are the mate of my spirit," he said brokenly, overriding the power of his lust, forcing himself to be gentle with her. "I am not whole without you."

His hands stroked her lean, muscled buttocks and legs as he spoke, sending shudders the length of her body and molten silver coursing through her veins. His caresses and soft kisses stole her strength away until, had he not held her so close, her bared breasts firm and full, pressing into his naked chest, she would have fallen.

"I too felt only half-alive when I believed you dead," Cloud Dancer whispered in return, as White Hawk lowered her to the scattered garments upon the earth. Her hands continued to explore, to renew her intimate knowledge of his body, and found the rough ridge of flesh just above his left nipple where the Spanish miniball had torn into his body.

She kissed him there, lips caressing the still red, but healed flesh of the injury, until White Hawk pressed her down to the furs again and rolled between her thighs. He wanted her, needed her; his blood sang with the desire to unleash his hunger and satisfy it in her warm velvet depths. His hands found her breasts, fondling and caressing, taunting and teasing before he bent his head to cover one soft, rosy tip with his lips.

Sparks exploded behind her closed eyelids as he swirled his tongue in lazy, sensuous movements before his teeth nibbled gently, sending a new maelstrom of sensations surging through her body.

"Love me, White Hawk! Never let me go!" Cloud Dancer cried out as he shifted more fully into the cradle of her thighs, his manhood finding entrance and filling her with one abrupt thrust.

Cloud Dancer's eyes widened. A small sound of wonder escaped her throat as her hands slid frantically up his back, stroking, pleading for him to continue while she arched greedily against him, her own hunger rising wild and primitive within her to meet his.

Buried deep within her, White Hawk remained still, staring down into her beautiful face. Her lips were parted as she panted with desire, her skin flushed and heated at his ministrations.

She blinked, eyes staring up into his as she squirmed beneath him. Under their furs dried grasses prodded softly into her back, wildly arousing her already sensitized flesh.

He stared down into her eyes, seeing the fire there, knowing in that instant that they were truly one.

Gently at first, he began to move against her, feeling Cloud Dancer pick up the rhythm in counterpoint. He gasped at her fiery need. His hands roamed freely, fingertips memorizing every curve and texture of her beautiful body as he continued to move slowly in and out of her.

Breathlessly, Cloud Dancer received him, locking her arms around his neck, losing her small hands in his thick ebony hair, losing her strength before the onslaught of heady sensations careening through her body, losing her heart and soul all over again to this powerful Apache warrior.

Sweat glistening the length of her body, Cloud Dancer met White Hawk thrust for thrust. An uncontrollable tension grew within her body, the insistent throbbing between her legs only partially assuaged by the fullness of him within her as they strove together to break the earthly bonds and reach for the stars.

Like a lightning bolt out of the clear, glittering night sky, Cloud Dancer and White Hawk found their ecstasy together, each crying out before the power of the fevered sensations they had unlocked, one within the other.

The days that followed were filled with play, work and lovemaking. When the sky was clear and the sun shone brilliantly from the crystal sky, Cloud Dancer and White

Hawk rode great distances, exploring and hunting together. Cloud Dancer continued to learn, White Hawk praised her sharpening skills as a hunter, and they ate well from the results.

With startling speed the days rolled away one after the other. Cloud Dancer most enjoyed the days when the heavy snows fell and they remained inside the tepee, their horses sheltered within the lean-to White Hawk had fashioned. During those long, lazy days they talked and planned the future, played and made long, luxurious love between the buffalo robes. It was a quiet time of peace that Cloud Dancer would store in her heart forever. She did not want to think it would ever end, but knew it soon must.

"Come!" White Hawk called one day as he entered the tepee, the morning sun brilliant at his back. "It is a good day for riding. We will journey toward the Great River and see what stirs there."

His dark skin bronzed by the cheerful glow of the campfire, the subtle play of skin tones heightened by both daylight and firelight, and the graceful movements of his powerful body all combined to make White Hawk a striking figure in his male beauty. Animated as he was now, he was an even more powerful force.

Cloud Dancer rolled to her feet in one lithe, graceful motion and picked up her bow and arrows, ones precisely fashioned at White Hawk's instructions for truer flight.

Dressed warmly against the cold, they left their camp, Cloud Dancer astride Bonita and White Hawk astride Dark Sky. After a day's confinement because of the snow, both horses were eager to go and stepped out briskly, skimming through the light, dry snow along the path White Hawk chose, skirting the deep drifts that had accumulated.

"The sun dances in your hair," White Hawk said softly as they rode. "Too bad it did not snow again today." He gave her a playful leer. "But if it had," he mused, "then I would not have seen the sun dance in your hair."

Cloud Dancer laughed at his circuitous reasoning. "And I would not have seen the sun upon your face—and this strange light in your eye."

"You would have seen the light in my eye," White Hawk countered. "I do not think it is ever far when I am near you."

Cloud Dancer thought of the tales the older Apache women had told her of their honeymoons as they had prepared her for her marriage—of lying tense next to their new husbands, so shy and fearful they were nearly afraid to breathe. Cloud Dancer compared those tales to what she shared with White Hawk.

"It is a good thing we spend these first days far from the camp of the Apache!" Cloud Dancer teased. "Too many, I fear, would know that look in your eye."

"Oho, wife! You think you know me so well...." White Hawk led the way into a small thicket, tying his stallion before turning to drag the puzzled Cloud Dancer from Bonita's back. "Come, the day has taken a sudden chill," he joked. "We must share the warmth of our bodies."

She ducked beneath his outstretched arm in a move designed to elude him, but found herself caught in the circle of his warmth. She laughed, softly pushing at him, as his hand settled upon her hip, fitting her smaller, rounded body against the angles of his own. She murmured, "I suspect, husband, that warmth is not the only reason you would have me near!"

He pretended to ignore her words and breathed deeply of the fresh scent of mint lingering upon her skin from the crushed leaves that had been rubbed over her body to prepare her for her wedding night.

"Umm. You smell of fresh mint and wildflowers, my wife."

Cloud Dancer giggled as happily as a child. "And you, my husband, smell of buckskin and smoke."

He looked at her, pretending shock, the light of gentle teasing in his eyes. "That does not please you?" The comic mixture of surprise and apprehension mixed upon White Hawk's angular features brought a new softness to his face Cloud Dancer had not seen before.

"Everything about you pleases me, my husband," she responded, laughing, and a moment later found herself cradled in White Hawk's arms, drifting slowly downward toward the earth.

Their joining was hurried and explosive, filled with the power of Ussen and kissed by the pale winter sun high in the clear sky. Their voices rose together in soft cries of ecstasy, and the fire in their blood warmed them even as White Hawk had said it would, their bodies entwined in the graceful dance of love.

It was some time later, Cloud Dancer blushing though there were none to see, when they mounted their horses and continued their exploration.

With a gentle touch of her heel, Cloud Dancer urged Bonita to an easy lope and White Hawk paced Dark Sky alongside. The snow flew in billowing clouds from beneath the horses' churning hooves as they moved downslope toward the west and the Great River, though it was doubtful they would reach the river itself if they intended to return to their camp before nightfall.

Slowing again to a walk, White Hawk pointed into the distance. "Look, what do you see?"

Cloud Dancer followed the direction of his gaze and slowly swept the area until her eyes found a darker patch among the trees beyond the sprawling valley where they rode. Then she saw the deer, a large-buck, still as stone beside the towering trunks of the great pines. She did not raise her bow since they did not need meat, but enjoyed the beauty of the regal animal.

"Did you see his tracks?"

"No," Cloud Dancer admitted.

"I saw them earlier, then again just before I pointed him out to you. He had been running. The tracks were widely spaced and the snow had blown over some. I am not surprised you did not notice." White Hawk continued to test her knowledge.

"And behind him—do you see what is there?"

Sitting straight and still on Bonita's back, Cloud Dancer stared into the trees. With the help of the exceptionally bright sunlight she was able to pick out the rock formations concealed in the tall trees behind the stag. "It looks like the opening to a canyon," she said.

"Yes. I have been here before." White Hawk gestured toward the barely visible opening, where it looked as if a small bit of hillside had been torn away by a giant hand. "It is good that you saw it. Few notice it hidden as it is by the trees. It is very large, the ground covered with tall green grasses in the spring, but I have found only one way in or out. The walls beyond the mouth of the canyon are steep and rocky. The stag might be able to scale them, but Dark Sky cannot."

Cloud Dancer smiled. "The stag has probably sheltered his family there against the winter. If the grasses were deep in the spring they will still lie beneath the snow."

"He fears we have seen him and will follow him to his home," White Hawk agreed. "Come, let us leave him in peace."

They rode on to the west, admiring a red hawk circling on the winds high above, following briefly the trail of a bear to where he marked a tall tree with great grooves in the bark from his claws. When they found a partially exposed hillside still crowned with dried grasses where the horses could graze, they stopped briefly to allow the horses to eat their fill, then traveled on.

The sun was past its zenith when both Cloud Dancer and White Hawk spotted the movement farther to the west, beyond the fringe of shorter trees that gave way to much more open country, dotted only with occasional stunted pines and scrub brush, farther west.

People! And they were riding, not afoot. Cloud Dancer and White Hawk worked their way closer, keeping well clear until they could identify the men who rode a slower, but parallel course to their own. Then, over the soft quiet of the day, rose the distinctive noise of soldiers on the march.

"Spanish!" Cloud Dancer spit the word in disgust.

Grimly, White Hawk nodded. "Spanish," he agreed.

There were eight men riding. Seven were garbed and outfitted as soldiers. The eighth was dressed like the holy man responsible for Perez de Ortega's death. Behind them, on lead ropes, trailed two more horses carrying food and supplies.

White Hawk's jaw clenched, a flame leaping into his eyes. "They are not moving fast. It would be a great coup for us to return to the camp of our people and bring men to take their horses from them."

"We are here now. If we wait until the sun goes down and they camp, we would not need more men to take their horses from them," Cloud Dancer suggested. "It could be accomplished by the two of us alone."

"You have not raided before," White Hawk said simply. He had known her desires since she had arrived among the Apache, yet now, faced with the reality of what it truly meant for her to join him in this dangerous pursuit, in his heart he hesitated. Not because he doubted her abilities— they were as sharp as any young, untried warrior's—but because of the danger he knew she would face and the possibility, ever present, of losing her.

She stiffened, but did not take offense, understanding his fear, for she, too, feared losing him again. "There must be a first time," she said firmly, the words coming out in a harsh whisper.

"You will raid for the horses and not for vengeance?" White Hawk met her gaze directly and waited for her answer. Her reply would determine whether this was indeed a raiding party for Cloud Dancer, or if it was a war party seeking blood for blood.

"We will take only their horses, not their lives," Cloud Dancer assured him. "If we wait until they huddle around their fire, they may not even notice we have come and gone until the morning."

White Hawk sighed his relief, careful not to let Cloud Dancer see. It was the answer he sought. He did not care for the Spanish lives one way or another. He did not wish to spare them out of any compassion he felt for them. Rather, he did not want the greater risk to themselves if they went in to kill, causing the Spanish soldiers to feel a killing frenzy. White Hawk was not a coward, and even a raiding party intent upon stealing the horses of the Spanish was not for the weakhearted, but he did not want Cloud Dancer to learn more about bloody killing on their marriage trip.

"Then we will wait until dark," White Hawk agreed.

Holding their horses to a slower pace, Cloud Dancer and White Hawk followed the path of the Spanish.

Little Fox held Falling Leaves close to him, lying in the shelter of a clump of winter-nuded elderberry. The scrubby brush offered perfect concealment.

"You are in my blood, a part of me..." he whispered hoarsely, well aware of the risk they were taking by slipping off alone together. They had seen nothing of Prairie Wolf, but that did not lessen the risk.

"I love you, Little Fox!" Falling Leaves returned, her hand slipping up to rest behind his neck. "I want to be all you expect in a woman. I want to learn the ways of the Kere that Cloud Dancer spoke of."

"Shh, my love. The risk we are taking is already great." His hands trembled as they moved over the neat, tight curves of her slim body where it pressed so intimately to his own.

Falling Leaves pressed a finger to his lips to silence him. "We will marry soon. You have asked for my hand and my parents have granted it. If we were in Acoma would you not love me?"

"We are not in Acoma," Little Fox protested, but he could feel his will and restraint slipping away at Falling Leaves's gentle nearness and flaming caresses. "I need you, Falling Leaves. I want to fill you with the honey of my love, but I do not want to hurt you. I would not disgrace you." His hand was gently stroking her side, bringing a wave of heat to her face and a soft shudder rolling over her body.

"Neither are we in the camp of the Apache," Falling Leaves breathed, surprised by her own boldness and wondering at the sweet yearning she was feeling throughout her body.

Little Fox groaned as he tried to maintain his self-restraint. He loved her deeply and at this moment she was pressing him almost beyond endurance. He barely had the strength to resist what she so innocently offered.

Then he realized he had not only a responsibility to Falling Leaves, but to these Apache who had taken him into their tribe; they were his people now and he would honor their ways.

In their sheltering thicket, beads of sweat shone on Little Fox's face as he smiled down at Falling Leaves, gently touching her face while he bent to kiss her softly. Then he looked into her eyes and spoke seriously.

"I cannot endanger our future happiness with the fleeting joy of this moment. We will wait. I have said it." Little Fox hadn't believed he had the power to utter the words, but was relieved when he did. He drew her tightly against him, not giving her the chance to turn away in shyness. "Our union will be sweeter for the waiting, you will see."

She shook her head in reply. Little Fox had been so patient and it made her love him all the more. A warm glow clung to them both.

Falling Leaves snuggled against him a few moments longer, reveling in the wonder of their love, then sat up. "We must get back to camp before we are missed."

They had risen and were ready to leave the concealment of their secluded spot when voices stilled their movements. Little Fox's arm stole around Falling Leaves and drew her close.

"Prairie Wolf and Standing Buffalo!" she gasped and huddled closer to Little Fox as if attempting to make herself smaller and less visible.

"Shh. Do not move and they will not see us!" Little Fox stood as still as the rocks and held Falling Leaves close as the voices came nearer, the words becoming more distinguishable. Then the two men appeared at a distance.

"She is a witch," Prairie Wolf said sharply to Standing Buffalo. "How swiftly your brother, White Hawk, married her! She has bewitched him! In truth can you say White Hawk has been himself since she arrived here?"

"I never approved of the marriage, but it was not for me to say. The Pueblo people are weak," Standing Buffalo said with some disgust. "They are but farmers. You say the one called Cloud Dancer is a witch. You have said so before, but where is your proof?"

Prairie Wolf's chest swelled with self-importance. "It is not easy to catch a witch at her evil, but I know she is a witch. If you will help me we will prove it and break her bond with your brother."

Standing Buffalo fell silent for a moment, considering. "What would you have me do to help get this proof?"

"Her hold over White Hawk is strong. To break it we must make him see the truth. If you were to go to her and let her know you desire her, she would seek to control you, to bewitch you as she has White Hawk. Though she might seem to fight you, she would join with you to cast her power over you."

Falling Leaves gave a soft gasp that was quickly silenced by Little Fox's arm tightening about her in warning.

"If White Hawk sees her give herself to you, the bond between them will be broken."

After another reflective silence Standing Buffalo spoke. "You are quick to accuse, yet there is some truth to your words. She has a strange power, that one. I, too, have felt it. She would draw me to her." Standing Buffalo had cursed himself in the past when the overwhelming wave of desire had rolled over him at Cloud Dancer's nearness. Now he wondered. Could the fault be hers and not his? "Still," he added, "I am not as sure as you."

"If we do this together, we will be sure," Prairie Wolf returned. "Cloud Dancer will reveal the truth. You are powerful in the tribe. You will expose her for the witch she is if you do this thing."

"And if she is not a witch," Prairie Wolf added in a more soothing tone, "then we will know that, as well."

Falling Leaves and Little Fox watched anxiously as Standing Buffalo slowly nodded his agreement and the two men began moving away.

"We must do it soon. Immediately after their return to camp..." Prairie Wolf's voice trailed off into the distance.

Little Fox held Falling Leaves in the concealment of the brittle brush, hoping they would not be seen.

"Prairie Wolf says she is a witch! He says he will soon prove it!" Falling Leaves spoke frantically.

"Cloud Dancer is not a witch," Little Fox replied calmly. "He has accused her of it before. Prairie Wolf will not be able to prove she is a witch when she is not."

Falling Leaves's eyes swam with unshed tears. "Prairie Wolf will make it seem Cloud Dancer is not faithful to White Hawk! There are others things he will accuse her of when she is exposed for the act of adultery, but that alone could be enough to have her nose cut off and to cast her from the tribe—or even to have her killed! It will break their bond and cause White Hawk to put her from him!" Falling Leaves's face twisted with fear and her hands worked quickly, one within the other. "You must do something, Little Fox!"

He nodded, thinking. "Things are different among the Pueblos, but not as Prairie Wolf interprets them. Cloud Dancer would not betray White Hawk with another."

"But Standing Buffalo thinks to save his brother from a witch! How can we tell how far he will go?"

Little Fox remained silent for a moment, thinking. He had been adrift when he had escaped after the horrors of Acoma. It had taken Cloud Dancer's arrival at Isleta to make him face reality and see that he needed to find a new life. He had found that life here among the Apache, as had she. She was like a sister to him. He had to find a way to stop Prairie Wolf.

"I will talk to Standing Buffalo."

"No! If you do they will know we heard them talk. And you yourself are from Acoma. They will simply say you were bewitched by her as well, more proof that she really is a witch, or they will accuse you of sorcery as Prairie Wolf will accuse Cloud Dancer." Falling Leaves shifted nervously on her feet, looking away, then back to Little Fox. "Cloud Dancer is my friend, but Prairie Wolf is my brother! I don't know what to do!" She peeped at him from beneath the sweep of long, black lashes.

Little Fox looked around nervously, bold black eyes evaluating every rustle of dried leaves and rattle of dead branches. He wanted to continue talking to Falling Leaves to reach some sort of a solution, but he feared for her should they be caught together like this, alone far from camp and chaperons. He was not sure how severe the punishment might be after Falling Leaves's vivid description of what might befall Cloud Dancer.

Little Fox's primary worry was for Cloud Dancer and White Hawk, but he feared Falling Leaves would also endanger herself. He looked down into her face, so deeply lined with concern for her friend. He laid his hand, strong and roughened, along her cheek, marveling at the softness of her skin, cupping her face in his palm, then let his hand fall away.

He smiled down into her worried fawn eyes. "If we cannot turn Standing Buffalo from this lie, then I will have to talk to White Hawk and hope he will believe his own brother would join with Prairie Wolf in a plan against him."

"I do not know," Falling Leaves said in a small voice. "Standing Buffalo has never had any great love for the people of the pueblos. I have heard him say often it was a mistake to be their allies when our men could be raiding their villages for plunder as others of our Apache brothers did. After what happened at Acoma he was even more bitter. I tremble to think what he would have turned into had White Hawk died. I think he already half believes Cloud Dancer must be a sorceress to have captured his brother's heart so completely. He did not favor their marriage and was not silent in declaring it was much too soon."

"White Hawk and Cloud Dancer have not yet returned. There is still time. I will think about what we can do. But now you must get back to camp. Go the way you came, and I will circle and enter camp from another direction." Little Fox gave Falling Leaves a gentle shove. "Now go. Hurry! Before someone sees us here together."

Falling Leaves hesitated a moment, painfully shy and embarrassed again, despite or perhaps because of the closeness they had shared such a short time before. She raised her eyes to meet those of Little Fox. Then, swift as the hummingbird in the spring, she lifted a small, dainty hand to return his caress, letting it flow from brow to cheek to chin before she turned and ran swiftly back to camp.

Chapter Seventeen

If not for the glow cast by the crescent moon and reflected by patches of pristine white snow upon the earth, darkness would have been complete. Leaving their horses on the far side of a hill behind them, White Hawk and Cloud Dancer crept closer to the camp of the Spanish on foot. White Hawk moved with the sure grace of a forest creature, while Cloud Dancer glided lightly beside him. Furtively they shadowed their way up the hill beyond which they knew the Spanish were camped. The soft, orange glow of the campfire beyond the hill crest lit up the night, marking them for any to see.

"They have left the horses as I said," Cloud Dancer whispered as they lay on their bellies behind some winter-dead brush watching the encampment below.

"There is only one man standing guard near the horses," White Hawk agreed. "And he is more interested in what is happening near the fire. I think he would rather be near its warmth." He turned toward Cloud Dancer, blue-black shadows dancing over his face in the night. "You must do as I say without question. You must give me your word."

"I will do as you say," Cloud Dancer murmured without hesitation. She had practiced and prepared for this, her first raid, but she had no experience. White Hawk was experienced and competent. He would not put her in jeopardy, yet she was confident he would not keep her from taking part. "They have tied their horses all to one line," she observed. "They have made it easier for us to take them."

White Hawk grunted. After this night the Spanish would have learned a lesson about leaving their horses so unprotected—and about the way of the Apache. It was a source of great pride to White Hawk that he had often raided without the victim's even suspecting he was near until it was far too late. It would be his pride now to teach Cloud Dancer.

"Their bellies are full and the fire warm," White Hawk said softly. "We need wait a little longer and they will be sure they are alone in these hills." He raised his head a little to be sure he could see all of the Spanish party with none beyond his sight. "When they begin to seek their blankets, we will take their horses."

White Hawk could see Cloud Dancer's eyes gleam with excitement even in the darkness. The cold of the winter night was biting, the wind rising out of the north to whisper across the hilltops and rattle the dried branches of the brush like old bones, but Cloud Dancer felt warm with anticipation as she lay beside him in waiting.

"How will we do it?" she whispered.

"They have tied their horses near a cleft in the hill behind." White Hawk gestured to the darkness behind the peacefully picketed horses. "We will take our Bonita and Dark Sky around behind and leave them in that cleft. Then we will creep forward and attempt to lead their horses back into the darkness without rousing the Spanish. It will be slow, but the time spent will be worth it if we succeed in silence. If not," he said with a shrug, "then we will free their horses, regain our own and chase the freed horses up between the hills. If we must do that, however, it will be very dangerous. The Spanish will use their thunder sticks, and they will follow us if they can. We will have to be sure we get all the horses. If we can do it by stealth, we will be able to lead the horses away, then keep to the hard, rocky ground where there is little snow and they will not be able to follow the tracks."

"We should go somewhere before we return to the camp of the Apache, hide the horses there and wait to see if the Spanish follow. Was the valley you told me about where the stag hid among the trees large enough?"

White Hawk grinned. "You learn quickly, Little One," he said with fondness in his voice. "That is where I had decided we would take them. Part of the trail will be rocky, and for part of the distance I will be able to cover our tracks. The rest—perhaps Ussen will send snow to cover what I miss."

"If the snow does not come, we will still have all the horses; it will take them a long time to find us."

"Come," White Hawk said in gentle teasing, his quiet strength covering the growing tension, "let us move to where we may better see and prepare ourselves."

Cloud Dancer's answer was to nod and move alongside him as his shadow. They reached their horses, and in silence made their way around the base of the hills behind which the Spanish party sheltered. Their well-trained mounts, Dark Sky and Bonita, remained silent; only the soft scuffing of their hooves over the earth marked their passing, as they walked, heads lowered, beside the man of the Apache and the woman of the Kere.

The bracing cold put color high in Cloud Dancer's cheeks and numbed her fingers. She blew upon them and rubbed them together periodically to keep them limber should she suddenly have need of her weapons. Though it was dark, the crescent moon shed enough light to see by, and if that was not enough, White Hawk seemed to have the eyes of an owl. He moved with an easy assurance, dodging shadowy brush and avoiding flushing any nocturnal animals that might alert the Spanish to their presence. Cloud Dancer did not question or swerve from the path he chose. They tethered Dark

Sky and Bonita far up the cleft behind the Spanish horses and continued on cat feet, sliding down the draw as quiet as a cloud across the moon.

The tension and excitement of the task they had undertaken constricted within Cloud Dancer like a tightening knot. Here, at last, was an opportunity to take from the Spanish as they had taken from her people. Her senses were alive as they had not been since that last terrible day at Acoma. Her eyes had adjusted to the darkness of the night and she could see clearly in the faint moonlight. The Spanish sitting near the fire would not have that advantage should they notice their horses disappearing. Staring into the dancing flames as they were, would blind them for many moments if they attempted to turn their attention abruptly to the darkness. The knowledge bolstered Cloud Dancer's confidence as she and White Hawk waited in the cold of the winter night.

White Hawk, too, felt the growing tension. He had felt it since they had spotted the camp of the Spanish and begun to make their plans. He had come to terms with his fears for Cloud Dancer in such a dangerous undertaking, but that did not stop the churning in his gut when he looked upon the camp of eight armed men and then upon his love, Cloud Dancer. She was sleek, well taught and as ready as any young warrior might be for a first raid—even more so, for she had seen bloody battle. He tried to tell himself he would be concerned for any young warrior on a first raid, and that much was true; but it was not the same with Cloud Dancer.

They waited in the dark and cold until the fire began to die and the Spanish soldiers sought their blankets in a tight cluster near the warmth cast by the coals. The holy man was the first, curled up near the fire and dead asleep long before the others followed his example. The single soldier left to stand watch was not alert. His head nodded upon his chest as he huddled in the folds of a heavy blanket far from the fire's warmth. Both Cloud Dancer and White Hawk noticed his weapons were not in his hands, but upon the ground beside him. Despite the unlikeliness of their being heard, White Hawk had switched entirely to sign language to communicate with Cloud Dancer.

The wind was rising out of the north and a few clouds whipped across the night sky, hiding the moon, then revealing it again. Stars began to blink out behind the increasing collection of clouds and White Hawk sensed a change. The snow he had hoped for could be coming. The air was heavier, the cold more penetrating.

With hastily delivered hand signs, White Hawk directed Cloud Dancer to move off toward the east and cover their flank while he took out the guard. From that point, too, she would be able to help with the horses, untying her end of the long tether line, and keeping the horses together.

They moved in on the Spanish camp like wraiths of fog borne upon the rising wind, both moving separately to accomplish their tasks.

White Hawk slipped up on the guard and used the butt end of his knife to club him into unconsciousness. Had this been a war party, he would have slit the man's throat instead and damned him and his companions for the fools that they were. But this time they would take plunder, and taunt the enemy. Their skill and the horses they would obtain would be their source of pride. To take vengeance for Cloud Dancer and her people was a strong urge when White Hawk was within range of the Spanish guard, but they had agreed this raid was only to take horses, not lives, and he would carry out that end.

With the guard slumped upon the cold, hard earth, White Hawk paused, taking stock of his surroundings, ears attuned to every small sound of the night. He heard nothing other than the scurryings and flutterings of the night creatures and the rising promise of a coming storm. Cloud Dancer did not betray her passing. He could see her form in the darkness, crouched low, slipping silently along the course he had indicated to her.

In a few more moments Cloud Dancer reached the end of the rope the Spanish had tied to tether their horses. The animals nearest her shifted their feet, snorting softly against the background of the wind as they picked up her unfamiliar scent. Cloud Dancer could see the camped Spanish clearly, each one sprawled or curled in his blankets close to the quietly burning fire. They were closer to the horses than had first appeared when she and White Hawk had seen them from the hilltop, and she waited a moment for the horses to quiet before she reached to untie the rope.

Her fingers trembled slightly and her breath clouded upon the air before her as she worked at the strange knots. She kept sending furtive glances in the direction of the sleeping men, searching for a sign that one of them might rouse as the wind continued to rise. The horses were expressing their uneasiness, and when she glanced toward White Hawk, she found him gesturing for her to hurry; he, too, was feeling the growing uneasiness of the animals and the leashed power of the threatening storm.

Cloud Dancer's fingers flew despite their cold stiffness, and the knot came free the same moment a clump of wind-borne brush rolled out of the darkness like some hulking beast of prey. A horse toward the center of the line whinnied in fright, half-rearing and twisting against his tether.

Panic was infectious, and the horses to either side of the one that had whinnied joined in, jerking back on the ropes that secured them and stamping their feet. Before acquiring Bonita, Cloud Dancer had been frightened of the large animals, but now she held her ground, her grip firm upon the rope as her eyes swung again to the sleeping Spanish.

She saw one stir and sit up, then another. White Hawk had frozen to stillness like one of the firmly rooted trees that dotted the hills; like Cloud Dancer, he held his end of the rope tight against the pull of the frightened horses. A small dust devil swept past bearing bits of twigs and a twisted cloud of sand. Then, for a moment, the wind quieted. Cloud Dancer watched in silent horror as the Spanish soldiers who had awakened spoke softly between them, then climbed to their feet, weapons in hand.

The first white flurries of snow, mixed with freezing rain, fell in the deadly calm that had followed the wind.

"Jorgé," one of the dim shadow figures called out softly to the one who could only have been the guard. He got no response.

Every muscle in Cloud Dancer's body had gone rigid. Her fingers were curled and stiff around the rope. Her eyes sought some signal from White Hawk.

"Jorgé!" The voice was louder this time, timbred somewhere between anger and confusion. More sharp, guttural words followed the first, words of which Cloud Dancer, despite Perez's teachings, understood little. But there was no mistaking the Spaniards' actions. They were armed and heading straight for the horses.

In a moment, Cloud Dancer knew, she and White Hawk would be seen. She could not see White Hawk's signal, but they were of one mind, rising as one, not relinquishing their hold upon the tether line of the horses, and turning toward the dark cleft between the hills looming as their escape.

The boisterous yells of the Spanish soldiers roused the rest of the camp, bringing more of the men out of their blankets and into the bracing cold of the falling rain and beginning snow.

There was no more time—or need—for stealth. White Hawk pulled sharply on the rope, trying to force the horses into motion, but they balked, frightened by the growing commotion and strange smells around them. Cloud Dancer pulled at her end of the rope and the horses moved a little, then balked again, confused by conflicting signals.

Guttural and grating, one of the Spanish voices rang out above the others, and there could be no doubt he was directing the attention of the others toward the horses.

An instant later a thunder stick spoke, its belching roar rending the fabric of the storm-laden night. Cloud Dancer felt the hot kiss of a miniball's close passage over her shoulder, and she cringed in memory of that other time when the shot had been truer and the lead had knocked her from her feet, taking her strength.

Another shot. This one not so near.

The horses threw up their heads against the restraint of White Hawk and Cloud Dancer's combined strength and bolted. What the two of them had not been able to accomplish, the Spanish had, with the sharp cracks of their guns: the horses were surging toward the deeper darkness of the cleft where the hills met.

White Hawk and Cloud Dancer ran on either side of the frightened horses. The turmoil of the Spanish camp rose behind them like a second approaching storm, as mixed rain and snow fell more heavily, beginning to coat the ground underfoot. Thunder rolled off the surrounding mountains to mix with the booming blasts of the Spanish guns.

"Climb on!" White Hawk yelled above the din.

Cloud Dancer had mounted Bonita on the fly before, just for the sheer exhilaration of it, but these horses were strange to her. They did not know her. She drew a deep breath, changed her stride to better match the horse closest to her and vaulted up, making use of their combined momentum to place herself squarely on the horse's back. White Hawk followed suit on another mount.

These horses were not accustomed to taking commands without saddle or bit, as Dark Sky and Bonita had been trained to do. But although they were difficult to manage, they kept moving up the narrowing draw formed by the hills on either side.

The narrowed passage made it impossible for the horses to remain strung out, trotting eight abreast. Cloud Dancer nudged her mount, using hands, legs and feet, urging it to take the lead and draw the others along behind it.

More gunshots followed the first; even in the darkness they came dangerously close to the fleeing pair and their booty of horses. One ball grazed the rump of the horse beside Cloud Dancer, causing it to shriek its fear and bolt against the restraining line. Cloud Dancer held on grimly, the rope burning her hand as a length slid between her fingers. Her heart pounded fiercely within her chest, and her breath rasped against a throat dried by fear.

She had known fear at Acoma, and this matched it. At Acoma many of her actions had been dictated by circumstance. Death and fighting had been all around her. She had been prepared to follow her family into death, extracting from the Spanish a dear toll in retribution before she died. Now, here with White Hawk, she must overcome her fear and act with reason—a reason Acoma and her inexperience had not allowed.

This then was what it meant to be a warrior, what all the training had prepared her for: to fear, and yet to think and function in spite of that fear, to rise to the demands of danger and emerge victorious in spirit, if not in fact. She was still prepared to die, if need be, but not with the same fanatic zeal she had felt in Acoma. White Hawk had given her reason to live.

"There!" Cloud Dancer called over her shoulder. "Bonita and Dark Sky are waiting!"

They wrestled their stolen remuda of Spanish horses to a stop. Cloud Dancer leaped off the end horse she had mounted, and darted for Bonita. The heavy sounds of booted feet running were close behind. Cloud Dancer and White Hawk had not been able to move with any great speed while attempting to maneuver the horses they had taken from the Spanish, but now Cloud Dancer jerked free the rope that tied Bonita and swung up on her back. Then she pulled Dark Sky's rope free and turned quickly toward White Hawk.

Behind him, coming over the arch of the hill, barely visible in the curtain of falling snow and rain, appeared a Spanish soldier, his pistol raised in his hand.

"White Hawk!" Fear gave Cloud Dancer's voice volume, and White Hawk dived for the ground without second thought as the pistol spit its sharp report and the soldier ran toward them.

Cloud Dancer clung to the rope connecting the Spanish horses and Dark Sky's rope, swinging White Hawk's horse and Bonita sideways across the draw to prevent the captured horses from bolting. Somehow she contained them while White Hawk, rising to his feet, his knife concealed in his curved palm, caught the full charge of the Spaniard.

The soldier was not decked out in his full battle regalia, leaving him vulnerable to White Hawk's knife. They toppled together to the cold, soaked earth, snow and rain driving down into their faces as White Hawk's knife found its mark before Cloud Dancer could notch an arrow to her bow.

Not caring whether the man lived or died, White Hawk roughly shoved the Spanish soldier from him. Then he rolled to his feet and saw that in those brief moments he had grappled with the soldier, Cloud Dancer had moved to control the horses and protect his back against further attack.

"Here!" Cloud Dancer tossed the end of Dark Sky's rope to White Hawk, blind to the Spanish soldier who approached her from the side through the thickening curtain of falling snow until he grabbed her leg and tried to jerk her from Bonita's back.

Her heart leaped into her throat and, her pulse pounding in her temples, she stared down into his dark visage, every detail of his face imprinting itself upon her memory. The black, damning eyes, the sharp beak of a nose and the pointed cheekbones above a heavy shock of beard. She saw the straight, even teeth, tobacco-stained and one broken off to a nub, and the thin white scar that slashed from ear to jawline.

Another thunder weapon of the Spanish growled its threat, spewing a lead ball over White Hawk's head as he grabbed Dark Sky's bridle and spun to aid Cloud Dancer, who was grappling with the stout soldier. Her hand was curled around the hilt of her knife, pulling it from its sheath, and she struck as a hunting eagle struck with its talons. At the last second the soldier saw her intent as the blade glinted in the silver light of the storm, and he threw up his arm to protect his face and neck. The blade slashed across his arm, drawing blood, and he lunged for her again.

"Use Bonita! Turn her. Turn her!" White Hawk shouted, his heart squeezing tightly in his chest at the sight of Cloud Dancer fighting the Spanish again. His love for her hit him with the force of the rolling thunder, and for an instant he knew a dizzying fear for her. If he lost Cloud Dancer he would no longer be whole. He could not lose her a second time.

He reeled toward her, giving up his hold on his horse's reins, knowing the rest of the Spanish soldiers were only seconds behind the first.

Cloud Dancer reacted out of instinct, following the guidance of White Hawk's shouted command. Pulling sharply on Bonita's reins, she drew the mare in a tight circle, throwing her attacker off balance and freeing herself from his grip.

"Hurry!" Cloud Dancer cried, spying the rest of the approaching Spanish as the last of the rain changed into snow. Heavy white flakes fell in earnest now, wind sweeping them sideways as the air reverberated with pounding thunder and the sky glimmered with muted lightning.

"Go!" White Hawk yelled. He vaulted astride Dark Sky, snatched up the dragging rope attached to the other horses and put his heels to Dark Sky's sides to urge him forward.

With their own familiar mounts beneath them, Cloud Dancer and White Hawk were better able to manage the stolen horses. They surged forward into the teeth of the storm, Cloud Dancer in the lead and White Hawk bringing up the rear, yelling and whooping to urge the horses forward at a faster pace, rapidly putting distance between themselves and the frustrated Spanish. A few more lead miniballs whistled past them as some of the soldiers managed to reload on the run and fire again—and then they were running free.

Once the Spanish were safely behind them, White Hawk drew the horses into a tight knot so that he could speak to Cloud Dancer above the rising pitch of the storm.

"It will get much worse soon!" he bellowed. "We have to reach the valley before we cannot see enough to find our way!"

Cloud Dancer nodded and bowed her head against the wind, her hair catching and holding the thick white flakes of snow. The thunder was dying, but the wind continued to rise.

"What of our camp?"

"We will return there later—if we get to the valley," White Hawk returned grimly. "I have been to the valley many times. Dark Sky knows the way almost as well as I. We'll lead. Hold on to the rope. Do not let it go slack."

"The Spanish will not follow!" Cloud Dancer spoke the only reassuring words she could find.

White Hawk grinned at her through the falling snow, his eyebrows and hair thick with the fat flakes. "No, they will think only of shelter, as we should."

Both White Hawk and Cloud Dancer knew well the dangers of traveling in a storm such as this. Vision was limited, and the potential existed for the snow to blossom into a blizzard that could blind them completely.

Together they bowed their heads against the elements, White Hawk taking the lead with Dark Sky, putting the powerful stallion to a brisk trot, and drawing the rest of the string along behind.

The heavy snow continued, filling in their tracks even as the horses made them. White Hawk and Cloud Dancer covered ground quickly, running before the full impact of the storm, fearing if they hesitated even a moment the worst of it would catch them.

It was the season of the falling snow. It came swiftly, could bury a village for days, then melt just as quickly. This was one year when Cloud Dancer would welcome the coming of the spring and new life with even more joy than in all her years past.

White Hawk unerringly found the entrance to the valley and led the way inside. There the wind was not so strong and the snow drifted in long slopes against large rocks and stone walls, leaving other patches of ground nearly bare, dried grasses exposed. Snow swirled and eddied without the full driving force of the wind behind it, collecting slowly here and there into deep drifts.

"I did not expect this when we started out this bright and sunny morning past," White Hawk remarked ruefully. "First we must shelter the horses, then we will find shelter for ourselves. Come, there is a place not far from here we can use to wait out the storm. I have been there before."

Farther ahead the valley narrowed, then widened again almost in hourglass fashion. At the widened end, rising in earthy red contrast to the falling snow, were mud walls in a configuration familiar to Cloud Dancer. It was apparent as they neared it that this place had long ago been abandoned, yet many of the structures remained at least partially intact. They looked as if her ancestors might have built them before abandoning them and moving south to the easier winters and more abundant waters of the Great River.

Cloud Dancer silently said a heartfelt prayer that they not disturb any spirits that might be lingering, then followed White Hawk, leading the horses into a shelter formed by three remaining walls and a partial roof. It had plainly been a large combination of rooms in the past, the dividing walls having crumbled into long hills of earth long ago. Great clumps of grass had apparently grown within the walls in summer, leaving at least some forage for the horses even now.

Quickly they secured the horses, then left to take shelter in a much smaller and more snug earthen building. White Hawk built a fire and Cloud Dancer drew out the leather pouches containing the emergency rations that a good Apache warrior was never without. They could not hunt, but they would not go hungry.

Cloud Dancer felt the first sweeping rush of the accomplishment. Her blood flowed through her veins with the force of a surging river, quickening the beat of her heart.

"We have taken from the Spanish as they have taken from our people! We have done what we set out to do!" Her eyes shone and the color flushed high in her cheeks.

"It did not go as I had planned," White Hawk admitted wryly, "but we accomplished what we intended." His eyes found Cloud Dancer's and she saw in them again that gentle strength of the forest stag. "And after today, wife, there is no one I would rather have at my back in battle."

"I was afraid I would lose you," she breathed, lowering her eyes to her hands in her lap. Shivering against the cold, she wished the fire would gain strength quickly and warm their small shelter.

"And I you," White Hawk admitted. "But you fought like the mountain lioness. You were strong and swift, and you did not freeze even though fear curled its hand about you."

"My friend, Little Fox, said I had the spirit of the mountain lion when he gave this to me. He honored me then and you honor me now." Cloud Dancer smiled and opened the small leather pouch she wore around her neck to remove the delicate, intricately carved lion fetish Little Fox had given her before they left Isleta.

As she slipped the stone fetish back into the pouch, White Hawk felt a twinge of jealousy that Little Fox had been allowed to see so much of her spirit, that he had recognized her lion heart and given her the fetish to honor it. But in a moment the jealousy passed. He put from him the thoughts of her people, the Kere, and their differing views on the relationships between men and women. Little Fox was her friend, no more. Cloud Dancer was his wife. She could have remained safely at the pueblo of Isleta with Little Fox, but her heart had drawn her on. She had chosen not to remain among the Pueblo peoples, but instead to turn to the way of the Apache even before she knew he still lived. And somewhere deep in the recesses of his soul, he had known she would come.

Cloud Dancer trembled again in the cold, and White Hawk moved to pull her firmly against him, wrapping his arm around her. "Here, wife," he growled softly in her ear, "I will warm you while we wait for the fire to fill this room with its heat!"

Her spirit soared. It was as if a stone had dissolved within her. Her heart raced as it had in battle, but not with fear or anger, rather with a sense of exhilaration so great she found it impossible to contain. The source of the feeling was so much more than having stolen some horses from the Spanish, their enemies. She felt that something was right with her life, that she had more than her love for White Hawk, that somehow, through their successful raid against the Spanish, she had regained some treasured modicum of control over her life and fate.

Laughter, bright and sparkling as the tinkling waters of a mountain spring, bubbled forth from Cloud Dancer, and she wrapped her arms around White Hawk, snuggling closer for warmth, and more.

"We will warm each other, husband!" She drank in the heady scent of him, felt the small room surging with the power of him.

Never had White Hawk felt so powerful, so whole, so right as when he held this small woman close to him. His hands came up her back to stroke and massage, sending a thrilling heat from his fingertips into her body.

"We have shared danger—now we will share triumph!" White Hawk tumbled Cloud Dancer to the soft sand near the fire, looming over her in the fire's soft glow while the storm continued raging.

A sense of tingling delight washed through her. She basked in the surging warmth of White Hawk's masculine hunger, saw the passion rising and flickering to flaming life in the depths of his sooty black eyes. Her pulse pounded with the strength, the feel, the scent of him, and she surrendered gladly to the tremors that shook her body as he pressed closely against her.

"You are still cold, wife?" White Hawk teased, nuzzling the side of her neck, sweeping aside the cascade of her shining hair to taste the smoothness of her slender throat. He slid his hand beneath her leather tunic, trapping the warmth of her small breast in his cupped hand.

Her pulse raced as her breathing became more uneven. White Hawk squeezed gently and drew the tunic higher until he freed her of it, quickly covering her body with his own.

Cloud Dancer clutched at his leather shirt, swimming in the dizzying sensations aroused by the rough-smooth surface of his leather shirt rubbing against her bared breasts. Her hands skimmed over the variety of textures his clothes and body offered, finally tugging urgently at his shirt, demanding the feel of flesh against flesh.

White Hawk did not wait to answer her unspoken demands. He rolled away and left her feeling bereft, even in that brief moment, then returned to her, freed of the constrictions of his heavy buckskin clothes. His nimble fingers went to the leather strings that held up her leggings and clout, quickly freeing them, laying her bare to his gaze.

For another long moment only the heat of his gaze warmed her, then he moved to cover her again, drawing her tightly against him, feeling the throbbing heat of her small, slim body beneath his. His desire was primitive, powerful and exciting. Her body was alive under his, softly twisting against him, seeking, demanding, reaching out to him.

Together they shuddered with the intensity and power of their desire. He pressed his belly hard against hers and gave a soft, deep-throated moan of passion barely leashed, his arousal already beyond the point of control.

Cloud Dancer molded herself to him, wanting more, moving against him, asking wordlessly that he give to her what she needed. Desire stole the breath from her throat and sent her blood rushing through her veins like hot lava.

White Hawk smiled at her wanting, but did not hurry. His hand followed the curve of her breast, stroking the underside. Then it drifted down across her hip before he rolled to his side, drawing her with him so that she was near the fire as his hands spread over her bottom, gently kneading the firm flesh and drawing soft gasps of pleasure from his wife.

One of White Hawk's hands slipped up her back and cradled her against him while the other slid the silky length of her thigh, drawing her slender leg up over his hip, opening her to his possession. Thunderbolts of desire arched through Cloud Dancer as his hard desire pressed against the softness of her femininity, seeking entrance. Cloud Dancer quivered and jerked in response to his tentative seekings, instinctively arching closer, drawing him tightly to her, but still he resisted. The hand no longer occupied with stroking her leg slid between them to touch the heated core of her desire. Never had he exerted such control to prolong a joining. Never had the waiting been such sweet torture. He throbbed with need and want, yet White Hawk drew Cloud Dancer on, knowing he would not be complete until she found the same pinnacle in their love as he.

Cloud Dancer moaned softly against White Hawk's neck, the soft brush of her lips sending new tendrils of warmth ripping through White Hawk's body. "You torture me, husband!" she cried in half protest as a new set of unbearably pleasurable sensations racked her body.

White Hawk chuckled, his breath a searing whip across her sensitized flesh while his fingers continued to do their war dance over her peak of desire. He inflamed her to the point of near delirium, and a savage hunger sprang to life within her.

"But I do not give you pain." White Hawk taunted her with silken words and soft, quick little gasps, his hands still working their magic.

"It *is* pain!" Cloud Dancer twisted against him, seeking, attempting to take for herself what he withheld, surprising him with her sleek strength. "But such *sweet* pain! It is an ache such as I have never felt. Come to me, White Hawk, and soothe this ache you have created within me!"

With one long, slow push, he buried himself deep within her, feeling Cloud Dancer go rigid against him, her leg tightening around his lean hip as she groaned against the sweetness of his invasion. The sensation of fullness trapped her breath in the back of her throat, cutting off her air. It was with effort that she dragged one ragged breath after another into her lungs to sustain her. She did not dare move yet she could not remain still.

She flexed her hips, her senses reeling at the sensations that exploded through her like a star burst. And then she felt White Hawk begin to move against her with a slow rhythm that quickened with each thrust as she adjusted to his possession. Seemingly in an eye blink he changed from gentle possession to savage demand, and what Cloud Dancer had thought to be her pinnacle became only the beginning. She hesitated, teetering on the brink of some new and wondrous discovery, something so powerful that it would control her.

White Hawk sensed her hesitation, felt the power building within her body as well as his own. "Trust me!" he whispered throatily, knowing the release they sought together would be like nothing either one of them had ever experienced before. "Trust me and let go! Together we are one. Together we will find the stars!"

As she had listened to him in all the other things White Hawk had taught her, Cloud Dancer listened in this. She cast off the last of her restraint and control, which she had fought so hard to attain. The first small convulsions began deep within her as a wave far out at sea, then she felt the answering ones in White Hawk's body. The wave of heat rolled the length of her slender body. Her head arched back, her mouth open in a soundless cry as she clung to him, the rushing of her own heated blood loud in her ears.

Exultation wafted through Cloud Dancer in heated, pulsating waves, and together she and White Hawk spiraled upward, riding a crest of savage victory and physical fulfillment in a dizzying, uncontrollable burst of joy.

Chapter Eighteen

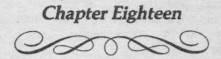

A Chinook wind had risen out of the south, beginning to melt the snow almost before it had stopped falling. The tall pines skirting the edge of the valley were dropping their heavy burdens of snow with soft plopping noises. Cloud Dancer and White Hawk had spent three cherished days in his hidden valley, the last of their time alone together, taking care of the horses they had stolen from the Spanish. Now their days of seclusion were over and they would return to the Apache village.

"I have tied the horses together, four in a string. We will be able to lead them easily." White Hawk stepped up beside Cloud Dancer, leaving the horses a few paces behind, and drew her tenderly into his arms.

Cloud Dancer sighed. "It is good we go home," she said softly, "but I will miss this place."

"We will return in the spring when it is green and the flowers are blooming," White Hawk promised. "Before the band moves east to find the buffalo."

The gently prevailing south wind felt almost balmy, the sound of running water loud. Cloud Dancer smiled. "I don't think spring is very far off."

"Then we will return soon."

Dressed warmly in her heavy buckskins, Cloud Dancer ducked back into the house of mud she and White Hawk had shared, retrieving their possessions for the return trip. She silently thanked the ancestors who had left this shelter for them.

Her heart swelled with pride when she emerged carrying the remainder of their belongings, her eyes again resting upon the bold, powerful form of her husband. She was proud, too, of their accomplishment. She doubted any other couple had ever returned from their honeymoon with a prize such as these horses.

She handed White Hawk his leather pouch of dried meat, fruits and nuts against the possibility of their being separated, along with his lance. His bow and quiver of arrows were slung over his shoulder as hers were slung across her own.

"I would like to give one of the horses to Little Fox for all he did for me before we found you again, and another to She Who Seeks Wisdom so she may use it to carry her heavy burdens."

"Four of the horses are yours to do with as you please. You are generous, wife." White Hawk said as they swung onto the backs of their horses, both Bonita and Dark Sky eager to be moving again.

They turned their horses to the trail. They would stop higher in the mountains to retrieve their tepee before returning to camp.

"And you, my husband, what will you do with your horses?" Cloud Dancer asked as they left the narrow mouth of the valley, their mounts moving easily through the snow, with White Hawk setting the course so they skirted the deepest drifts.

"One I will give to our chief. The others must be used to breed more horses so that our people will have an easier life, and so we, too, will be mounted if we must fight the Spanish."

Cloud Dancer nodded. "It is good. My two remaining horses will join yours. There will be more raids against the

Spanish, and soon there will be a herd so all will have a horse for their needs."

The snow was melting rapidly, turning most of the Apache camp into a sea of thick, gooey mud, though large drifts of snow still remained scattered about. Dogs began to bark at Cloud Dancer and White Hawk's approach. By the time they rode into camp it seemed every man, woman and child was there to greet them or to just watch their arrival. Word of the horses they brought spread before them in a wave, evoking much shouting and laughter from the gathered people.

When Claws of the Bear, chief of these Apaches, appeared before his tepee, White Hawk drew his horse to a stop and with solemn respect nodded his greeting to the chief.

"You return with your woman, leading many fine horses," Claws of the Bear said to White Hawk. "You have done well."

"*We* have done well," White Hawk answered, his voice full of pride as he nodded to indicate Cloud Dancer at his side. "My wife, Cloud Dancer, has proved herself to be a warrior. She was my right hand and my shield. My power is to see the future when Ussen wills it. Cloud Dancer's power is with the horses. They bow to her wishes, and she leads them like tame dogs upon a rope."

Cloud Dancer sat straight and proud upon Bonita's back, while White Hawk, the more seasoned warrior, did the talking.

"Come," Claws of the Bear stated, "we will build a council fire, feast, celebrate your victory and hear your story."

The day was brilliantly sunny, the air balmy enough to have the kiss of spring. They found a reasonably dry spot within the circle of tepees, the women bringing woven mats

of grass to lay upon the damp earth while the men gathered
wood for a fire.

White Hawk and Cloud Dancer moved to take care of the
horses while the council fire was prepared. Turning, Cloud
Dancer caught Prairie Wolf staring at her, his gaze flat, the
intensity of his eyes upon her a raw and savage thing.

Prairie Wolf was aware of every admiring male eye in the
camp focused upon Cloud Dancer. How could this have
happened? How could White Hawk take his new bride from
the camp as many Apache warriors had done in the past, but
return with a prize such as the horses they led? And White
Hawk was sharing the glory equally with Cloud Dancer.
Prairie Wolf blanched. It was a glory he should be sharing
in her stead! It was he who had been close to White Hawk
before she came, he who had been trained by the powerful
medicine warrior, White Hawk, he who should have shared
in the glory of this coup against the Spanish, for that was
where the horses had to have come from. He was being
cheated out of what he deserved—and by a woman. The
teeth of jealousy sank deep in Prairie Wolf's heart. Others,
warriors of the tribe, now looked upon Cloud Dancer with
more respect than they afforded him, yet he had been on the
four raids needed to make him a full-fledged warrior, and
she had not. She had power, that much was clear, but not
the kind of which White Hawk spoke. Soon all here would
know it. He would see to it. With Standing Buffalo's help,
he would unmask her as the manipulating sorceress she was.

Cloud Dancer shivered before the black intensity of
Prairie Wolf's probing, damning eyes, the dark cold of his
anger. From the beginning she had known she would not
necessarily be accepted by all the warriors of the Apache,
despite White Hawk's assurances that there had been
women warriors before her; but she had not expected the
pure contempt of one such as Prairie Wolf. She Who Seeks
Wisdom said he was a fool, but Cloud Dancer recognized he

was also a danger to her. She would have to find a way to deal with him.

"Prairie Wolf is angry," Cloud Dancer said softly to White Hawk as they turned their horses away.

"Prairie Wolf is always angry." White Hawk spared a quick glance in the younger man's direction, seeing the dark look in his eyes as Cloud Dancer had. "He behaves like a boy. He must learn to be a man."

He is a man, thought Cloud Dancer, *and he is a man who hates me.*

"Sit beside me." The invitation came from Claws of the Bear and was directed at both White Hawk and Cloud Dancer when they finished caring for the horses. They took their places beside him as the preparations for the celebration continued around them.

Already many of the other men of the camp were seated around the bonfire, which now burned brightly. Prairie Wolf occupied a place nearly directly across from Cloud Dancer. Standing Buffalo, White Hawk's brother, sat beside him, his face still as stone, his eyes appraising.

"You have brought many horses," Claws of the Bear began in his heavy voice of authority. "We who are gathered here would hear the story of how that came to be."

Cloud Dancer sat in awe of the dignified chief, the most respected man of the tribe. He was old, but not ancient. He had an erect carriage, a broad chest and a face deeply lined with the etchings of experience. There was no doubt as to his strength, both of the body and of the spirit.

By Apache standards Cloud Dancer knew she and White Hawk would be considered to be very rich, possessing the horses, and they would be owed respect in their own right. They would be honored not just for the horses they had procured, but for how they had done it; everyone knew it could only have been accomplished with bravery and daring. It was a great coup.

"We were riding in the mountains when we saw the Spanish," White Hawk began, speaking clearly and using his hands for emphasis. "At first we thought to return here to gather a raiding party, but we realized they would slip beyond our grasp in the time it would have taken to return here. So we followed and waited to see if the Spanish would expose themselves enough to allow my wife and myself to take the horses."

"And how many more horses could we have taken if you had returned here and gathered a raiding party?" Prairie Wolf's question was blunt, his words sharp, like knives. "If it had not been for the sudden coming of the snow, would you have led the Spanish back here—caused us to fight for what we had not shared in? Was it *her* thought that you raid alone?"

"Enough!" Claws of the Bear's voice cracked out across the gathering with the sound of a great tree branch snapping beneath the weight of heavy ice, its splintered edge aimed at Prairie Wolf.

Immediately there was total silence around the roaring fire. Cloud Dancer could feel the fury seething within White Hawk where he sat beside her, hear the anger in Claws of the Bear's voice, yet she was curiously without rancor at Prairie Wolf's remark. She glanced around the gathering and saw Falling Leaves, a look of absolute horror upon her face. Nearby, Little Fox sat cross-legged within the circle, his face set in tight, grim lines. Cloud Dancer smiled faintly at Little Fox, then turned that smile toward Prairie Wolf.

She had no way of knowing that her smile, combined with her calm, had the effect of strengthening Prairie Wolf's case to Standing Buffalo; they believed it reflected her complete calm and confidence in her power, the power Prairie Wolf attributed to a witch.

"I have asked White Hawk to tell his story, and he will tell it in his own time and way." Claws of the Bear's tone dared another interruption. "To you who have questioned it, I will say White Hawk is a respected warrior. There is no reason to question that he would have done what was best for his people.''

White Hawk raised his head after Claws of the Bear finished speaking, and met Prairie Wolf's gaze with the glow of pure fury in his eyes. He raised his hand and took a moment, tightly leashing his anger before he spoke.

"I will answer his questions," White Hawk said tightly, "so that no one here will doubt what Cloud Dancer and I have done. And if Prairie Wolf again questions my concern for my people, my abilities, my judgment...or my wife, we will fight.''

Prairie Wolf's eyes narrowed, but he said nothing.

The warning was plain. White Hawk continued. "No more horses could have been taken from the Spanish, for Cloud Dancer and I took all there were in their party. We left the Spanish just before the snow began to fall. On foot, in such a storm, it would have been difficult for them to follow us, and as the snow continued to fall, it covered our tracks. There was no trail to follow. We had decided not to return here until we were sure it was safe, so we stayed with the horses in a valley in the high mountains. We did not even return to our own camp until we left that valley with the horses.'' White Hawk's voice was a low rumble, his tone sharpening to emphasize a point or rising with remembered excitement. "The Spanish are near. They are always a threat. But they will not come because we have brought the horses.

"It was Cloud Dancer's thought that the Spanish would slip away if we returned here for more men for the raiding party, and I saw that it was true. We decided to take all the horses or none. There was nothing to be gained by waiting.''

White Hawk continued the telling of the story, his words steady, his narrative a colorful recreation of what they had experienced, the brief fight with the Spanish, the hair-raising moments that could have cost either or both of them their lives, and their race against the storm. The many gathered around the fire listened with rapt attention. Prairie Wolf kept his own council with sullen silence. Standing Buffalo's face was unreadable.

When he was finished with their tale, White Hawk looked at his wife, then turned his attention to those gathered. "Cloud Dancer proved herself to be all a warrior can be when we struck the Spanish and counted coup against them. She was inexperienced, and so did as I directed. She fought bravely when the Spanish caught up to us. She held the horses when they would have bolted and she was my shield. She fought as I saw her fight in Acoma—with bravery and with skill. She is strong and swift, her aim true." He looked directly at Prairie Wolf. "I advise caution to any who would ridicule or demean her, for not only would they face me, they would face Cloud Dancer."

"You have done well and spoken true," Claws of the Bear said in the silence that followed White Hawk's last words, as all eyes turned to Cloud Dancer's straight, proud form seated beside her husband.

Prairie Wolf's face twisted into a faint snarl, one corner of his lip lifting in disdain as he leaned close to Standing Buffalo. "There were none to see all he spoke of save White Hawk and his wife." He uttered the last words as if they tasted bitter. "She has clouded his mind. See how she smiled when she turned him against me, one of his own people. She could not have been all he said she was. She has not learned since childhood as our warriors have learned. He endows her with power over the horses. I say she has power over him!"

Standing Buffalo nodded slowly, watching his brother's face, weighing Prairie Wolf's words. He had seen much change in his brother since the woman of the Kere had arrived in the camp of the Apache. Prairie Wolf was young and without many coups counted as yet, but he knew the way of the warrior and his words rang more true than

Standing Buffalo could ignore. If she was indeed a sorceress, a witch, she must be exposed. He would test her as he participated in Prairie Wolf's plan. If she were a witch, or a willing adulteress—or both—she would be soon exposed and expelled from the tribe.

Falling Leaves was frightened, but she did her best to conceal it from Little Fox as they hovered at the edge of the dancers. They would not be able to speak long or they would be noticed.

"You have found a way to warn White Hawk and Cloud Dancer?"

"No. There have been too many near them." Little Fox spoke quickly in low tones. "And Prairie Wolf watches. I must do it when I cannot be seen, for if Prairie Wolf sees me and their plan is thwarted, he will know."

Falling Leaves shuddered. Her brother's wrath could be terrible. She turned clear, fawn eyes from Little Fox for a moment so he could not see the apprehension in them. Since Cloud Dancer and White Hawk had given Little Fox one of the horses they had returned with, her parents now looked even more favorably upon him as her suitor, but there was no telling what Prairie Wolf would do if he discovered that Falling Leaves and Little Fox betrayed him.

"Perhaps I will find a way to warn Cloud Dancer," Falling Leaves suggested.

"I will not tell you no," Little Fox said, but there was apprehension in his voice. "But you must be careful." Little Fox yearned to take Falling Leaves into his arms and hold her close, but he reminded himself, this was not Acoma. They would marry soon; that, however, would not excuse what the Apaches would view as an impropriety.

Falling Leaves nodded quickly, planning their strategy. She was no longer entirely the shy Apache maiden she had been raised to be. Cloud Dancer and Little Fox had changed that.

"Nothing can happen while the camp celebrates and honors Cloud Dancer and White Hawk. I will come to the circle and we will join the dancing." She dipped her head shyly in concession to her deeply ingrained upbringing, then added, "We will be able to see White Hawk and Cloud Dancer. There will be a time when we can warn them after the celebrating is over."

When Cloud Dancer and White Hawk were not joining in the dances Cloud Dancer sat at her husband's side, sharing the feast, or moved off to find She Who Seeks Wisdom and spend time with the other women. None she spoke to seemed to harbor any animosity at the respect Cloud Dancer now commanded from the men. Some commented they could probably do as well if it were not necessary for them to remain behind with their children. Cloud Dancer agreed with their assumption; there was no reason not to.

White Hawk spent much time talking to the men of their raid, describing the Spanish camp and discussing the virtues of the horses they had brought back.

"You are glad now we returned, wife?" White Hawk asked as he took his place again beside Cloud Dancer in the circle surrounding the brightly burning fire.

Cloud Dancer smiled impishly. "I am not sure. I think there are even more people than I remember. It is difficult to get time alone with you, husband."

He laughed affectionately. "It is no different with you. Many are proud of what you have accomplished and wish to speak with you. You are what you wished to become, a woman warrior. But you are also my wife. I think there will be moments that are difficult."

"I wish to thank you, my husband," Cloud Dancer said solemnly.

White Hawk's obsidian eyes glittered with humor and he cocked his head, giving her his ear in the teasing manner he had learned from his young wife. "What is it you wish to thank me for? I deserve thanks no more than you do. If it is for what I have taught you, remember that it is your learning of those skills that saved my life.''

"It is that," Cloud Dancer said, "but it is more. When we struck against the Spanish I was frightened, but through it I felt I regained some control of my life. Now, I may still be frightened, but I will never be less than whole. It is a wondrous gift. Thank you, my husband.''

The heavy beat of the drums rose again around them as the men began their chants and the dancing resumed. Cloud Dancer looked up at her husband and smiled, thinking of the future stretching out before them.

Chapter Nineteen

The celebration in honor of the great coup had already gone into the second day when many of the young men went hunting for more fresh game so that the revels could continue for the second night. It was a celebration intense in its joy and the participants were reluctant to give it up. It had been much the same, Cloud Dancer remembered, during the dances at Acoma after the harvest.

Cloud Dancer had slept little, finding herself alone with She Who Seeks Wisdom more than with her husband. The dancing continued with the music of the drums and the hypnotic chants of the men, their voices rising and blending in a vigorous singsong that rose and fell, powerful one moment, like a soft ghost sound the next.

"You are thoughtful, Daughter." She Who Seeks Wisdom settled her square form beside Cloud Dancer where she had taken refuge from the constant commotion of the exuberant celebrants. "This is not a time to be thoughtful. You should do no more than enjoy this revelry that is held in your honor. You do not have to think at a time like this. It is a time to feel."

"I am not so thoughtful as you give me credit for," Cloud Dancer said, grinning. "I am tired."

"There is more."

"I am tired. I must go to make sure the horses are all right, and White Hawk gambles with the men."

She Who Seeks Wisdom threw back her head and guffawed. "He is a man, all right."

Cloud Dancer nodded her agreement silently, then turned the conversation away from herself. "I have seen Little Fox and Falling Leaves together in much of the dancing. Will they be joined soon?"

"There is no doubt," She Who Seeks Wisdom said brightly, "and if there was any, your gift of one of the horses to Little Fox would have ended it. He will be one of the best hunters in the tribe with that horse." She patted Cloud Dancer's arm and gave her foster daughter a lopsided grin. "I have not even thanked you for my horse," she said softly. "You have saved this old back much strain with your gift. You are a good daughter!"

"You are most welcome. But I have the feeling that if I had not saved your back the strain this way, then we would have found another!" Cloud Dancer teased. "Much as Falling Leaves's parents sought a good match for her, you have been pleased with my choice."

"It is my lot that I am to be blessed with a golden old age. I must have done something to deserve it."

"You are wise in choosing your companions," Cloud Dancer asserted, gently teasing. "Sometimes that is enough." Then, before She Who Seeks Wisdom could retort, she asked, "Do you know where Falling Leaves is now?"

"She sleeps. I saw her mother drag her from the circle long ago. It will be dawn soon."

Cloud Dancer cast her gaze toward the starry heavens above. The crystalline sky was a canvas of black velvet, scattered with brilliant, twinkling stars. It was cold, but the cold lacked the edge it had possessed in days past; spring could not be far off. She looked toward the east and saw no sign yet of the dawn that She Who Seeks Wisdom had proclaimed was imminent, no rosy or golden glow to announce the sun's arrival. She could enjoy the cloak of the night's soft, gentle darkness a while longer.

"I will speak with Falling Leaves tomorrow," Cloud Dancer said, rising. "Now I will visit Bonita and the other horses, and then I, too, will seek my sleeping robes."

She Who Seeks Wisdom nodded, and Cloud Dancer slipped away on cat feet, moving in silence even in her unguarded moments.

Breathing in the rich, earthy smell emanating from the small herd of horses contained within the boundaries of the rope corral, Cloud Dancer smiled in the darkness, her blood throbbing with the beat of the drums in the background.

Bonita was beside her a moment after she arrived, reaching her glossy neck over the side to have her nose stroked.

"You do not like it when we do not go into the hills each day, do you?" Cloud Dancer spoke softly, reaching out to pat the warm, velvety nose, then to stroke the bow of Bonita's finely arched neck. "Well, I do not like it, either. Perhaps tomorrow..."

As Cloud Dancer spoke, some of the captured horses approached, squeezing in next to Bonita, seeking the gentle touch of Cloud Dancer's hand. They had learned quickly of her gentleness and penchant for bringing special morsels to even the most stubborn or ill-tempered steed.

"You are all like children!" Cloud Dancer chided them gently, amused, but not threatened by the press of large, warm bodies.

Suddenly Bonita's head came up and her ears flicked back and forth as her nostrils flared, catching a scent she was not comfortable with. She blew softly, her breath a sudden moist gale against Cloud Dancer's cheek, and tossed her head.

Cloud Dancer spun around, eyes accustomed to the darkness seeking some sign of danger. What she saw instead was a shadowy outline of a warrior moving toward her. There was a familiarity about the way the figure moved, but she was not quite sure.

"White Hawk?" Cloud questioned softly, surprised and a little chilled by the fact that she had not noticed the approach herself; it had taken Bonita to make her aware of it.

"No." The voice was dark liquid, the single word a telltale caress. "Am I so like my brother then that you cannot tell us apart?" Standing Buffalo asked as he came nearer. "Or is it something else?"

Cloud Dancer was puzzled, but even more, she was apprehensive. She had nothing to fear from White Hawk's brother, yet the nagging doubt would not leave her. He glided through the darkness to her side as a leaf skated upon the breezes of autumn.

"You wish something of me?" Cloud Dancer stayed where she was, hands hanging at her sides, a tentative smile playing at the corners of her lips. "Is White Hawk searching for me?" She did not care to ponder Standing Buffalo's last enigmatic question.

She could feel his eyes upon her in the dark, and something more as a strange chill of precognition raced up the length of her spine. It was elusive, but undeniable; there was trouble coming.

Cloud Dancer stood a little straighter, willing her hands, curled tightly at her sides, to relax. She could find no basis for her seemingly irrational fear. But this was not Standing Buffalo's way. He was not accustomed to addressing a woman boldly, directly, in the manner of the Kere, a manner that his brother had adapted to so easily.

Standing Buffalo held Cloud Dancer in the grip of his steady regard and tried to see beyond the beautiful face with its smooth, unblemished skin, rosy tan, and the small, stubborn chin and fathomless cat's eyes with their tilted corners. It was into those liquid, brown depths that Standing Buffalo peered for his answers, but came up wanting. He thought it was like looking into the silvered surface of a quiet pool, and those eyes affected him. Perhaps he was indeed facing a witch, as Prairie Wolf claimed.

"White Hawk is not seeking you," he said at last, breaking the heavily weighted silence between them.

His tone, his stance, the impropriety—in the eyes of the Apache—of his being here alone with her, rang persistent warning bells in the back of Cloud Dancer's mind. He stepped so close to her she was aware of the rich, earthy buckskin smell of him. She yearned to step back, yet she did not want to show weakness. She stood her ground.

"I have spoken with my brother and Bempol. I have heard much of the ways of the Kere," Standing Buffalo ventured, his words soft. "Our customs are very different, yet you have come to the Apache and accepted my brother. Have you accepted our ways as well?"

Where was this leading? Cloud Dancer wondered. "Yes," she responded, a little puzzled and even more alarmed when she realized Standing Buffalo's broad form was planted squarely between her and her return to camp. "It is why I came to be a warrior among the Apache. Your ways accept a woman warrior. The people of Acoma and Isleta could not accept it, and I could no longer stand by and watch helplessly when my people were attacked."

"You knew they would be attacked?"

"No."

Standing Buffalo's eyes were difficult to see in the darkness and impossible to read.

"Prairie Wolf says you are a witch."

"Prairie Wolf is a fool." The heat of anger flooded Cloud Dancer's face. Her eyes flashed, the spark leaping the darkness between them.

"Easy words to say. And a witch would not admit to being one. But why should I believe your words when I have seen with my own eyes that you have bewitched my brother—as you have bewitched me." His words were raw and taut as a bowstring, his movements swift and smooth as a striking snake as his arms reached out to draw her into his embrace.

"No . . ." Cloud Dancer tried to yell her denial but found herself pressed so tightly against Standing Buffalo's chest that her word was muffled in his buckskin shirt, and the breath for a new protest not allowed to enter her lungs.

Her impulse was to snatch her knife from the sheath at her waist and plant it in his heart—but this was White Hawk's brother! She twisted in his grip and fought furiously. Fear of Standing Buffalo, fear of where this was leading, knotted in Cloud Dancer's stomach. She felt Standing Buffalo's hands pressing her resisting body closer, and the strong, sinewy contours of his body pressed intimately to her own.

"Among the Kere, my brother has told me, a maiden may be alone with a man and not fear her reputation is ruined. She may even lie with a man before marriage and not feel the anger of her parents or her people." Standing Buffalo's hands stroked and promised as he spoke into the softness of Cloud Dancer's hair. "Are the men of the Kere not men? Would they see their woman with another man and do nothing?"

"No!" Cloud Dancer shot back, but her denial was lost in her struggles.

Cloud Dancer fought the encroaching hands and throbbing body with every ounce of her strength, but short of her drawing her knife and slipping it between Standing Buffalo's ribs, her smaller stature and strength were no match for him.

"Release me!" Cloud Dancer demanded ineffectually against Standing Buffalo's chest, her small fists pressing fiercely against him for release.

Her head spun in a dizzying whirlwind of fear, anger and doubt. Somehow Prairie Wolf had caused this! But what was she to do? If White Hawk came to check the horses as she had . . . if She Who Seeks Wisdom had told him where she had gone...if White Hawk found Standing Buffalo here like this with her... Cloud Dancer fought down a sob of frustration. She could not even think what White Hawk would do.

"Do not fight me," Standing Buffalo ordered gruffly. "I do not wish to hurt you. Give to me and I will not tell my brother. I must have you, for you are in my blood. It will be here as it was in your home in Acoma. All will be well."

"You do not know how it was in my home!" Cloud Dancer shrieked, the sound muffled and trapped between them. "You do not understand! You have heard about our customs, but you have not learned. You do not know!"

Reason found its way back to Cloud Dancer. She accepted Standing Buffalo's overwhelming strength. She could not free herself of him by pitting her own lesser strength against his. Cloud Dancer suddenly relaxed against him, gathering her strength, feeling half-smothered by his bear-like embrace.

Almost overcome by the gentle presence of Cloud Dancer within the circle of his arms, Standing Buffalo was not sure he could stop what he had started if he wanted to. And with each passing moment he less wanted to stop. This was not as he had planned it. Her sudden surrender sent the blood rushing through his veins like needles of ice. Could Prairie Wolf be right? Could this soft creature within the circle of his arms be a witch? He was half-convinced; but the other half railed against the accusation and damned him for what he was doing to his brother's wife.

Feeling the change in Standing Buffalo, the lessening of his tension, Cloud Dancer shifted her stance, planting one foot between his spread feet and shifted her weight suddenly. She intended only to trip him, free herself of his grasp and run, but it did not work as she had planned.

Standing Buffalo, caught unaware, fell heavily, but he did not release Cloud Dancer. They collapsed to the snow-crusted earth and rolled into the shadows. The horses shifted nervously, nickering uneasily and stamping their confusion.

Cloud Dancer struggled to free herself, but Standing Buffalo's hands were everywhere, his weight working to his advantage more now than when they had been standing. Twisting and turning, Cloud Dancer succeeded only in allowing Standing Buffalo to straddle her, one knee roughly thrust between her legs in an intimate posture that sent fury and terror washing over her in a wave.

Only a few days before she had thanked White Hawk for having helped return control of her life to her, and now it was being wrenched from her yet again.

"Witch!" Standing Buffalo groaned. "How could you have made my brother believe you would be satisfied with one man?" He held her pinned to the ground beneath him, the writhing of her body igniting fires he had never known burned so hot within him. "Witch," he murmured again, driven by his fanaticism.

Instantly realizing her movements only inflamed him further, Cloud Dancer froze, hating the sweat that sprang from every pore of her body, hating her weakness, at that moment hating Standing Buffalo with all her being.

"I am not a witch," she said, her voice thick with emotions clogged at the back of her throat. She had to keep control now, if not of the situation, of herself. If she gave in to the blind panic that tore at her she would lose everything. "If I were a witch, would I allow you to do this now?" she panted.

"No one knows the reasons of a witch. I burn for you as I have never burned for another. If you are not a witch, then why is this so? I am not a man to take my brother's wife."

"Because you are as much a fool as Prairie Wolf," Cloud Dancer managed in a flat, inflectionless whisper, the words forced between clenched teeth. But by her very tone she hoped to distract Standing Buffalo's attention from his self-centered arousal and make him feel anger, anger directed at her. "You are White Hawk's brother—I am his wife. You wish to destroy us all!"

Standing Buffalo went rigid above her. She could see the half snarl of anger curling his lips, and the cords of his neck stood out like sticks, pressing against the brightly beaded collar he wore. Cloud Dancer remained limp as deerskin beneath him, unmoving, breathing in short little gasps at the pressure of his weight upon her.

She would never know what picture she presented, with Standing Buffalo sprawled across her, one leg wedged between hers as she lay panting beneath him, nor was it a scene that lasted long. One moment Standing Buffalo was pressing her down upon the cold earth, grinding her back into the crusted snow, the next he was torn from her, reeling backward into the solid body of one of the Spanish horses.

The animal screamed and jumped back, as the other horses, disturbed by the commotion, danced away, leaving Standing Buffalo to sprawl just as suddenly in the dirt and snow.

Cloud Dancer was on her feet in an instant, leaping to White Hawk's side, grasping his rigid, corded forearm between her own smaller, softer hands. "Do not hurt him!" she burst out, terrified that White Hawk, obsidian eyes flashing, would attack his own brother for what he had done to her.

"Do not hurt him?" His chest heaved. His words crumbled over her. "I find you with my brother like this, and your first words are of concern for *him?*"

White Hawk stood still as the ancient trees, his face as sharp and unmoving as granite. In his eyes was a wounded look such as Cloud Dancer had never seen before. There was no yielding in the set of his body.

It took several long, painful seconds for Cloud Dancer to realize White Hawk did not believe himself to have rescued her, but to have dragged two lovers apart!

"No!" Cloud Dancer breathed, her hands still warm against the coldness of his flesh. "I came to see Bonita and the other horses—Standing Buffalo followed me here. He said I was a witch, that I had bewitched him and he could not stop himself from what he was doing. I fought him, but he was too strong for me."

"He was too strong for you, but the Spanish were not? You fight many and are victorious, but not over this one?"

The look of pure disgust on White Hawk's face when he finally turned his eyes toward Cloud Dancer was almost too much for her. She released his arm as if she touched fire. Pain rose in her chest, squeezing the breath from her lungs. Tears burned behind her eyes, but she did not allow herself to shed them.

"I knew the ways of the Kere were different from those of the Apache. I honored the ways of the Kere when I was at Acoma. You have said you would honor the ways of the Apache here, though I have said I would not expect it when we were alone. But this..."

Standing Buffalo climbed to his feet and stood straight and tall, unmoving, his eyes flat and expressionless.

Cloud Dancer's golden-brown eyes flicked from one brother to the other, a matching anger growing apace in her mind and in her heart. Her blood throbbed with it, her head swam with it.

She lifted her chin and pushed words at him in her clear, clipped voice. "Think what you will, husband. I have not dishonored the Apache or you. Nor have I brought dishonor upon myself. You say you honored the ways of the Kere. Such was easy for you, since the ways of the Kere allowed you more freedom than those of the Apache. It was no sacrifice. You came to Acoma as a respected shaman and warrior to a people who were in need of help and in awe of you. I came among your people as a woman determined to be a warrior." Her eyes flashed and her skin flushed. "You

did what you came to do at Acoma. I have done what I came
here to do.''

Her body stiff and aching, Cloud Dancer drew herself up
even straighter, her eyes meeting White Hawk's unflinch-
ingly. ''A warrior, even a strong warrior, can be defeated by
another. I bow to Standing Buffalo's greater strength. I will
say no more.''

Anger, fear and distrust hung in the air between them like
an invisible lance. Cloud Dancer gave an audible sigh and
let go of the anger, feeling it flow from her as from a wound
lanced, leaving her with nothing but terrible pain caused by
the doubt in White Hawk's eyes. Her pride would not allow her to beg White Hawk's understanding. She would not
have him if he did not trust and love her beyond what he
believed his eyes had seen. If he could not recognize the
truth, then she had lost him already.

Cloud Dancer turned her damning gaze upon Standing
Buffalo. ''You know what happened here. You will carry it
in your heart always.''

Her spine rigid, her heart breaking, Cloud Dancer turned
and walked away from both brothers. Fiercely, she dammed
the tears within her. Her throat ached and her eyes burned,
but her steps did not falter. She returned to the tepee of She
Who Seeks Wisdom.

White Hawk watched Cloud Dancer go. He felt as though
his heart were being torn from his breast. His eyes did not
even see his own brother. How could Cloud Dancer have
done this thing? He had known the ways of the Kere. He
knew they had not viewed the joining of man and woman
they way the Apache did. He had recognized that their ways
were much freer than those of the Apache and had even re-
joiced in those customs when Cloud Dancer came to him
and they were caught by the storm. Was that so long ago?
The winter had barely begun when they had first joined and
now the kiss of spring was in the air. They had not known

each other long or well, but they had become each a part of the other. Or had they been that even before their meeting?

Anguished, White Hawk watched Cloud Dancer's slim, straight back as she walked into camp. She had come to him in his visions. He had known her to be his from the time he had first spoken to her at Acoma. Yet they had been raised in different cultures. Could it be that the pueblo life from which Cloud Dancer came was too liberal after all, too easy, to allow them to live together in happiness? Would Cloud Dancer be forever seeking favors other than his?

His gaze moved to his brother, who had not moved since he had regained his feet. Whatever Cloud Dancer's crime, her guilt had to be shared by his brother. Standing Buffalo could claim she seduced him, claim she was a witch, but a man was responsible for his actions. If such was true, he would not have had to give in to her temptations.

"You are my brother," White Hawk said tightly, "but now I do not wish to look upon your face."

His expression was filled with disgust and anger. White Hawk walked stiffly to Dark Sky, slipped the rope bridle in his mouth and over his head, gathered the stallion's reins and guided him out of the rope corral.

"I will not want to look upon your face for a long time," White Hawk told Standing Buffalo as he vaulted astride Dark Sky.

"Prairie Wolf was right." Standing Buffalo rumbled the words, an edge of desperation in his voice. "She has taken away my will and drawn me to her, and now you curse me for it and turn from your own brother. She has blinded you. She truly is a witch. It will have to be decided what is to be done with her."

"No!" The single word was like a clap of thunder. Dark Sky jumped beneath White Hawk. "She is not a witch. And what is to be done *I* will decide." He turned Dark Sky and left at a gallop.

Standing Buffalo stared after his brother, breathing deeply, hands clenching and unclenching at his sides. Because of her, brother had turned against brother. She truly was a witch as Prairie Wolf claimed. She had to be...didn't she?

The answer he gave himself was not the one he sought. Her actions had not been those of a witch. She had not encouraged, nor had she fought him, and he knew she was capable of either. She had not turned brother against brother—that he had accomplished himself.

Dark Sky's retreating hoofbeats pounded at Standing Buffalo, and he faced the truth. Prairie Wolf was wrong. Cloud Dancer was no witch.

Chapter Twenty

Cloud Dancer was returning from the place where the horses were kept, her back straight, her face still as stone, when Little Fox caught sight of her. She carried herself stiffly, as though wounded, but he could see nothing wrong. Then he saw Standing Buffalo emerge from the dark shadows and Prairie Wolf intercept him as hoofbeats drummed off into the hills. Little Fox froze in his tracks. He knew what had happened. His heart tightened. How could it have happened so soon? Half the camp was in a stupor from the long celebration in honor of both White Hawk and Cloud Dancer. Others were still feasting and dancing.

The answer came to Little Fox even as he asked the question of himself. What better time? Few, if any, would take any notice of the exact whereabouts of others, save parents chaperoning the young and unmarried. There would be none to witness what took place.

Grimly, Little Fox took up his weapons, unwilling to leave the camp without them, and hurried toward the horses. If he hurried, he would be able to catch White Hawk and tell him of his knowledge of Prairie Wolf's plans. It would not undo the harm already caused, but it would allow it to proceed no further. Still, Little Fox felt a sadness in his heart. Knowing the truth, White Hawk would be able to forgive Cloud Dancer—for in reality there was nothing to forgive—but would he be able to find it in his heart to forgive his brother?

Catching the chestnut horse with the white stockings that Cloud Dancer had given him, Little Fox mounted and galloped into the fading night after White Hawk.

It was not difficult for him to follow White Hawk, for the stalwart Apache warrior did nothing to cover his tracks. In anger or hurt—probably both—he was riding blind, not watching for danger. Such behavior from White Hawk worried Little Fox, and he urged his horse to move faster. He had little doubt that if White Hawk did not want to be found, he would be nearly impossible to corner, but Little Fox knew he would catch up with him soon. He thanked the fates that had seen fit to provide him with a horse through Cloud Dancer's generosity, and he thanked the time he had spent with Cloud Dancer and Bonita, learning to ride. He hoped he could now repay those gifts that had been given.

He guided his horse up a steep incline, having some trouble with the animal that had been so recently liberated from the Spanish. The trees were thicker here than near the camp of the Apache, making it difficult to see far into the gathered shadows, but Little Fox pressed on, kneeing his horse forward, slapping his heels to the chestnut mare when she hesitated.

White Hawk rode on at a dangerous speed, driven by the devils of his anger and pain. How could Cloud Dancer do such a thing? They had not even spent a night alone together in camp, and she was in his brother's arms. How could she turn to Standing Buffalo when they had shared such joy in each other's arms?

He hesitated, drawing back on Dark Sky's reins, causing the horse to dance beneath him. Cloud Dancer *would not!* A part of him shouted the denial and he nearly turned back.

But he had seen them! Before his eyes he had seen them together on the ground! Cloud Dancer was lying calmly beneath Standing Buffalo. His eyes had not deceived him.

He gave Dark Sky his head again, becoming aware of someone following him. His eyes burned with anger, and muscles knotted in fury's tension. His attention was divided. Could it be his eyes had seen what was not truly so? That could only mean Cloud Dancer had not wanted what had been occurring between her and Standing Buffalo; if he accepted that it meant his brother had been attacking his wife. White Hawk's thoughts recoiled at the idea.

He heard again the sound of pursuit. With a heavy hand he drew Dark Sky into the brush and waited.

Little Fox's progress had been slowed by the trees, but he was still advancing at dangerous speed when a dark shadow, large and menacing, erupted out of the brush before him. It blocked his path and startled his chestnut mare, causing her to rear, throwing him to the ground. His breath knocked out of him, Little Fox gained one knee, weapons ready. Then he recognized White Hawk seated upon Dark Sky, glaring down at him.

"Why do you follow me?" White Hawk demanded angrily.

In the meager gray light of dawn Little Fox could not see very clearly, but he did not miss the flash in White Hawk's dark eyes.

Lowering his drawn bow, Little Fox relaxed. He climbed to his feet to face the imposing Apache warrior. "I have much to tell you," he said urgently. He began his tale, relating all he and Falling Leaves had witnessed between Prairie Wolf and White Hawk's brother, Standing Buffalo.

"How do I know you speak the truth? Cloud Dancer is your friend." The tone in his voice made it plain he wondered again if Little Fox were more than her friend. "Her ways are your ways, and you would lie to protect her." White Hawk spoke stiffly, his hands gripping Dark Sky's reins so tightly the umber skin across his knuckles whitened. But Little Fox's words had about them the ring of truth. What he had seen began to make more sense. Still, he wished to believe neither that his wife would betray him nor that his brother would force himself upon her.

"Her ways are *your* ways," Little Fox corrected him. "That was so even before we found you and the camp of your people." The rich timbre of his voice brooked no doubt; the truth of his words lay bared in the depths of his bold, black eyes for White Hawk to see. "It is you she loves. She would take no other. Even the ways of our people that you speak of would not allow a married woman to flit from man to man—even if her bond to you were not so strong. If you still do not believe me, you must talk to Falling Leaves."

White Hawk shook his head wearily. "You then accuse my brother of attacking my wife, and I can find no reason to doubt you," he said, racked by the pain in his heart. "I saw it when I found them together, but I refused to accept my brother's betrayal."

White Hawk's grief weighed heavily upon Little Fox. "No," he said firmly, "your brother's fault is in his concern for you. Prairie Wolf was able to twist Standing Buffalo's caring to his own purpose. Your brother shares the guilt, but he did not originate it."

"I have driven Cloud Dancer from me," White Hawk said in a voice as cold as his eyes had become upon realizing the truth of Little Fox's words and of what he had done. "She will not forgive me for what I believed when I saw her lying beneath my brother."

The image returned to White Hawk's mind sharp and clear in every detail. His body tightened, his stomach knotted into a hard fist of fear. Had he lost what had been a part of him since he had seen his first vision? Had he truly driven Cloud Dancer from him?

"She did not fight Standing Buffalo. Why not?" White Hawk searched Little Fox's face for the answer, studying the bold eyes beneath heavy brows, the proud square chin. "Her skill with a knife matches that of most of our young men. She might have been able to kill him."

"She has great love for you," Little Fox answered simply. "She would not attempt to kill your brother—no matter what he did."

White Hawk groaned. The answer wrenched his heart. "Standing Buffalo is stronger—and he is my brother. I will return to Cloud Dancer and explain. My brother will pay for what he has done, as will Prairie Wolf."

Little Fox flung himself once again astride the chestnut mare. He did not like to think of what White Hawk's plans for his brother might include. The warrior's pain and fury were etched in fine lines around his brooding eyes.

Turning his mare, Little Fox saw a frozen look come upon White Hawk's face. He followed the direction of the spirit warrior's gaze and felt everything go dark and silent within him, even as the first rosy streaks of dawn reflected in his eyes.

The drift of the wind brought the sounds to their ears. The faint, distinctive noise of armed Spanish soldiers reached them, as the string of mounted men passed in the distance. The tiny figures of the soldiers moving steadily on a course toward the Apache camp were barely visible from the steep hilltop in the gray mist of the dawn. That they moved with purpose was readily apparent. But they could not know that ahead lay the camp of the Apache who had stolen their horses. It was only chance that the Jicarilla camp was the one they would find in their determination to bring punishment for the act. But that did not lessen the danger to the people in the camp. When the Spanish struck many would die.

White Hawk's face hardened, his eyes glittered like ice. "They are riding toward our camp." He bit the words out, anxiety clawing at the back of his throat, making it difficult to draw a steady breath.

"They are too far ahead of us!" Little Fox spoke in a bitter rush. "We cannot get back in time to warn the people—to warn Bempol to gather the warriors!"

"We will beat them." White Hawk wheeled Dark Sky, directing the horse down an even steeper incline than the one Little Fox had ascended such a short time ago.

The stallion took off at a plunging run, angling only lightly on the downslope under White Hawk's able direction. Little Fox was not as experienced a horseman as White Hawk, but he did not consider; he just followed.

White Hawk chose a path on instinct, knowing that direction, though a more treacherous route, would cut the distance they had to travel back to camp. If they were lucky, if neither horse fell, they could get back in time to give precious minutes of warning to the people. He could hear the pounding hooves of Little Fox's mare coming on behind and urged Dark Sky to even greater speed.

The great stallion complied. Moving as one, man and horse dodged down the slope, careening past bare winter skeletons of trees, jumping deadfalls and skirting crusted patches of ice that would have spelled their downfall. Despite the cold of the day White Hawk broke into a sweat as they plummeted down the hillside in a barely controlled headlong rush of man and beast. White Hawk moved with the stallion, shifting his weight, lifting Dark Sky's great head with the reins when he faltered. He wrapped long, slender fingers in the heavy mane when a jarring misstep nearly catapulted them head over heels.

And all the time, White Hawk could hear Little Fox pounding down the slope behind him. His ear was tuned to the heavy crash that could spell the death of both the young warrior from Acoma and his horse; but miraculously that sound never echoed through the icy stillness.

White Hawk's mind raced. Scenes of Acoma flashed through his mind in a sickening kaleidoscope of blood and death. Women and children of the Apache camp were unsuspectingly in the path of the Spanish thunder weapons. Cloud Dancer was there. She would fight. If she died now, she would die thinking her husband believed her unfaithful with his brother!

The heat rushed up White Hawk's neck and into his face, his pulse racing with the breakneck pace of the horse beneath him. They had to beat the Spanish soldiers. Bempol was a great war chief—White Hawk had to believe that somehow he would rally the warriors for the attack with only a moment's warning. He could accept nothing else.

Dark Sky struck flatter ground in a lunge that was more a deerlike leap than the solid stride of a powerful stallion, snapping White Hawk's head back upon his neck, jarring his jaws against each other. Then they were flying over the more level ground, taking the dips and swells easily in the stallion's stride, the distance falling away quickly beneath driving hooves.

White Hawk was aware of Dark Sky drawing steadily away from Little Fox's chestnut mare, but the young warrior from Acoma had completed the harrowing descent without mishap several strides behind White Hawk. The only thing of importance now was warning the village. Once, White Hawk glanced over his shoulder toward Little Fox to see him coming on strong, and waving for White Hawk to go ahead. White Hawk tightened his legs around Dark Sky and pressed his heels against him, asking for more. Like the great power of the earth itself, the horse gathered himself and leaped forward, strides lengthening, head outstretched, dragging vast amounts of air into his laboring lungs. At any other time the sheer power of the stallion would have thrilled White Hawk. He would have thrown his head back and given voice to his throbbing war cry, but not this time. This time White Hawk sat far forward, easing the horse's burden, leaning close against his heated neck and praying to the gods.

* * *

"He will come to his senses," She Who Seeks Wisdom said gently to Cloud Dancer, her words barely more than a whisper as they sat close together before the small fire, in the wake of Cloud Dancer's unhappy tale. "White Hawk was surprised, but he is not a fool like Prairie Wolf. He will think about what he saw and he will return to you."

"If he trusts me so little, do I want him to return?" Cloud Dancer sighed the question, asking it as much of herself as of She Who Seeks Wisdom.

"And if you had seen White Hawk as he saw you, what would you think?"

Cloud Dancer met the older woman's steady gaze. "I trust White Hawk."

"Yes, in your heart. But what if your eyes saw what his saw? Would it not take time for the trust that is in your heart to understand what it was your eyes had seen?"

Cloud Dancer softened, but she was still worried. "But what of Standing Buffalo? He believes now as Prairie Wolf, that I am a witch."

"He believes that only because my brother, Prairie Wolf, has convinced him of it." Falling Leaves ducked into the tepee and bowed her head respectfully toward She Who Seeks Wisdom. "Forgive me for not asking leave to enter," she apologized softly, "but I had to speak to you. I have heard talk that there was trouble and White Hawk rode off." She knelt and sat gracefully back upon her heels before the fire. "It was not an accident that Standing Buffalo followed you when you went to the horses. Prairie Wolf and he planned it. It was intended that it would break the bond between you and White Hawk, so that he would not trust you and would see you for the witch Prairie Wolf claims you to be. I wanted to warn you, as did Little Fox, but you were gone with White Hawk, and when you returned with the horses—" Falling Leaves's voice rose to a thin wail "—we did not think they would do such a thing while the entire tribe honored you!''

"Little Fox knew of this?" Cloud Dancer smiled faintly, her hand going to the leather pouch around her neck that contained the small carved lion fetish.

Falling Leaves nodded. "And he has gone after White Hawk. But what if White Hawk does not believe him?" Falling Leaves cried and buried her face in her hands.

Cloud Dancer raised her liquid brown eyes, dancing with amber lights reflecting the fire's glow, to She Who Seeks Wisdom. The old woman's words had been firm and reassuring, but the doubt remained.

Without warning, before any of them could say another word, pandemonium erupted outside. Hooves thundered against the frozen earth, and rough calls ricocheted across the Apache camp where it lay beneath the gold and rose dawn. It was a call to arms and they had no time to organize. The Spanish were only moments away. Bempol's voice rose in bellowing command, directing a defense too hastily called.

Cloud Dancer sprang to her feet as the flap of She Who Seeks Wisdom's tepee whipped open. Framed in the doorway against the gold-streaked dawn stood Prairie Wolf. His eyes swept the tepee's interior, hardening when they touched his sister, then flicked away, finding Cloud Dancer.

"You are a warrior! Bring your weapons! White Hawk has ridden with a warning. The Spanish are close behind!''

The sharp crack of a Spanish pistol gave Prairie Wolf's words emphasis and ended further conversation.

Prairie Wolf expected Cloud Dancer to hang back, but she did not. Her spear in her hand, her bow and arrows slung over her shoulder, she brushed past him into the full onslaught of the attack. Women screamed. Children ran, and warriors rushed to cover their escape. The crack of the terrible Spanish thunder weapons split the air and a warrior fell, spilling his blood upon the earth.

For precious moments Cloud Dancer hesitated, then she stuck her head back into She Who Seeks Wisdom's tepee. Prairie Wolf smirked at her apparent reluctance to join in the melee—the show of cowardice he had been sure would surface when she was confronted by the shadow of death without White Hawk to stand between it and her.

"Run!" Cloud Dancer shouted at She Who Seeks Wisdom and Falling Leaves. "Take to the arroyos and follow them into the hills! Scatter! Hurry, before the warriors cannot hold them back. I'm going for the horses!"

There was no time for more. She Who Seeks Wisdom raised her hand in protest, but Cloud Dancer spun back outside and turned her attention to the horses. "They must not get the horses!" she yelled at Prairie Wolf, though the Spanish soldiers were pouring into the camp from the direction of the rope corrals, firing their weapons as they came on.

Cloud Dancer bolted from his side, long, graceful strides carrying her swiftly into the heart of danger, and Prairie Wolf followed.

Astride Dark Sky, White Hawk was more of a match for the Spanish soldiers though he knew the stallion was exhausted after the hard run to warn the camp. He guided the great horse with his knees and plunged into the battle, his war cry upon his lips.

The Spanish soldiers fell before the force of White Hawk's charge, his lance flinging them from their horses though it did not penetrate the armor they wore. Other warriors, on foot, leaped in to attack the soldiers White Hawk unhorsed. Behind the ragged line the warriors held, White Hawk was aware of the women and children sprinting for the safety of the higher hills. The acrid smell of gunpowder hung heavy upon the morning air. The warriors would follow the women in retreat; they were no match for the Spanish thunder sticks. White Hawk heard the cries of battle all around him; he saw men fall. He tried not to think of Cloud Dancer, for there was no hope of finding her now.

A miniball whistled past White Hawk's ear and he spun Dark Sky to meet the new threat, raising his war ax after he lost his spear, toppling another soldier from his horse. The stallion plunged ahead at White Hawk's urging, colliding with the Spaniard's horse, which staggered before Dark Sky's heavier weight, almost falling to its knees. With a cry that echoed across the battle, White Hawk swung his war ax, connecting solidly with the soldier's helmet in a stunning blow.

Beyond the fallen soldier, White Hawk's eye caught a flash of movement. Cloud Dancer raced toward the rope corrals and the horses. Right behind her ran Prairie Wolf.

Cloud Dancer was small, her fleetness taking Prairie Wolf by surprise. He went in the same direction as she, pressing hard to catch up with her, dodging with nimble speed through the battleground that had earlier been their peaceful camp. He, too, did not wish to see the horses lost—no matter how they had been acquired or by whom. He watched Cloud Dancer rush headlong into the Spanish soldiers, as they worked to bring down the rope corral and free the horses.

The fleeting thought crossed Prairie Wolf's mind that nothing could be better than for Cloud Dancer to be killed in battle while her husband believed her to be unfaithful to him with his own brother. Then there was no more time for thought, as Prairie Wolf, too, was swept into the tumult of battle.

"Bonita!" Cloud Dancer called to the little mare and the horse jerked against the Spanish hand that held her. "Bonita!" Cloud Dancer called again.

Well trained, the horse jerked her head up and, when she was not immediately free, reared, pawing at the air and the soldier who held tightly to her rope.

Cloud Dancer did not call again, but instead went for the man who held Bonita. He looked at her and grinned a wolfish smile. Cloud Dancer did not know what he expected of her, but she could see the surprise in his eyes.

With lightning speed she attacked, her lance lashing forward to catch an unprotected arm, ripping flesh and spilling blood. The dark-skinned, black-bearded young soldier yowled and dropped the rope, staggering back as another soldier gained Bonita's back and one of his companions grabbed Cloud Dancer from the rear. Her weapons were knocked from her hand and she was hoisted belly down across Bonita's withers in front of the Spaniard who had subdued her horse.

Cloud Dancer tried to throw herself from the mare's back, but the man who held her down was too strong. He pressed his hand into the middle of her back and galloped out of camp, the cries of battle falling quickly behind.

A light of satisfaction touched Prairie Wolf's eyes as he saw Cloud Dancer being carried off, but only for a moment. Then the sound of a thunder stick exploded in his ear and a searing pain whipped across his left temple, sending him cartwheeling into oblivion amid an explosion of bright lights.

He was unaware of being hauled across one of the horses before the Spanish, replete with a number of captives and the horses they had sought to recover, withdrew from the Apache camp.

In the silence that came with the end of battle, White Hawk followed the retreating Spanish, keeping them in sight, but maintaining a respectful distance. He had no doubt the Spanish soldiers were aware of his presence and that they would use the thunder sticks if he moved within range. He had seen the Spanish take Cloud Dancer and others captive.

"You have not won," he said with conviction, though no one was close enough to hear. "We will return our people to their families—and the horses will be ours."

He fought the frustration and anger that threatened to strangle him at his inability to launch the rescue now, on his own. Finally, reluctantly, he turned Dark Sky back toward camp. He would raise a war party. The tracks of the Spanish would not be difficult to follow.

The keening wail of the Apache women for their dead was the first sound that met White Hawk as he rode back into camp to assess the damage and gather men to follow the Spanish.

She Who Seeks Wisdom's hand touched Dark Sky and drew White Hawk's attention as his eyes roved over the destruction of their homes. "What of Cloud Dancer?" the old woman asked.

"The Spanish have taken her and a number of others, some wounded." His face was tight with worry, twisted with anxiety over what he would find here, among his people. "All is well with you?"

"I am unharmed, but Falling Leaves is among the captives," the old wisewoman replied, glumly casting her eyes around the wreckage of the encampment. "It was the words of Cloud Dancer that drove us to action and saved us. Falling Leaves turned back. I think she feared some treachery from her brother, Prairie Wolf, who came to call Cloud Dancer to battle, saying you had brought the warning."

"It was not soon enough," White Hawk replied. "We have lost too many."

"Many more could have died. You did what could be done."

"It does not make it easier." White Hawk glanced up, spotting Claws of the Bear near the remains of his smoke-blackened tepee. "I must go," he said hastily. "Tell those you see I am raising a war party to avenge the dead and return the captives to their families."

She Who Seeks Wisdom nodded and stepped back to allow White Hawk passage. White Hawk's heart and mind reeled with the shock of Cloud Dancer's loss. Later he would find it impossible to remember the words he had just exchanged with the old woman. He had one driving force now, which made his heart pump when he felt it would shrivel and die. They would get their people back. He would hold Cloud Dancer in his arms again. She would forgive him for those terrible moments when he had seen her in his brother's embrace and had not understood. He had to believe that, or he would go berserk and attack the Spanish party single-handedly.

He led Dark Sky among the debris strewn by the raid as he walked toward the center of camp. Claws of the Bear was there, too. Little Fox, battered and torn, appeared from the edge of camp, walking strongly, his spear in his fist. The war chief, Bempol, strode forward from the east. Standing Buffalo went to join them. Others arrived, returning after the fight, regrouping, coming together to do what must now be done.

With the wail of the living for the dead in poignant backdrop, they met and planned.

"The Spanish were going west with their captives," White Hawk reported, "but I am sure they will turn south when they reach the banks of the Great River."

Little Fox agreed. "When we first saw them, that was the direction from which they came. They probably believe we will not attack after they have hurt us so badly and with our people in their hands."

Other members of the gathering nodded solemnly in agreement with Little Fox, looking upon the young warrior from Acoma with new respect since they had seen him fight the Spanish with uncommon bravery.

White Hawk listened, but his eyes were locked with those of his brother, Standing Buffalo. "It is my vow that I will bring back my wife, Cloud Dancer, and the others taken captive with her, or I will give up my life in the attempt,'' White Hawk's words fell like pebbles in the flowing waters, his dark eyes challenging his brother. "There are only two horses remaining in our camp, my stallion, Dark Sky, and the chestnut mare Cloud Dancer presented to Little Fox. Still, those who accompany us must be able riders, for we intend to return not only with the captives, but with the horses as well.''

Bempol nodded his head in agreement and satisfaction. He was war chief of this band of Apache, but his position was not threatened when another spoke up to raise a war party for revenge and succor. It was the right of any member of the tribe to do so.

"Those who remain behind must move the camp,'' Bempol remarked. "It must be to a place where the Spanish cannot find it. It was only because we were so exposed that they found us now.''

"Who, then, will join the war party and who will remain?'' White Hawk threw out the question, the rich, sincere timbre of his voice leaving no doubt that both tasks were equally respected.

"I will go with White Hawk.'' Little Fox spoke with quiet ferocity. "I will not wait for another to return Falling Leaves to her family.''

"I will go,'' another person said.

"And I.''

"And I.'' Standing Buffalo added his voice to the others, his heart heavy with the grief he had given his brother before this tragedy. Cloud Dancer was not a witch. He knew that now for a certainty. In the face of White Hawk's rage she had wrapped herself in the cloak of her dignity, she had bowed before the hurt of White Hawk's mistrust of her. Hers had not been the acts of a witch. She had not sought to hurt in return, to strike out, to turn brother against brother.

"I have done my brother a great wrong," Standing Buffalo said quietly, his words carrying to all those gathered by its tone instead of volume. "I believed Cloud Dancer to be a witch, but I know now that this is not so." His voice was heavy with self-recrimination. "In my blind fear for my brother, I unwittingly become a pawn of Prairie Wolf's jealousy. I have much to answer for when our people are again together, but now I would accompany White Hawk and be his right arm in bringing back his wife, Cloud Dancer. I will swear to give my life in place of hers if I am called upon to do so. I await my brother's answer. I will not go if he does not wish it."

White Hawk drew a deep breath, his eyes softening. The anger toward his brother was still a raw, open wound, but there were the beginnings of forgiveness in his heart.

"I accept you," White Hawk said with a curt nod.

"Then we go," Bempol said sharply, climbing to his feet, and he threw back his head to give his piercing war cry.

One after another the Apache warriors gained their feet, brandishing weapons above their heads, and gave voice to full-throated battle cries.

Chapter Twenty-one

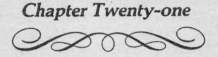

"Do not be afraid," Cloud Dancer whispered to Falling Leaves. "White Hawk and Little Fox will catch up with us before these Spanish can take us back to be slaves." Her eyes swung around the perimeter of the Spanish camp, probing for weaknesses. She was quickly rewarded. The Spanish soldiers did not know how to make camp like the Apache. Their terrible thunder sticks made them powerful and to be feared, but they depended upon that single strength, leaving openings in their defenses that made them vulnerable. Cloud Dancer had learned much among the Apache; her adopted people knew how to take advantage of such vulnerability.

Falling Leaves turned large, trusting eyes to her friend. "What if they cannot?"

"Then we ourselves will find a way to escape." Cloud Dancer patted her high, soft leather boot, where her knife still nestled in its sheath. "But we will have help, do not worry. The warriors from our village will follow, and the Spanish are not gods. They fall in battle as do our warriors."

Falling Leaves managed a wan smile, but trembled. "I wish I could be as sure as you, Cloud Dancer. I fear Little Fox has been hurt . . . or worse." Her voice quavered.

"Little Fox is a brave warrior. I saw him still fighting when the Spanish withdrew. We have many brave warriors in our village. I have learned from many of them, and White Hawk speaks highly of most. They will not allow this... White Hawk and Little Fox will not allow this." Cloud Dancer spoke with more bravado than she felt. She had faith that White Hawk and the other warriors would follow, but with their thunder weapons the Spanish took a terrible toll.

Cloud Dancer remembered some of the Spanish language Perez had taught her in their brief days together. She could understand bits of what these Spanish soldiers said to one another and that knowledge sent a chill up her spine. As punishment for the theft of their horses they intended their captives to be slaves for many years to come. Cloud Dancer would not accept now the fate she had escaped at Acoma.

"You understand their words!" Falling Leaves said in some surprise, noting Cloud Dancer's rapt attention whenever the Spanish soldiers spoke near them.

"Shh." Cloud Dancer pressed her fingers gently to her friend's lips. "Some of them understand our words," she cautioned.

"But—"

"If we speak very softly, they will not hear."

Fallen Leaves held her silence until she was sure none of the soldiers was within earshot, then said, "If they were after the horses you and White Hawk took from them, how did they find our camp? They could not have followed you through the snow."

"It was chance," Cloud Dancer assured her. "Another group of soldiers found the ones we had left on foot after the storm. They came looking for any encampment of the people. Ours was nearest to the Great River in their path. They must have been surprised we had the horses they sought—though it made little difference. They would have attacked us had we not had the horses."

"They spoke of this?"

Cloud Dancer nodded, her eyes sweeping the camp time and again, probing for further weaknesses. "One or two of the soldiers from that group accompanied this one. They say they will leave here in another day—then it will be much more difficult to escape."

"What are we to do?" Falling Leaves asked apprehensively with a deep sigh. "We are but women and wounded."

Cloud Dancer caught and held Falling Leaves's gaze. "I have caused the thunder to roar from the Spanish thunder stick. If I can get one, I can use it. We will tell the women that this is no different from any time they are forced to pick up weapons and defend their homes. They will have to fight if they do not wish to face life as a slave far from their homes and families. Tell them this when there are no Spanish soldiers near to hear. But for now we must help the wounded, so they will be strong enough to run or fight when the time comes."

"What will the soldiers do if we try to help the others?" Falling Leaves asked nervously.

"Nothing. They are wary of our warriors, but they do not fear the women. Come."

Cloud Dancer's words quickly proved to be accurate. The soldiers raised dark eyebrows when Cloud Dancer and Falling Leaves began moving among the captives, but did no more than watch when they realized their objective was to nurse the wounded. They had seen no real demonstration of Cloud Dancer's fighting abilities before she was captured and they wanted to return with as many live captives as possible, to force them into slavery as punishment for thievery against the Spanish crown; therefore, they ignored the women's ministrations to the wounded.

Cloud Dancer did not feel strong after their long journey, having been forced to remain on Bonita, belly down, mile after jarring mile, but she was much better off than some of the wounded.

Many of the captives Cloud Dancer did not know well, but they were familiar faces, many friendly, all having shared some of the never-ending work of the village. Cloud Dancer and Falling Leaves moved among them, helping where they could, binding wounds, often shocked by the damage the Spanish bullets did to human flesh. Cloud Dancer was relieved there were no children among their numbers. At least White Hawk's warning had come soon enough to prevent that.

Stepping over a young warrior whose broken leg Cloud Dancer had braced as well as she could, she murmured her warning to be ready to seize an opportunity when it came, then bent over another warrior. At first she saw only the deep, bloody furrow gouged across his temple and deep into his hairline. It took a few more seconds for her to recognize Prairie Wolf.

Quickly she tamped down the fury that arose within her at the sight of him. For the good of herself and all who shared her fate, any score she felt she had to settle with Prairie Wolf could be settled when they did not have to fight the Spanish.

She gently touched the wound, cleaning it with some of the water the soldiers had given them to drink. Instantly Prairie Wolf's eyes popped open.

He brushed her hand aside and sat up, squinting and peering at his surroundings. "Where are we? What has happened?" he demanded sharply, his words like the snarl of a wounded animal. He dashed his fists against his eyes in an effort to clear his badly blurred vision.

"We are captives of the Spanish," Cloud Dancer replied tightly, watching his actions closely. As the seconds passed she realized that he could not see well, for he could not distinguish the Spanish soldiers all around them. "There are eleven of us—all women or wounded. The children escaped capture."

Prairie Wolf grunted.

"Falling Leaves is here. Between us we are nursing the wounded and warning them to be ready, when the time comes, to escape."

"And who will lead this escape—you?"

"Speak more softly!" Cloud Dancer snapped. "There are those among the Spanish who speak the tongue of the Kere. No doubt there are those who speak the language of the Apache as well. I will lead," she added steadily, "until one better able to do so takes the responsibility."

Prairie Wolf swung his blurred gaze toward Cloud Dancer, amazed at the way her countenance wavered and blurred before his eyes, but he thumped his chest with one close fist and said, "I will lead!"

"We will catch them by the time darkness falls," Little Fox remarked to White Hawk. "They are powerful and I fear the thunder stick."

"As do we all," White Hawk agreed. "A man who does not fear is a fool."

"That is true, for he may easily lose his life, but it also makes him powerful—and the Spanish have little fear of us."

"They will learn to fear us," White Hawk said grimly. "And they will not fear us for our weapons, they will fear us as men."

The pace of the Apache warriors was steady and swift. United by their goals—to liberate their people and retrieve all that the Spanish had taken from them—they followed at a determined jog the clear trail the Spanish had left. Only White Hawk and Little Fox rode horses, since the Spanish had taken not just their own horses, but the few the Apaches had acquired before White Hawk and Cloud Dancer's raid. Yet even though the rest of the warriors were on foot, the Apache were long accustomed to covering great distances swiftly on foot and they pressed on.

A swift runner scouted ahead, returning to give reports on what he had found. "The trail is fresh. We are getting closer to them."

"They will camp early for the night," White Hawk predicted. "They will not expect us to attack this night, and many will shed their armor in camp when the fires burn. They will be vulnerable to our arrows then." He spoke to all the warriors with them, then turned his attention to the scout. "Go ahead of us, but be careful that you do not run upon their camp that they might see you. Warn us when we are still well away from their camp."

The scout nodded and raced off across the rolling hills to carry out his instructions.

Bempol stopped beside White Hawk's horse. "He is a brave warrior and one of the best among us to follow the tracks. He will know when to slow his pace and creep up upon the camp of the Spanish."

"This I know," White Hawk agreed. "I but remind him, because it is strong within me to hurry and I must not allow myself that."

"Your heart is troubled because of Cloud Dancer."

"Yes. I have wronged her and I would not have her die not knowing I know my error and would put it right."

"We will find their camp by the time the sun goes down behind the far western mountains," Bempol echoed Little Fox's prediction earlier. "We will war against the Spanish, and you will put right this wrong you have done her." His words left no room for argument.

White Hawk looked toward the distant mountains, his heart aching, and wished he could seek a vision before they fought the Spanish. His power was strong, but he could feel nothing of the coming clash with the Spanish. His love for Cloud Dancer was so deep, his anguish so complete, that his sense for the future could not rise up within him. He comforted himself with visions past—those he had seen before he had met Cloud Dancer. He had seen her fall in battle once and had not lost her. It could not be that they had both been spared to have their lives end now at the hands of the Spanish.

With Bempol's words echoing in White Hawk's ears, they hurried on in the wake of their scout, racing the sun.

"I cared for only one warrior who was wounded too badly to travel unaided. He is Crooked Knife." Falling Leaves spoke very softly when she and Cloud Dancer sat down again together after moving among the wounded.

"Would one of the women be able to hold him upon a Spanish horse?" Cloud Dancer asked, noting the fading gray light of day's end.

"I...I think I could," Falling Leaves volunteered. "I have ridden one of the horses in camp before. None of the other women with us has been upon a horse's back."

Cloud Dancer gave a short shake of her head. "I will have to help him. It would be better if you help your brother, Prairie Wolf. His vision has been clouded by his wound. I cannot tell how much. He pretends he suffers from no more than a pain in his head."

Falling Leaves heaved a deep sigh, her eyes troubled. "I will try, but I do not think he will allow me to help him."

"He has more pride than brains!" Cloud Dancer snapped.

"That has been true all his life," Falling Leaves admitted sadly, giving Cloud Dancer a queer little smile. "He wishes to be the bravest warrior, the greatest hunter, the most respected of our tribe."

Cloud Dancer softened, her eyes speaking of her regret at her hasty words. "I am sorry, Falling Leaves. He is your brother."

"That does not mean that he has not been cruel and sometimes foolish."

Cloud Dancer turned her thoughts away from Prairie Wolf to how they would escape the Spanish with the burden of their wounded.

"There are many guards posted," White Hawk observed, as he, Bempol and Little Fox lay belly down behind a screen of scrubby brush no more than twenty-five yards from the Spanish camp.

The night was a cloak of black velvet, the stars large and brilliant against it. The pale light was all that was necessary, but the large Spanish campfire cast a yellow-orange glow over the entire camp. It was a clear night, with no scent of a storm upon the air. They could easily spot the small knot of captives, sequestered from the rest of the camp with guards near them. The horses were not far beyond.

"The soldiers have taken off their armor as you said," Bempol said to White Hawk. "All but those near the horses." The other Apache warriors who had come with the war party crowded closer at Bempol's gesture. "If we are not able to take the horses from the Spanish soldiers we must free our people and scatter in the direction of the four winds," he said earnestly. "Give them many trails to follow and rejoin our people in the high mountains."

Several warriors grunted their acceptance of Bempol's sage words; other merely gave curt nods.

On cat feet the Apache warriors spread out in a great fan, concealed in the darkness behind bits of scrub brush and the crests of small hillocks. In silence they waited as the Spanish soldiers settled down for the night.

White Hawk's heart lurched as he drew the cold night air deeply into his lungs to steady himself. His bow and quiver of arrows were at his hand. The others who accompanied him were in position and ready. All who had come on this raid had lost ones they loved to the Spanish thunder sticks, or hoped to rescue a loved one from the camp below.

Standing Buffalo stood ready but did no more than listen and follow orders.

White Hawk knew Cloud Dancer waited below, with the other captives. She would expect the warriors to come. She had not lived long among the Apache, but she would know that. He could see the captives huddled together, but he could not pick out her slim form in the closely gathered group. He swallowed hard. White Hawk wished the captives were not so close together. If, when the Apaches attacked the Spanish camp, the soldiers turned their terrible weapons on their prisoners, many would die.

"Cloud Dancer," he murmured beneath his breath, "I am here. I was wrong and my heart cries out for your forgiveness."

As strongly as anything he had ever done in his life, White Hawk willed Cloud Dancer to know what was in his heart, to feel his presence and to know, before the war party struck, how much he loved her.

He drew a deep breath and raised his hand to signal the attack.

"They are here," Cloud Dancer said softly to Falling Leaves. "I have heard them in the hills and I have seen movement in the brush." She turned from Falling Leaves, shielding her next words from the young girl. "I hear you, my love," she whispered. He was there, and because he was, he had seen the truth of Prairie Wolf's treachery. She knew it to be so.

"I have seen nothing, heard nothing," Falling Leaves protested, a shiver of apprehension crawling up her back that they would soon be forced to action.

Cloud Dancer turned back to her. "The coyotes crying in the hills are not coyotes. One has the voice of White Hawk. Be ready. It will be very soon."

The words were barely out of her mouth when the first arrow whistled into camp, taking one of the Spanish soldiers guarding the captives full in the chest. He fell in silence except for the heavy thud when his body hit the earth.

Falling Leaves jumped and looked to Cloud Dancer for guidance.

A second arrow found its mark as the Spanish encampment erupted into chaotic and violent action. The attention of the Spanish soldiers was ripped from their unarmed and less threatening captives. The arrows fell now in a shower of death, men crumpling to the earth as guns began spewing their thunder in response.

Out of the night the Apaches came like phantoms borne upon the chilled night wind. The attack continued with the guttural shouts of the defending Spanish, joined by the ear-piercing war cries of the Apache warriors. Blood colored the earth, and the air reverberated with the sounds of fighting and dying.

"Now!" Cloud Dancer told Falling Leaves. "Get the others moving now!"

In the first frenzied moments little attention was paid the seemingly docile captives, but that did not last long. Cloud Dancer could feel attention shifting toward them.

"Go!" Cloud Dancer yelled, putting Falling Leaves to flight at last.

At the Indian maiden's urging, many of the prisoners were on their feet almost instantly. Those who could helped others. A couple of the younger girls panicked, dashing for the safety of the night's concealment as more reports from the thunder sticks shook the air.

"Help the wounded!" Cloud Dancer shouted above the din. "Go for the horses!"

Palming the knife the Spanish had not found in her moccasin sheath, Cloud Dancer half rose to go assist the badly injured warrior, but found her path blocked by Prairie Wolf.

"I will give the orders!" he bellowed, his eyes appearing distant and unfocused. "You are not Apache! You defy me!"

"There is no time for this, Prairie Wolf!" Cloud Dancer spit in return, her body rigid with the expectation of receiving a Spanish miniballs. "Go! Our people die while you fight with me! You are half-blind. I am your shield as I am theirs! Now go!"

Throughout the camp the arrows continued to fly, and the whistling screams of the small lead balls spewed by the thunder sticks thudded into earth or flesh. The heat of battle flashed through Cloud Dancer's veins.

Falling Leaves pulled frantically on her brother's arm, trying to free Cloud Dancer from his grasp, to pull him with her in a mad dash for freedom and life.

Cloud Dancer jerked her arm free, sending Prairie Wolf reeling into his sister...and felt the heavy hand of a Spanish soldier upon her shoulder.

Discounting her as any threat, the soldier flung Cloud Dancer to the ground and lunged for the wounded Prairie Wolf.

"No!"

Falling Leaves's shrill voice pierced Cloud Dancer's momentary fog at the stunning blow, and she rolled into the soldier's legs without thought. She did not analyze the fact that she was protecting Prairie Wolf, who had made himself her enemy. She moved to protect one of her people, as any warrior would.

Her weight, though slight, was enough to throw the soldier off balance and bring him into the dirt with her, short of his target. Her knife in hand, Cloud Dancer struck, but the stocky Spanish soldier saw its flash in the dim orange glow of the campfire, and quickly as a snake he intercepted her blow.

Cloud Dancer gasped as his hand chopped brutally down upon her wrist, knocking the knife away from him, but she did not relinquish her grip on the hilt of the knife. She rolled away from him, her mind working frantically for a way to use her smaller weight and size to advantage.

Terror sent her heart racing and brought sweat out on her face, but she would not let this enemy see her fear. She put it in the back of her mind, allowed it to pump up her senses to a tingling awareness, but not to overwhelm her. White Hawk filled her heart and mind—White Hawk, who touched her life with his strength and wisdom...and love. She feinted and fell back, avoiding the Spaniard's grip. She could not die now and be torn from White Hawk with so much unsettled between them—she could not!

Prairie Wolf blinked frantically against fuzzy vision, trying to focus on the fight before him. Cloud Dancer had risen up to defend the people from the fury of the Spanish, and now she was defending him! The sharp blade of anguish turned over within his gut. In that instant he recognized the leering face of his own jealousy and what it had cost Cloud Dancer—what it had cost him. She was no witch; she was no threat to the people. She was a warrior. Her actions left no doubt. His head spun sickeningly, but he knew he must help her. He, too, was a warrior.

"Come away!" Falling Leaves cried desperately to him. "Come away, or all she has done will be for nothing!"

"No!" Prairie Wolf told his sister with quiet authority amid the chaos of battle. "Quickly, to the horses. Bring Bonita if you can! I will help Cloud Dancer."

"Your sight—"

"I see well enough!" he snapped. "Now go!"

This was a different Prairie Wolf, giving orders and lunging toward where Cloud Dancer had gained her feet opposite the stocky Spaniard. Falling Leaves raced toward the horses to do his bidding, dodging the fights between Apache warriors and Spanish soldiers. She had to get Bonita. Bonita knew her. The mare would come readily with her. But others were ahead of her in reaching the rope corral of the Spanish....

Cloud Dancer gained her feet in a tumbling roll that took her just out of the Spanish soldier's grasp. Dirt clung in damp clumps to her buckskins and streaked her exposed hands and face. She whirled, knife at the ready, and felt a tingling shock run through her body at recognition of her adversary. She was confronting the same Spanish soldier who had almost torn her from Bonita's back when she and White Hawk had taken the horses. She could not forget that dark face, slashed from ear to jawline with a thin white scar. She remembered the beak of a nose and straight yellowed teeth, one broken to a nub, gaping at her from behind the bush of his mustache and beard. He had to have come with this band of soldiers seeking the missing horses.

Recognition dawned in his eyes as well, and he grinned at her, exposing even more of the tobacco-stained teeth.

Another soldier broke from the fighting and ran their way, drawn by the threat to their horses as more Apache warriors poured into the camp from the west. Most of the captives were safely away. There remained only Cloud Dancer, Prairie Wolf, Falling Leaves and the wounded Crooked Knife.

"Yahh! Yi-yi-yi-yi-yi!" Prairie Wolf's fierce war cry slashed through the night. Others, more distant, answered as he leaped across Crooked Knife's prostrate form to confront the second soldier, weaponless. He drew the breath sweepingly into his lungs. It chilled and invigorated him! This was what it meant to be truly a warrior! This was what Cloud Dancer had learned before him. The heat of battle flowed molten through his veins. He felt immortal. His eyes flashed and he felt he possessed the strength of three men.

For the briefest instant Cloud Dancer's eyes met Prairie Wolf's and she saw the clarity of them. There was in that moment an understanding between them. For an instant they were one, Apache warriors fighting to protect their people, their lives.

Then Cloud Dancer's entire attention was again commanded by the Spanish soldier before her. She feinted with the knife, moving with the agility and swiftness of a hummingbird, darting in and gliding back. He wore no armor and he moved with an agility that was surprising. Cloud Dancer resolved not to underestimate him, rose on the balls of her feet and moved in again.

White Hawk exploded into the enemy camp from the west with warriors intent upon reaching the captives and horses. For a moment the chaos of the battle was disorienting, as he grappled with a soldier, succeeding in turning his small thunder stick upon him and firing the weapon into him. A surprised look on his face, the soldier crumpled to the earth and White Hawk plunged on.

Little Fox appeared out of the melee on his right, and he and White Hawk spotted Falling Leaves rushing toward the horses and into danger.

"Falling Leaves!" Little Fox bellowed.

She turned, the movement saving her life as White Hawk hurled his knife into the throat of a Spanish soldier who'd been running for Falling Leaves.

Both Little Fox and White Hawk were beside the trembling maiden in a moment.

"Cloud Dancer?" White Hawk's eyes were wild.

"There!" Falling Leaves waved her arm back toward the place she had been running from. "She and Prairie Wolf are fighting for their lives and that of Crooked Knife! I was to take Bonita to them!" She spit out the words in a frantic rush, her face white and twisted in fear.

White Hawk was moving before Falling Leaves finished speaking. He could make out Cloud Dancer's slight form now, and that of Prairie Wolf, locked in combat with the Spaniard.

Cloud Dancer jumped in closer and ducked as the soldier's arm swept toward her, passing over her in a blow that, had it connected, would have broken her neck. She glided in swiftly again to sink her knife into his exposed chest, but realized her mistake too late. The Spaniard anticipated her movement; he had baited her into it and was ready for it.

He stepped forward as she did. Too close! She could not wield the knife! One hand fastened upon her wrist above the knife, the other closed upon her neck. Instantly Cloud Dancer's breath caught in her throat, trapped inside her body, and she felt the blinding pain of her windpipe collapsing beneath the terrible pressure. Darkness swam before her eyes as Prairie Wolf dodged his armed adversary and, seeing Cloud Dancer's peril, slammed full force into the Spaniard who threatened to choke the life out of her.

Cloud Dancer's knife spun to the earth and she and the soldier toppled before the blow, but he did not give up his grip on her throat. Her senses dimming, Cloud Dancer heard, as if in a dream, the piercing sound of White Hawk's battle cry.

In an instant he was upon them, his strength doubled by the fear in his heart at the sight of Cloud Dancer in the Spaniard's grip. He wrapped the bend of his elbow around the Spaniard's neck, jerked and twisted. The crack of the soldier's neck was audible even above the surrounding sounds of battle.

White Hawk's woman rolled free, gasping and coughing, but very much alive, and he wheeled toward Prairie Wolf. The young warrior was holding his own against the Spaniard, poised and moving with the swift savagery of the wolf for which he was named. He dived for the ground, snatched Cloud Dancer's knife from where it had fallen and came to his feet in a moment. With his war cry echoing in the night he attacked savagely. The knife found its mark and the Spaniard slipped to the earth.

"We must go!" said Prairie Wolf, meeting White Hawk's gaze levelly. For an instant White Hawk saw what Cloud Dancer had seen. He nodded.

Little Fox appeared, leading Bonita and Dark Sky. Falling Leaves, mounted on his own horse, hovered at the fringes of the darkness surrounding the camp. "We have the horses! Our people are free and we have taken vengeance! Now we must leave this place!"

"Hurry!" Cloud Dancer called in agreement, turning to lend her help to the young warrior Crooked Knife.

"Yahh! Yi-yi-yi-yi-yi!" Prairie Wolf threw his head back and again gave voice to his war cry in rapid staccato, as White Hawk and Little Fox used their combined strength to swiftly boost the injured warrior onto Dark Sky.

The thunder sticks of the Spanish barked once—Prairie Wolf jerked around, diving for Cloud Dancer, hurling his body into hers to drive her to the ground. Then the gun cracked again. The miniball meant for Cloud Dancer found its mark in Prairie Wolf. His face dissolved into a crumpled mask of surprise as he fell to his knees, dragging Cloud Dancer down with him, his war cry dead upon his lips. Then he toppled without another sound.

"He is dead," White Hawk said, bending over him. His words were expressionless, but his voice trembled with a tangle of emotion he did not understand.

Falling Leaves's wail of grief rose above the abating sounds of battle.

Cloud Dancer scrambled to one knee, snatched the knife Prairie Wolf had used from the dirt where it had fallen and threw it as her husband had taught her. End over end it split the air, finding its mark in the Spanish soldier who had killed Prairie Wolf as he tried to reload the weapon that had taken the Indian warrior's life.

Little Fox swung up on Dark Sky behind the wounded Apache, holding him tightly, and blocked Falling Leaves's path to her brother's body. The look on his face stopped her from attempting to get nearer.

White Hawk and Cloud Dancer mounted Bonita. Together they all left the bloody battleground with pounding swiftness, as the Spanish, once more afoot, turned away in retreat, no longer eager to test the ferocious fighting skills of the Apache.

The crust of old snow crunched beneath the hooves of their horses as they moved slowly toward the high mountains above the pueblo of Taos. Little Fox was still holding the injured warrior before him on the horse. Falling Leaves uneasily rode Little Fox's horse, grieving her brother's death in pained silence.

White Hawk and Cloud Dancer rode together upon Bonita's back. For now, Cloud Dancer was content to put aside her role as warrior and relax with that of woman and wife. Soon they would be rejoining other members of the war party led by Bempol and Standing Buffalo, and ultimately the rest of the tribe, who were awaiting the return of the warriors and freed captives in the newly located camp in the high mountains.

Cloud Dancer sighed in contentment and leaned back against White Hawk's strong frame.

"You are like the great cat of your totem," White Hawk murmured into her hair. "You purr when you are content."

Cloud Dancer giggled like a young girl, leaving behind their recent struggle as a butterfly sheds its cocoon. She snuggled closer, enjoying the feel of his warmth and strength wrapped around her.

"You and Prairie Wolf found understanding before he died," White Hawk remarked.

"Yes." The thought of his brave death brought sadness to Cloud Dancer's heart.

"And you had forgiven me before I asked it."

"Yes." The single word was a whisper.

"You could not have known I would know the truth when I came with the war party against the Spanish."

Cloud Dancer twisted around in his arms to face him, laying her small hand against his cheek. "You came for me,

White Hawk. I knew when you were near. You were angry and hurt when your eyes saw me in your brother's arms. She Who Seeks Wisdom said you would know the truth when the anger faded. In my heart I knew she was right."

"You are my heart, my woman, my shield. How could I live without you at my side?" White Hawk's words were roughened by emotion. "Little Fox came after me, but I had begun to see the truth before he came—even before my anger died."

Pure joy made Cloud Dancer feel light-headed. She squeezed her eyes tightly closed against tears that threatened. "For a short time, before I saw She Who Seeks Wisdom, I thought I had lost you. We have so many differences, White Hawk, but I love you."

"I love you, Cloud Dancer. The differences are as sands upon the wind. They will be gone in time. We will grow together more with the passage of each day."

"You will not hold anger in your heart against your brother, Standing Buffalo?"

White Hawk shook his head. "No. The time before us will not be easy for the Apache tribe. The mark of the Spanish is upon the land. Much will change. All of us must find the understanding that touched your heart and Prairie Wolf's before his death. I will not hold anger in my heart for my brother. We will find our understanding again."

Cloud Dancer sighed her pleasure and turned to face forward, gazing toward the distant mountains looming majestically before them as she rocked gently upon Bonita's back in her husband's arms. "It is good. Together we will face what comes, my heart, my husband, my shield."

* * * * *

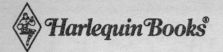
Harlequin Books®

GREAT NEWS...

HARLEQUIN UNVEILS NEW SHIPPING PLANS

For the convenience of customers, Harlequin has announced that Harlequin romances will now be available in stores at these convenient times each month*:

Harlequin Presents, American Romance, Historical, Intrigue:

> May titles: April 10
> June titles: May 8
> July titles: June 5
> August titles: July 10

Harlequin Romance, Superromance, Temptation, Regency Romance:

> May titles: April 24
> June titles: May 22
> July titles: June 19
> August titles: July 24

We hope this new schedule is convenient for you.

With only two trips each month to your local bookseller, you'll never miss any of your favorite authors!

*Please note: There may be slight variations in on-sale dates in your area due to differences in shipping and handling.

*Applicable to U.S. only.

HDATES-RR

A CENTURY OF
1890s AMERICAN 1990s
ROMANCE

A CENTURY OF AMERICAN ROMANCE has taken you on a nostalgic journey through time—from the turn of the century to the dawn of the year 2000.

Relive all the memories . . . the passions . . . of
A CENTURY OF AMERICAN ROMANCE.

1890s #345 AMERICAN PIE by Margaret St. George
1900s #349 SATURDAY'S CHILD by Dallas Schulze
1910s #353 THE GOLDEN RAINTREE by Suzanne Simmons Guntrum
1920s #357 THE SENSATION by Rebecca Flanders
1930s #361 ANGELS WINGS by Anne Stuart
1940s #365 SENTIMENTAL JOURNEY by Barbara Bretton
1950s #369 STRANGER IN PARADISE by Barbara Bretton
1960s #373 HEARTS AT RISK by Libby Hall
1960s #377 TILL THE END OF TIME by Elise Title
1970s #381 HONORBOUND by Tracy Hughes
1980s #385 MY ONLY ONE by Eileen Nauman
1990s #389 A > LOVERBOY by Judith Arnold

Harlequin Intrigue®

QUID PRO QUO

Racketeer King Crawley is a man who lives by one rule: An Eye For An Eye. Put behind bars for his sins against humanity, Crawley is driven by an insatiable need to get even with the judge who betrayed him. And the only way to have his revenge is for the judge's children to suffer for their father's sins....

Harlequin Intrigue introduces Patricia Rosemoor's QUID PRO QUO series: #161 PUSHED TO THE LIMIT (May 1991), #163 SQUARING ACCOUNTS (June 1991) and #165 NO HOLDS BARRED (July 1991).

Meet:

Sydney Raferty: She is the first to feel the wrath of King Crawley's vengeance. Pushed to the brink of insanity, she must fight her way back to reality—with the help of Benno DeMartino in #161 PUSHED TO THE LIMIT.

Dakota Raferty: The judge's only son, he is a man whose honest nature falls prey to the racketeer's madness. With Honor Bright, he becomes an unsuspecting pawn in a game of deadly revenge in #163 SQUARING ACCOUNTS.

Asia Raferty: The youngest of the siblings, she is stalked by Crawley and must find a way to end the vendetta. Only one man can help—Dominic Crawley. But will the son join forces with his father's enemy in #165 NO HOLDS BARRED?

Don't miss a single title of Patricia Rosemoor's QUID PRO QUO trilogy coming to you from Harlequin Intrigue.

QPQ-1